The Beach Café

LUCY DIAMOND lives in Bath with her husband and their three children. When she isn't slaving away on a new book (ahem) you can find her on Twitter @LDiamondAuthor or on Facebook at www.facebook.com/LucyDiamondAuthor.

Novels

Any Way You Want Me

Over You

Hens Reunited

Sweet Temptation

Summer with my Sister

Me and Mr Jones

One Night in Italy

The Year of Taking Chances

Summer at Shell Cottage

The Secrets of Happiness

Novellas

A Baby at the Beach Café

Ebook novellas

Christmas at the Beach Café

Christmas Gifts at the Beach Café

Lucy Diamond

THE BEACH CAFÉ

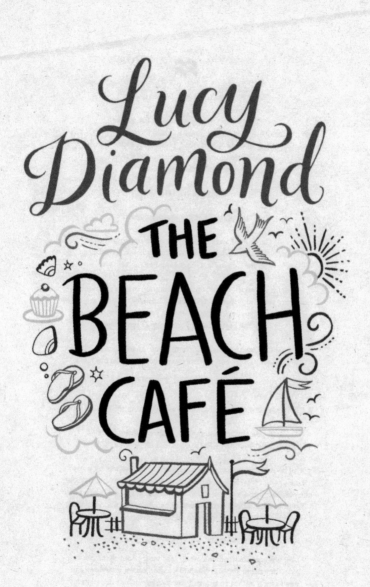

PAN BOOKS

First published 2011 by Pan Books

This edition published 2016 by Pan Books
an imprint of Pan Macmillan
20 New Wharf Road, London N1 9RR
Associated companies throughout the world
www.panmacmillan.com

ISBN 978-1-5098-1110-6

579864

A CIP catalogue record for this book is available from the British Library.

Typeset by Set Systems Ltd, Saffron Walden, Essex
Printed and bound by CPI Group (UK) Ltd, Croydon, CR0 4YY

Visit **www.panmacmillan.com** to read more about all our books
and to buy them. You will also find features, author interviews and
news of any author events, and you can sign up for e-newsletters
so that you're always first to hear about our new releases.

To Mum, Dad, Phil, Ellie and Fiona

for all the happy memories of childhood holidays in Cornwall

Acknowledgements

Huge thanks to Jenny Geras for her editorial input, and to the rest of the team at Pan for being so wonderful – Thalia, Chloe, Ellen, Michelle and Jeremy. Thanks to Simon Trewin at United Agents for helping me develop the original idea, and to Imogen Taylor, who said that all-important first 'yes' to this book.

Finally, my thanks as always to Martin, for the pep talks and support, for the willingness to discuss my characters with me as if they were real people, and for holding the fort so admirably when I went off to Cornwall to research the perfect beach and write about it. Did I tell you I'm planning to set my next novel in the Seychelles?

Chapter One

Family legend has it that on the day I was born, when my elder sisters, Ruth and Louise, came tiptoeing in hand-in-hand to see me for the very first time, my mum said to them, 'This is your new baby sister. What do you think we should call her?'

Ruth, the oldest twin, thought hard, with all the wisdom she'd gained in her mighty three years of life. 'We should call her ... Baby Jesus,' she pronounced eventually, no doubt with a lisping piety. Ruth had taken the Goody Two-Shoes role to heart from an early age. Either that or she was angling for extra Christmas presents.

'Mmm,' Mum must have replied, probably in the same I-don't-*think*-so way she did throughout my childhood, like the time I told her I had definitely seen the tooth-fairy with my very own eyes, and no, it absolutely wasn't me who had wolfed half the chocolate biscuits – it was the others.

'Louise, how about you?' Mum asked next. 'What should we call your new sister?'

Obviously I was only hours old at the time, so I don't remember anything about this touching bedside scene, but I like to imagine that Louise made the little frowny face she still does, where her eyebrows slide together and the top of her nose wrinkles. According to Mum, she said with the utmost solemnity, 'I think we should call her ... Little Black Sheep.'

Little Black Sheep indeed. I'm not sure whether this was a 'Baa, Baa, Black Sheep' reference or something to do with the fact that I had remarkably springy black hair from the word go. Whatever the reason, you've got to love my sister's astonishing foresight. Because guess what? That was pretty much how I had ended up at the ripe old age of thirty-two, with not a mortgage, full-time job, husband or infant to show for myself – the quintessential black sheep of the family. Spot on, Louise. Uncanny prescience. I was the freak, the failure, the one they muttered about in patronizing tones, trying not to sound too gleeful as my shortcomings were discussed. *Oh dear. What ARE we going to do with Evie? I'm worried about her, you know. She's not getting any younger, is she?*

Hey-ho. I wasn't too bothered by what they thought. It was better to be an individual, surely, someone who had dreams and did things differently, rather than be an anonymous, ordinary ... well, *sheep*, obediently following the rest of the flock without a single bleat of dissent. Wasn't it?

We have photos from that day, of course, grainy, brown-tinged photos with the rounded-off corners that seemed to be all the rage back then. There I was, cuddled in Mum's arms, wearing a teeny pink Babygro, with Ruth and Louise leaning over me, both in matching burgundy cord dungarees (this *was* the Seventies, remember), their eyes wide with what I like to think of as wonder and awe. (No doubt Ruth was already plotting her pocket-money scam, though, which went on for several years.)

I can't help thinking that there's something of the Sleeping Beauty fairytale about the picture. You know, when the fairies come to bestow their gifts on the little tot and they're all really excellent bequests, like how clever and talented and pretty she will be — until the evil old fairy (who hasn't been invited) rocks up, bristling with malice, and wrecks everything with her 'She shall prick her finger on a spindle and DIE!' contribution.

This image tended to come back to me every time I sat in a hairdressing salon, until I began to wonder if Louise's 'Little Black Sheep' remark had somehow been a curse, straight from the realms of finger-pricking voodoo. Because throughout my entire life my hair had been frizzy, woolly and black, with a mad, kinky curl to it. Just like your average black sheep, in fact, albeit one who appeared to be immune to the powers of miracle hair conditioner and straightening devices.

And so it was that on a certain Saturday morning in early May I was sitting in a big squishy vinyl chair at a hairdressing salon on the Cowley Road, the scent of hairspray and perm-lotion tingling in my nostrils, as I pondered whether I had the bottle to get the sheep sheared into a radically different style. 'I think your face could take a short cut,' the stylist said enthusiastically. 'You've got the cheekbones for it – you could totally rock an elfin look. Maybe if we add an asymmetrical fringe – yeah. Very cool.'

'You don't think it would be too … boyish?' I replied hesitantly. I stared at my reflection, unable to make a decision. I'd come into the salon fired up with brave plans to request a head-turning Mia Farrow crop, but now that I was here, I couldn't help wondering if such a cut would make me look more like Pete Doherty. I wished for the thousandth time that I had hair like Ruth and Louise – long, tawny, Pantene-advert hair, which swished as they walked. Somehow I had missed out on that particular gene, though, as well as the perfect-life chromosome.

The stylist – Angela, I think her name was – smiled encouragingly. 'You know what they say: a change is as good as a holiday,' she replied. She had aubergine-coloured hair in a wet-look perm. I really shouldn't have trusted her. 'I'll make you a coffee while you think it over, okay?'

She clip-clopped off, bum waggling in a too-tight bleached denim skirt, and I bit my lip, courage leaking out of me by the second. She was probably only suggesting an elfin cut because she was bored with trims and blow-dries. She probably couldn't care less how I'd look at the end of it. And I wasn't convinced by the 'a change is as good as a holiday' line, either. I'd spent two weeks camping in the Lake District the year before, and it was not an experience I wanted repeated in a haircut.

My phone rang as I was mid-dither. I rummaged in my bag for it, and saw that 'Mum' was flashing on the screen. I was just about to send it to voicemail when I got the strangest feeling I should answer. So I did.

'Hi, Mum, are you all right?'

'Evie, sit down,' she said, her voice quavering. 'It's bad news, darling.'

'I am sitting down,' I replied, examining my split ends. 'What's up?' My mother's idea of bad news was that her favourite character was being written out of *The Archers*, or that she'd accidentally sat on her reading glasses and broken them. I was hardened to all her 'bad news' phone calls by now.

'It's Jo,' she said, and I heard a sob in her voice. 'Oh, Evie ...'

'Is she all right?' I asked, making a thumbs-up sign at Angela as she dumped a coffee in front of me. Jo was my mum's younger sister, and the coolest, loveliest, most fun aunt you could ever wish for. *Must give her a ring*, I thought, making a mental note. I had been a bit crap about keeping in touch with everyone lately.

'No,' said Mum, in this awful, shuddering wail. 'She's been in a car crash. She ... She's dead, Evie. Jo's dead.'

I couldn't take in the news at first. I sat there in the hairdresser's chair feeling completely numb as memories of Jo deluged my mind. As sisters, she and Mum had been simultaneously close, but worlds apart. Mum, the sensible older one, had gone to university, become a teacher, married Dad, raised three daughters, and had lived for years in a nice part of Oxford. Jo, on the other hand, was more flighty and free-spirited. She'd left school at sixteen to have all sorts of adventures around the world, before settling in Carrawen Bay, a small seaside village in north Cornwall, and running her own café there. If Mum could be summed up as an elegant taupe, Jo was a screaming pink.

I'd loved childhood holidays in Carrawen. Jo's café was set just back from the bay and she lived in the flat above, so it was the most magical place to stay. There was something so exciting about waking up to those light, bright mornings, with the sound of the sea and the gulls in your ears — I never tired of it. Days were spent with my sisters, running wild on the beach for hours on end, being mermaids, pirates, smugglers, explorers, finding shells, rock-pooling and building enormous castles in our exhilarating-but-impossible attempts to stave off the incoming tide. In the evenings, once we'd been sluiced down in Jo's tiny bathroom, our parents let us stay up thrillingly late, sitting on the balconied deck of the café with one of Jo's special Knickerbocker Glories and three long silver spoons, while candle-lights flickered in storm lanterns, and the sea rushed blackly behind us.

Back then, Jo had seemed like a girl herself — way younger than Mum, with her hair in blonde pigtails, freckles dotted over her face like grains of sand, and cool clothes that I secretly coveted: short skirts, funky bright trainers, cut-off denim shorts, and jeans and thick fisherman's jumpers when the weather turned cold.

As an adult, I'd loved going to stay with her too, whatever the season. Somehow, the bay seemed extraspecial in winter, with the wide, flat beach empty of holidaymakers. I was there one memorable Christmas Eve, when what seemed like the whole of the village — from grannies leaning on sticks to babes in arms — congregated on the beach in mid-afternoon and sang carols together. Jo brought along warm, floury mince pies and steaming mulled wine, and everyone toasted each other's good health, then a fire was lit and children danced around with red and gold tinsel in their hair. It was like being part of the best secret club ever, a million miles away from the frantic, sharp-elbowed crush of Oxford's High Street and its stressed-out shoppers tussling over last-minute presents.

But now Jo was gone, wiped out in a moment, it seemed, hit by a lorry driving too fast down the winding lane that led to the bay. Never again would I sit at the bar of her café while she tempted me with lattes and sugar-sprinkled shortbread; never again would we chat together while the sun cruised slowly across that expanse of Cornish sky; never again would she drag me into the sea for a bracing early-morning swim, both of us shrieking and splashing each other as the icy water stung our bare skin . . .

No. It couldn't be true. It simply couldn't be true. Mum must have got it wrong. Or my imagination was playing weird tricks on me. She couldn't have died, just like that. Not Jo.

'Have you made up your mind yet?' Aubergine-Angela hovered behind me, scissors and comb in hand.

I blinked. I'd been so steeped in memories that it was a shock to find myself still in the salon, with Leona Lewis trilling away from the speakers above my head and the gentle snip-snipping of hair all around. 'Um . . .' I couldn't think straight. 'You choose,' I said in the end, my mind blank. Hair seemed very trivial all of a sudden. It didn't matter. 'Just – whatever you think.'

Matthew dropped me round to Mum's later on because I was still too freaked out about Jo's car crash even to think about getting behind the wheel myself. 'I won't come in,' he said, pecking me on the cheek. 'I'm not very good with crying women.'

'Oh, but –' I broke off in dismay. 'Can't you just stay for a bit?'

He shook his head. 'Better not. I've got to pick up Saul later, remember.'

Saul was Matthew's seven-year-old son who usually came to ours at weekends. He was adorable, but right now, all I could feel was disappointment that Matthew couldn't stay with me. I'd managed to keep it together as best as I could at the hairdresser's – still in massive shock and denial, I think – but had been absolutely bawling my heart out by the time I got home. 'Bloody hell,' Matthew had said, his face stricken as he saw me sobbing there in the hall. His eyes bulged. 'Well, it'll grow back . . .' he said faintly, after a few moments. 'I mean, it's not *that* bad.'

'I'm not crying about my *hair*,' I'd shouted. 'I'm crying because Jo's died. Oh, Matthew, *Jo's died!*'

I'd been with Matthew for five years and I knew he

found displays of emotion embarrassing and awkward, but he was really lovely to me then. He held me tight, let me cry all over his shirt, made me a cup of tea with two sugars and then, when I wouldn't stop weeping, poured me a large brandy too. I felt as if something in me had died along with Jo though, as if a huge, important part of my life had been snuffed out, like a candle-flame.

Guilt and self-recrimination were setting in – a trickle at first, which swiftly became a flood. I hadn't visited Jo for ages. I hadn't even phoned lately. Why had I left it so long? Why hadn't I made time? I was such a selfish person, such a rubbish niece. I couldn't even remember the last conversation we'd had, and had no idea what our last words to each other had been. Why hadn't I paid better attention? Why had I let her slip away? Now she was gone, and it was too late ever to speak to her again. It seemed so utterly, horribly final.

After the brandy had burned its way into my bloodstream, I felt an ache to see my mum, and Matthew insisted on driving me there, which was absolutely unheard of, as my parents' house was only a mile and a half away. Normally he'd have given me a lecture on the evils of short car journeys made by lazy, inconsiderate drivers, if I had dared pick up the car keys rather than my bike helmet.

But now I was here, and he was driving carefully away from me, eyes fixed firmly on the road, hands at an exact ten-to-two on the wheel, just as his instructor had taught him once upon a time. I wished he hadn't gone. I stood there in the street for a moment, hoping stupidly that he would turn the car round and come back – 'What was I thinking? I can't possibly leave you at a time like this!' – but the sound of his engine grew quieter, then faded away to nothing.

I rubbed my swollen eyes and went up the drive to the house.

Mum opened the door. Normally my mum is what you would call well groomed. She has smart shoes that match her handbags. She has a wardrobe full of tasteful clothes in shades of ecru, cream and coffee, and always accessorizes. She knows how to drape a scarf and how to do big hair, and she smells very expensive. She wears full make-up even when she's gardening.

Not today, though. I had never seen her in such a state. Her face was puffy from crying, her eyes were red-rimmed and sore-looking, with rings of mascara below them, and her hair was bouffed up crazily where she'd obviously been raking her hands through it. She opened her arms wide as if she was about to fling them around me, then froze and let out a shriek of horror instead. 'Your hair! What have you done?'

'Oh God, I know,' I said, putting a hand up to it self-consciously. 'I was in the hairdresser's when you rang, and afterwards I just . . .' My voice trailed away. Even now, at this awful time when we'd just heard about Jo, I felt stupid, the only moron in the family who'd say something cretinous like 'You choose' to an overenthusiastic hairdresser. She'd left me with inch-long hair all over, apart from a long, wonky fringe; and yes, I did look like a boy. A stupid, sobbing emo-boy.

'Oh dear,' she said. 'What a day this is turning out to be. Jo going . . . You arriving like an urchin—'

'Mum, stop it!' I said sharply, cringing at how she could equate the two things. Why did she even care about my hair anyway? It was growing on my head, not hers. And, newsflash: her beloved sister had just died tragically. Wasn't that slightly more important?

Dad was hovering in the background and gave me a warning-look-cum-grimace, so I bit my tongue and kept back the rant that was brewing inside. 'Hello, love,' he said, hugging me. Then he let go and stared at my haircut. 'Goodness,' he said, sounding dazed, before seeming to rally himself. 'Louise and Ruth are already here. Come and have a cup of tea.'

I followed him into the kitchen and my sisters gawped at me. 'Fucking HELL,' Louise squawked, jumping up from the table and clapping a hand over her mouth.

'Language!' Ruth hissed, covering Thea's ears immediately. As a modern-languages teacher at one of the posh secondary schools in town, Ruth only ever swore in foreign languages in front of her children, so as to protect them from the Anglo-Saxon equivalents. Curly-haired Thea, two, was the youngest of Ruth's three children and already showing signs of precocity. 'Kin-*ell*,' she now repeated daringly, flashing a gaze at her mum to check her response.

'Thanks a lot, Lou,' Ruth said, then glared at me, as if it was my fault. Obviously in her eyes it *was* my fault, for daring to enter the Flynn family home with such a ridiculous haircut. What *had* I been thinking?

Ruth and Louise weren't quite identical, but they had similar faces with matching high cheekbones and large hazel eyes, the same long, straight noses and porcelain skin. They were easy to tell apart, though, even to an outsider. Ruth always looked as if she'd stepped out of a catalogue – her hair glossy and perfectly blow-dried, her clothes boringly casual and always spotless. On this day, for instance, she was wearing crease-free chinos, a Breton top, a navy silk scarf around her neck and brown Tod loafers.

Louise, on the other hand, generally scraped her hair back into a ponytail, although she never seemed to tie it quite tight enough, as tendrils always worked their way loose, falling about her face and neck in wispy strands. She rarely wore make-up (unlike Ruth, who'd never leave the house without a full face of credit-card-expensive slap), and had a permanently dishevelled, confused air. Her clothes seemed to have been thrown on at random – she would team a smart navy Chanel-style skirt, say, with a brown polo-neck jumper from Primark. Still, she got away with it, by being the Family Genius. Too brainy to think about style, that was Louise.

'Hi,' I said pointedly now, as neither of my sisters had actually greeted me yet in a remotely conventional fashion.

Louise recovered herself and came over to kiss my cheek. 'That's quite a look you've got going there,' she commented, her mouth twisting in a smirk. 'What's that in aid of? Midlife crisis? Homage to Samson?'

I huffed a sigh, feeling irritable and petulant. 'For crying out loud! Is that all you lot can talk about, my flaming hair? What's wrong with you?'

Silence fell. Mum, Ruth and Louise all exchanged glances, and I folded my arms across my chest defensively.

'Flaming hair,' Thea whispered to herself in glee. 'Flaming *hair.*'

'I'll put the kettle on,' Dad said, ever the diplomat, as Ruth scowled at me across her daughter's flaxen curls.

We drank tea and talked about Jo, and Mum cut us all slices of crumbly fruitcake. 'Oh, I shouldn't,' Louise said with a sigh, but managed to get through two fat wedges of it nonetheless. Then Dad produced a bottle of Merlot and we polished that off too, as the memories of Jo kept on coming.

After a while — I had lost track of time by now, but we'd somehow emptied a second bottle of wine — Ruth's husband, Tim, arrived with their other two children (perfect Isabelle and angelic Hugo) in tow, then left again with Thea. The rest of us stayed put around the table in what felt like a bubble.

'Do you remember that Christmas we stayed at Jo's, and there were reindeer prints on the beach on Christmas morning?' Louise said dreamily, her face flushed from the wine. 'And those marks she said were from the sleigh runners?'

Mum smiled. 'She got up at the crack of dawn to make those prints on the wet sand,' she said. 'But that was Jo all over, wasn't it? Anything to make the day extra-special.'

'I loved it when we were there for my birthday one year, and she did a treasure hunt all around the beach that led to my present,' I said, remembering the delicious excitement of racing across the sand in search of clues, before finally finding a wrapped parcel tucked behind a tumble of black rocks. I'd ripped it open to find a new doll and lots of clothes for her that Jo had made herself. Bella, I'd called her. Bella the Beach-Doll. Suddenly I wished I'd still got her.

'She was amazing,' Mum said, her voice wobbling. 'A one-off. And too damn young and lovely to die.' A tear rolled down her cheek. 'God, I'm going to miss her.'

Dad held up his glass. 'Here's to Jo,' he said.

'Jo,' we all chorused.

Chapter Two

The funeral was the following Friday, down in Carrawen Bay, and I felt conscious of just how long I'd been away as I struggled to remember the turn-off I needed for the village. 'Um . . .' I faltered, slowing to a crawl and peering through the windscreen.

'Do you want me to check the map?' Matthew asked. It was a four-hour journey from Oxford and he had driven the first leg to the Taunton Deane services, where we'd switched. I'd confidently said I'd drive the rest of the way, but somehow the lanes were becoming confused in my memory, and all the fields of grazing sheep looked exactly the same.

'No, I think it's just a bit further,' I blagged, feeling guilty for having forgotten. It wasn't all that long ago that I'd known these roads like my own face; had been back and forth to Jo's all the time from Plymouth, where I went to drama school, especially when I'd fallen in love with gorgeous Ryan, the sexy surf-dude who had captured (and then broken) my heart.

I pressed my lips together as I thought about him now. He had shaken me up, all right, Ryan. Ryan Alexander, that was his name. I was nineteen, and he and I had spent the most perfect, romantic summer together in Carrawen Bay, me supposedly working for Jo to earn a few quid, but actually spending quite a lot of time sneaking off with lover-boy for romantic trysts and secret knee-tremblers in deserted spots along the coastal path and in the steeply shelving sand dunes. Oh yes. Nothing like the gritty sensation of sand in your nether regions to make you feel desired. And in need of a bath. Happy days! Well, until he buggered off travelling with his mates, and I never heard from him again, that was. Whenever I thought about Ryan now – which wasn't often, honestly – he remained young and god-like in my mind, tanned and muscular, forever nineteen. He was probably shacked up in Australia or Hawaii, I reckoned, still chasing the surf, still hoping to catch that elusive perfect wave.

I braked sharply, just in time to make the turning. 'Bloody hell, watch it!' said Matthew, jerking forwards in his seat.

'Sorry,' I said. 'Here we go. Carrawen Bay, one mile. Nearly there.'

I fell silent as I steered into the narrow lane and drove slowly along, mindful of Jo's accident in this very road, tears seeping from my eyes for what felt like the hundredth time since I'd heard the news. It didn't seem possible that she wouldn't be in the village when we got there, wouldn't be waiting for me with one of her huge, tight hugs, her cheerful smile, that twinkle in her eye.

'It's very pretty,' Matthew said politely as we rounded a corner and caught our first glimpse of the sea, a bright luminous blue, stretching out into the horizon. There was the familiar golden sweep of the bay, the dunes, the piles of rocks with their seaweed-fringed pools full of treasures to be discovered. Jo's café was a timbered building with huge windows and a deck, just visible on the far left.

'Mmm,' I said, my voice trembling as I fought back the tears. It struck me as absurd that Matthew had never accompanied me down here. He'd always preferred walking holidays to beach ones, was never happier than when climbing a huge bleak mountain, buffeted by gale-force winds. Me, I was in my element with my feet in the waves, the sun on my face, the screech and flap of seagulls in the sky. 'I'd call it beautiful, rather than pretty,' I said after a moment as we reached the village's first straggle of white-washed cottages and old stone farm buildings, their slate roofs speckled with yellow lichen. 'Devon and Dorset are pretty. Cornwall's too wild and rugged to be anything other than *beautiful*.'

From the corner of my eye, I saw Matthew raise his eyebrows at my nit-picking, but he didn't say anything.

Matthew and I had met five years ago. I was working as a waitress in a cocktail bar ... No, not exactly. I was working behind the bar of The Plough, a so-called gastro-pub in the centre of Oxford, although a gastroenteritis pub might have been a more fitting description, given Jimmy the mad chef's lack of basic hygiene. A cocktail bar it was not. (The owner, one florid-faced Len Macintosh – or Big Mac, as everyone called him, due to his darts-player physique – was from Doncaster and thought that cocktails were for poofs, as he so charmingly put it.)

Big Mac clearly had a fetish for girls in stupid costumes, which was why throughout the whole of December he had the female bar staff in ridiculous elf outfits, all seemingly designed for maximum discomfort and embarrassment. Mind you, it wasn't just us girls who suffered. The male members of staff had to wear furry reindeer antlers with jingling bells on. Not the most masculine get-up, as my colleague Lee kept moaning bitterly.

So there I was one night, in my elf combo, which consisted of a nasty pea-green dress of purest nylon, a bright-red belt and, to top it all off, a daft green-and-red hat. I was feeling a prize prat and heartily glad it *wasn't* Christmas every day, or even every month, when in came Matthew with an office-party posse, there for their annual knees-up.

The romantic in me would like to say that our eyes met across the beer pumps and I melted like an advent-candle under a burning flame after one soul-searching look from his deep-brown eyes. In all honesty, I was so frazzled with the massive bar order, and the fact that my elf dress was bringing me out in a sweaty rash, that I didn't give him a second look. It wasn't until he swung into heroic action later on that I did a double-take.

Yes – swung into heroic action! You read that correctly. Now we're talking proper romantic stuff, right?

Matthew's group were quite pissed when they came in. There were sixteen of them, all working for the same IT firm. (You got it. Mostly geeky blokes with bad dress sense and even worse complexions, pontificating earnestly about complicated computer stuff as they shovelled in their disgusting turkey risotto. I'm not selling Matthew very well so far, am I? Bear with me.)

I went to collect their crockery once they'd finished and had to reach across the table to collect one guy's plate. He was being particularly unhelpful by not passing it to me (I suspect he was hoping my breasts would fall out of the elf dress) and I had to really stretch to pick it up. As I was already balancing a stack of plates on my left arm, I had a blind-spot on this side, which was why I leaned right over one of the Christmas candles Big Mac had put on the tables to make the place look cheery and festive.

Whoomph! went the bright, hot flame as it roared straight up my nylon dress.

Smash! went the plates as I dropped them all over the table. I was screaming, other people were shouting, everything seemed to be happening in slow motion. And then there was Matthew, leaping to his feet, throwing his coat around me and putting out the flames in an instant. (See? Tell me *that's* not heroic.)

'Oh my God!' I croaked, feeling completely hysterical and freaked out by my very own Joan of Arc moment. 'Oh my *God*.'

'Are you okay? Are you burned?' he asked. His arms were still around me, as was his big black overcoat. I felt like a Jane Austen heroine, swooning in his grasp.

'I . . . I think I'm okay,' I said, weakly. I opened the coat to see the remnants of my costume hanging in black, charred tatters. I closed it again hurriedly, not wanting the pissed geeks to notice that my bra and knickers didn't match. My hands were shaking. 'Bloody hell . . . I can't believe that just happened. Thank you.' I blinked, then looked properly at him for the first time. He had a smooth pink face, conker-brown hair and grey eyes that were fixed on me in concern. My rescuer. 'Thank you,' I said again, still swaying with shock.

Big Mac had waddled over by then, ice bucket in hand as if he'd been about to chuck the contents over the elf inferno. 'Flipping heck, love,' he said, his normally mottled face drained of colour. 'Are you all right? Are you hurt?'

'Of course she's not all right!' Matthew raged, rounding on him. 'She shouldn't be wearing a dress like that around naked flames. She's a walking fire hazard. You're lucky she's not been badly burned.'

Whoa! Hero alert. I'd never seen Big Mac so chastened-looking, so ... small. Matthew had told *him*, all right, shooting up even higher in my estimation.

Still, silver linings and all that. From that night on, the elf costumes were taken away and never seen again. Yes, okay, so we all had to wear the stupid jingly reindeer antlers now, but frankly, even that was progress, despite the dim sensation of tinnitus after a four-hour shift. Furthermore I was in love with – and forever in debt to – the man who'd saved me from hideous third-degree burns. Remarkably, I was utterly unscathed. He'd acted so quickly, so instinctively, that he'd completely extinguished the fire before it had had a chance to burn into my skin. He was my saviour.

Five years down the line, and ... Well, things had changed, sure, but that was what happened to all couples, wasn't it? You couldn't be a swooning Jane Austen heroine 24/7, just as you couldn't be a full-time damsel-in-distress-rescuing hero. And so he'd discovered (quite quickly actually) that, unlike him, I was a dreaming drifter with no life-plan mapped out as far as my pension (er ... what pension?), and I'd realized that he was ... not *tight* exactly, but careful with his money, shall we say. And that he was actually quite serious about pensions and ISAs and career prospects, and got tetchy with me for not being interested. He even had spreadsheets charting his finances on our PC at home, which he spent hours laboriously updating.

There was common ground too, of course. We both liked long cycle rides out of Oxford, we liked pubs and the cinema, we liked each other's friends and families (well, most of the time) and, for all our differences, we got along pretty well together. Predictably, my parents absolutely adored him. 'We're so glad you've found someone like Matthew at last,' Mum had said, almost collapsing with relief after she'd met him for the first time. 'He's so much more sensible and *nice* than those other boys you've been out with. He's just what you need, Evie.'

Sometimes, very occasionally, I wondered if she was right about him being just what I needed. Sometimes (again very occasionally), I worried in private that we weren't the perfect match everyone said we were. My parents might not have been crazy about my ex-boyfriends – the conceptual artist who lived on a houseboat near Iffley Lock and took too many hallucinogens; the drummer who had tattoos and a motorbike and was very experimental sexually; the playwright who was so shy he would literally hide behind his own hair – but in many ways I'd felt a kinship with them. They'd been black sheep too, like me. Even if I didn't fit in with my family, I'd fitted in with them on some level.

Every now and then I wondered, disloyally, what I would have been doing if Matthew and I had never met. At the time of the perilous elf-meets-Guy-Fawkes incident, I'd been saving up to go to India and Nepal with a couple of mates. They'd gone six months later, and returned with beautiful saris, silver jewellery and colourful hair braids, as well as tales of spliffs on perfect sunset beaches, mountain treks, bustling city adventures, the Taj Mahal and the worst diarrhoea ever. Me, I'd spent that time at secretarial college, learning keyboard skills and Powerpoint. 'It'll open up so many more jobs to you,' Matthew had advised.

I wished I had gone to India now and not just because I hated typing. But anyway. He *had* saved my life. And we were happy. We were together. I was living in his house and he was going to put me on the mortgage any day now.

Concentrate on the road, Evie, I thought, remembering almost with surprise that we were in Carrawen village. Yes. Jo's funeral, of course. I dragged myself hurriedly back from my wanderings down Memory Lane and slowed to twenty miles an hour.

There was the tiny old school, the farm where Jo had bought her milk and veggies, the surf shop – Waveseekers – which had a rail of wetsuits outside and gaudy surf-boards in the windows, the Tardis-like grocery shop and the gorgeous old stone cottages. I had so many memories of this place and couldn't quite believe how familiar it all looked, when everything had changed.

I caught sight of my parents' silver Golf parked outside the pub, just along from the squat stone church where the funeral was to be held. I squeezed into a space in front of theirs, narrowly missing scraping their bonnet as I misjudged the angle, then cut the engine and took a long, deep breath. And now for the funeral. This was going to be tough.

I clambered out, feeling crumpled and unkempt after being stuck in the car for so long, and tried to tidy my hair and smooth down my black skirt on the short walk to the church. I put my hand into Matthew's, wanting comfort, as we walked inside the old stone building. I still couldn't believe this was actually happening.

The church was absolutely packed, everyone in black, heads down, tissues to their bloodshot eyes. Mum gave a reading, as did the local vicar, a weather-beaten man with white hair, who spoke movingly about how much Jo had meant to the Carrawen community.

After we'd sung 'All Things Bright and Beautiful' and, for once, I hadn't giggled over the line about 'the purple-headed mountains', Jo's best friend Annie stood up to give an emotional speech about what a wonderful person Jo was, and how badly she would be missed by everyone. 'For her kind heart, her wicked sense of humour and for knowing all the gossip,' she finished. 'And don't get me started on how much we'll all miss her famous carrot cake.'

Later, as we stood in the cemetery watching the coffin being lowered into the ground, with a faint breeze bowing the branches of the ancient yew trees, it really hit me that she was gone, gone forever. She'd only been 57; way too young to die. I couldn't remember ever feeling so sad.

The village pub, the Golden Fleece, had put on a buffet for the occasion and kept the booze flowing freely all afternoon. It was dark and cosy inside, with low ceilings and small cottagey windows. The walls were decorated with old fishing nets, gleaming horse brasses and paintings of fishing boats.

Mum and Dad went off to the solicitor's to discuss the will, but the rest of us — Matthew and I, Ruth and her husband Tim, and Louise and her husband Chris — were there for the duration. Their children had been palmed off on various friends and mothers-in-law for the night, so our conversation was punctuated by several phone calls checking up on them. 'Could you remind Hugo to practise his violin tonight? He's got his Grade Two exams next week,' Ruth said loudly into her mobile, as if hoping to impress the rest of the pub with her infant prodigy.

Louise, meanwhile, had to sing 'Twinkle, Twinkle, Little

Star' down the phone to her youngest, Matilda, who didn't seem very happy about Mummy being away. The first two times she sang it quietly, hunched over her phone as if deeply embarrassed by the request. 'Louder? That *was* louder,' she sighed when Matilda wasn't satisfied. 'Oh, all right,' she muttered, rolling her eyes. 'If I must.' She drained her glass of wine and belted it out, much louder this time, earning herself several bemused stares from the other punters. 'Kids!' she exclaimed comically as she ended the call.

Louise was plastered within an hour, her cheeks pink, her hair dropping out of her ponytail by the minute, and her gesticulations becoming progressively wilder. She had the hump with Mum, she told us. 'Can you believe it, she's only gone and entered Josh in the Cats' and Dogs' Home "Pet Lookalike" competition – with Monty,' she sniffed indignantly. 'I mean, honestly! How rude is that? Her own grandson – and she's basically saying she thinks he looks like a flaming Yorkshire terrier!'

Despite the circumstances, I burst out laughing. Josh was Louise and Chris's earnest seven-year-old and yes, now that I came to think of it, he did have the same shaggy brown hair and mischievous eyes as Monty, Mum and Dad's grumpy pooch.

'I wouldn't have minded so much if she'd actually asked us first,' she spluttered. 'But she just went and sent off photos of them both without a word. What a cheek!'

'What's the prize?' Matthew wanted to know. 'Could Josh win himself a year's supply of Pedigree Chum?'

Louise swatted him with a beer mat. 'No, he bloody can't,' she said. 'The prize is twenty-five pounds to spend in the Cats' and Dogs' Home shop. That's handy for us, seeing as we have neither a cat nor a dog, don't you think? I wonder who'd end up spending that!'

Ruth – who, as the sole teetotaller of the group, was the only one not slurring her words at this point – patted Louise's hand. 'If it makes you feel any better, Mum thinks she's paying Josh a compliment, likening him to Monty,' she said. 'I'm serious!' she added, as we all (with the exception of Louise) roared with laughter again. 'You know how much she dotes on that wretched mutt. Josh must be golden boy for her to have chosen *him* for the competition.'

There was a note of envy in Ruth's voice, and I tried not to groan out loud. She was fiercely competitive with Louise – always had been. Ruth had all but suffered a nervous breakdown as a teenager trying to match Louise's grades in school, whereas Louise was one of those naturally brainy types who floated through life, passing everything with ease, with only the most cursory flick-through of revision notes necessary. Worse, she didn't even seem to notice Ruth snapping frantically at her heels. Even now it rankled with Ruth, clearly.

I was about to change the subject to safer grounds when

Mum and Dad came back into the pub. Everyone stopped laughing abruptly, feeling self-conscious and remembering why we were all there. Mum flashed me a look, then sat down, her face pale. She seemed uncharacteristically quiet.

'Are you okay, Mum?' I asked, reaching over to take her hand. It had been worst for Mum, of course, losing Jo. She looked as if she'd hardly slept since we'd heard the news. I knew that today must have been a horrendous ordeal for her.

'Um ... yes,' she said after a moment, giving me the same quick glance, as if she was wondering whether or not to tell me something.

'What is it?' I asked. 'What's happened?'

'Well ...' she said, twisting her rings on her fingers and not looking at anyone for a second. Then she turned to Dad. 'You tell them,' she said. 'I'm still taking it in.'

Dad cleared his throat. 'We've just been talking to the solicitor about your aunt's will,' he began. 'And it's a bit peculiar, shall we say.'

He paused, and I felt my heart step up its pace. It wasn't like jokey, affable Dad to look so grave. Had Jo died horribly in debt? Was there some dark secret in her will, a love-child, maybe?

His gaze fell on me. 'She's left you the café, Evie,' he said bluntly, and handed over an envelope with my name typed on it. 'Here – this is for you.'

'She's *what?*' I stared at him, and then at Mum, half-expecting them to laugh and tell me they were joking. They didn't. 'What do you mean, she's left me the café?' I said. 'Are you serious?'

Mum nodded. 'That's what the will said, love.' She nodded at the letter I was holding. 'Why don't you open it?'

'Bloody hell,' Ruth said tightly. 'There must be some mistake. She's really left the beach café to *Evie?*'

I looked down at the envelope dumbly, then ripped it open, my fingers fumbling on the paper, my mouth dry all of a sudden. I shot a look at Matthew, who appeared as bewildered as I felt. Ruth was right; this had to be a mistake, my brain reasoned. Had to be. Some silly misunderstanding, some cock-up, or ...

I pulled out the letter and felt a pang at the sight of Jo's loopy writing there on the page. It was dated four years earlier, and I gave a choking sort of cry. 'But this was written ages ago. Surely this can't be ...'

Then I fell silent as I read.

Dearest Evie,

    I've just had the loveliest weekend with you here in the bay. You remind me so much of myself at your age – full of life, full of dreams, sparkling with energy and enthusiasm. I love seeing you here – you always seem at your happiest and most relaxed when you're down by the sea. And yet I sense that you're not truly fulfilled, that you haven't yet found your heart's desire, the peace that comes with pure, deep contentment.

You might not ever read this letter — maybe life will take some unexpected twists and turns for us both, and my words will become meaningless. But I'd like to state, here and now, that in the event of my untimely death, I am leaving you the café in my will.

I stopped reading, unable to take the words in. The sentences were jumbling up before my eyes, and I felt dulled by wine and shock. No way. This couldn't seriously be happening, could it?

'What does it say?' Ruth urged. 'Evie?'

'Hang on,' I mumbled, turning my eyes back to the paper.

Yes, beloved niece, you read that right. You know that you have always been my favourite girl, the daughter I never had. You are the only person to whom I would entrust my precious café, because I know you will look after it with the love and care it deserves. I've always felt you have a kinship with this place, and I know you can do it.

Excuse an old girl her fancies. As I said, you might never read this letter. But maybe, just maybe, one day you'll hold it in your hands and I hope you'll understand and respect my wishes.

Much love

Jo xxx

I swallowed, my cheeks burning hot suddenly, as blood rushed into my face. Then I folded the letter quickly, not wanting my sisters to read the bit about me being 'the favourite'. Nor did I want Matthew to see the lines about me not having found my heart's desire. If Jo had written this four years ago, I'd have been going out with him by then. It was the sort of thing that would get his back up, bring a bitter gleam to his eye.

'Wow,' I said, gazing around the table. For a second, a wild fantasy bubbled up in my head: me behind the counter of the café again, serving the most incredible food, being awarded Michelin stars, lauded by all the restaurant reviewers in the broadsheets, queues stretching out of the front door . . .

Louise was grinning broadly. 'Priceless,' she said. 'Oh, she was a devil, wasn't she? Bonkers!'

'She wasn't bonkers,' I said, stung.

'That's not a nice way to speak of the dead,' Mum snapped. 'Admittedly, I don't know what she was thinking, leaving such a responsibility to Evie, but—'

'Well, Evie can just put it on the market, can't she? Make a few quid, get a nice place in Oxford,' Ruth put in dismissively. Her voice had a falsely bright topnote betraying how furious she really was that I'd been singled out for special attention.

'I *am* sitting here, thank you very much,' I reminded them. 'And I've got a nice place in Oxford already, remember.'

'Well—' Matthew began, and I stiffened as I sensed he was about to correct me.

'All right, *we've* got a nice place,' I said, before he could get in first. 'Oh, all right, for heaven's sake, *Matthew's* got a nice place that I'm living in, then.'

There was an awkward pause. Sore point.

'I didn't mean—' he started defensively.

'*Anyway*,' Ruth said over him. 'That's not really relevant, is it? Personally, I don't think it's fair that Jo gave you the café. There *are* three of us, after all.'

'Ruth!' Dad exploded. 'Poor Jo's not been in the grave five minutes. How dare you start bitching about the will? You haven't been forgotten, don't worry, there's something left for you.' He looked crosser than I'd seen him for years. 'Honestly!'

Ruth lowered her eyes to the table and Tim put an arm around her. 'Sorry,' she muttered to nobody in particular.

Mum looked anxiously at me. 'Evie, this is obviously a surprise to us all, but there's no rush to do anything. Dad and I can help you with the legalities of getting the café onto the market, and—'

'Who said I wanted to sell it?' I blurted out. Everything seemed to be moving so quickly. People were making assumptions, making decisions for me. I hadn't yet had time to work through my own thoughts on the bombshell.

Matthew stared at me. 'What do you mean?' he said. '*Don't* you want to sell it?'

'I...' I began, then stopped. The words of Jo's letter were still running through my mind; I could almost hear her saying them out loud to me. My fantasy world popped up inside my head again – ker-ching! – with a vision of Matthew and me in matching aprons behind the counter, smiling happily at one another as I frothed the milk for cappuccinos and he sprinkled on the cocoa powder in a heart shape. We could do it, couldn't we? We could run away to Cornwall and live here, and...

'Because it's not exactly practical, is it?' Matthew went on, as if reading my mind. 'I mean, we both live and work in Oxford.'

He was right, of course. Completely right. It was ridiculous to daydream about running away. Silly. Childish. My daydream vanished immediately, like smoke in the wind.

'I just need a bit of time,' I said. I rubbed my eyes, feeling drained. *You are the only person to whom I would entrust my precious café*, Jo had written. *You can do it.* And here was everyone flogging it, before I'd even had a minute to think. My family, honestly. This was them all over. Couldn't take the black sheep seriously, even when a fully fledged business had fallen into her lap. 'I've got to get my head around this. I haven't taken it in yet.'

'I'm not surprised,' Mum said kindly. 'It's been one hell of a day. There's no rush to make any decisions – certainly not tonight anyway. There's plenty of time to sort everything out.' She gave everyone a tired smile. 'Let me tell you what else the will said...'

She and Dad began relating what the others had been bequeathed, but I tuned out, unable to stop my mind whirling and spinning with the news. Jo had given me the café. It was mine. I owned a business, a building right here in Carrawen!

There was only one thing I could think of doing. I necked my glass of wine and got to my feet. 'My round,' I said. 'Who wants another?'

Chapter Three

'Evie, have you finished that letter yet? I need it as soon as possible.'

'Evie! Mr Davis wants coffee.'

'Evie, I've left a pile of filing on your desk. And don't forget that the stationery order needs putting through today.'

It was the following Monday morning, and Carrawen Bay seemed a long, long way away now; a shimmering, unreachable oasis in my mind, a dream I had once had. I was back in Oxford, in a dingy office block near the Clarendon Centre, where I was midway through a two-month temping job for the most bad-mannered, ill-humoured group of people in the world, who all seemed to think I had superhero abilities when it came to my Everest-like intray.

I hadn't had the most illustrious career, it had to be said. After drama school, I'd wanted to tread the boards (or be flung into Hollywood stardom, let's be honest), but after five years when I only managed a few minor roles in theatre productions, and a sole appearance in *Casualty* as an extra (Overdose Victim), I grudgingly accepted that I was always going to be more *Hollyoaks* than Hollywood, and reluctantly knocked that dream on the head. Then I tried to make it as a photographer, followed by a stint singing in a band, but those career options didn't pan out too well, either. That was the point at which I met Matthew; and then, with Matthew's encouragement, I'd quit my pub job, gone to secretarial college and had been temping ever since. And bored out of my wits. Recently I had finally resigned myself to doing what my parents and sisters had been brainwashing me to do all along – go into teaching.

Personally I wasn't convinced I would make the most illustrious teacher. I didn't have a lot of patience at the best of times, became quickly irritated by whingeing children and, worst of all, couldn't bear the sound of chalk squeaking down a blackboard. My sisters reassured me that it was all whiteboards these days and amazing computer trickery, but I still felt on edge at the thought of being in a classroom again. (And don't get me started on my lifelong fear of school toilets.) However, I'd grudgingly come to the conclusion that perhaps taking a teacher-training course might actually be a tad more interesting and worthwhile than staying in Temp Hell for the rest of my days. And, frankly, I'd run out of other options. My family had been relieved, to say the least.

'You're making the right decision,' Ruth told me, nodding her head with sage approval. 'Teaching's not only rewarding, but you've got the security of work for life. And then, of course, you've got your pension too – never too early to be thinking about that.'

I completely disagreed. In my opinion, taking a job for pension reasons when you were still in your thirties was so mind-bogglingly old-fartish that it should be punishable by law. Besides, I wasn't sure I even *wanted* 'work for life', either – the very phrase filled me with dread. Where did following your dreams and taking chances fit into 'work for life'? What happened to fun and spontaneity?

The thing was, arguing with Ruth was like arguing with a moving bulldozer; you were always going to be squashed eventually, whether you liked it or not. You could protest all you wanted to about fun and dreams and risk-taking, but get her on the subject of mortgages and family responsibilities and she was unstoppable.

So, duly flattened, I'd done the safe, sensible thing and applied for a place on a course at Oxford Brookes. Much to my surprise, I'd actually been offered one. I'd almost laughed in disbelief when the letter had arrived. They really thought I was a suitable candidate for being a teacher? Clearly my acting skills had been magnificent during the interview. Suckers!

Anyway, the course started in four months' time, in September, and originally, knowing how intensive and full-on-exhausting a PGCE was meant to be, I'd had vague plans to take some time off before it started and enjoy my last months of freedom. I could decorate the house, dig out my camera and do some photography, sort out the garden, or maybe even take a last-hurrah holiday somewhere hot and exotic – perhaps I could squeeze in an India trip after all . . .

'It's probably better for you to get as much work as you can before September,' Matthew had pointed out, though. 'If I'm going to put your name on the mortgage, you've got to pay your way, really. She who pays, stays, and all that.'

I'd never heard that particular maxim before, but I supposed he was right. It wasn't fair to expect him to cough up for everything while I took a year off work in order to do the course, and I was a liberated twenty-first-century woman who was happy to pay my share of the bills, and what-have-you. So no, I wasn't in hot, dusty India, with my hair in braids, sporting a henna tattoo as I haggled in a market for a silver bangle. I wasn't on a palm beach either, engrossed in a fat blockbuster novel and soaking up the rays. Instead, I was typing and photo-copying and filing and coffee-making for the slave-masters and -mistresses in the torture dungeon – I mean offices – of the Crossland Finance Solutions company. And yes, it was every bit as dull and demeaning and *dire* as it sounded.

There was one guy there, Colin Davis – Mr Davis to me – who particularly drove me nuts. He was a fat slug of a man in a tight brown suit, with greasy hair, bulging eyes and bright-pink skin that always seemed to have a sheen of sweat. He must have been nearing fifty, but acted more like a twenty-year-old lout, forever making derogatory remarks about the female members of staff, and churn-ing out endless macho twaddle about who he'd like to 'do' (Katie Price, Alesha Dixon and Cheryl Cole usually, although there were many variations) and what, exactly, he'd like to do to them. More recently, he also seemed to have taken a liking to my bottom, grabbing it, patting it and pinching it whenever he got the chance, which wasn't often, if I could help it. I had perfected the Colin Davis swerve pretty quick, I can tell you.

(I know what you're thinking: why didn't someone report the slimeball to management, and get him sacked? That was the problem. He *was* management, and he wasn't going anywhere – other than to prowl around my desk and perv.)

I kept begging the temp agency to find me another

position, but they weren't sympathetic. 'We haven't got anything else suitable,' they would say each time I phoned in desperation. Of course they'd say that. They were getting a juicy commission, after all, for every hour I suffered working in that hole. Why would they want to pull the emergency cord on this particular gravy train?

'I *said*, I needed that letter as soon as possible! How long does it take to type a few pages?' There he was now, buzzing through from his office on the intercom. Horrible toad of a man. How I wished he'd hop off.

'Sorry, Mr Davis,' I replied insincerely. 'It's coming right up.' Then I muffled the intercom speaker quickly, not wanting to hear his inevitable 'gag' about something else that would be 'coming right up', if I was lucky. Ugh.

I bashed out the letter – something very boring about tax rates – while visions of Carrawen Bay swam through my thoughts. Waking up hungover to the back teeth on the morning after the funeral in a too-hot B&B bedroom hadn't been a lot of fun, but there was no better place to have a hangover than on a beach, in my opinion. I knew that all it would take would be a blast of that bracing, briny air against my skin, the sea breeze ruffling my hair and cleansing my lungs, and my spirits would be well and truly lifted.

It had been drizzling, but after breakfast Matthew and I had pulled on our coats and tramped down to the bay to walk off our stodgy fry-ups. Sure enough, I felt better within minutes as the blustery air slapped me about the cheeks. Ozone-tastic!

It gave me a jolt to see the café again as we reached the sand dunes and headed down the steep, twisting path to the bay itself. The events of the previous day skidded into my head (the will, the letter from Jo, the shocking news that I'd inherited the business) and I found myself staring at the café – my café – as if seeing it for the first time. *My café*. It seemed dream-like, unreal, as if I'd imagined the whole thing.

We'd reached the bottom of the path by now, and stepped onto the beach. It was low tide, and the waves had left curved ripples, like scales, on the wet sand. Clumps of bladderwrack lay black and glistening where the tide had dumped them, and the wind tugged at what was left of my cropped hair, tickling the back of my bare neck. The beach was empty, except for us and a man with a lolloping black Labrador and two little blonde girls in spotty wellies, who were shrieking and running around with the dog.

I couldn't help veering towards the café, drawn help-lessly to it. Mum and Dad had stayed overnight up in Jo's flat there, as Mum had wanted to make sure all the practicalities had been taken care of: the fridge emptied, the heating turned off, the windows securely locked, that kind of thing. 'Come on,' I said to Matthew. 'Let's go in, have a cup of tea and talk to the staff.'

He wrinkled his nose suspiciously. 'Evie, wouldn't it be better not to get caught up emotionally in this? What are you going to say? I mean—'

I knew what he meant. He wanted me to get shot of the whole caboodle as quickly as it had landed in my lap. Why say anything to anyone? Why get involved? Maybe it would be easy for *him* to do that without becoming sentimental, but me, I wasn't made like that. 'Matthew, the café was Jo's. How can I react any way other than emotionally?' I snapped. I wished he didn't have to be so down on the place. I wished—

'Evie, Mr Davis has asked for coffee *again*. How much longer are you going to be?'

A sharp, nasal voice broke into my thoughts. I looked up from my computer screen to see Jacqueline, Mr Davis's PA, glaring at me between her thickly mascaraed false eyelashes. It was like being confronted by Bambi with a bad attitude.

'Two minutes,' I said evenly, trying not to rise to her goading. It struck me as ridiculous that Mr Davis couldn't actually drag his fat arse to the kitchen to make his own coffee, if he was dying of thirst; and presumably Jacqueline, who was only a glorified secretary herself, felt it beneath her too. What was so demeaning about – gasp! – flicking a switch on a kettle with your own finger, for God's sake, or walking to the Starbucks on the High Street, even?

Jo had never treated her staff like scum, never bullied them, never made them feel crap. You could tell from the way they'd all turned up at her funeral with lowered heads and tears in their eyes. According to Mum, the café had been closed for a few days after her death out of respect, and when we dropped in on Saturday, the staff who were working there still looked shell-shocked. My gaze had automatically flicked to the counter, expecting to see Jo at the coffee machine, sharing a joke and a laugh with a customer. Of course she wasn't, though.

The café wasn't huge, but it gave the illusion of space, with its high timbered ceiling, and the large windows and glass doors that opened out onto the deck. Inside, there were eight tables, and a couple of booths by the windows. Outside, there were wooden tables and chairs, with colourful beach umbrellas that provided shade when the sun was blazing down. On hot days, the glass doors could be folded back so that the breeze floated inside, although on cooler days the doors were shut tight, and the place felt cosy and warm, especially when you saw the white-headed waves churning tempestuously as they rushed foaming up the beach.

Jo had always made the cakes and pastries herself, and it gave me another pang to see the cake counter empty that day. Clearly nobody had felt up to filling her shoes when it came to providing the most sinfully delicious chocolate brownies in Cornwall, or the yummiest fruity flapjacks. Oh, Jo ... It seemed impossible that she wasn't ever going to walk out of the kitchen again with a tray of freshly baked goodies. 'Get one of these down you,' she'd always say.

I wondered how the staff were feeling about working in the café now. Cornwall didn't exactly have high employment rates, and they were surely worrying about their future job prospects. One of the girls behind the counter looked barely sixteen, with her fresh little face and henna-red ponytail. What would she do if the café closed? What would any of them do? It wasn't just a business I had inherited, it was people's lives too.

I tried to shake the red-haired girl's face out of my head and return to the real world, this Oxford office world, as I waited for Mr Davis's letter to print. It was taking ages, I registered dimly, glancing over at the printer. Then I noticed that a red light was flashing ominously. PRINTER ERROR, the display panel read.

My phone was ringing. Emails were pinging. Jacqueline was looking pointedly at the clock, and Mr Davis was heaving himself out of his chair and lumbering towards me, no doubt with images of my bottom dancing before his eyes. Oh God. I only just managed to bite back the scream of frustration that rose inside my throat.

'I really, really, *really* hate working in that office,' I moaned later, to my best friend Amber. We'd met after work for a drink in The Bear, a cosy ye-olde-type pub in town, and it had taken me a large gin and tonic and a packet of peanuts to feel even slightly less harassed. 'I hate it, hate it, hate it.'

Amber wrinkled her nose. 'How long's your contract for?' she asked.

'Another month. Four sodding weeks. Twenty bloody days. I can't do it, Amber, I just can't. I've started hiding the filing in a cupboard, because I'm so behind on it, and have been fantasizing about bottom-armour to protect myself from Evil Colin's molesting hands.' I sighed. 'That's not good, is it?'

'That's not good, babe,' Amber agreed. 'Nothing else come up from the agency?'

'Nope,' I said gloomily. 'They don't care. As long as they're getting their cut, they're just leaving me to get on with it.'

'Well, you know what I'm going to say,' Amber began, her dangly earrings swinging as she leaned nearer to me. 'Life is too damn short to waste it in that boring office.

Think of all the other stuff you could be doing. Fun stuff! Stuff you enjoy! Stuff that makes you happy!'

'I know,' I said, but she was on a roll. Once Amber's in full flow, you might as well drink your drink and let her get it all off her chest.

'I mean, there *are* other jobs in Oxford,' she reminded me, slapping a hand down on the table in emphasis. 'Plenty of other jobs. It's not like you *have* to work there because there's nowhere else.' Another slap. Our glasses wobbled. 'Tell them to eff off and walk out, that's what I would do.'

'I know you would, but—' She would, too. Amber had been through even more careers than me. We'd met at drama school, so she'd suffered the actor-wannabe torture as well, although, unlike me, she'd never truly given up on her dream. She'd had bit parts in *EastEnders* and *Emmerdale* to show for it, lucky thing, as well as several seasons in panto, and various roles in local theatre productions. Sure, she'd also been a till-monkey in a museum shop, tried a stint as a commis chef in the Randolph, set herself up as a freelance events organizer (for all of six months) and, more recently, was working in a florist's over in Jericho, but she was still auditioning, still hoping, still learning lines and stepping into other characters' shoes. I wasn't sure if she was dedicated or deluded, but she could at least claim to have ambition, which was more than I could say for myself these days.

'But nothing, Evie!' she interrupted now. She flung up her hands and her chunky silver rings glittered in the pub lights – one, two, three, four. 'Where's your bottle gone? Come September, you'll be slaving away at college and you'll wish you'd done something more exciting over the summer.'

'Matthew thought it would be a good idea to save up ...' I started saying, but she raised an eyebrow, and nothing else came out of my mouth.

'Remember India? He thought it was a good idea for you to do something boring then, too,' she said, drumming a stubby-nailed finger on the table. 'And you totally missed out!'

'I know,' I said wretchedly. 'I hear what you're saying. But ...'

'I'm getting us another drink,' she told me. 'And then we'll come up with a plan. I'll be right back.'

I watched as she strode to the bar. Amber was tall and skinny, with long, flame-red hair that tumbled down her back in waves. She had blue eyes, a wide full-lipped mouth, and a dirty, throaty laugh. She wasn't classically beautiful, but there was something about her – some invisible energy, or effervescence – that meant people noticed her, turned their heads and looked at her, wherever she was. As usual, she was wearing skinny jeans that showed off her skinny bum (a 'copper's arse' I used to tease her – as in 'Call the cops, someone's stolen her arse!'), a scoop-necked black top and a jumble of scarves and jewellery around her neck. Her silver-sequinned baseball boots twinkled with reflected lights as she walked back, bearing full glasses.

'What about that café, then?' she said, when she sat down again. She pushed a gin over to me and took a slurp of her own red wine. 'What happened when you were down there?'

'Well, I had a chat with the staff,' I said. 'There are just three of them at the moment because the season hasn't started yet. So there's the chef, Carl, who seems a total prat, and then two teenagers, Seb and Saffron, who only work there on Saturdays. I told them that, as the new owner of the café, I would look after them and make sure nothing happened without giving them plenty of notice, but . . .' I shrugged. 'I was a bit vague, really. Matthew told me I shouldn't have spoken to them until I had clearer plans, but I felt I had to say *something*.'

It had been pretty awkward, actually. The red-haired girl, Saffron, had practically glared at me, so suspicious did she look when I told her I'd inherited the café. 'Right – so you're going to be running this place, from two hundred miles away?' she'd asked disbelievingly. 'How's that gonna work?'

I'd forced a smile, not liking the chippy look on her face. 'Well, I'm not sure yet,' I confessed. 'I guess I'll need to take on a manager, someone who'll be here during the week, unless, Carl, you could serve the customers as well as cook for them...?'

Carl, who was lanky and olive-skinned, with oily brown hair tied back in a ponytail, looked scornful. 'Right,' he drawled. 'So you want me to serve customers, cook, wash up, ring up the till – all on my own? All for the same pay? No chance, love.'

My cheeks burned at the patronizing 'love'. I was at least ten years older than him, the cocky shit. 'Fair enough, it was only a suggestion,' I said coldly. 'Okay, in that case, I'll advertise for somebody else. In the meantime, I guess the café will have to be closed during the week.'

'Great,' Carl snapped. 'So I'm losing four days' work, just like that? Brilliant.'

'Well, what's the alternative?' I asked, through gritted teeth.

'Oh, all right,' he moaned. 'But I want a pay rise if I'm going to have to do more.'

Seb, the other member of staff, hadn't spoken all this time. He looked about seventeen and had a pleasant pimply face and a thatch of straw-coloured hair. He wore a bright purple T-shirt with the slogan I AM NOT A GEEK. I AM A LEVEL-9 WARLORD printed on it. 'I was hoping to take on more shifts when it's half-term,' he said when I turned questioningly to him. 'That's when the café starts getting busy, and Jo usually needs more help. So maybe Saff and I could pitch in that week, and—'

'Speak for yourself,' Saffron interrupted rudely.

I sighed. This wasn't going very well. 'Look, I know it's not great for anyone, but let's try and pull together, shall we? For Jo's sake? Seb, that would be brilliant if you could come in over the half-term week, I really appreciate it. That's the end of the month, yeah? Great. Carl, I'll be in touch about pay once I've gone through the books.'

And that was the best I could offer. I'd taken away masses of paperwork to decipher and had been wading through it ever since, attempting to keep up with the bills and wages and untangling various correspondences. The reality of having inherited a business had suddenly become very daunting.

'Whoa,' Amber said, when I told her all of this. 'You've got your hands full, then.'

'I know,' I replied. 'It's a massive job. And everyone keeps on at me to sell up and be done with it, but I don't know if it's the right thing to do. Jo loved that place – it was her life. And for me to just stick up a "For Sale" sign, and—'

Amber wrinkled her nose. 'Yeah, but realistically, what else can you do? Run the place from Oxford? That's never going to work,' she said bluntly.

'It might do,' I countered. 'If I found the right manager, if I could get someone like Jo to run it for me . . .' I trailed off, not even convincing myself. Jo was one in a million. She was irreplaceable.

'And, if you *did* decide to sell up, you wouldn't need to temp any more, would you?' Amber went on. 'You'd be quids in! You could tell that Colin to sling his hook, and walk out of there tomorrow. Have yourself a little holiday. Maybe even take your best mate along too . . .' She leaned back in her seat triumphantly, clearly viewing this as the trump card. She had a point. The thought of sticking it to Colin was so tempting that my fingers twitched at the prospect of flinging themselves into V-signs. The thought of Amber and me hanging out on a beach was even better. I had a sudden vision of us tanned and drunk, clinking glasses of ouzo together on a Greek island, or cold beers on the Costa del Whatever.

Then I felt guilty for imagining a holiday without Matthew and tried to Photoshop him into the vision, but he just started complaining about the heat and worrying about the food hygiene. 'You know what my dicky tummy's like,' I heard him say in my head, and cringed.

Amber, meanwhile, was warming to her theme. 'Yeah, I reckon that's your best option. Sell the café, make yourself a wodge of cash — and Bob's your uncle, college paid for and sorted. That's what I would do.'

'Would you?' I was surprised she was being so business-like about it. 'What, just like that?'

'Absolutely just like that,' she replied. 'I mean, providing you definitely want to do this teaching thing, of course?'

'Ye-e-es . . .' I said, more hesitantly than I meant to.

Her eyes narrowed. 'Evie, you don't sound very convincing,' she told me. 'Because if you've changed your mind, you could always get down to Cornwall instead and run the café yourself. What's stopping you? A beach summer would be amazing!'

I was just about to say that there were lots of things stopping me, of course – like Matthew and Saul and work, and . . . well, everything else, *obviously* – when in the nick of time my phone went and I snatched it up, oddly grateful to have been interrupted. It was only my mum asking me round for Sunday dinner, but it meant I could duck out of Amber's fierce line of questioning, thank goodness. A beach summer in Carrawen *would* be amazing, but I couldn't possibly consider it.

After I'd hung up again, I went straight in with a query about the new production she was auditioning for at the Playhouse, and kept well away from the subject of my career for the rest of the evening. It felt safer that way.

Chapter Four

It got me thinking, though. Amber was right about one thing — however emotionally attached I was to the café, it would be difficult to look after it properly all the way from Oxford. But, if I sold it (sorry, Jo), then I wouldn't have to stick out my awful temp job any more. I'd have money and freedom, and I'd be able to do whatever I chose for a while. I could even postpone the teaching course, which was looming unpleasantly ahead of me, however positively I tried to think about it.

Back at home that evening I turned on my laptop, then connected to a property website.

'What are you up to?' Matthew asked, coming to stand behind me and massage my shoulders. 'Not planning to move out, are you?'

'No, of course not,' I said. 'I'm just curious to know what prices are like in Cornwall. I mean, for the café.'

'Ahh.' He sounded approving. Good girl, Evie, doing the sensible thing — bravo. 'Obviously you wouldn't be able to sell it straight away: paperwork, et cetera, and—'

'Yeah, I know,' I interrupted, typing in the postcode and pressing Search, 'but I just want to get an idea. I was thinking . . . Well, I might be able to leave my job. Which would be nice.' I gave a short laugh. 'More than nice, actually. It would be a bloody godsend.'

'Ah,' he said again. This was a different kind of 'Ah', though – less approving, more wary. 'Obviously you can't bank on selling quickly . . .'

'Obviously,' I agreed, leaning closer to the screen as the first ten results appeared.

'And obviously there would be the estate agent's commission to pay, and—'

'All right, all right, I know!' I said, irritated by the way he was speaking to me – as if I was some kind of half-wit, as if I didn't have a clue. Just because he had actually bought a house before, while I'd been a terminal renter all my life, didn't give him the right to patronize me with all his 'obviously's.

The massaging stopped abruptly. 'No need to bite my head off,' he said huffily, walking away. 'Only trying to be helpful.'

'I know, but . . .' I began, although he was already out of earshot. 'I can manage,' I mumbled, staring at the screen again and scrolling down the results. Nothing. Then

I scrolled down the next ten. And the next. Hmm. There were lots of pretty cottages and luxury apartments for sale, but nothing that resembled Jo's place in the slightest.

I frowned. Well, what had I been expecting? Jo's café was unique. Of course there wouldn't be anything similar on the market. I'd have to contact an estate agent directly and get them to give me a price estimate. Not that I had made up my mind to sell yet – I hadn't. I just wanted to know the facts before I made any decisions.

I jotted down a couple of numbers and went to make peace with Matthew.

The next day in the office I waited until everyone had gone for their lunch breaks and then phoned one of the estate agents, who was based in Padstow, a few miles from Carrawen. I spoke to a very friendly bloke, who took down all my details and sounded extremely interested when I said I'd inherited the café and was wondering what to do with it. I could almost hear him rubbing his hands with glee in fact, when he told me he knew the very café I meant, and that it would be a splendid investment for a businessperson or a company – it was a prime spot of land, and absolutely ripe for redeveloping.

'What, you mean a buyer might just . . . knock it down and build something else there?' I said uncertainly. I hated the idea of someone ripping apart the beautiful old building, tearing down the wooden frame, dismantling the windows and doors. I had a vision of all the tables and chairs, the coffee machine, even the framed photos from the walls being dumped in a skip, and winced. I didn't like the thought of the café being anything other than what it already was.

'Absolutely,' he enthused. 'Obviously any purchaser would need to apply to the council first, in order to change the use of the building, but I wouldn't think it would be a problem. It's a wonderful beach; I'm amazed the area hasn't been developed further before now, to be honest. When you look at what has happened to Padstow and Rock, the opportunity is there for the taking, frankly.'

'Yes, but . . .'

'We also get lots of clients interested in second homes in Carrawen Bay,' he went on, not seeming to hear me. '*Lots* of clients. And it would be very easy for someone to turn the café into a luxury holiday home, for instance. Those views would make it a very special property.'

I squeezed my eyes shut, feeling disloyal to Jo as his words gushed into my ear. I could just imagine the look of horror on her face if she could hear me having this conversation. 'Right,' I said. 'Only – well, there are people working in the café at the moment, you know, they have *jobs*, so I wouldn't want them to lose out if I sold the place. And if I *was* going to sell it, I'd definitely want it to carry on being a café, so—'

He gave a cheerful laugh. 'It doesn't really work like that, I'm afraid, Miss Flynn,' he replied. 'It would be up to the buyer to do what they liked with it, once a sale had gone through. Do you want me to pop round, have a proper look at the place and give you a valuation? I could drop in later this week, if that's convenient. Then, if you're happy with the price, we can get the ball rolling, measure up, take some good photos and book in some viewings. I can think of at least five clients off the top of my head who'd be *very* interested. Yeah?'

I hesitated. This was all happening too quickly. I only wanted to sell the café if ... Well, if someone like Jo was going to be there at the helm, keeping the place just as it had been run for all those years.

I sighed. I was dreaming, wasn't I? I was kidding myself.

'Miss Flynn?' the estate agent prompted. 'I could drop in on Thursday if—'

'No,' I interrupted. 'No. Um ... I need to think about this for a bit longer. Thanks for your help, though.'

'Well, if you change your mind, give me a call back; my name's Greg, and I'd be delighted to have this property on our books.'

I bet you would, Greg, I thought miserably, replacing the

receiver. Greg wouldn't care about the kind of person he sold it to. He wouldn't vet all the potential customers to make sure they were nice, decent people who would be custodians of the café, look after the staff and the building properly, would he? No. He'd be all too happy to flog it to the richest person who came along with plans to turn it into a spa complex for swanky types, as long as he got his big fat commission.

I sighed again and put my head on the desk. I couldn't let that happen. I wouldn't let that happen. But what was I supposed to do?

I slammed the front door behind me, threw my bag onto the floor and kicked off my shoes, sending one smacking against the hall radiator with a dull clang. 'That bloody, bloody, bloody, BLOODY sex-pest,' I fumed.

It was Wednesday, and I'd just had the worst day in the office ever. I'd overslept and then had a bike puncture on the way to work, making me doubly late, and meaning a bollocking from Jacqueline, followed by a ton of punishment filing. A crampy PMT had kicked in halfway through the morning, then at lunchtime I'd managed to wrench my ankle on one of the cobbled lanes off the High Street, and snapped the heel of my shoe clean off. Just to put the icing on the cake, later that afternoon Fatso Davis had 'accidentally' brushed his hand against my breast in the lift, making my skin crawl. I had jerked away from him in revulsion, but the smirk on his face let me know he'd copped a good old feel.

'Bloody, bloody, BLOODY DISGUSTING – Oh. Hello, Saul.' I broke off my tirade as I stormed into the kitchen and saw him at the table there, doing a jigsaw with Matthew. Saul was the absolute nicest kid in the world. He usually stayed with us on Wednesday and Saturday nights, and even in my worst PMT-and-sex-pest rage, just the sight of him was enough to make me feel better, as if the world had shifted onto its rightful axis again.

He jumped off his chair and ran over to hug me, and I wrapped my arms around him, kissing his lovely tufty brown hair.

'I forgot it was Wednesday. Oooh, am I glad to see you, it feels like ages. Are you okay?'

'Yep,' he said. 'I finished that Lego dinosaur, you know – do you want to see a picture of it?'

'Too right I do,' I replied, giving him a last squeeze before letting him go. It had taken Matthew a full six months to tell me he had a son, when we started seeing each other, and when he'd finally broken the news he'd been a bag of nerves, apologetic even, that there was this child in his life, this boy from his doomed first marriage. He shouldn't have been nervous or apologetic, though: in my eyes, Saul was nothing but wonderful. Since I'd been introduced to Saul, my life had grown accordingly to encompass the joys of Lego, Play-Doh and football, and more recently Gogos (small plastic alien-type creatures), Match Attax card-collecting and *Beast Quest*. I loved it.

'Hey, Evie, your hair's gone all short,' he said, his eyes wide as if he'd only just noticed. 'You look really cool, like a boy.'

'Thanks,' I said, knowing that this was surely the ultimate compliment.

'Hi,' Matthew said, coming over to kiss my cheek. 'Everything all right?'

I kissed him back and a heavy sigh gusted out of me. 'Not the best day of my life,' I told him, withholding the full details as Saul's bright, interested eyes were still fixed on me. I hoped he hadn't heard my earlier shout. Matthew would kill me if Saul went back to his mum tomorrow and asked, 'Mummy, what's a sex-pest?' in his innocent, piping voice. Emily, Matthew's ex, would be on the phone within five seconds and I'd be in the doghouse for at least a year.

Matthew went to finish some work while I got on with making dinner. I wasn't the most accomplished cook, it had to be said. I had wrecked several saucepans in the past, the most memorable occasion being the time I forgot about the egg I was boiling and left the pan on a flaming gas ring for several hours. The water had boiled dry, the egg had exploded, and the pan was giving off a foul burning smell by the second hour. 'How can anyone forget that they're boiling an *egg*?' Matthew had shouted in exasperation. 'You only have to remember for three flipping minutes, Evie!'

'I know,' I'd said sheepishly. 'I just … forgot.'

The one and only time I'd tried to cook a roast, I'd given us food poisoning ('This chicken is so raw it's practically still alive!' Matthew had realized after the first fatal mouthful). The birthday cake I'd attempted to bake for Matthew had mysteriously vanished into the bin after that first revolting slice we'd each had (it seemed to taste of curry powder; I had no idea why or how). And I'd never been able to make a cheese sauce without having to sieve the lumps out of it.

I could do toast, though, and a half-decent fry-up. And anything that just needed putting in the oven I was mostly okay with. Luckily Saul's favourite food was pizza. Even I could manage that.

We decorated the pizza together in our traditional way, leaving a quarter of it as a margherita for Saul, arranging mushrooms and ham on my section, and olives and pepperoni and extra cheese on Matthew's. Saul loved spending ages lining up the shiny olive halves in patterns, and sprinkling the grated cheddar just so. 'It's snowing cheese,' he said, as he let the pale-yellow curls fall from his fingers.

'Or maybe it's sand,' I suggested. 'Cheesy sand, on a cheesy beach.'

He grinned. 'Dad said you'd been to the beach at the weekend. Did you go rock-pooling?'

I lifted the pizza carefully and slid it into the oven. 'Not this time, no,' I said. 'Do you like rock-pooling?'

'Yeah!' he said, as if that was the most stupid question he'd ever heard. 'Course I do! It's my favourite thing on holiday. My aunty Amanda lives by the sea. She is soooo lucky, lucky, lucky.'

'Mmm,' I said distractedly, shutting the oven door. 'My aunty used to live by the beach too. She loved having the sea as her next-door neighbour.'

'When I'm a grown-up, I'm going to live right *on* a beach,' he told me, wiping his cheesy hands on his school trousers before I could stop him. Oops. Emily wouldn't thank me for that. 'I'm going to build myself a sand *CASTLE* to live in – do you get it, a real castle, made of sand? – and I'm going to go rock-pooling *ALL DAY*.'

'That sounds good,' I said, 'but only if I'm allowed to visit you.'

He nodded. 'I'll build a special bit of the castle just for you,' he promised. 'A whole wing!' He laughed. 'Hey, isn't it weird that castles have wings, like birds do? As if they could fly away!'

I ruffled his hair, a surge of love for him stopping me speaking for a moment. 'You're a sweetheart,' I told him. 'Now — are we going to set this table, or what?'

I dreamed of the beach at Carrawen that night. It was a cold, crisp day in my dream, with that pale-blue early-morning light you get at the coast in winter. The sea was luminescent, sleek and calm, the weak sunlight glittering on its rippled surface like a million sequins. I was the only person there and I stood right in the centre of the bay, gazing out at the indigo-blue line of the horizon, letting the peace and stillness fill me all the way up. I was so happy. So content. So calm . . .

Then the radio sprang into life beside my head, burb-ling DJ nonsense and shattering that perfect peaceful moment. I groaned, stretching out a hand and fumbling to hit the Snooze button. I wanted to slip back into my dream, wanted to be swallowed up again by the empty calm of that winter beach, but annoyingly I couldn't return a second time.

I rolled over towards Matthew's side of the bed, but it was empty and I guessed he must already be up and having breakfast with Saul. He had to take him in to school on Thursday mornings, and lived in fear of running late and thereby suffering the wrath of Emily. She had spies at the school, according to Matthew; a crack team of mums who clocked what time he arrived with Saul and reported back every detail of the viewing.

Emily was always perfectly civil to me, if not actually *friendly*. She was a nurse: a brisk, uber-organized sort of a person, who seemed to iron everything that had a crease in it (even Saul's pants, for goodness' sake), and generally ran her house, and life, like clockwork. Hospital corners on all of *her* beds, I bet. I got the impression that she judged our household accordingly. (Not a whole lot of ironing attempted, and not a single properly made bed, needless to say.)

Matthew and Emily had split up five and a half years ago when she'd gone off with a dashing young paramedic called Dan, whom Saul (and presumably Emily) idolized, although Matthew professed to loathe him, disparagingly calling him 'Doctor Dan' whenever he was forced to refer to him. A fleeting shadow passed over Matthew's face whenever Saul talked about Dan, and I sympathized – it must have been hard for Matthew, having his son grow up with another man. Not just that, but another man who, according to Saul, told the best jokes ever, was brilliant at football, and had spent an entire weekend painting a really cool *Doctor Who* mural on his bedroom wall as a birthday surprise.

I went downstairs now to find Saul munching his way through a bowl of cornflakes in the kitchen, while Matthew made his school lunch. I watched Saul carefully spoon in more cereal, his face dreamy with the early hour, his eyes absent, jaws working mechanically. He was gorgeous. It was the one thing I envied Emily for – that he was hers, properly hers, and not mine. I pretended for a moment what I always did: that he was my son, mine and Matthew's, and we were a happy family waking up to another happy day. Forget my parents and sisters, this was one family scenario where I felt I truly belonged.

Temp Hell that day was … well, hellish. I started a tally of how many times I was asked to do a particular job without anyone saying 'please', and was up to twenty-seven by midday. Then the intercom buzzed and the SlugMan spoke. 'Can you come into my office for a minute,' he said.

Twenty-eight.

'Sure,' I replied, trying not to wilt too visibly. I knew he'd be watching me from his glass-walled Office of Power in the corner and that the slightest grimace or eyeroll would be noted and held against me.

'Oh, and bring your notepad and a pen,' he added as an afterthought.

Twenty-nine.

'Sure,' I repeated tonelessly, feeling like a robot.

Mr Davis had the best office in the whole building, with huge windows along one side of the room, giving him a perfect view of the city centre, packed with the domed roof of the Radcliffe Camera and various church spires and college towers, all in the beautiful mellow Cotswold stone. It was just as well he had the view, because he hadn't exactly done much to doll up the rest of the space. He had one of those I'm-the-boss-style desks, vast and imitation mahogany, with a smart black laptop open on top, alongside a framed photo of what looked suspiciously like his mum. There were shelves crammed with files behind his head and dull grey filing cabinets below the windows, one of which sported a sickly looking aspidistra with dust on its parched leaves.

'So, Miss Flynn,' he said, his voice smarming over my name. I hated his affectation of refusing to call me Evie like any normal person would. 'You smell very nice today. New perfume? Or is it what they call pheromones, eh?'

My face felt hot at his words. Pheromones indeed. In his dreams. I tapped my pen against the notepad, determined to get this over with quickly. I didn't want to hang around here exchanging innuendo-loaded chit-chat with this creep for any longer than I absolutely had to. 'You said you wanted me for something?' I asked briskly.

There was a horrible juicy silence. Damn. That had come out wrong.

'I did, didn't I?' he replied after a pause just long enough that my cheeks had turned scarlet with embarrassment. Oh God. He was actually licking his lips. 'I do want you for something, Miss Flynn, believe me. I've always wanted you, Miss Flynn.'

I inadvertently took a step backwards and bumped into a filing cabinet. My flesh was goosebumping all over at his words, but I uncapped the pen and held it over the pad, willing him to give me my orders and let me go again. I badly needed some fresh air.

'Miss Flynn,' he began. 'I'd like you to take down...' then he paused and looked right at me, bug-eyed and leering, 'your knickers. I *mean* – a letter.'

Blood pounded in my ears. I couldn't believe he had actually just said that. *I'd like you to take down ... your knickers.* The dirty, lecherous bastard.

He was smirking, his lips parted in a way that I could see his horrible red tongue in the wet cavern of his mouth. 'I don't think so,' I managed to say after a moment of stunned shock.

He sneered. 'Oh, right, lost your sense of humour, have you? Feeling frigid today? Very well, let's get on with it, if you're not going to play. Dear Mr Baxter, I am writing in reference to your letter of—'

I shut my eyes briefly as he began rattling off the letter, and had an image of the beach in my dream the night before. The glittering water, the cool blue morning, the calmness that had descended upon me. I gripped my pen, unable to bring myself to move it across the paper. I didn't want to be here any more. Amber was right. Life was too damn short.

'It is with great pleasure that we ...' he droned, then looked up and noticed that I wasn't doing anything. 'Miss Flynn! Are you listening?' he snapped. 'Have you written a single word yet?'

I stared him full in the face, hating him. 'No,' I said softly. 'I haven't.' Adrenaline spiked through me, and then the music from *Working Girl* suddenly started up in my head, Carly Simon singing 'Let the river run ...', the chords swelling louder, stirring me into action. Sod this for a life. I'd had enough of being a working girl, if it meant putting up with creeps like Davis. I chucked my pen and notepad onto his desk.

'I quit,' I told him. 'You are the most disgusting and vile person I've ever had to work for. You repulse me, you and your ... your sweaty hands and your horrible froggy eyes.' Yikes. I wasn't quite sure where the froggy-eyes bit had come from, but they looked as if they were about to explode out of their sockets right now. I stared him down. Moral high ground – I *owned* it. 'So I quit,' I said again, turning away, nose in the air. 'You can shove your job somewhere painful.'

'Miss *Flynn!*' he spluttered, but I didn't wait to hear the rest of it. I walked out, head high, straight back to my desk where I wasted no time in turning off the PC and gathering up my possessions. My phone started ringing, and the intercom was flashing, but I ignored them both. Not my job any more.

Jacqueline appeared by my side like a heat-seeking missile. 'Where do you think you're going?' she snapped. 'Bit early for lunch, isn't it?'

'Get stuffed, Jacqueline,' I replied. 'I'm off. You'll have to get a new skivvy from now on. Oh yeah, and by the way, I've left something in the cupboard for you.' I indicated the spot where I'd dumped a huge armful of filing earlier that week. 'Have a nice life.'

'Wait!' she shrieked. 'You can't just walk out!'

'Watch me,' I said, and swished past her, right out of the door before she could argue.

My heart was galloping, I was shaking all over and my breath was coming out hard and fast, as if I'd just run up six flights of stairs. Oh my God, Evie, I thought, as the cool air of the morning hit me outside. What just happened in there? What did you just *do*?

I cycled over to Matthew's office on the other side of town and phoned him. I was alternating between euphoria at having quit and shock at how quickly and theatrically it had happened. But nobody with an ounce of sanity or self-respect could have stayed on working for King Sluggo, especially after the take-down-your-knickers remark. You had to know your bottom line, as my mum might have (inappropriately) commented. And when that line was crossed, it was time to make a stand.

Well, I'd done that all right.

'Hi,' I said, when Matthew picked up his phone. 'Fancy skiving off for half an hour so you can meet me for a quick coffee?'

There was a moment's silence, when I could imagine him blinking in surprise. Silly me. Matthew wasn't exactly the skiving type, and especially not on the spontaneous whim of his work-shy girlfriend. 'I mean – you could call it your early lunch break,' I put in helpfully, 'or—'

'What do you mean? Where are you?' he asked.

'I'm outside your office. Just—' *Just walked out of mine*, was on the tip of my tongue, but suddenly I bit it back. I knew a revelation like that wouldn't go down terribly well, blurted out over the phone. 'Just fancied a break,' I lied.

'Um ... Well, I'm right in the middle of something,' he said. He was still working with the same IT geeks from the Christmas party all those years ago, as a programmer for a technical software company. 'Sorry.'

'It's kind of important,' I told him. 'Please?'

'So is this,' he replied. 'Sorry, Evie, maybe later on.'

'Okay,' I said, trying not to feel deflated. I had all the time in the world, after all, now that I was unemployed. 'I can wait. I'll be in Marian's, so come and join me when you can.'

Marian's was a café over the road from Matthew's office. It was dingy inside, with the ceiling still stained tobacco-brown from the pre-smoking-ban years, and every other surface bore a lingering trace of chip fat. My tea came in one of those stainless-steel teapots that couldn't actually pour the tea without spilling it everywhere – a pretty basic design flaw, I'd always thought – and the UHT 'milk' was served in little plastic cartons that were practically impossible to open. I went crazy and bought a packet of shortbread fingers as well, but they were way too chunky and made my mouth feel as if it were full of cardboard when I bit into one.

I couldn't help contrasting it all to Jo's café: the sea breeze versus the drone of a grubby ceiling fan, the sandwiches made from fresh bakery bread instead of anaemic-looking mass-produced slices, the cakes and biscuits warm from Jo's oven rather than factory-made, and then wrapped in cellophane for God knows how long ... There was no comparison. The two were poles apart.

You are the only person to whom I would entrust my precious café.

I remembered Jo's words from her letter, and I felt a pulling sensation inside. Then I knew exactly what I should do. No, not just 'should do' – *needed* to do.

The girl behind the counter put on the *Mamma Mia!* album just then and I heard Amanda Seyfried's clear, high voice sing 'I have a dream...'

I left the rest of my tea and got to my feet. Matthew hadn't showed up, but I couldn't wait any longer. I had plans to make, I had packing to do. Cornwall was calling me and, for the first time in ages, I had a dream.

Chapter Five

Dreams are all very well in the heat of the moment, but by the next morning they can look different. Mine certainly did. The night before I'd been fired up with a vision that I'd honour Jo's memory by taking on the café and making it better than it had ever been. I'd get it redecorated, perhaps even build an extension, expand the business. I'd hire a brilliant new manager who'd run it on a day-to-day basis, while I, as the owner, would drop in every month to give my devoted staff pep talks and inspiration. Perhaps I'd suggest new additions to the menu, or throw parties for the villagers to thank them for their custom. And together we'd build up a devoted clientele, who came from miles around to sit and admire the views and enjoy the mouth-watering delights on our menus. No longer would the customers be people merely drifting up from the beach – oh no. I would put Carrawen Bay on the map. Holidaymakers would choose to go there especially because I'd made the café such a success.

'Your aunt would have been proud,' the villagers would say when they came in. 'We can't believe how well you're managing the café without her – and all the way from Oxford, too!'

By the time I was halfway to Cornwall the following day though, I wasn't so sure if it was that I *had* a dream, or that I was *living* in a dream. Boring reality was trickling in, dampening all my big ideas. I couldn't even run my own bank account, let alone a full-grown business. I didn't have a clue about managing staff or giving pep talks. And Oxford was a bloody long way from Cornwall. Too far to be popping back and forth all the time.

Matthew had put it more bluntly. 'What sort of normal person quits their job to babysit a beach café two hundred miles away?' he'd asked over dinner the night before. 'I just think this is a bit ... reckless, Evie. I don't think you've thought it through properly.'

Well, if I *was* being reckless, it felt surprisingly good. Dangerously good in fact. To hell with boring reality. There I was in the car, with my overnight bag packed, the keys to the café and the knowledge that I never had to answer the phone with 'Crossland Financial Solutions, Evie speaking, how-may-I-help-you?' for the rest of my days. I'd never have to be in the same room as Colin Slime-bucket Davis again. And every time I imagined Jacqueline's look of horror when she discovered that massive wedge of filing I'd left her, I couldn't help but laugh to myself. It was Friday, the sun was beaming down, I was singing along to the radio at the top of my voice and, best of all, I was heading for the beach. My beach. Yes, all in all, I was in way too cheerful a mood to be having any sort of crisis. I felt as if I'd just unlocked a cage and set myself free. Now I was stretching my wings, taking flight, and—

BEEEEEP!

A white van was blowing its horn and flashing its lights behind me and I realized I'd been so absorbed in my daydream that I'd slowed to fifty miles an hour. I had to concentrate, I was nearly at Exeter and always managed to get in the wrong lane when the motorway ended.

'What are you going to *do* down there anyway?' Matthew had asked when I'd begun packing up a case of clothes and toiletries.

'Well, you know,' I'd replied airily. 'Make sure everything's running smoothly and the staff are managing okay. Help out in the kitchen, or—'

'You? In the kitchen?' Matthew had snorted. 'Anyway, I thought you were going to *sell* the cafe?' He sounded suspicious, as if I was planning to trick him in some way. 'I thought you'd decided?'

No, Matthew, I said inside my head. *You'd decided that. But I hadn't.*

I'd shrugged, tucking in a few paperbacks I'd been

meaning to read for ages. 'I just need to be there at the moment, that's all,' I replied. I knew this would sound irritatingly flaky to Matthew, who had no truck with whims and fancies, so I added, 'Look, humour me, will you? It's something I want to do. I'll be home again in a few days, and life will go back to normal.'

His lower lip seemed to be sticking out. Surely he wasn't going to sulk about this?

'I'll bring you back a Cornish pasty, how about that?' I said, trying to lighten the mood.

He sneered. He *was* sulking. 'I don't even like them,' he muttered, huffing out of the room.

I'd felt a tiny bit bad, but not nearly bad enough to stop me going. And why the hell shouldn't I go? This was a big deal, this inheritance. Way more important than a crappy temping job with the Human Slug. And yes, okay, so I didn't have a game plan as to what I'd actually do when I got to Cornwall, but that didn't matter. I just needed to make sure everything was ticking along as it should be. I could make up the rest when I got there.

I sighed, thinking back to when Matthew and I had said goodbye that morning. It hadn't exactly been on the best of terms. Neither of us had slept well the night before. I'd tried to snuggle up to him, hoping to make friends again, but he'd turned his back on me. Sex wasn't on the cards then – not that *that* was any big surprise. It had been weeks. I was beginning to think Matthew had gone off me lately. There were only so many times a bloke told you he was 'too tired' before a girl started taking it personally.

Over breakfast we'd both been quiet – me, because I felt vacant and spacey from tossing and turning all night, and him because ... well, I got the feeling he was still in a tremendous strop with me. He grunted when I asked if he wanted a coffee and barely looked in my direction. Was he trying to guilt-trip me into changing my mind and not going? I wondered. If so, it wasn't working.

'What's up?' I asked after a while. 'Is this about me heading off to Cornwall? Because I do need to get this sorted out, you know. Whatever happens – whatever decision I make – I do actually have to go there at least once more. And now seems a good time.'

'What with you having flounced out of your job, you mean,' he put in, rather too caustically for my liking.

I glared at him, fed up with his sulks. 'Yeah, that's right,' I said. 'What with me flouncing out of my job. I don't know *what* came over me. It was such a great place to work, as well. I must have been mad.'

He stood up, even though he hadn't finished eating. 'Suit yourself,' he grumbled, leaving the room.

I ground my teeth as I heard him stomping upstairs. He was a fine one to talk about flouncing anywhere. And –

I broke off from my train of thought as I realized I'd been in completely the wrong lane for the A30, and was now heading merrily into the centre of Exeter instead. Bollocks! I thumped the steering wheel in frustration, blaming Matthew entirely for my slip-up.

It took almost five hours to get down to Carrawen Bay, including an impromptu lunch break in Exeter, and then twenty minutes swearing furiously as I tried to find my way back to the Cornwall road, with the rain lashing down in buckets all the while, so hard I worried that my wipers were about to fly off in their vain attempts to clear the screen. Then, just as I'd passed Launceston and was thinking I was onto the home straight, I got stuck behind a muck-spreader, which crawled along at fifteen miles an hour. I didn't have space to overtake for ages and could feel impatience bubbling inside me as it trundled along, leaving clods of mud on the road in its wake.

But at long last, the muck-spreader turned off at Pendoggett, and then my spirits lifted as I had my first glimpse of the Atlantic, dark and grey though it was. Now the trees were becoming more hunched over, forced into growing in strange, bent shapes by the battering wind that swept across from the sea. The black-and-white Cornish flag fluttered from the tops of pubs and B&Bs and, just ten minutes later, I was heading into Carrawen, and the storm seemed to be blowing itself out.

It was only as I passed the grocery shop – Betty's Pantry – that I realized I'd brought absolutely no groceries with me, not even a carton of milk. I pulled over to the side of the road and hesitated. There would probably be stuff at the café I could use, but it didn't seem right just to start helping myself. So I turned off the engine, grabbed my purse and dashed into the shop to pick up a few things.

Betty – if that was the stout, pinny-wearing, blue-rinse lady behind the counter – raised her eyes from the copy of *OK!* magazine she was flicking through as I hurried in and stared at me for a moment, as if trying to place me. Then she gave a loud snort of derision and turned back to her page.

I felt slightly discomfited – was the snort aimed at me? – but assured myself quickly that no, of course it wasn't. Betty didn't know who I was, so why would she be snorting at me? It was probably some shenanigans in her magazine that had caused the noise of contempt. Misbehaving celebrities, no doubt, or drunken members of the aristocracy. Fair enough. They often warranted a snort from me, too.

I began loading my basket. Cereal, bread, butter, cheese,

milk, teabags, a huge slab of chocolate – well, why not? It was kind of a holiday, wasn't it? . . . Then I heard the mutter. 'That's her over there, Jo's niece.'

'What, the one who—'

'Yep. Her.'

I spun round in surprise. Betty was leaning on the counter talking to a younger woman with a short peroxide-blonde bob, wearing a pink velour tracksuit. Both were staring quite openly at me, with scornful looks on their faces.

I stared back for a moment, my heart thumping. 'Are . . . are you talking about me?' I asked eventually.

'Yep,' Betty replied, folding her doughy arms in front of her. Her dark, piggy eyes glittered with dislike. Bloody hell. I felt like I'd wandered into a Wild West saloon all of a sudden.

'I'm surprised you can show your face around here,' the blonde woman tutted, looking down her sharp little nose at me. 'What a nerve!' She turned her back pointedly and addressed Betty. 'Twenty Lambert & Butler for me, love.'

I gaped, completely confused. 'I don't know what you're talking about,' I said, feeling hot all over. 'But you've got it wrong, whatever it is. I've just come down here to—'

'Oh, you don't need to explain,' Betty interrupted, without deigning to look at me. She handed over a pack of cigarettes to the blonde woman and took the money.

'We've heard all about it. And let me tell you, Jo would have been ashamed of you. Downright ashamed.'

I stood there, still utterly in the dark. 'Look, there's obviously been some misunderstanding,' I tried wretchedly, but Betty wouldn't let me finish.

'Save your breath,' she snapped, 'but understand this: you're not welcome in my shop. So you can just put those things back on the shelf right now, because I won't be serving you.' Then she counted the change into the blonde woman's hand. 'Eighty, ninety, five pounds. Thanks, Marilyn.'

The blonde woman left the shop and I went up to the counter. 'Please can you just tell me what this is all about?' I asked, hoping to appeal to any shred of decency that the old bag might possess.

She merely jerked a thumb at the door. 'How many times do I have to tell you? Out! Hoppit!'

I gave up. I left my basket of groceries on the floor – she could dream on, if she expected me to meekly put them all back – and walked out, feeling bruised by the encounter and still baffled. What the hell was all that about?

'Okay,' I muttered to myself as I got back into the car. 'So . . . I'll just go straight to the café then.'

It was mid-afternoon and the village seemed quiet. I drove past an old man leaning heavily on a stick and a young guy walking a collie, but there was barely another soul around. The houses and pavement glistened wet from the rain as the church clock tolled the half-hour, and I felt self-conscious, imagining curtains twitching as my car went by, and the whispers of contempt: *There she goes. Her. What's she doing here anyway? Doesn't she know she's not welcome?*

I tried to snap out of my paranoia. I was being silly. Betty had got the wrong end of the stick about something, but that didn't mean the rest of the villagers would have it in for me. Rude old cow. I'd steer well clear of her shop while I was down here, that was for sure. I imagined she packed a hefty right hook.

I rounded the corner, almost through the village now. There was the sea in front of me, wild and choppy-looking, with white crests on the cold, grey waves as they crashed into the bay. The seagulls were keening above the water, their harsh cries like spiteful laughter as they dipped and swooped. I unrolled my window, suddenly needing to breathe in the fresh sea air after the disconcerting experience in Betty's shop, and the cold wind burst inside, wrapping itself around my burning face.

And then, at last, there was the café – thank goodness. It sat there like a place of refuge; I couldn't remember ever feeling so glad to see it, so relieved to be back. I was somewhat apprehensive too, though, as I pulled into the small car park tucked behind it. I still hadn't quite got my head around all of this — me owning the café, and Jo no longer being there. And, like Betty, the staff hadn't exactly been pleased to see me the last time I'd been in. In fact, Carl and the red-haired girl, Saffron, had been pretty rude. But I was sure all that would change once we got to know each other, and we could work together to keep the café busy and successful like one big happy f —

Oh. I had just noticed how much litter there was strewn around the car park. The wind sent a couple of crisp packets whirling about off the ground, like blue-and-green butterflies. And ... Gross! One of the dustbins had fallen over and its bin bag had been half-dragged out — by the yobbish seagulls probably. It had been ripped open, and the contents had spilled everywhere.

I frowned. Not exactly the best first impression for the place. Back when I'd worked for her, Jo had been super-strict about fastening the bin lids on tightly. I'd teased her about it, calling her obsessed, but maybe she'd had a point.

Oh well. Perhaps it was too much to expect the staff to carry on doing everything perfectly without her. They were probably under a lot of strain, trying to keep the place going without her guidance. I bet they missed her loads. I couldn't be too hard on them right now.

I got out of the car and locked it, then began walking towards the front of the café. Something rustled behind me and I swung around just in time to see a long, scaly tail flick behind the bin and vanish. Oh God. A rat! I really hated rats. And I was pretty sure that the Environmental Health people weren't all that keen on having them hanging around cafés, either. Shit. I was going to have to play Bad Cop with the staff, and remind everyone to clear up the rubbish properly. That would go down well.

Shuddering, I hurried round to the front of the café. The beach was deserted after the recent storm, and the sea looked furiously grey, bursting over the rocks with great fountains of white, lacy spray. Wooden steps led up to the decking area outside the café, and as I climbed them, the first thing I saw was an old drink carton lying right in the middle of the deck. More rubbish. Brilliant.

I tutted and picked it up, then noticed that the outdoor chairs had all been left upright during the recent cloudburst and had rain puddles on their seats. Shaking my head crossly, I went around tipping them against the tables so that the water would drain away. God, this wasn't a good start. I hoped things were better inside.

I took a deep breath, trying to give Carl and the staff the benefit of the doubt. The drink carton might have been dropped just a minute or so ago after all, by someone leaving the café, or perhaps had been blown there by the wind. The bins ... Well, it was easy to forget them, I supposed. Hopefully once I had given everyone a reminder, it wouldn't happen again. No real harm was done.

I went inside, badly in need of a reviving coffee after my long journey, but winced immediately at the sound of loud reggae blasting out from the kitchen. Jo had always had the radio on – a cute retro radio that she kept perched on the counter. It wasn't there any more though. (Had it been nicked? I wondered darkly.)

The café wasn't busy – an elderly couple sat nursing a pot of tea on a table for two, and a family with two squirming little girls were in the far corner. A petite woman with ash-blonde hair was at the counter and she rolled her eyes when she saw me. 'Don't hold your breath for the service,' she said. 'I've been waiting here five minutes already. Think he's having his own private party in there, or something.'

I felt dismayed, and cross too, at this. 'Sorry,' I said, going behind the counter and dumping my bag there. I grabbed an apron from the nail and briskly put it on. 'What can I get you?'

The girl goggled in surprise. 'Oh! Do you work here?' she asked.

'Not really,' I said. 'Well, sort of. What would you like?'

'Two white teas, a black coffee, a latte and a Coke, please. And have you got any cakes?'

It was only then I noticed that the plates where Jo's magnificent cakes were usually displayed were empty, save for a few stale crumbs. Nice. 'I'll find out,' I said, scribbling down the order. I felt slightly dazed. I hadn't expected to get stuck in to hands-on café life quite so quickly. 'Give me a minute,' I said. Then I went into the kitchen.

The reggae was even louder in there, making the windows vibrate with the booming bass. Carl had his back to me, stirring something pungent and spicy at the hob, completely oblivious to anything else.

'Carl!' I said, bristling with annoyance. What was he playing at? And what was he cooking, anyway? It smelled like curry, and I knew that wasn't something Jo had ever had on the menu. 'Carl!' I said again, when he didn't seem to hear.

I snapped off the stereo at the wall and the room went quiet. He swung round instantly, and did a double-take as he saw me there.

'What's up? What's going on?' he asked.

'I could ask you the same,' I replied. My voice sounded snotty and cold, but I didn't care. 'There's a customer out there, said she's been waiting for five minutes. And the music's too loud, and I saw a *rat* outside, and there's litter everywhere!' I stopped abruptly as his face darkened. Oops. So much for not going in on the attack.

'Chill out, man,' he said, waving a hand. 'It's all under control.'

'Really,' I said flatly. 'That's not how it looks from

here.' I folded my arms across my chest, feeling my face turn pink. I wasn't good with confrontation at the best of times. 'Anyway, can we get these drinks for the customer, please? Oh, and is there any cake?'

'Cake's all gone,' he said. 'Not my thing. What drinks does she want?'

I rattled off the order, not liking the way he looked at me so sneeringly. 'I'll get the Coke,' I said.

He turned down the heat under the pan of curry and wiped his hands on his apron. 'I'll just do everything else then, shall I?' he said.

I stared after him, fuming at his rudeness. 'Well, that is your *job*,' I muttered savagely under my breath. Honestly! How had Jo ever managed to work with such a tosser? Two minutes of being in a confined space with him and I was spitting tacks.

I stuck my head in the store cupboard, wondering what else I could offer the girl, seeing as there were no cakes. The stock seemed very low, I thought, scratching my head as I gazed around. Back when I had worked there, the cupboard had always been full of boxes of different-flavoured crisps, and cartons and cans of soft drinks, as well as industrial-sized packets of tea, filter coffee, sugar and all Jo's baking ingredients. Today most of the crisp boxes seemed empty – apart from a few lonely packets of prawn cocktail – and there seemed to have been a flour explosion on the floor. And what had happened to all the soft drinks? I couldn't see any.

Thankfully there were still a couple of cans of Coke in the fridge behind the counter, so I took one out. 'I'm afraid we're out of cakes, but we have some crisps, if you want those?' I asked my customer, holding up a pink packet in each hand.

'Um . . .' Her face fell, and she shook her head. 'No, don't worry about it. I'll get something from the shop up the road, thanks.'

'Sure,' I said, my smile feeling like an ache.

'Two teas, two coffees, one black, one white,' Carl said, dumping them on the counter. 'Anything else?'

'No, thanks,' she said, glancing from me to him. She paid and left, and Carl stalked back into the kitchen, where the music started up again, pounding at top volume.

I stood for a second, wondering what I should do next. What I really wanted was to take my things upstairs to the flat, unpack and have a quick shower to blast away the grubby feeling I always got after a long car journey. But I could already imagine Carl muttering something sarcastic if I slipped away, and didn't want him to have any reason to have a go at me. No, I needed to stay here, get my hands dirty and show that I meant business.

I noticed that the old lady had winced as the music came back on and was pulling a face at her companion.

Neither of them appreciated it, by the looks of things. I bustled over to their table, with damage limitation in mind. 'Is everything all right?' I asked.

'Well, no,' the lady said apologetically. 'Could the music be turned down a bit, do you think? We can't hear each other.'

'Sure,' I said. 'Right away. Can I get you anything else while I'm here?'

She shook her head. 'We were hoping to have a cream tea, but it seems to be off the menu. Will you be getting more scones in tomorrow? Only we always treat ourselves every year when we're down here on holiday, and . . .'

'I've just got here today, but I'll see what I can do,' I promised her. I'd make the flipping scones myself, if I had to, I vowed. If they'd been coming here on holiday for years, looking forward to a cream tea at Jo's, it felt crucial they could still have that. *The show must go on!* bellowed Freddie Mercury in my head.

I marched into the kitchen and turned down the stereo. 'It's really loud out there,' I said to Carl. 'A couple of people have complained.'

He just shrugged. *Don't care. BOTHERED!*

'What are you cooking there, anyway?' I asked. 'Is this a new dish for the menu?' It was good that he was taking the initiative, I told myself. Great that he was experimenting.

'I've got some mates coming over tonight,' he replied. 'Said I'd do them something to eat.'

I stared at the greenish-brown curry, then up at him. 'What — here, in the café?' I asked. 'But I thought it was always closed after five?'

Another shrug. *What's it to you?* 'Friday night is poker night,' he said. 'I told the lads they could come over here.'

I pursed my lips. 'Right. So this curry you're making — it's not even to sell, is it? It's got nothing to do with the business.'

He gave me a look of disdain. 'Have you got a problem with that?'

I ran a hand through my hair. 'Well, yes, I have actually, Carl. This is work time — you're meant to be serving here in the café. And I don't want this place turned into a . . . a gambling den in the evenings, for you and your mates.' Snotty, snotty, snotty. I sounded like an ice-princess, but I couldn't stop myself. Was that where all the soft drinks had vanished to? I wondered. Carl's mates coming round, helping themselves?

'Look, love,' he said, loading the word with sarcasm. 'You can't just waltz in, telling me what to do, giving me the I'm-the-boss line. It's not been easy here, you know — running out of stock, bills coming in.' He spread his hands wide, glaring at me. 'Where were you then, eh?'

'I'm sorry, I—' I tried, but he was in full flow now, unstoppable.

'Yeah, exactly. You weren't here. You don't know the half of it, so don't start dishing the shit before you've got the full story.'

'Okay,' I said. 'You're right, I *don't* know the full story, but when I come in and see the place in such a state, I can't help but jump to conclusions.'

He made a *tch* noise between his teeth and I took a deep breath.

'Look, let's start again,' I said. 'We've got off on the wrong foot, but I'm here now, so let's try to straighten things out.'

There was an uneasy silence and for a split-second I thought he was going to tell me to eff off and storm out. Then he nodded. 'Okay.'

'Good,' I said briskly, trying not to show my relief. 'Look, it's quiet at the moment. Why don't we both grab a coffee and have a chat.'

'Sure,' he said. 'Milk, two sugars for me.'

Right. So I'd be making them then. It was on the tip of my tongue to say '*Please*', in the way that my mum had always done when we were kids, but I held it back and went meekly to the coffee machine. 'Um...' I said help-lessly, wondering which button to press. This was a much whizzier model than Jo had had when I'd worked here all those years ago.

He'd come out behind the counter and was watching me. 'Christ, can't you even work a coffee machine?' he snorted. 'I'd better show you, if you're going to be sticking around. Watch and learn, Boss Lady.'

Gritting my teeth, I stepped to the side while he showed me how to make cappuccinos, americanos and espressos. 'No problem,' I said haughtily, although I'd already forgotten half his instructions. I'd swot up with the machine's manual later on, I promised myself, not wanting to give him the satisfaction of my asking for any more help.

Just then the dad from the family in the corner appeared at the counter looking really pissed off as he held a plate of half-eaten sandwiches. He had rimless rectangular glasses and a prominent Adam's apple, and he was wearing a pastel-pink polo shirt. 'Excuse me,' he said, his Adam's apple jerking as he spoke. 'The ham in these sandwiches – I think it's off. It smells awful.'

I peeled back the bread of one of them, noting the measly scrape of margarine and the soggy shreds of lettuce, and held the plate up to my nose. Then I recoiled in disgust. 'Bloody hell,' I said. 'That smells vile.' The ham was shiny and bright pink, really nasty, cheap-looking stuff. 'I think you're right,' I said. 'I'm so sorry. Let me make you another.'

His lips tightened to a bloodless line. 'The thing is, my daughter's already eaten half of it,' he said. 'And if she comes down with food poisoning, I'm not going to be happy. In fact, I'll be going straight to the council. I'm really appalled that you could even serve this up in the first place.' His Adam's apple was moving so agitatedly now that I felt mesmerized by it. 'What's happened to this café? We've been coming here for years and always loved the food. But now . . .'

I felt like crying. I couldn't look Carl in the eye. Didn't he have a clue about food hygiene? Even an idiot could see that the ham looked dodgy. 'I'm really sorry,' I said again. 'Let me make you something else. Carl, have we got any more ham?'

He shook his head. 'I said, didn't I, we've been running out of stock?' he muttered, as if that was any excuse.

'Yes, but . . . Look, we'll talk about this later,' I hissed, before turning back to the man. But he'd already returned to his wife and kids.

'Don't eat another mouthful,' I heard him saying to them. 'Let's go and find somewhere else to have tea. This place has gone way downhill.'

My face burned with shame as they walked out, one of the kids bursting into tears as they went. 'But I'm hungreee,' she sobbed, tears plopping from her big blue eyes. I was just about to bung them the prawn-cocktail crisps –

'On the house!' – but by the time I'd snatched up the packets, they'd left.

Oh God. I felt myself drooping against the counter with dismay. The man was right. The café *had* gone downhill – worryingly downhill. At this rate, I wouldn't be able to stop it before it crashed all the way down to rock bottom.

Chapter Six

I got the feeling Carl wasn't very keen on taking orders from me. Even though I tried to be supportive of him that afternoon – asking in a kindly, managerial manner how I could make things better in the café, and what needed doing – he still wasn't accepting any responsibility for the way he'd let things slide. That was all my fault, he kept implying, for not being around to look after the place. And yeah, you guessed it, it ended up being me who went outside to clean up the car park later that afternoon, keeping a nervous eye out for ratty interlopers, while he sloped off with his vat of curry, to rearrange the wretched poker night for an alternative venue.

'How's it going?' Matthew asked when I called him that evening. 'Have you got Rick Stein worried yet?'

'Ha,' I said. 'Not quite. Oh God, it's been really shit actually,' I went on, unable to stop myself from breaking into a wail. I poured out my woes: the reaction from Betty when I'd walked into her shop, the litter; the music, the poker night, the ham sandwich, the hundreds of pounds I'd just shelled out at the cash-and-carry to give us any kind of stock. As I reeled them off, the problems all seemed to close in around me like black clouds. What the hell had I got myself into? What kind of fool was I, thinking I could come down here and pick up the reins, just like that?

'Bloody hell,' Matthew said, when I'd finally finished. 'What a nightmare.'

'I know,' I said. 'It almost makes me want to go back to work for that pervert at Crossland. It's that bad. I mean, what if the little girl is really ill after eating that revolting ham sandwich? It could be curtains for the café. History. I'll be sued, and bankrupt, and—'

'Talking of Crossland,' he interrupted, ignoring my dramatics. 'Your temp agency rang, wanting to speak to you. I've given them your mobile number, they didn't seem to have it.'

I pulled a face. There was a reason they didn't have my mobile number. 'Oh God, they're probably ringing up to bollock me for walking out of that other job. Great. Well, that's something to look forward to.'

I must have sounded thoroughly miserable because his tone softened. 'Evie – you don't have to put yourself through all this, you know. You can just—'

'Sell it, yeah, I know. I've been bloody tempted today,

believe me.' I heaved a sigh. 'I'd better go, anyway. I need to make some scones for tomorrow.'

'You?' He was laughing now. 'You, make scones?'

'Yeah, all right,' I said, feeling defensive. 'Don't scoff.'

'I won't, don't worry,' he assured me, still laughing. 'Not if you've baked them, anyway.'

I laughed as well. 'Very funny,' I told him. 'I'll talk to you tomorrow. Love you.'

'You too,' he said.

I put the phone down, and sank back into the sofa. Jo's sofa. It still smelled faintly of the Issey Miyake perfume she'd always worn, and I felt a pang of missing her as I breathed it in. She'd lived here for years and years – for some of the time with Andrew, a guy with whom she'd had a long and complicated relationship before he'd died of throat cancer a few years ago. They'd had terrible arguments about this place, though; he wanted her to sell up and for them to take on a bigger and fancier restaurant in Newquay together. She hadn't wanted to. 'Never confuse business with your love life,' she'd been fond of saying. 'I'm not going anywhere.' And she hadn't.

Andrew hadn't been the only one on her case. I'd found out in recent years that my grandparents – Jo's parents – had always been disapproving of her decision to settle in Cornwall and live the beach life. Back in the day, they'd been keen for her to marry the young vicar from the

Hampshire village where Jo and my mum had been brought up, and couldn't understand it when Jo went off gallivanting around the world instead. Jo and Andrew had never married, and were unable to have children, and therefore Jo had failed in her parents' eyes. Forget the fact that she was happy, that she had her own successful business, that she was living the life she'd always wanted – that didn't seem important to them.

'Well, I thought you were brilliant, Jo,' I said aloud now as I remembered the tight, pinched expression on my grandmother's face whenever Jo had been discussed. 'I thought you got it spot on.'

It was weird being in the flat without her; it didn't feel right at all. The room I was in, her living room, had the most perfect view overlooking the beach and sea – the sort of view you could never tire of gazing at. She'd painted the walls a warm creamy-white and kept the decor simple and unfussy: a seascape painting over the fireplace, a couple of blue-glass vases and . . . My eyes widened as they fell on a collection of framed photographs above the low white-washed bookcase. Hey! I recognized those.

I went over, smiling. There were three photos, all of the beach in different lights. One was a sunrise shot, with the first pinky rays reflected in the calm water. One was of a stormy day, much like today, when the beach was grey and deserted, and the waves looked wild and uncontrollable.

The third was the classic sunset scene, the sky striped in swathes of apricot, rose and fuchsia, long shadows spreading over the sand.

Tears misted my eyes suddenly, because they were all photographs I'd taken when I'd been staying with her. She was the one who'd first told me I had a good eye for a photo. 'You frame the shot perfectly,' she'd said. 'You're a natural.' She'd encouraged me to make a go of it, she'd believed in me; the only person in my entire family who wasn't trying to shoehorn me into a teaching career. She'd known how I'd felt.

I loved thinking of her walking past my photos every day, maybe straightening them or dusting them now and then. It made me want to get out my camera again, rediscover that triumph of capturing the perfect evocative shot. I'd given up on photography, just as I'd given up on so many other things, but I wished now that I'd taken other pictures for Jo, maybe of Oxford and the Cotswolds, compiled a whole album for her: *The Evie Flynn Collection*. It would have made a great birthday or Christmas present. Too late now, though, of course.

Anyway. This wasn't the time for what-might-have-beens. I had scones to make, and bloody good ones they had to be too, if the old couple had been looking forward to them all year. No pressure whatsoever, then.

*

Previously I'd never been much of a cook, but I'd always flattered myself that it was just because I couldn't really be bothered with all that chopping and grating and whisking. I mean, anyone could *cook*, couldn't they? Anyone could bung a few things in a bowl and stir them and then stick them in the oven. I was sure I could make wonderful roast dinners and amazing soups and elaborately iced cakes too, if I absolutely tried my very hardest, concentrating fiercely and not being distracted by the radio or a text from a mate.

The thing was, now that I was actually in Jo's kitchen, frowning at her handwritten scone recipe, it seemed a lot more difficult than that. The butter wasn't mixing properly with the flour — most of it seemed to be stuck under my fingernails — and I wasn't sure if golden caster sugar was the same as caster sugar. As for buttermilk...? What the hell was buttermilk? Was it butter and milk mixed together, or what? I'd never heard of it before. I bit my lip, wondering if it would be okay to slosh in some ordinary milk, or if that was a terrible *faux pas*. Would the scone-loving old lady bite into one of my efforts and look shocked at the no-buttermilk taste? 'I'm sorry, dear, but these aren't *proper* scones,' she might say. 'What a shame. This always used to be such a *nice* café, too.'

Aargh. Why was it so complicated? Why hadn't I paid

more attention when I worked here, asked Jo to give me a few baking lessons? I dithered, my hands still in the mixing bowl as I wondered if it would be too embarrassing to phone my mum and ask her advice. Mind you, she wasn't a great baker herself. In fact, her advice would probably be 'Just buy your scones from Waitrose, of course.'

I was fast coming to the conclusion that this might actually be the best option for everyone concerned when I was stopped in my tracks by another glance at the recipe. The paper was sun-faded and creased, there was a greasy fingerprint on one corner as if it had been held by a buttery hand, and there were even traces of flour still visible. This was a recipe that had clearly been well used and well loved. I had a vision of Jo standing right where I was, pinny on, humming to the radio, weighing and mixing and rolling out her scone mixture.

I couldn't just turn my back on this recipe as if it didn't exist, and go to Waitrose instead. This recipe was part of the café's history – it symbolized everything that was real and good about the place.

I took a deep breath and read through the instructions once again. I wouldn't be defeated by a scone recipe. I would bake the perfect batch if it was the last thing I did.

That's my girl, said Jo in my head.

*

On Saturday morning I woke at six, with the sun streaming in through the window. Right. Big day today. The café's busiest day of the week. Up and at 'em!

I shut my eyes again, exhausted. I'd been up for hours the night before in my quest to make the best scones in Cornwall. Or even some that were vaguely edible.

The first lot hadn't risen at all, for some reason – they just looked like pale, doughy blinis. Yuck. Straight in the bin with them; start again. The second lot of scones *had* risen, gratifyingly, but most of them had burned (less gratifying). I managed to salvage three that looked okay, but I wasn't sure that would be enough. What if we got a rush on cream teas? What if the first customer who tried one said, 'My God, these are amazing, I need to buy up your entire scone collection?' My old lady might not get to taste the fruits of my labours. I couldn't let her down.

The third batch were perfect. No, really, they were. Okay, so they were slightly wonky, but they rose at least, and were a lovely golden-brown. They were so yummy-looking, in fact, I almost sat down with a pot of raspberry jam and some clotted cream and started tucking in myself. The old lady would be pleased. It would make her holiday. That was if she even turned up, of course. She'd better bloody turn up after all this, I thought with a sudden fierceness. If she didn't, I'd be searching through the village for her with a megaphone.

Giddy with my success, I decided to make a carrot-and-walnut cake next. Jo had always served up carrot cake in the café, she had been famed throughout the village for it. She'd made a three-tier version with lovely fluffy cream-cheese frosting, which had taken pride of place on the counter. I had to get it back on the menu, I told myself. It was what she would have wanted. It was what the customers wanted too, surely.

It was only when I'd put the cake tins into the oven (finally! I never wanted to grate a sodding carrot again, my fingers were in shreds) that my thoughts turned to the icing. That was the moment I realized we didn't have any cream cheese. Not even a smidgen. Damn – could I get away with ordinary icing? No. Would anyone around here be open and selling cream cheese at eleven o'clock at night? No.

I felt like letting out a great howl of frustration. No doubt Carl would snigger at my un-iced cake in the morning. Word would get back to Betty Doom and she'd look scornful at this further proof that I wasn't cut out to be here. *She* wouldn't serve me any cream cheese, would she? She'd probably spit at me if I tried to ask for it. Well, I'd just have to get up at the crack of dawn the next day and go out of the village on a cream-cheese-buying mission.

That had been the plan, but now it *was* the next day,

and the thought of cream cheese made me feel distinctly queasy. But I heaved myself out of bed nonetheless and stood under the shower until I felt slightly more alive. Come on, Evie. Jump to it. A whole day with Carl-the-Jerk to look forward to. Bring it on...

By nine o'clock I was ready. The carrot cake had been iced (icing was great — it covered up all the dimples and scorched bits of sponge, I realized), the kitchen and dining areas were spotless, I'd had a practice run with the coffee machine and reckoned I could get by on a wing and a prayer, and I'd replenished all the stock we held behind the counter. Oh, and I'd also chalked up a sign on the blackboard saying: TODAY'S SPECIAL: CORNISH CREAM TEA — £2.95. If that didn't get the punters racing in, I didn't know what would.

There, Jo. That all right for you?

Humming to myself, I unlocked the front door, turned the sign to 'Open', put up the parasols on the outside decking and stood for a moment, gazing out at the beach. It was a beautiful morning. The sky was a soft, misty blue, patterned with small white clouds — a mackerel sky, Jo would have said if she'd been standing there with me. An elderly couple were walking slowly across the sand together, arm-in-arm. A male jogger in a red singlet and shorts thudded along, iPod on, face blank, arms swinging to a soundless beat. I heard the sound of exuberant barking and then a chocolate-brown dog hurtled onto the beach, its tail wagging in joy as it galloped over the sand.

'Lola! Come on, then.' A man had followed the dog onto the sand and was holding a green ball up in the air.

Hearing her name, the dog turned and barked again. The man bent his arm back and hurled the ball, which sailed like a green dot through the air. The dog chased wildly after it, head up, watching its arc, her powerful legs propelling her across the damp sand, leaving a trail of prints.

The café was on the left side of the bay as you looked out to sea and, to reach it from the beach, you had to climb up ten wooden steps. I wanted to stay watching from my vantage point, but didn't want the man to turn and see me staring, so I reluctantly returned inside. Right. Show on the road ... Tick! The beach café was open for business. Just time to make myself a quick cup of tea before the customers began flooding in.

'Hello?'

I stiffened as I heard a shout a few minutes later. Oh! Here came the flood already. Or was it Betty and her lynch mob? Then I heard a low, rumbling woof and guessed that it was the man from the beach, and his dog.

I re-emerged from the kitchen into the serving area. 'Hi,' I said. 'What can I get you?'

He was tall, and in his late thirties, I guessed, with short dark hair, brown eyes and a hint of stubble around his mouth. He was wearing a sun-bleached blue T-shirt and knackered-looking jeans. Through the doorway I saw that the dog had been tied to the wooden balcony outside. She was lying down with her head on her front paws as if worn out by her beach antics.

The man smiled. A wide, easy smile that showed perfect, even teeth. 'A cup of tea would be great, please. And some water for the dog, if that's okay.'

Phew. So he hadn't been sent by Betty to set his hound on me, at least. I made us both a tea and put some water in an old margarine tub, carrying it outside and setting it down by the dog.

'So,' the man said conversationally when I returned, 'you're the bad niece then.'

My hackles rose. Maybe Evil Betty *had* sent him after all. 'I'm the what?' I asked, folding my arms across my chest.

He grinned. 'The bad niece. That's what they've all been saying in the pub anyway.'

'In the pub?' I was like an echo. 'I don't understand. Why are people saying that? What do they think I've done?'

He sipped his tea. 'Well, you're selling this place, aren't you? They've all got their knickers in a twist about it. Someone wants to turn it into a luxury second home, apparently, and there are enough second-homers here already, and it's wrecking the village, and they're upset about your aunt dying, and they'd hoped that you'd take it on...' He'd clearly been doing some major eavesdropping. 'No skin off my nose what you do, obviously. None of my business. But the rest of 'em – they're up in arms. Can't talk of anything else.'

My cheeks were scarlet. 'Well, it's not even true! The café isn't for sale!' I shook my head, reeling from this information. I could just imagine them all moaning about me in the pub; I was surprised my ears hadn't burned to a crisp. No wonder Betty had been so frosty. 'No one's talked to *me* about turning it into a luxury second home,' I said indignantly. 'No one's asked *me* if they can buy it. It's all gossip. Meaningless gossip.'

He shrugged. 'You know how word gets around these places,' he said. 'Chinese whispers. I suppose I should be grateful they're not discussing *me* for a change.' He eyed me over his tea. 'So, you're saying you're not selling?'

I took a deep breath, feeling flummoxed. 'I ... I haven't actually decided what I'm going to do yet,' I confessed, leaning back against the tiled wall. It felt cold under my palms. 'Maybe I will have to sell it eventually. I live in Oxford, so it's not exactly practical for me to run it. But that's why I came down here, to work out what to do. I don't know why everyone's already jumped to conclusions and started slagging me off, when I haven't even decided anything yet. God!'

My voice shook, and he held his hands up. 'Sorry,' he said. 'I should know better than to pass on gossip. I should have known it was cobblers, after the rubbish they invented about me.'

'What's your story then?' I asked, to change the subject. 'Why have you been gossiped about?'

'Oh, lots of reasons,' he replied carelessly. 'I haven't lived here for the last two hundred years, so obviously I'm a suspicious outsider, like you. And I've driven them nuts, not telling them much about myself, so they've had an utter field day − a field *month* − speculating and guessing about who I am and why I'm here.' He grinned. 'They thought I was some kind of fugitive at first, apparently, on the run from the law. Why else would I be hiding in their village out of season?'

I grinned back. 'I'm surprised no one made a citizen's arrest,' I told him.

'You and me both,' he said. 'The truth is far less exciting, though. I'm dog-sitting for a mate while he's working abroad for a couple of months. Getting away from it all, you know.'

'Ahh,' I said. 'And...' I was about to ask exactly what he was getting away from when a young couple came in with a baby in a sling. I smiled at them politely. 'Hello,' I said. 'What can I get you?'

By the time I'd served them, the man was getting to his feet. 'Thanks,' he said, bringing over his empty mug. 'How much do I owe you?'

'Oh God, did I forget to charge you?' Embarrassment coursed through me. I wasn't going to win Professional Businesswoman of the Year if I kept giving out freebies. 'Oops. One pound fifty, please.'

He handed over the money. 'Nice to meet you,' he said. 'I'm Ed.'

'Evie,' I replied. 'Nice to meet you, too. And you can tell those gossips from me they've got their facts wrong.'

'Will do,' he said, then turned and strode out. 'Come on then, Lola,' I heard him say. 'Time to go.'

I had a straggle of customers to deal with – teas, coffees and a couple of rounds of toast – but it was ten o'clock before any of the other members of staff put in an appearance. Seb was first, the lad who helped out at weekends, and he looked horrified to see me there. 'Sorry I'm late,' he said, turning bright red. 'I didn't think we'd be open yet. Last week, Carl said – '

He didn't finish his sentence, but I could guess the rest. Carl had said not to bother coming in at the usual time as he wouldn't be opening up till later. No doubt he'd antici-pated a hangover after the poker party.

'No worries,' I said lightly. I was too relieved to have someone else behind the counter to be really cross with him.

Just then a couple of twenty-somethings came in for a coffee and bacon roll each. Seb and I looked at each other. 'I'll do the coffees,' he said.

'Right,' I said, hurrying into the kitchen before anyone could see the panicked look on my face. It was only *bacon*, I reminded myself. I could cook that. Anyone could fry up a bit of bacon, even me. It was just ... Where was Carl? I hadn't expected to have to do any actual cooking while I was here; it was hardly my specialist subject. Stress!

I made the bacon rolls without any disasters, and after that we had a steady stream of people in for hot drinks, toast and brunchy things. I could feel myself getting hotter and sweatier as I slipped behind with the orders. Seb's handwriting was so appalling, I kept having to run back to the counter to double-check what he'd scrawled on the order slips, and he kept muddling things up, forgetting who'd asked for what. Then he burned himself on the milk frother and went so pale and trembly I thought he might faint.

Saffron, the sulky redhead, finally showed her face by eleven o'clock, and she was slightly more efficient at least, but her customer service was the pits. Even from my hell-ish bacon-frazzling, toast-burning nightmare of a kitchen, I was aware of the rude, uninterested way in which she spoke to people. 'Brown or white toast?' she'd snap. 'Do you want milk in that tea?'

I felt scared for the customers, imagining her shining a dazzling light in their faces as she interrogated them. And guess what? No one – not one single person – had bought a slice of my cake, or asked for a cream tea yet. Ungrateful sods.

Just as I was starting to have a meltdown over the ninety-seven thousand sandwiches I'd been asked to make, Carl rocked in, looking whey-faced and shambolic in the same T-shirt he'd been wearing the day before. Had he *slept* in it? I wondered, narrowing my eyes at him. 'Carl, where have you been?' I cried. 'How come you're so late?'

He shrugged. 'I knew you'd be here,' he said. 'I didn't think there was any rush.'

I felt like whacking him over the head with my greasy spatula. 'That's crap, and you know it,' I retorted. 'For all you knew, I could have gone out somewhere today. This wasn't the deal – that you can slack off when I'm around. I'm not going to be here forever, you know.'

'Thank God for that,' he said, washing his hands. He dried them on a tea towel before picking up a spatula of his own and ambling over to the cooker, where four pink rashers of bacon were sizzling and spitting. 'I'll take over here.'

I scowled. 'Very big of you,' I muttered, spreading margarine on the bread.

'Don't mention it,' he said sweetly.

It was the longest, hottest, most bad-tempered working day I could remember in a long time. Saffron had a stand-up row with a teenage girl who came in – her arch-enemy, apparently, not that I cared about *that* – and called an elderly gentleman 'a deaf old giffer' when he didn't answer her 'D'ya want milk with that?' immediately. Carl was rude and unpleasant the entire day. We ran out of milk, we ran out of bread, we ran out of cheese and, to top it all off, Seb managed somehow to drop my cake. Yes, my carrot cake, my pride and joy, the one I'd slaved over until midnight. I felt like bursting into tears when I saw it split into umpteen spongy shards on the floor.

'Oops,' Saffron said wickedly, eyes glittering as she turned her sharp little face towards mine. 'That icing's going to be a bugger to get off the lino.'

Seb looked as if he might cry too. He must have apologized at least fifteen times. I wouldn't have minded so much if the cake had been almost finished, or at least sampled by somebody, but it was the first slice he'd been asked to cut all day.

Don't even *ask* how many cream teas we sold.

'Well, that was a total fucking nightmare,' I said bitterly as we cleared up at the end of the day. 'Tell me it's not always like that.'

'It's always like that,' Saffron replied, just as Seb said, 'It isn't usually that bad.'

'It's not good, though, is it?' I asked, pausing in the middle of wiping a table. 'I mean, we just about scraped through by the skin of our teeth, but I don't think Jo would have been too thrilled if she could have seen us.'

Seb, who was sweeping up, looked as if he'd been slapped, whereas Saffron stuck her pointy nose in the air. 'If Jo had been here, things wouldn't have got so bad,' she countered. 'She'd have made us all laugh, made it fun, rather than stamp about looking pissed off all day.'

The cow, I thought. I'd give her stamping about, looking pissed off. 'What I mean,' I said, deliberately ignoring her jibe, 'is that if this is going to work, we've all got to pull together. Be a team.'

Seb nodded meekly, but Saffron looked so scornful that I felt like throwing the spray gun at her. 'A *team*. Pull *together*,' she scoffed. 'How can you say that to our faces, when we all know you're planning to sell this place?'

I sighed. 'Oh, not you as well,' I said.

She put her hands on her hips triumphantly. 'Yeah, we're not stupid. Word gets around, you know. Lindsay at the pub heard you all talking about it after the funeral. Then we've had some prat from the estate agent's poking around – you recognized him, Seb, didn't you?'

'He sold my nan's house for her,' Seb explained. 'Spotted him straight off, I did.'

'Cheeky so-and-so, did he really come in here?' I asked, table-wiping forgotten. 'Are you sure he wasn't just dropping in for a pasty?'

'No,' Seb said shyly. 'He had a bloke with him, and I heard him telling the bloke how easy it would be to convert the café into a big, fancy house.'

I shook my head. The nerve of the man! 'Great,' I muttered. 'You know, you could just have asked me, instead of jumping to conclusions—'

'Well, we're asking now,' Saffron interrupted. She was very brazen, it had to be said. 'Are you selling this place or not? Cos we need to know.'

There was silence as she and Seb stared at me. It had all gone quiet in the kitchen too, where Carl was no doubt eavesdropping.

'Well, I'm . . .' I began. My heart was thumping. This felt like a really big moment. Should I be honest – tell them I hadn't a bloody clue what I was doing? Or would that make them all down tools and walk out? 'No,' I said finally. 'I'm not selling. Got that?'

Chapter Seven

Sunday was another busy day in the café. I was up with the lark – or rather the gulls – trying to make a vegetable soup that would warm up anyone mad enough to go swimming in the still-icy waves. How hard could a soup be, after all?

I chopped and cooked the veggies, added some herbs, then whizzed the whole lot up in a blender, but the resulting mixture looked like – well, the contents of a baby's nappy, if I was honest. Sludgy, sloppy and brown, and not at all the sort of thing you'd want to put anywhere near your mouth.

I put a lid on the soup and went to open up, but when I stepped out onto the deck, something gave me a start. Lying curled up, pressed against the café wall, was a girl in a sleeping bag, her eyes shut. I must have made some kind of exclamation, because her eyes suddenly flicked open and, when she saw me, she was up on her feet, yanking the sleeping bag under one arm and hurrying away down the steps to the beach.

'Hey!' I called. 'Are you okay? Come back!'

She paid no attention, just scuttled off up the sand, her long blonde hair flying out behind her. She only looked about sixteen, poor kid. Where had she come from, and how had she ended up sleeping on my deck? Maybe she was on holiday here and had been to a beach party the night before? I wrinkled my nose doubtfully. No, surely I would have heard a beach party if it had gone on right under my nose.

I wrapped my arms around myself as a cool breeze blew straight off the sea, making goosebumps prickle up on my bare skin. The girl had vanished from sight now, off who knew where. I hoped she had a home to go to.

Once again my first customers that day were Ed and his dog, Lola, who curled up in the same corner of the deck as she'd done previously. 'Hi there,' I said, feeling pleased to see him as he strode in.

'Morning,' he said, smiling at me. He had a dimple in one cheek, I noticed. Then his smile vanished. 'God, what's that awful smell?'

I must have looked dismayed because he immediately apologized. 'Sorry. That was a bit rude.' His mouth twitched as if he was amused. 'But, if you don't mind me asking, what *is* that smell?'

'That awful smell,' I replied, unable to stop a certain

haughtiness in my voice, 'is the Soup of the Day actually.' Then I gave up on haughtiness and sighed. 'It didn't quite turn out the way I wanted it to,' I admitted. 'In fact, it looks as revolting as it smells. My advice is: don't have it. We've got scones, though, still very nice, just baked yesterday – well, the day before that, I suppose ...?' My voice trailed away and hot colour surged into my cheeks. 'No, okay. Bit early for scones. What can I get you?'

'A coffee and a bacon roll, please,' he said. 'The scones do look good, though,' he added kindly. He leaned a tanned arm on the countertop as I reached for a clean coffee mug. 'Are you doing the cooking now here, then?' he asked. 'Have you given that Carl bloke the boot?'

'I wish,' I said without thinking, then slapped a hand to my mouth. 'Oops. I didn't say that. And I don't wish I was doing the cooking at all. It's not exactly my strongest point.' I explained the situation to him while I made his coffee. 'So you see,' I said, stirring in the frothed milk, 'it's all rather up in the air. I haven't a clue what's going to happen next.' I slid his coffee over to him. 'Right. One bacon roll coming up.'

'Could you toast the roll for thirty seconds or so, and could I have it with a scrape of butter, please,' he said. 'Oh, and the bacon should be crispy. I'll do the ketchup myself.'

I stared at him.

'If that's okay,' he added quickly. 'Please.'

I blinked. 'Sure,' I said, trying to recover myself. 'You're very precise with your bacon-roll preferences.'

He shrugged. 'I just know what tastes best,' he replied mildly.

I went into the kitchen and bunged a roll under the grill and slapped a couple of rashers in the frying pan. Then I realized he was peering through the door at me. 'The bacon's better if you grill it,' he said. 'If it's not too much trouble.'

I tried not to show my exasperation. He was like the male Sally from *When Harry Met Sally*. In a minute he was going to criticize the way I buttered the roll, and I would have to throw it at him in a fit of pique. *Deep breaths*, I told myself. *Deep, calming breaths.*

I took the bacon from the pan and put it under the grill instead. 'No problem,' I said evenly. 'Why don't you sit down and I'll bring it over when it's ready?'

He had the grace to look sheepish at least. 'In other words, stop interfering and shut up,' he translated, and laughed. 'Sorry. I'm a bit of a perfectionist about food.'

You're not kidding, I thought, but gave him a serene smile. Then I did some more deep, calming breaths – so deep and calming, in fact, that my nostrils began to vibrate. Even though he was now sitting down, I still felt stressed out. How long had that roll been under the grill? Yikes, one side was slightly scorched. He would definitely notice if I didn't slice the offending black bits off. Bloody hell! It was like having Egon Ronay in for his brunch.

Then I stiffened. Oh God, what if he *was* a food critic, taking notes about the place? Was that why he was so pernickety?

My fingers seemed to be all thumbs as I took my knife to the charred bits of roll, then buttered it. A 'scrape' of butter, he'd asked for, like he was some kind of supermodel on a diet. Still, the customer was king, et cetera, et cetera. A scrape of butter was what he'd get.

The bacon was sizzling and crispy-looking by now, so I gingerly removed it from the grill and laid the rashers reverently on the roll. Yum – it smelled amazing, at least. I put the whole thing on a plate and carried it through to him, feeling like a lowly minion serving a prince. As I approached, I saw him scribbling something down on a piece of paper and then stuffing it in his jacket pocket when he saw me. Oh, my goodness. He *was* a restaurant critic. Suddenly this bacon roll seemed like the most important thing in the world.

'Cheers,' he said as I set it down on the table. He opened the roll, squirted a circle of ketchup onto the bacon, then closed it, bit into it and chewed.

I realized I was holding my breath. Ridiculous. Get a grip, Evie!

'Bloody delicious,' he pronounced, sticking a thumb up. 'Perfect.'

My breath rushed out in relief. 'Good,' I said, trying to sound casual, as if this wasn't at all surprising to me. Put that in your review and smoke it, I thought, with a secret smile.

The door opened just then, and in came a Japanese family, all with sun visors and raincoats, who went on to make the most convoluted and complicated order I'd ever taken, full of changed minds and crossings-out. They were followed swiftly by a couple who'd quite clearly just emerged from a shag-fest, all tousled hair, hand-holding and soft-focus dreamy smiles. And then, by the time I'd served them, Ed had gone, before I could say anything else to him. I just caught sight of him leaving with his dog, and felt intrigued. He probably *wasn't* a restaurant critic, on reflection, but I couldn't help wondering what he was doing down in the village, and how he'd been able to come here for two months' dog-sitting. Did he not have a job?

There was no time to dwell on it, though, as more customers were turning up, with breakfast orders coming in thick and fast. Surprise, surprise – all my staff were late again.

Saffron burst in last of all, stinking of patchouli, with thick kohl rimming her green eyes, and a phone in her pocket that kept ringing and ringing. Yet did she think,

Oh yes, I'm at work now, better not answer this? Or even, *Oh yes, I'm at work now, better switch it off altogether?* No, she did not.

'Saffron!' I cried in the end, exasperated, as I returned from wiping tables and clearing crockery, only to find her once again leaning against the wall, deep in conversation and completely ignoring our queuing customers. 'Can you turn your phone *off*, please. You're meant to be working, not yacking all day.'

Her eyes narrowed to slits and the usual hardness came over her face. With a scowl of displeasure, she stuffed her phone into her pocket. 'Yes?' she snapped at the luckless customer who happened to be next.

She really wasn't the greatest waitress to have working for you, I thought, noticing her deftly palm a five-pound note that she was clearly intending to slip straight into her jeans pocket. I went and stood next to her pointedly, until I saw with my own eyes that she'd put it into the till.

Mind you, she wasn't the only problem. Seb was as big a klutz as ever, spilling a pot of coffee down himself and scalding his leg. Tears glistened in his eyes as if he wanted his mummy to comfort him. As for Carl ... I was still smarting from his rude comments about my soup.

'We can't serve that slop,' he'd jeered. 'Evie, thanks, love, I know you're trying to be helpful, but leave the cooking to me for God's sake.'

'I just thought—'

'Yeah, well, don't,' he'd interrupted. 'Just don't. I'm the chef, all right? I'm the man in the big hat. You do your thing and I'll do mine.'

My cheeks had flamed as I'd stormed out of the kitchen on the pretext of needing to serve someone. The man with the big hat had a big blooming ego too, I thought, gritting my teeth. He was so bloody patronizing! So horrible. How had Jo ever stood working with him for so long?

At four o'clock, just as the café was quietening down and I was starting to think about closing up for the day, Annie came in. Annie was Jo's best friend in Carrawen Bay and I'd known her for years. She was a cuddly, squashy sort of person, with the kindest smile you could imagine. I'd been meaning to get in touch with her ever since I'd come down, but with one thing and another, I hadn't managed to pick up the phone yet.

'Hello!' I exclaimed, swerving out from behind the counter and rushing over to hug her. Her hair was henna-bright, with big, springy curls framing her round face.

'Hello there, stranger,' she said, giving me a squeeze. 'How's it going? I heard you were down here, looking after the place. Is everything okay?'

'Well –' I began, then stopped abruptly. I didn't want to launch into a moan about how badly things were going right in front of my staff. 'I'm getting there,' I said after a moment. 'Bit of a steep learning curve, but I'm getting there.'

'Good,' she said warmly. 'It's lovely to have you here, especially now that Jo –' She broke off and I saw tears appear in her eyes. 'It's what she would have wanted,' she said eventually. 'But anyway. I was just popping in to invite you round for dinner one evening. When are you free?'

I smiled. 'That would be really nice,' I said gratefully. Much as I loved staying in Jo's flat, it was kind of lonely, being there on my own. 'I'm free ... well, every night, to be honest. Whenever's best for you.'

'How about tonight, then?' she asked. 'We're still at the same place – number ten Silver Street. Why don't you come over at six? We can have some food and a good old catch-up.'

'Thanks, Annie,' I said. 'That would be great. I'll see you at six.'

Annie lived in a small terraced house along a quiet road. Long plumes of feathery pampas grass swayed in one corner of her tiny front garden, and there was a collection of bone-white seashells by the front door. I rapped the brass knocker twice and waited.

'Hello, come on in,' Annie said, beaming as she pulled

the door wide. There were glorious cooking smells wafting through from the kitchen: roast chicken, lemon, garlic. 'Perfect timing,' she said. 'I've just put the peas on.'

'Lovely,' I said, following her down the narrow white-painted hall. I could hear music playing somewhere upstairs, a cheerful bass throb through the ceiling. She led me into the kitchen, which was small and unfussy, with a couple of pans boiling merrily on the gas stove, and a chicken cooling under foil on the worktop.

I passed her a bottle of wine. 'Here,' I said. 'This is really kind of you, having me round.'

'Oh, it's my pleasure,' she said. 'I know how much Jo adored you, so it's nice for me, too, feeling as if I've still got some connection with her by inviting you.' Tears filled her eyes and I clutched her hands. 'I'm sorry,' she said, making a sound that was half-sob, half-laugh. 'I still really miss her. I just can't believe she's gone, Evie, I really can't.'

'I know,' I said. 'Me too. It was such a horrible shock.'

Annie nodded. 'She played a big part in this community,' she said. 'It's not the same without her. Everyone misses her.' She took a big breath. 'Still,' she went on, 'it's lovely that you're here, taking over the place. I think people will be happy about that.'

I rolled my eyes. 'Not everyone,' I replied, and told her what had happened with Betty. 'I haven't dared go back in there since,' I admitted.

Annie opened the wine and poured us each a glass. 'Betty is ... Betty,' she said gnomically. 'She's a law unto herself. But honestly, Evie, her bark's worse than her bite. She was just worried you were going to flog the place to a developer, that's all.' She passed me a glass of wine. 'Cheers. We're not too good at change around here, I'm afraid.'

I clinked my glass against hers. 'Cheers,' I echoed. 'Here's to Jo. I wish more than anything that she could be here with us right now, but we'll never forget her.'

'I'll second that,' Annie said. 'Although – ' she glanced heavenwards briefly, then went over to her cooker, 'if she *was* here right now, she'd probably be reminding me to get the roast potatoes out of the oven and stop gassing, and bloody well carve the chicken.'

I laughed, because I knew she was right, and Jo would indeed have said just that. She was never one to forget about something as important as food. 'I'll give you a hand,' I said.

I hadn't had such an enjoyable evening for ages. Martha, Annie's seventeen-year-old, who was willowy and doe-eyed, all legs and long blonde hair, was sweet and giggly. The food was delicious, Annie was a great host, and we talked about everything and nothing – Annie's job (she worked in a health-food shop in Wadebridge, although she was feeling the pinch ever since her hours had been cut), Martha's upcoming exams (she was particularly dreading French) and her boyfriend, Jamie, whom she went gooey-eyed over whenever his name was mentioned. 'He's an artist,' she said, with the same reverence in her voice as if she were talking about Picasso. 'He's really good.'

'Wow,' I said, exchanging a secret smile with Annie. Bless her, she seemed besotted. 'Is that what he does to earn a living?'

Her face fell slightly. 'No,' she said. 'He works in the pub too. It's really hard to make it in the art world, though,' she added defensively.

'Oh, I know,' I replied. 'I've been there myself, tried to be a photographer for a while, but...' I shrugged. 'Like you say, it's hard. You need a lucky break, but that's not always possible.'

'He's showing his work in this north-Cornwall summer exhibition soon,' she went on. 'We're really hoping that'll be his big break. Fingers crossed!'

'Fingers crossed,' I echoed, holding mine up to show her.

'He's actually pretty good,' Annie said. 'His stuff is a bit different from the traditional seascapes you usually get down here. That's one of his up there.' She pointed to the wall where a small square canvas hung, and I stood up to take a closer look. It was a dreamy scene depicting a shoal of fish underwater, with their bodies picked out in luminous, acid-bright colours, and the sea around them blended shades of soft blue and green. The overall effect was startling – it completely drew you into the underwater world and lent the creatures a magical aspect.

'I really like that,' I said. 'I love the colours he's used.'

I thought Martha was going to explode with pride. 'He's done a whole series of them,' she said. 'Not just fish, but sharks and dolphins and turtles too – all sorts of sea creatures.'

'You'll have to let me know when his exhibition's on,' I said. 'I'd love to go along and see the rest.'

'I will,' Martha said. 'I'll get you a ticket when they go on sale.'

We cleared the table, then Annie brought in dessert – a huge chocolate cake with hazelnut and chocolate frosting. 'Oh my goodness,' I said, one hand on my stomach. 'I'm really regretting that extra roast potato now. Why did I stuff myself to bursting point with the first course, when the second one looks unbelievably yumptious too?'

Martha laughed. 'Mum's cakes are amazing,' she said, flashing an affectionate look at Annie. 'None of my friends dare come round when she's made one, especially if they're on diets. They all know it'll be utterly irresistible.'

Annie picked up the cake knife. 'So, Evie, are you telling me you're too full for a slice?' she asked, the blade hovering over the icing.

'No way,' I replied, horrified that she could even think I'd pass on a helping. 'I'm full, but I'm not *that* full.' I grinned. 'And I don't have far to waddle home, at least. I'd love a slice, please.'

I could feel myself salivating as she cut me a piece of cake that resembled something a giant might use as a doorstop. 'Well, I'm glad *I'm* not on a diet, as it would be well and truly out of the window by now,' I commented, taking a forkful. 'Thanks, Annie.' Then the sweetness of the chocolate hit my tastebuds and there was a crunch of hazelnut, and my brain registered just how perfectly fluffy the sponge cake was.

'Oh my GOD,' I sighed, leaning back in my seat and shutting my eyes. 'This is delicious.' I swallowed, my fork already eagerly carving out the next mouthful. 'Really, Annie, it's amazing.' I smiled across the table. 'I wish I could make cakes like this. Honestly, the disasters I've had . . .'

I stopped talking suddenly as a brilliant idea slammed into my head. 'Annie, you should bake for the café! Can I hire you? Will you be my new cake-baker?'

She blinked in surprise. 'Well, I wouldn't want to step on Carl's toes,' she said doubtfully.

'Oh, who cares about him? He's a jerk, Mum, we all know it,' Martha argued.

'Carl doesn't seem to have picked up a cake tin since the day Jo ... since ... for ages,' I said, stumbling over my words. 'He's more bothered about making horrible curries for his mates. We really need a proper cake-maker, Annie. And you said yourself that the shop job wasn't paying fantastically, so ...'

Annie still looked taken aback. 'Are you serious about this? You're not just being polite because you've had dinner here, and a few glasses of wine?'

'I am totally serious,' I said. 'Obviously we'd need to sort out the details, how much you'd charge and how many cakes we'd want a week, and what sorts, but ...' I was nodding so hard I almost gave myself whiplash. 'But in theory, if we were both happy with the arrangement, then yes! Why not?'

'Yeah, why not?' Martha chimed in. 'You should do it, Mum. You love baking, and everyone in the world loves your cakes. And you'd be helping out Evie. Jo would want you to do it.' She winked at me.

That was the clincher, it seemed. 'Well, when you put it like that, O wise daughter of mine, then you've got a point,' Annie said. 'Evie, I'd absolutely love to be your cake-maker.'

She held out a hand and we shook. 'Brilliant,' I said,

unable to stop smiling. 'I can't tell you how relieved I am that I'll never have to make scones again. The only downside,' I went on, wedging another bit of cake onto my fork, 'is that I'm going to put on at least a stone every time I'm working there and serving up your cakes all day.' I grinned at her. 'But hey, it's a price I'm willing to pay. When can you start?'

Chapter Eight

I felt more optimistic that evening as I went back to the flat. Not only was I full to the brim of good food and wine, I was also buzzing with plans for the future of the café. My new cake-maker and I were both completely open to seeing how things went, and either upping or decreasing the orders according to sales, but initially Annie had agreed to provide two large cakes every two days, with a batch of cupcakes, brownies or flapjacks too. Oh, and scones. She made lovely light scones, according to Martha. I could have kissed them both at the news.

'So, let's see, if I bring you a chocolate cake, a lemon cake and a batch of fruity flapjacks first thing Tuesday,' she said, scribbling it down, 'and maybe a carrot cake, and a Victoria sponge for Thursday, with some chocolate brownies. How does that sound? And then something else on Saturday? We can see what's most popular, obviously, over the first few weeks, and tailor the orders accordingly.' She smiled, her cheeks flushed with the wine and excitement. 'Evie, I'm so thrilled about this, you know. I love baking, but with just me and Martha here, I have to rein myself in. But now I've got an excuse to bake and bake and bake – and get paid for it. Perfect!'

'It's pretty bloody perfect for me, too,' I told her. 'And the customers. They'll be relieved they don't have to try any more of my experiments, that's for sure. And Carl might buck his ideas up too, if he hears I'm bringing you in as my right-hand woman.'

Oh yes, it was a win–win situation all right. I could feel Jo smiling down at me as I got into bed that night. With Annie on board, I was definitely going to get the café back on track.

I woke up on Monday still in a good mood. Jo had never opened the café on Mondays unless it was a bank holiday, or school holidays, and I knew Carl wouldn't be coming in, so I figured I could give myself a day off too, and catch up on the paperwork and stock levels.

Once I was showered and dressed, I made a tray of breakfast things and took it outside to the deck. For the first time since I'd arrived in Cornwall, I felt as if I was on holiday. Raining cats and dogs in Oxford, Amber had said when I'd phoned for a gossip the night before – well, not here. The sky was a bright, clear stretch of blue, and the sun shone down, making the water glisten and sparkle. The breeze was cool as it ruffled my hair, and I put my feet up and leaned back against the warm wooden steamer-chair to drain the last of my coffee. This was the life, breakfasting with such a view! I could see why Jo had loved living here.

Afterwards, on the spur of the moment, I locked up the café and headed down to the beach, kicking off my flip-flops and leaving them at the foot of the steps.

The sand was cool and grainy under my bare toes, but it felt good. I strode towards the sea, the wind cold against the back of my neck, and tucked my hands in my pockets. I walked until I reached the first foaming curls of waves, gasping as the icy water hit my feet. Then I paddled through the shallows, feeling invigorated as the waves splashed my ankles, soaking through the bottoms of my jeans. The wet sand was silky smooth here, squeezing between my toes.

Come home, Matthew kept saying on the phone – but home seemed like another land now. It was hard to imagine Monday morning in Oxford at this moment: the Cowley Road a busy stream of cyclists, buses and cars, kids being walked to school, Matthew and I eating breakfast in our small, rather dark kitchen, with Radio 4 burbling in the background. Was it still raining there, I wondered, envisaging the hiss and scrape of windscreen wipers, puddles in the roads, umbrellas and coat hoods put up in self-defence.

Here in the bay the light was almost unnaturally bright and the sea glittered with the golden rays of early-morning sun. I felt utterly alive; keenly aware of myself and my surroundings, all my senses charged up to the max. I felt like running along, whooping and yelling like a kid with the glory of it all. I wished I had my camera with me.

My phone began buzzing and vibrating in my pocket, and I pulled it out to see an unfamiliar number on the screen. An unfamiliar Oxford number. 'Hello?' I said warily.

'Hi, Evie, this is Sophie from Pearson Recruitment,' came a high-pitched, breezy voice. I couldn't help my shoulders sinking. Damn.

'Oh, hi,' I said failing spectacularly in my attempt to muster up a shred of enthusiasm. My toes had dug themselves into the sand with sudden tension and I wiggled them free.

'I've got some great news — we've got a new placement for you,' she burbled. 'It's a two-month temporary post as admin cover for a pharmaceutical company just off the ring road ...'

I pulled a face while making a non-committal 'Mmm' sound. A pharmaceutical company off the ring road? I wasn't exactly hearing Thrillsville, Tennessee.

'It's full-time, thirty-five hours a week, slightly better

pay than you were receiving at Crossland, and they want you to start at nine o'clock on Wednesday,' she said. 'So shall I give them a buzz and say you're on board?'

My eyes were transfixed by the light sparkling on the waves; I had to drag myself back to what she was saying. 'What – this Wednesday?' I asked. I glanced at the café. Oh God. That would mean leaving tomorrow, and there was still so much I needed to sort out.

'Yes, that's right, this Wednesday,' she replied. 'It's really lucky something's come in so quickly for you, isn't it? I knew you'd be pleased.'

Pleased? I didn't feel pleased. I felt ... torn. Confused. I stood gazing helplessly out to sea, unsure how to reply.

'So I'll give them a buzz then, yeah?' she said, breaking the silence. 'And I can email you their address, and the company website, so you can read all about them. Yeah?'

My toes were curled into the sand again, as if they were trying to root me into the beach. But real life was calling too, like whispers in the wind: Matthew, Saul, cold hard cash ... 'Yeah, okay,' I said finally, unable to help the sigh slipping out with my words. I had to go back to my real life sometime, didn't I? I couldn't stay here forever, tempting though it was. 'I'll be there on Wednesday.'

I clicked off the call and immediately felt as if I'd made the wrong decision. I wished I could rewind the last two minutes, spool back to where she said 'Yeah?' and reply, 'Well, no, actually'. Just as I was feeling more at home in the bay, I was going to leave again.

But at least I'd get to see Matthew, I consoled myself – and my mum too. It was her birthday on Friday, and we were all meant to be going out to dinner in Jericho to celebrate. Oh, yeah. Real life was edging back into my consciousness. It was right that I went back, really. And once in Oxford, I'd get to see Saul too – even better. The thought of his small, beaming face was consolation enough to finally loosen some of the knots in my stomach.

All holiday feelings had vanished now and I strode back to the café, lists of things I needed to do multiplying in my head.

On Tuesday morning, just before nine, Annie arrived with her first cake order. Both of the large cakes looked perfect – the chocolate cake had thick, glossy icing and smelled heavenly, and the lemon cake looked deliciously moist. It was all I could do not to cut off a slice of each there and then and cram them into my mouth. 'And flapjacks too,' she said, passing me a square tin. 'Twenty plain, and twenty with fruit in. Let me know which go down best, for future bakes.'

'Annie, you're a legend,' I told her, unpacking them onto plates. They were lovely and sticky, and didn't fall apart like the flapjacks I remembered making at school. 'Thank you. Listen, I've got to go back to Oxford today, so . . .'

Her face fell. 'Oh no! So soon?'

I nodded. 'Afraid so.' I sighed, wishing more than ever that I had turned down the temp job. I just didn't feel ready to leave Cornwall yet, especially now that we had such amazing-looking cakes to sell. I wanted to see people's faces as they bit into them, wanted to get that vicarious thrill of watching their pleasure. 'I don't know when I'll be back either, unfortunately. As soon as I can, obviously, but . . .' I shrugged. 'It's really difficult trying to juggle two lives, here and Oxford.'

'I understand,' she said. 'Do you still want me to go on baking, even though you won't be here?'

'Oh God, yes, absolutely,' I replied. 'I'll leave instructions with Carl, and make sure you get paid. Here – ' I scribbled down my mobile and home numbers for her – 'and keep in touch, won't you? Let me know if there's a problem. I'll speak to Carl about how the cakes are selling, and ring you about new orders. Is that okay?'

I hoped it *was* okay. Managing the café by telephone was not remotely ideal, but it was the best I could do right now. Thankfully she nodded. 'Of course,' she said. 'Well, I can't pretend I'm not sad that you're off again. I was looking forward to us working together, and it was lovely to have you round on Sunday night — Martha and I were both saying how much we enjoyed it. But I do understand. Make sure you come back soon, won't you?'

I gave her a hug. 'You bet I will,' I told her.

By noon, I was loading my case into the car with an odd sense of foreboding about leaving.

'I'll be down again before long,' I promised Carl. 'Hopefully a weekend during half-term at the least.' I'd persuade Matthew that we could bring Saul down for a little holiday, I vowed. Sell it to Emily as some time off for her and Dan, then pretend he was my boy for a few days, and we were a happy family having a seaside holiday together. He'd love the beach, I knew it already. I could just imagine him, skinny white legs sticking out of swim-shorts as he dug the most humongous castle for his Gogos to take up residence in.

'See ya then,' Carl said, arms folded in front of him. I felt his eyes on me as I got into the car and started the engine. I hoped he wasn't about to start texting his mates the moment I was gone, with POKER PARTY BACK ON messages.

I drove away, trying not to think about that. I'd only been in Cornwall a few days, but already I was used to life there: the amazing light first thing in the morning, the glorious fresh air, the spectacular scenery, the slower pace of life. It was a shock to my system, getting back on a busy A-road and being surrounded by traffic again. I tried not to think about the calmness of my beach in comparison, the rhythmic rolling of the waves, the vast openness of the sky.

At least the first reaction to the cakes had been good, I tried to comfort myself. There had been some genuine oohs and aahs when people saw them, and we'd sold quite a few flapjacks at elevenses time too. I was sorry not to be there for the afternoon, that time of day when every person in their right mind fancied a bit of cake. They wouldn't be sorry if they came to *my* café with a sweet-tooth craI thought proudly.

I arrived in Oxford four hours later, drumming my fingers on the steering wheel as I hit the gridlocked ring road. Cars queued back from the roundabouts, nose-to-tail, all the drivers looking frustrated and fed up. It was a warm day and I'd rolled down my windows, but quickly wound them up again as the smell of diesel wafted in around my nostrils. 'Come *on*,' I muttered under my breath, feeling impatience creeping through me. 'Hurry up!'

Another twenty minutes of stop-start driving and I was pulling up outside our house. Home. I heaved my bags out of the car and let myself in. Then I stopped and stared. Everything seemed ... different. It smelled very clean and the hall looked unusually tidy. The coat-rack was normally completely overloaded with coats, scarves, hats and umbrellas, but it seemed to have been thinned out in my absence. All that remained were a couple of jackets, my fawn-coloured mac and a single umbrella, neatly rolled.

Whoa. If it wasn't for the fact that I recognized the spatter of mud along the bottom of my mac, I'd have had to double-check I was in the right house. I raised my eyebrows, wondering if the fact that Matthew had resorted to tidying up in my absence was a sign that he had missed me desperately. I hoped so. I smiled, liking the image of him busying around, making our home look even nicer to distract himself from his boredom. There was something kind of romantic about that.

Further in, the house looked even cleaner. Spookily clean, in fact. It was as if Kim and Aggie had paid a surprise visit, or Matthew had become best friends with Mr Muscle and invited him round to demonstrate his products. I wandered through the rooms, wide-eyed and holding my breath. The chunky wooden coffee table in the living room – usually scattered with magazines, news-papers, books, letters, empty mugs – was spotless and suspiciously glossy-looking. I bent down and sniffed it, breathing in the unmistakable scent of beeswax. Beeswax! He *had* been bored.

Elsewhere in the room the CDs had all been put back in their boxes and were lined up on the rack. The mantelpiece – which tended to be a resting place for photos, bills, invitations and other important stuff – was empty save for a couple of candlesticks and the clock. It had even been dusted, I noted, raising my eyebrows in surprise.

The kitchen was similarly pristine – the kettle and toaster both gleaming, the draining rack empty, the fruit bowl full of bright Granny Smiths and perfect bananas. I knew without checking that the wrinkled old grapes that had lurked there previously would now be history, consigned to the compost heap along with the elderly, shrunken clementines that I'd somehow not got round to eating.

'Good work, Matthew,' I murmured, staring around in awe at all his slaving. It must have taken him *hours*. I gingerly picked up the kettle and filled it, then wiped my fingerprints off the sparkling chrome with a tea towel. While it began boiling, I took my bags upstairs.

Walking into our bedroom gave me a start. I hadn't seen it so spotless since the day I'd moved in. My eyes boggled at the cream-coloured armchair that stood in one corner. It was usually covered with heaps of my clothes – but not now. They had vanished, presumably all put away for the first time ever. I'd almost forgotten there was actually a chair there beneath them.

The bedside tables were both empty too. I blinked in

surprise at mine: when I'd left a few days earlier, there had been a teetering tower of paperbacks on it, a clock and several old glasses of water. Now there was ... nothing.

I found that my arms had wrapped themselves around my body. Surprise and delight had turned to an uneasy feeling. Standing in our bedroom felt like being in a depersonalized, sterile hotel room. It didn't feel like my home any more.

I don't know how long I stood there (I didn't dare sit down on the bed for fear of creasing the duvet cover), but the next thing I knew, a key was turning in the front door and I heard Matthew come in. His footsteps were sure and heavy — one, two, three ... and then I heard a moment's silence. Ahh. He'd clocked my denim jacket on the coat-rack, I guessed. The mess-maker had returned. I wasn't even sure what his reaction would be. Pleased, surely? Pleased that I, his long-standing girlfriend, was back in our home — yes, of course. But did a ripple of annoyance also go through him as he noticed that I'd left my handbag on the floor by the shoe basket? Did his fists clench when he saw that I'd dumped the day's post skew-whiff on the hall table?

I shook myself. I was being ridiculous. Utterly ridiculous. This was *Matthew*, my boyfriend, after all, the man who'd saved my life!

'Hiya,' I called out, hurrying to the top of the stairs. 'You okay?'

He was standing there in the hallway and it was like seeing a stranger for a moment. Then he smiled. 'You're back,' he said. 'Hello.'

I ran down the stairs and hugged him. 'I barely recognized the place,' I said, my face against his shirt. It was slightly damp with sweat from his cycle ride home. 'You've been busy.'

He gave me a squeeze. 'Well, I had to do *something* while you were away,' he said lightly. 'I'm glad you're home.'

'Me too,' I said. I squeezed him back with rather more enthusiasm. 'We should go out tonight,' I suggested, the idea popping into my head. 'Have dinner together somewhere nice and romantic, catch up properly. I feel as if we haven't seen each other for ages.' My spirits rose at the thought of dressing up and finding a table in a cosy, intimate bistro or restaurant. And having food cooked for us and brought to us too – even better. I'd had enough of my own kitchen nightmares recently to warrant a visit from Gordon Ramsay.

His arms loosened around me. 'Mmm,' he said. 'But with your job starting tomorrow, you should probably have an early night,' he added. 'And we *are* going out on Friday, remember, for your mum's dinner. That's going to cost a fortune. I'm not sure we should go out tonight as well.'

I hesitated. He was probably right. Almost certainly right. Best to be sensible and not rock up to meet the pharmaceutical boffins tomorrow at my new workplace stinking of night-before wine and garlic. Good first impressions, and all that. And yet ... part of me wished that for once, just once, he would throw caution to the wind and say, *Yes, let's be spontaneous, let's go and find a party we can crash, let's go and do something really fun and outrageous together. NOW!* We both knew that wasn't going to happen, though.

'True,' I said. 'Lucky I've got you to keep me on the straight and narrow, isn't it?'

'Very lucky,' he said.

I had the distinct impression there was something else going on behind this conversation – a subtext, as if some other, unspoken dialogue was taking place between us concurrently – but I couldn't quite grasp what, couldn't tune into it.

Once again I gave myself a brisk shake. It was probably just the fact that we hadn't seen each other properly for ages, that was all. Give it a few hours and everything would be back to normal, I was sure.

Chapter Nine

'So, how's the new job going?' Ruth asked on Friday night. We were sitting in Brasserie Blanc on Walton Street for Mum's birthday dinner, and there was a familiar gleam in her eye as she sensed another 'Evie fucks it up' story in the offing. She knew me so well.

'Crap,' I replied baldly, skimming through the menu. *Asparagus, soft-poached egg, lemon butter sauce.* Yum. Just the way the food had been described on the menu made it sound delicious. Back at the café, Jo had chalked everything up on the board, so there hadn't really been a menu as such. It was a case of: *Pasties: trad Cornish, beef & ale, chicken & veg.* Maybe when I was next there I could make them sound more enticing, I thought to myself: take a tip from Raymond and glam the list up a bit.

'What do you mean, crap?' Ruth persisted. She was sitting opposite me and leaned forward, her long rope of jet beads swinging against her glass of water with a clink. She looked almost hungry to know about my latest failing.

I was surprised she wasn't rubbing her hands with glee in anticipation.

'Oh, just dull,' I replied, waving a hand dismissively. This was the understatement of the year. My new colleagues were so boring and uptight they made the Crossland gang look like a bunch of party animals. I did not want to think about them on a Friday night. Time for a swift change of subject. 'I'm going to have the soup to start, and the fishcake for a main. What's everyone else having?'

Thankfully everybody started discussing food options and we could veer away from my career. There were eight of us – Mum and Dad, me and Matthew, Louise and Chris, Ruth and Tim. But despite the fact that it was Mum's birthday and she should be the main focus of attention, and despite the fact that Ruth usually liked talking of nothing other than Ruth-world, the conversation kept bouncing back to me and the café and my job, as if these were topics they were all completely fascinated by.

'How did it go, Evie, when you were in Cornwall?' Mum asked, calling down from her position at the head of the table. She looked slightly tipsy already. 'Are you still thinking of selling up, or—?'

'No,' I interrupted. 'Not selling.'

'*Really?*' Louise put in, wide-eyed. 'I thought you *were*

selling? I thought she *was* selling?' This last to Matthew, as if I wasn't to be trusted to speak for myself.

I suddenly felt tired of this conversation, which I seemed to have had about a million times by now with every single member of the family, and half the population of Carrawen Bay too. 'No,' I said firmly. 'I'm not selling. Not until the summer's over, anyway. And it went fine, Mum. Had a great time. So . . .' I cast about for something to change the subject. Again. 'Has anyone—'

'But how are you going to manage it, all the way up here, if you're not selling?' Ruth wanted to know. 'No disrespect, Evie' – yeah, right, I thought, not much – 'but how is that going to work? I just don't understand.'

My fists were tightly balled and I hid them under the table in my lap, trying to keep my temper. 'Look, I don't know, all right? I don't know how it's going to work, but it just *will*. I know you're all desperate for me to make a tit of myself, as usual' – a clamour went up at that, of course, all of them denying it hotly – 'but I'm just going to give it a try, see what happens. It's what Jo wanted, after all. And now, if you don't mind, can we talk about something else for a change?'

Silence fell and I realized I'd practically shouted my last sentence. Several diners from other tables had turned to stare at me. I drained my glass of wine with a gulp and glared them out. 'Yes, have a good look,' I said meanly. 'Okay? Angry woman on table nine. Seen enough? Right.'

'Evie!' hissed Matthew, his hand on my arm. 'Behave yourself!'

Behave myself. Like he was my dad, for God's sake. I wrenched my arm away from his like a stroppy teenager. Whose side was he on, anyway?

'Well, I'm sure we're all very sorry for being *concerned*,' Ruth said sarcastically. A victorious smile played on her lips. *And Evie falls for it once again. The black sheep proves that, yes, for the hundredth time, she is well deserving of her title.* 'I'm sure we're all deeply *sorry*—'

'All right, Ruth, that's enough,' Dad mumbled.

'. . . If we've offended you by *asking* after you, like normal families do,' Ruth finished, ignoring Dad.

Normal families. Ha. That was a laugh.

'We're going to be down there over half-term,' Tim said. He had a big, bland face, Tim, as if he'd been made in a factory. The Nice-but-Dull-Husband model. 'Cornwall, I mean. We can pop in, make sure things are okay, if you—'

'Can we?' Ruth asked sharply. His face fell, and I felt sorry for him. Poor sod. He was only trying to wave an olive branch around. Ruth had just snatched the olive branch and broken it over her bony knee.

'Thanks, Tim,' I said pointedly. 'That's really kind of you.'

Ruth gave a huffing noise, glaring daggers at anyone foolish enough to make eye contact with her.

'This *is* meant to be a happy occasion,' Mum said, seeming nettled that she'd been temporarily forgotten about. 'Do we have to argue on a birthday? Come on, girls.'

'Sorry, Mum,' Louise said, patting her hand and shooting stop-it looks at Ruth and me. 'Your hair looks gorgeous, by the way. Have you had it done this week?'

Mollified, Mum began a long explanation of her latest style and the inspiration behind it, and what the stylist had said (quite a lot about how young it made her look, blah-blah) and where the stylist was going on holiday (Morocco with his boyfriend for a week in June) and how she'd tried a new thickening spray, and it had been wonderful.

The subject of the black sheep was dropped. But not forgotten, judging by Ruth's contemptuous glances, which punctuated the meal. I found myself sinking into a mood of drunken gloom that not even half-hearted sex with Matthew at home could lift.

'I wish you'd stuck up for me,' I said when it was over and we were lying there, back on our separate sides of the bed. My voice sounded small in the darkness.

'Mmm?' he said, not moving. I could tell he was on the verge of sleep; his breathing was deep and slow, his voice far-away.

I hesitated. Was there any point in pursuing this? You couldn't force someone to be on your side, or stick up for you in an argument, after all. 'Nothing,' I said in the end. But it didn't feel like nothing. It felt like a problem that kept me awake, wondering and worrying, for hours into the night.

Matthew went off to the gym the following morning, and I knew he'd be gone hours, so I phoned Amber and arranged to meet her for lunch in Fratellis. Then I kept myself busy, sorting out washing, and tidying up (my possessions seemed to have spread themselves all over the house again within the few days of my being back), before sitting down and sorting out the business banking.

I tried not to wonder how things were at the café without me. I also tried not to think about the night before. Every time Matthew's 'Behave yourself!' flashed into my head, I did the mental equivalent of sticking my fingers in my ears and singing 'La-la-la, I can't hear you'.

I wouldn't talk about my feelings (what feelings? what problem?) with Amber, I decided. She had never said as much, but I kind of knew that she had never been as blown away by Matthew as I had. Naturally I'd really wanted the two of them to get on, and in the early months of our relationship had arranged all sorts of pub nights and dinners where they could get to know each other, but it hadn't exactly panned out as I'd hoped. He thought she was irresponsible and immature, and she thought ... well, she'd always been very careful to say she thought he was 'nice', but I knew deep down that he wasn't her cup of char in the slightest.

Once, when she and I had both been ratted on a girls' night out, she'd let slip something about him being boring, but had then looked as if she wanted to chew off her own hand at such a gaffe. 'Oops,' she'd muttered. 'Sorry. Rewind, delete ... I never said that, right?'

I'd laughed it off, but the words had stayed with me, clear and sharp as print, even through the fug of my next-day hangover. And I'd wondered what else she thought of him but hadn't wanted to admit.

So, no. I wouldn't say anything, I vowed as I strolled down the road later on to meet her. I'd bury the feelings of doubt, put on a happy face. I didn't want to open up a seething can of worms.

But then again, I'd never been any good at bottling things up. I was useless, in fact, at bottling things up. Which was why, despite my best intentions, as soon as we sat down, I found myself blurting out, 'Matthew and I aren't getting on very well', before I even knew the words were coming.

We were in the courtyard garden, with a bright May sun beaming down on us. Amber lifted her shades and looked me in the eyes. 'What's happened?' she asked.

And that was all it took for my worries to come spilling out. Our different views on the beach café and what I ought to be doing for the rest of my life; the way he'd cleaned the house so spectacularly while I'd been away that I seemed to have been scrubbed out of the place; and the argument last night at the restaurant.

'Hmm,' she said, popping an olive into her mouth. 'And how's your sex life? Has it survived all this, or——?'

'It's crap,' I told her gloomily, dropping my gaze. I had my elbows on the table and propped my chin up in my hands. 'I initiated a shag last night because I felt a bit ... needy, I guess. And he went along with it, but, you know, there's no passion any more. No *Phwooarr, come here, you big gorgeous thing, let's...*' I shrugged, aware that the woman at the next table was listening in. 'You know.'

'Hmm,' she said again. 'So have you told him how you feel? Have you talked about this?'

I shook my head. 'I keep putting it off,' I confessed.

The waiter brought us a couple of beers, misted with cold, and I raised mine to my lips and took a long, cool slug of it, not bothering with the nicety of pouring it into a glass.

'I feel as if I just ... exasperate him,' I found myself saying. 'Like I'm some kind of inconvenience. Honestly, last night, the way he spoke to me, it freaked me out. "Behave yourself," he said – like I was a kid. I'm surprised he didn't tell me to go and sit on the naughty step, or send me up to my bedroom.'

'That's pretty naff,' Amber said carefully. 'You're meant to be equal partners, after all, not—'

'I know!' I interrupted. The beer was sinking through me very pleasantly and loosening my tongue. 'It was so patronizing, so ... putting me in my place. I'd never dream of speaking to *him* like that, so why does he think he's got the right to boss *me* around? And honestly, Amber, the whole thing with the café – it's been like pulling teeth, trying to get him to see my point of view.'

I was off into rant mode. No stopping me now. All the niggles and irritations I'd felt towards Matthew came streaming out in a tirade, from A to Z. The way he cleared his throat so loudly. The way he never forgot things, and always knew exactly where he'd left his house keys. The way he was always early for everything. Even the way he breathed sometimes annoyed me.

I only stopped when our food arrived; the mushrooms glistening black, garlicky and pungent, the sardines silver and oily, a large bowl of crisp green salad leaves and a basket of bread. I had drunk my beer already and clocked the waiter raising his eyebrows.

'You want another?' he asked.

'What the hell,' I mumbled. 'Yes, please.' Well, it was Saturday and I was having a major crisis. It was allowed, wasn't it?

'Okay,' Amber said, as we divvied up the food. 'Now tell me the good stuff about him. You've been together years — there must be loads of things you love about him too.'

'Oh, sure,' I said, spearing a fat mushroom. 'Well, there's Saul, of course, and . . .'

Amber shook her head. 'Evie,' she said, 'you can't count Saul. He's not Matthew. Carry on.'

I was starting to feel bamboozled by the beer and the sunshine and just how serious this conversation was. 'Okay,' I said. 'Good stuff about Matthew. Well . . .' The problem was, whenever I tried to think of what I loved about Matthew, Saul's face kept appearing in my mind, smiling back at me. 'Um — well, he's practical,' I said after a moment. 'Reliable . . .'

'You're making him sound like a Ford Focus,' Amber pointed out.

'He makes me laugh,' I added quickly.

'Does he?'

I chewed a bit of sardine while I thought about it. 'No, not really,' I admitted. I slumped in my chair. 'God, this is terrible.'

'Do you still fancy him?' Amber pressed. 'Do you look at him and think *Hell-o!*, and give his bum a cheeky squeeze when he walks by?'

I hesitated. 'I do love him ...'

'You're not answering the question,' Amber said, jabbing her fork in my direction.

'I ... I don't know,' I said. 'But he did save my life, remember. I love him for *that*.'

'Hmm,' she said. She didn't say anything else.

We ate in silence for a few moments. 'Hypothetically speaking,' she said after a while, 'if you and Matthew ... went your separate ways, what would be your gut feeling?'

I bit my lip. 'Don't say that,' I replied. 'Just because I'm having a moan, it doesn't mean we're about to split up, or anything.'

'Of course not,' she said, waving a hand. 'But what if you did ... ?'

I couldn't meet her eye. My first thought had been how much I'd miss Saul. How awful of me was that? Missing Saul before I missed his dad – how traitorous could you get?

'If we did go our separate ways,' I said slowly, testing out my feelings as I spoke, 'I would be ...' I frowned, trying to digest the scenario. Breaking up with Matthew would mean being single again and I'd kind of assumed that one day Matthew and I would have a family of our own, would get married. The idea of facing the rest of my life on my Jack Jones, and those things being taken away from me, made me feel queasy. 'Well, my whole life would be totally up in the air,' I said. I put my knife and fork down as conflicting emotions swirled around my head. 'I'd feel – lonely. And sort of . . . scared about what to do.'

I took some bread and munched it. 'Let's not talk about this any more,' I said. 'It's making me feel strange.'

'Okay,' she said. 'But you know I'm here, don't you, if you ever do want to talk about it?'

'Yes,' I said. 'I know.' Despite my words, I was already mentally slamming the door I'd inadvertently opened, trying to lock away the conversation so that I didn't need to think about it. I imagined myself sliding great metal bolts against the door: thud, thud. There.

'So, how are things with you?' I asked. I slipped my shades back onto my nose as I took a forkful of salad. I didn't want her to see the troubled light that I knew must be in my eyes.

Chapter Ten

The conversation with Amber kept ringing around my head all weekend, making me feel discombobulated and out of sorts. Oh, we had a nice enough time – Saul came to stay on Saturday night, which was lovely as usual; and then on Sunday, after we'd dropped Saul back at Emily's, Matthew and I took the bikes out along the river, with a picnic in a sunny meadow on the way. Underneath all the pleasantries, though, something felt different. It was as if I was standing outside myself, watching our relationship with a critical eye. I wasn't sure that I liked what I saw.

Once upon a time we might have got a bit frisky in this meadow, I thought sadly as he produced a Thermos flask from his backpack and poured us both cups of tea. We'd have lain there snogging, giggling and whispering like teenagers, unable to take our hands off each other. Now we were sitting there, eating cheese sandwiches and drinking tea on our M&S travel rug, like a boring old married couple.

I toyed with the idea of pushing him down on the rug and straddling him, but then had visions of him complaining about his bad back, or giving a startled yelp as he was scalded by his tea. So I didn't.

Even spending the previous evening with Saul had seemed to take on a new poignancy after talking to Amber. He'd brought some Lego with him, and the two of us spent ages making a castle together, with turrets and secret doorways and dungeons. 'This room is for you and Daddy,' he said, pointing it out. 'And there's Mum and Dan's room. My room is right in the middle, see?'

'Perfect,' I said, but it cut me to the quick. *Hypothetically speaking*, I heard Amber say in my head, *if you and Matthew went your separate ways, what would be your gut feeling?*

Sadness, I thought in the next second. Sadness that I'd no longer be able to do this with Saul. If Matthew and I did separate, would I ever see my boy again? He would grow up without me, maybe make castles with another of his dad's girlfriends, build a different woman a Lego suite with Matthew instead of me . . .

'Evie, are you crying?' I heard Saul ask in astonishment.

I wiped my eyes hastily. 'I think it's just hay fever,' I told him. 'So, who's going in the dungeon, then?'

Later that evening, after he'd had his tea and a bath, we snuggled up on the sofa together and I started reading him my childhood copy of *Finn Family Moomintroll* while

Matthew leafed through the newspaper. Saul's hair was in damp strawberry-smelling spikes as he leaned against me, and once again I felt that same piercing happiness laced with sadness as I read. I'd kept loads of my favourite books from when I was his age – the Roald Dahls, the Helen Cresswells, the Enid Blytons – and there was something lovely about sitting here, reading the Moomins to Saul, just as my mum had read it to me. There were still so many books I hadn't read with him, though. Would I get the chance to, now?

I shook myself. I was being maudlin, acting as if Matthew and I had already decided to split up, when nothing of the sort had happened. Probably just PMT, I told myself, trying to shake off my weird mood.

Everything seemed to have changed lately, that was the thing. Jo dying, me inheriting the café, and the uncomfortable feeling that perhaps Matthew and I weren't as rock-solid as I'd always thought. It felt as if someone had taken my life and shaken it up, jumbling all the elements so that they didn't quite fit back together as they used to.

The next week passed with dreary familiarity. My temp job was still mind-bogglingly awful, and the situation between me and Matthew felt disjointed and somewhat fragile. I kept trying to work up to having a Big Conversation with him, about where we were going and what the future held for us, but found the idea so paralysingly stressful every time that it hadn't actually taken place.

I popped round to my mum's one evening and found her looking suspiciously red-eyed as she pored over one of Jo's old photo albums. 'I still can't believe she's gone, Evie,' she sniffed, as I put my arms around her and hugged her. 'I feel lost without her somehow, as if the world's not right any more.' She blew her nose and turned the page, and we both looked at the photos of a very young Jo wearing a bikini on a palm beach somewhere exotic. She was beaming into the camera, her arm around some strapping bloke in shades, as if she was having the time of her life.

'You know, I always envied her for having the guts to do her own thing,' Mum said, dabbing at her eyes. 'She was so ... brave. Much braver than me. Especially the way she stood up to our parents the way she did. I've been going through her letters and there are some really quite nasty ones from Granny and Grandad, almost bullying her for the choices she made.'

'Oh no,' I said. Granny and Grandad had never been the cuddliest grandparents, even when I was little. They were prim and proper, liking children to be quiet and well behaved rather than noisy and fun-loving.

'Yes,' Mum said. 'I felt that too. How anyone could try to crush their child like that, push them in a direction they really didn't want to go, then turn against them for not conforming, is beyond me.'

I said nothing, and after a rather loaded silence, she looked at me in concern. 'Evie – you don't feel that Dad and I have ever done that, do you?' she asked. 'I know things haven't fallen into place for you quite as easily as they have for Ruth and Louise, but you do know that we just want what's best for you, don't you?'

I hesitated. I wasn't sure I *did* know that, but didn't want to hurt her feelings by saying so. 'Well . . .' I began, searching around for the right words.

'Because we'll always love you, whatever you decide,' she said, putting her arm around me. '*Whatever* you decide.'

I twisted my fingers in my lap. 'I might not have done everything perfectly, like Ruth and Lou,' I began, 'but—'

'There *isn't* a perfect way, though, Evie,' she said. 'And you know – you may not believe it, but I think deep down they've always rather envied *you*, in the way that I envied Jo.'

I gave a snort. 'Yeah, right,' I said sarcastically. 'Because there's just so much to envy.'

'I'm serious,' she said. 'Neither of them would ever dare break away from what's expected of them, just like I never did. Whereas you – you're gutsy, like Jo. And I think that's a really admirable quality, love. I genuinely do.'

'Wow,' I said, checking she was serious. She was, and

it made me feel slightly lost for words. 'Um … thanks, Mum.'

'I suppose Jo dying so suddenly has made me think about life, and what's important,' she went on. 'And it's brought it home to me: life is short. You can't waste it doing things you don't enjoy.' She blew her nose again, then smiled at me. 'So I, for one, am going to have a glass of wine and drink a toast to Jo, who lived every minute to the full. Will you join me?'

I smiled back at her. 'Damn right I will,' I said.

My head was reeling as she poured the wine. Whoa. My mum had never said anything like that to me before. It made me feel different about myself somehow, the fact that she thought I was gutsy, like Jo.

'Cheers,' she said, passing me a glass. We clinked them together.

'Cheers,' I echoed thoughtfully.

On Thursday, I had a phone call from Annie while I was at work. 'Hi, Evie,' she said. 'I'm sorry to bother you, but there's a problem. The café hasn't been open for the last few days, and—'

'*What?*' I asked. Denise, the clerk with a perfect blonde ponytail and pale eyelashes, who worked nearest me, shot a nosy sideways glance my way and I lowered my voice. 'What do you mean?'

'Well, I went along to deliver the cakes yesterday morning and the place was all closed up,' she said. 'I had to go to work, so I couldn't hang about, unfortunately. Then I tried popping back last night, but it was still closed. It hasn't been open today, either. I don't know what Carl's up to, but I thought you should know.'

'Oh, shit,' I groaned, earning myself another look from Denise, and one from Tweedy Brian, the office manager, who stood up and glared sternly at me over the partition between our desks. 'Just what I didn't need. I'll give Carl a ring to see what he's playing at. Thanks, Annie.'

'All right,' she said. 'Let me know if I can do anything to help.'

'Cheers,' I said, ringing off. I got to my feet. 'Just nipping out for some fresh air,' I said. 'Anyone want a coffee?'

Tweedy Brian eyed the wall clock. *Jobsworth alert.* 'Morning break isn't for another twelve minutes,' he said, all prim and disapproving. His fleshy chin wobbled as he spoke and I had the sudden urge to flick a paper clip at it.

'Ah well, I won't tell if you don't, Bri,' I said, smiling brightly and walking through the office.

'Wait,' he said. 'Excuse me, Miss . . . um . . .'

'I think her name's Eva,' Denise put in, sounding thoroughly uninterested, as if she was talking about sanitary towels.

'It's *Evie*,' I said, without breaking my stride, 'and I'll be back in five minutes, okay?' I could hear Tweedboy protesting, and there were a few indignant sniffs as I went through the door, but I ignored the lot of them. I hated office politics. All that pettiness about who owned which stapler, and who hadn't replaced the toner in the photo-copier, and who had the cheek to walk out of the office twelve minutes before morning break. *For God's sake*, I felt like shouting. *None of this matters!*

Outside the office, I perched on a wall and dialled Carl's mobile number. It was eleven in the morning, so he should have been in the café for the last hour, but he sounded as if I'd woken him up, once he finally answered. 'Yeah?' he said.

'Carl, it's Evie,' I said crisply. 'Annie's just phoned and told me that the café hasn't been open for the last few days. I was wondering—'

'Oh, yeah, I meant to tell you about that,' he said, his voice sounding thick and groggy. I heard him puffing on a cigarette and hoped it wasn't anywhere near my stock. Where was he?

'Tell me what?' I snapped. 'Because—'

'Excuse me,' came a loud male voice from behind me.

I looked up to see a burly security guard leaning out of the reception door. 'Can't sit there, love. Could you move along, please.'

Move along, please. Like he was a flaming police officer. 'I work here,' I said huffily. 'I'm just making a quick phone call, that's all.'

'Yeah, well, whatever you're doing, can you do it somewhere else, please. Thank you.' He had one of those potato faces, piggy eyes and jowly cheeks. He was tall and overweight, and looked uncomfortable in his uniform; the kind of man you could imagine perspiring pinkly on warm days. 'Now, please,' he prompted when I didn't move.

I tutted and rolled my eyes. What was it with these jobsworths anyway? This office seemed to attract them, with strange magnetic powers. Then I stood up, taking my time to walk all of two feet away from the office door. 'Are you still there, Carl?' I asked. 'Sorry about that. So, as I was saying...'

'I was gonna ring you later anyway,' he interrupted. 'Tell you that I've quit.'

I stopped dead, as if someone had just shot me with a tranquillizer gun. 'You've ... quit?' I repeated. The word rebounded around my head like an echo. 'What do you mean? You can't just quit on me.'

I heard him puffing out the cigarette smoke – puff, puff, puff – as if blowing smoke rings. 'Well, sorry,' he said. 'But I got a better offer. I'm working at a place in Tregarrow. Started yesterday.'

'Nice of you to tell me,' I said, feeling helpless with

frustration. I wanted to scream. 'You need to give me more notice than that, Carl, you can't just walk out!'

There was a pause while I imagined him shrugging. 'Well, I just did,' he said.

I gritted my teeth. 'So you did,' I said, wanting to strangle him. 'I guess that's that, then.' I hung up, then kicked the wall so hard, I thought I'd broken my big toe. 'Fuck!' I yelled into the car park. 'SHIT! And BOLLOCKS!'

'I've got to go down there,' I said to Matthew that night. 'I've just got to. There's no chef now Carl's walked out, which means there's no money coming in. I've had Annie making cakes that aren't going anywhere – it's a disaster. I've got to sort it out.'

He nodded as if he'd been expecting this. We were sitting having a Chinese takeaway (his choice) in front of a TV talent show (my choice). He watched dispassionately as a so-called talking Pekinese dog remained mute, much to its spangly-dressed owner's despair. 'Come on, Ruffles,' she cooed. 'Tell everyone your name.'

'I mean, I've got to,' I said, waving my fork in the air. Several grains of rice fell from it like tiny snowflakes. 'When I rang Annie back, she said she'd keep any eye on the property for me, but all the same, I can't leave it abandoned.'

He opened his mouth as if he was going to ask about my temp job, but then closed it again. He already knew the answer.

'Come on, Ruffles,' the despairing granny trilled on the telly. 'Just say your name, darling. Say "Ruffles" for the nice people. Say "Ruffles".'

BUZZZ, went one of the judges, pressing a button to vote her off.

'And ... to be honest,' I said, 'I might have to stay there for some time. Hire a new chef, keep everything ticking along.'

Matthew was sitting there as mute as poor old Ruffles. It made me feel edgy. 'Why aren't you saying anything?' I asked.

He sighed and put down his fork on his congealing chow mein. 'Evie, if you go ...' he said, and then pressed his lips together without finishing the sentence.

My heart boomed painfully inside me. I knew what he was going to say. And I kind of wanted him to say it, yet at the same time was terrified of hearing the words.

BUZZZ, went the second judge on the TV panel, Simon Cowell, rolling his eyes and looking impatient.

'Matthew,' I said quickly, before he could go on. 'Maybe—'

'I think you should go,' he said, as if he couldn't hear me. 'I can tell that's where your heart is.'

His old-fashioned terminology made my eyes prickle. 'My heart is here too,' I tried saying. 'But—'

BUZZZ, went the third judge on the telly, the sweet actress whose name I could never remember. 'Sorry, darling,' she said to the old lady. 'But I'm afraid it's a No.'

I flicked the telly off with the remote and stared at Matthew. 'What are you saying?' I asked hoarsely. 'Are you saying . . . ?'

'I think we should make a clean break,' he said. 'I'm sorry, Evie. I've been thinking about it for a while, and I'm just not sure where we're going any more.'

I squeezed my eyes shut, unable to look at him. My fork fell out of my hand and I heard it thud down on the carpet. More mess. I could imagine the rice sinking stickily through the pile. No wonder he wanted shot of me.

'I . . .' I began. Oh God. It was happening. *Hypothetically speaking*, Amber intoned for the umpteenth time in my brain. The voice of Doom. No need to be hypothetical now, though, eh?

He took my hand. 'Evie, I'm sorry,' he said again. 'I'm really, really sorry.' *But I'm afraid it's a No.*

Tears were sliding down my face, dripping onto my plate. *This is it*, I thought melodramatically. *This is really it. We're actually breaking up.* And then, with a lurch, *I'll never see Saul again.*

'Say something,' he implored. He sounded genuinely pained. 'How are you feeling?'

'I . . .' I began. Part of me wanted to rail against him, to tell him he'd got it wrong, that we were good together, we were right together. But at the same time I knew I wouldn't be able to say those things with any conviction. 'I feel really sad,' I managed to get out. That was true. Sad, and frightened that I was all on my own now. Scared that I wouldn't have Matthew to organize me any more. I'd be a mess without him, I knew it. And I was heartbroken that I was losing my boy, my borrowed son, whose company was like a bright, golden light sparkling into my life twice a week.

'I'm going out,' I said, getting up. I couldn't look at him. 'I need to clear my head.' I wanted to escape from this awful, toxic conversation, have a good cry on my own, try to make sense of what was going on.

'Wait,' he said. 'Don't you want to talk about this?'

I shook my head. 'And say what?' I asked. 'Look – I get it, okay. It's over. I kind of knew it deep down too, to be honest. You deserve someone clean and tidy and sensible, and—'

'It's not about being clean and tidy and sensible,' he said – almost shouted, in fact. I thought he was going to cry too, then. 'It's more that . . . I think I'm holding you back. This café — it's really under your skin, I can tell. I know it's important to you. And it won't work, with you having a foot in two different worlds. You've got to do it. So I'm ... I'm letting you go.'

I sat down again, flung my arms around him and sobbed. 'It doesn't mean we have to split up, though,' I said, weeping into his shirt.

'It does,' he said, stroking my back. There was a new gentleness in him. It felt, for a moment, almost romantic, this scene between us, until I remembered that actually he was dumping me. 'Evie, it does. I really hope the café is a success — honestly, I do. But we've grown apart: you must see that. I'm just being realistic.'

'I know,' I sniffled. I clung to him, feeling dazed. God. This was *real*. We were splitting up. We were actually splitting up. No more Evie-and-Matthew. No more Matthew-and-Evie. What was I going to do now?

Good question.

Chapter Eleven

'Oh, shit.' Amber said, when I phoned the next day to tell her that Matthew and I had split up. 'Oh, hon, I wasn't expecting that.'

I gave a hollow laugh. 'Yeah, right – that's not how it sounded on Saturday.'

'I didn't seriously think ... Oh, shit. Are you okay? Do you want to move in with me for a bit?'

I blew my nose. I'd been blubbing since I'd woken up that morning. 'I'm okay,' I said.

This was so patently a lie – in fact I stammered over the 'okay', turning it into about five syllables – that she said, 'Shall I come round? It's very quiet in the shop, I'm sure Carla will let me pop out.'

'Honestly, no, I'm fine,' I began, and then changed my mind. 'Actually ... would you?'

'Of course,' she replied. 'Give me five minutes.'

I put the phone down and went on with my packing. I was sorting out all my stuff, piling my CDs and books into boxes, leaving sad-looking gaps in the shelves. I turned my head away, not wanting to look at those miserable empty spaces. Those spaces represented me – my presence gradually being removed from the house. It wasn't a happy thought.

I forced myself to turn back and carry on, after a moment. This was the right thing to do. Matthew was being brave, forcing things to their inevitable conclusion. The relationship had been going nowhere for a long time. It was a mercy killing.

My plan for now was to pack up, load as much stuff as I could into the car and take myself off to Cornwall for the summer. And after that: who knew? Somewhere else that took my fancy. *Life is short*, my mum had reminded me. *You can't waste it doing things you don't enjoy.* And with those words of wisdom from my own mother ringing in my ears, I'd canned the temp job first thing that morning, earning myself a frosty silence from the recruitment consultant. 'I see,' she'd said eventually. 'This is very short notice, so I'm not sure we'll be able to offer you anything—'

'That's fine,' I'd said. 'I've got my own business to run anyway. Bye.'

My hand hovered on *Finn Family Moomintroll* when I came to it on the shelf. I hadn't finished reading it to Saul, and had been looking forward to reaching the chapters with Thingumy and Bob, as I knew they would make him laugh. And now . . .

A tear rolled down my cheek. Now I would have to leave the book, for Matthew to read it to him. I grabbed a pen and wrote on the title page, 'Dear Saul. You are the coolest. I hope you like the rest of this story. Love, Evie.' Then I had to put it down hurriedly before my tears blurred the ink.

Thankfully the doorbell went just then and it was the most ginormous relief to see Amber standing there with her bike, a bunch of white tulips and a huge slab of Dairy Milk. 'These are from Carla,' she said, thrusting the flowers at me. 'And the chocolate's from me. Come here,' she said, putting her arms around me. 'I'm really sorry to hear what's happened.'

At least I still had Amber, I thought gratefully as she hugged me. 'Come through,' I said. 'I'll put the kettle on.'

We went into the kitchen and I found myself looking at it with new eyes, scanning the room for what I needed to pack. It seemed petty to take down the Andy Warhol calendar, even though I'd been the one who'd bought it, or to drive off with the set of non-stick saucepans (mine), leaving Matthew to do without. Having said that, there was no way I could leave behind my old striped milk jug, or the 1970s sunflower plates I'd picked up from the junk shop, or the bright red teapot . . .

One thing at a time, I reminded myself, filling the kettle.

'So what are you going to do?' Amber asked, leaning against the worktop. 'I meant it about moving in with me. You can have the spare room for as long as you like.'

'Thanks,' I said, getting down some mugs. 'But I'm going to take off to Cornwall for a bit, I think. Throw myself into the business, distract myself from my broken heart . . .' I gave a hollow laugh. 'You know.'

'Really?'

'Yeah, really.' I told her about Annie's phone call the day before — was it only yesterday? It felt much longer ago than that — and how, with Matthew and I splitting up, it made sense just to head off there as soon as possible and get stuck in. 'At least I won't be moping around here,' I said, dumping teabags into the pot. 'And I actually feel a tiny bit excited about going. Almost as if I've been set free.'

'Wow,' she said. 'God.'

'Yes,' I said, warming to my theme. 'I really do. Not that I was in a prison, or anything before, but it's like new possibilities have opened up. And it's scary being set free, and I don't know what the hell I'm doing, but I actually *like* the thought that I can do what I want again.' I rubbed my eyes. 'I mean, I'm really sad about Matthew, and everything, too. It's not that I like having split up with him. But...' I shook my head. I couldn't find the right words this morning.

'I'll make the tea,' Amber said. 'Sit down and eat some chocolate. And have a few deep breaths before your head explodes.'

I did what I was told. Chair, chocolate, deep breaths.

'Here,' she said, putting a steaming mug in front of me and sitting down at the table with one of her own. 'Listen – about going to Cornwall. Do you want me to come with you for a few days? Just to keep you company and give you a hand in the café? I don't want you driving off all tearful, and then feeling lonely and not having anyone to talk to. I'm not saying it'll be *like* that,' she added hurriedly. 'I mean, you'll probably be fine. Have a great time. But just in case...'

'Seriously?' I said. 'You'd really come to Cornwall with me? What about work?'

She made a pfff! noise. 'Sod work. For starters, it's the bank holiday, so the shop's shut on Monday anyway. And for seconds, Carla owes me some holiday – and she owes me a favour too, with the number of wedding flowers I've done for her in the evenings the last few weeks,' she said. 'Besides, her daughter's always angling for some extra shifts. Carla won't go short-staffed.' She squeezed my hand. 'If you *want* me to come, that is. I totally understand if you just want to be on your own, get your head straight, do some primal screaming on the clifftops, or whatever it is that you had in mind.'

I broke off another square of Dairy Milk and popped it into my mouth as I thought. I'd barely slept the night before, I'd been so stunned by what Matthew and I had said to each other, so overwhelmed by all the tasks that lay ahead of me. I'd hoped I could keep myself together enough to pack up and leave, not wanting to dwell on the ache that I knew I'd feel inside, despite all my brave talk of being set free. Making a new start in a new place would be exhilarating, yes, but lonely too. So did I want Amber to come with me and hold my hand?

You bet I did.

'Are you sure?' I asked. 'Are you absolutely, totally sure?'

Her eyes sparkled. 'You know me,' she said, wrinkling her nose as she smiled. 'Love a mini-break. So, what time are we off?'

Four hours later we were in the car and heading out of Oxford, with bin bags of my clothes and other assorted, hastily packed possessions in the boot. It was strange, shutting the front door and wondering if I would ever go back. Amber had already offered to pick up the stuff I'd inevitably left behind, so unless Matthew and I had a passionate reunion further down the line, this was it for me and number twenty-three. It wouldn't be my home from now on; I didn't belong any more. I wasn't sure *where* I belonged.

I hesitated, then dropped the keys through the letter box, feeling slightly sick as I heard them clink to the floor inside. There seemed such a finality to the moment. Another bridge burned. No turning back now.

'Ready?' Amber said gently.

I still had my hand on the letter box and felt reluctant to remove it. It was as if by letting go, I would sever my last connection to the house. Was this really the right thing to do? Should I dash over to Matthew's office instead and try to talk him round, persuade him to give us another try?

'I'll wait in the car,' Amber said when I didn't reply.

The sound of her footsteps walking away broke the spell. 'Goodbye,' I whispered to the house, running my fingers along the cold brass metal flap of the letter box, as if caressing a lover's face. And then, with a deep breath, I turned away, got in the car, started the engine and drove off down the street. I didn't look back.

'You okay, Thelma?' Amber asked, glancing over at me as we headed for the ring road.

'I'm okay, Louise,' I replied, flashing her a quick smile. 'I'm glad you're here with me. I'd probably be weeping along to 'Stand By Your Man' if you weren't.'

'Whereas now,' she said, switching on the radio and

fiddling with the dial, 'you've got me, and...' We both started to laugh as 'Freedom' by George Michael suddenly blasted out. 'Ah, George,' she said fondly, cranking up the volume. 'I couldn't have put it better myself.'

The further we got from Oxford, the better my mood became. The sun came out from behind the clouds, and it felt as if we were driving towards a happier place. There was something satisfying about being proactive; about getting up and leaving to start afresh. Amber was in a great mood, too, with her sudden holiday lying ahead of her, and was the best kind of company, making me laugh, finding good songs for us to bellow along to on the radio and chatting away about this and that.

'It's ages since we've done anything like this,' she said after a while. 'Just the two of us, I mean, having a little adventure. We've both been a bit coupley, the last few years, haven't we – me with Jackson and then Bill, and then that jerk Neil, and you with Matthew ... I really like the idea of us having some girl-time again.'

'Me too,' I said, envisaging the two of us in fluffy dressing gowns on the sofa at Jo's, facepacks on, curlers in, watching a chick flick and eating chocolate. Yes, girl-time was exactly what I needed.

'We can get all dressed up, go out on the razzle, dance round our handbags,' she said dreamily, puncturing my image of chilled-out serenity in an instant. 'Mind you, I'm guessing the nightlife isn't too hot over in Carrawen Bay?' she added after a moment.

I shook my head. 'It's not exactly rocking,' I told her.

'Well, who better to start livening it up, than me and you?' she asked.

I pulled a face. 'I'm not sure I really want to liven things up right now,' I protested weakly.

She took out a pocket mirror and expertly applied some fresh lipstick. 'We'll just see about that,' she said.

Once we arrived in Carrawen Bay it was almost eight o'clock, and becoming dusky. Lights were on in all the B&B windows along the high street and, as we drove past the pub, it looked bustling and full of life. 'Fab,' Amber said appreciatively. 'It's really pretty here. Oh wow, and there's the beach. Gorgeous!'

Even in the filmy half-light, I had to agree. The sand looked a smoky grey and the water navy-blue, darkening to black on the horizon, but there was no disguising the generous sweep of the bay, and the huge slice of sky. Gorgeous indeed. I felt proud of it, as if I'd made it with my own bare hands. 'It *is* lovely,' I said. 'And here's the café.'

I pulled into the car park and turned off the engine. Neither of us spoke for a moment, then Amber said in a stage whisper, 'I can hear the waves.'

I grinned at her. 'Yeah,' I said. 'Nice, isn't it?' I meant it too. For the first time all day, I felt calmness wash over me with the sound of the breakers. I was back here in the bay, and everything was going to be all right.

We'd picked up fish and chips in Polzeath and took the hot paper packets onto the café deck, the salt-and-vinegar scent mingling with the sea's briny tang. It was shadowy up on the deck, with a few old cigarette butts blowing around like leaves. A polystyrene cup rolled in a slow semicircle and I grabbed it. 'Bloody Carl,' I said, not for the first time. 'Of all the unreliable, useless, rude, lazy—'

'Ah, you're well shot of him,' Amber said. 'He's history, and us two are the future. Right, are we going in, then?'

I unlocked the door and flicked on the lights. Surprise, surprise, Carl hadn't bothered clearing up before he jumped ship. Plates and cups had been left on the tables, and the floor was sandy and crumb-strewn. I clenched my fists. He was totally getting a slap the next time I set eyes on him.

'Wow, it's amazing in here,' Amber said, gazing around. 'Must be lovely in the daytime with the light streaming in. God, Evie, I can't quite believe it's all yours.'

I smiled at her despite my annoyance. 'I know,' I said. 'I can't, either. It looks even better when it's been cleaned.'

'Oh, that won't take us long,' Amber said. 'But first things first, where are your plates? And do you have any ketchup for these chips? Let's eat, and then we can do everything else.'

It was the right thing to do. I found us a couple of cans of Diet Coke from the fridge and we sat in the corner booth, and put the lot away. I realized with a jolt halfway through that I hadn't thought about Matthew for ages. By now, presumably, he'd be back at the house. It must have been weird for him, walking in on his own, realizing that I'd cleared out. Maybe he'd half-expected me to be there, tearful and pleading, *Don't leave me, I can't go on without you* . . .

I imagined him sitting there all alone in the living room, and felt a pang of sadness. Was he missing me? I wondered. Or was he stretching out on the sofa with a celebratory beer?

I blinked, aware that there was a suspicious wetness in my eyes. I also realized that I'd managed to eat the rest of my chips without tasting them.

Amber had finished hers too. 'I'm stuffed,' she said, stacking the plates and getting to her feet. 'Why don't we unpack the car, and then you can show me round. I can't wait to check out the rest of it. Then we'll make a start on the cleaning up.'

'Okay,' I said, smothering a yawn. My sleepless night

was really catching up on me now that I'd managed the drive here safely, and all the food had made me dozy. I could feel my energy levels plummeting.

'Two go wild in Cornwall,' Amber said, trotting off to the kitchen. 'This is going to be *fun*.'

'Definitely,' I called after her, trying to sound enthusiastic. Inside my head a flood of images were appearing one after another, like a personal slide show: Matthew saying he wanted to break up, Ruth's gloating face, Saul and I cuddled up reading the Moomins, my dusty, dirty café . . .

Oh, what had I done, leaving everything behind in Oxford for this? What had I DONE?

Chapter Twelve

By eleven o'clock that night we'd unpacked most of my stuff, cleaned up, emailed an ad for a new chef to the local press, ordered a cash-and-carry delivery online (arriving on Monday) and sunk almost two bottles of wine between us. Oh, and experimented with the dodgy liqueurs we'd discovered at the back of Jo's drinks cabinet.

I'd been tempted to close the café until we'd got a chef and were fully stocked up again, but Amber persuaded me that we should open as normal the next day. 'It *is* Saturday tomorrow, and the forecast is for amazing weather,' she said, her head lolling on the sofa. 'And hey, I've done a bit of cheffing in my time, haven't I? I can muck in with that side of things.'

I had my doubts – especially because, as far as I could remember, Amber's job at the Randolph had largely involved slicing vegetables rather than cooking very much (albeit slicing vegetables in that swift, impressive way that chefs have) – but the wine was making me agreeable and overconfident. 'Oh, what the hell. We'll manage,' I said. 'I'll nip out first thing and stock up for what we need over the weekend. It'll be a laugh.'

Unfortunately those words would come back to haunt me more than once the following day.

After a hot, drunken night of little sleep, I woke with a splitting hangover at eight o'clock and the realization that: Oh bollocks, I was meant to have gone out much earlier than this to buy the groceries we need for the next few days. And then I remembered everything that had happened all over again: Matthew and I breaking up, me moving out, the scarily big number of things I needed to do to get the café up and running...

These thoughts flashed into my head one by one at a sickening speed. It was like seeing a trailer for my life imploding – a trailer that I couldn't turn off or blot out, however hard I tried. I let out a whimper and shut my eyes again. The sun was bright through the thin curtains and made my head ache. (Yeah. Because it was all the *sun's* fault. Nothing whatsoever to do with the gallons of Pinot Grigio that Amber and I had necked, or that weird blue liqueur that made my eyeballs fizzle.)

I wondered what Matthew was doing this Saturday morning. He was probably up and about, already having breakfasted on something healthy and sensible like porridge. He'd set-off for a five-mile jog along the river, then would probably buy lots of wholesome vegetables from the farmers' market, still with clods of earth on, in that just-dug-from-the-ground style. Then perhaps he'd treat himself to some more cleaning and tidying until every single last trace of me had been scrubbed away, until I was completely removed from his life, before settling down with his spreadsheets for the evening.

Meanwhile here *I* was, stinking and hungover, a business failure before I'd even crawled out of my pit.

I dragged myself into the shower and some clothes, made two coffees that were as strong and punchy as a pair of boxing gloves, and went to wake Amber. The forecast had been correct for once – the sky was a faultless blue, and the sea looked frisky with white frilly waves. If it stayed like that, the beach would be heaving within a few hours, and so too would the café, if we managed to get our arses into gear and open up, of course. Right now, the only thing that was heaving was my stomach.

Two hours later – consisting of several sessions of dry-retching over the toilet, a mammoth shopping run, two cups of tea, a fry-up and a double espresso – I was flipping the 'Closed' sign to 'Open'.

'Let's do it, baby,' Amber said, flourishing a spatula. 'Beach Café Birds are GO.'

And we were off.

I'll tell you something: working in the café was a whole different experience with Amber in the kitchen instead of Carl. Even during our busiest hours over lunchtime, she was quick, efficient and actually pleasant when Seb, Saffron and I put through order after order. She buttered and filled zillions of sandwiches, cooked fry-ups by the panful, heated every single pasty I'd bought without a mix-up and, even after all that, she was still cracking jokes and singing along to the radio. The day was – astonishingly – actually rather enjoyable. I even managed to overlook Seb spilling lemonade over two little boys, who burst into shocked, sticky sobs.

It wasn't quite so easy to ignore Saffron's usual atrocious customer service, though. She shuffled in late – surprise, surprise – with the squinty eyes and bed-hair of someone suffering a humongous hangover, and kept bunking off in the stock cupboard when she thought I wasn't looking. I didn't have a shred of sympathy for her, however, when I'd just battled on through my own wine-and-dodgy-liqueur nightmare. Talk about a lightweight, I thought scornfully. The girl had no idea about *real* suffering.

We were busy that day, with queues of people stretching out of the door at times. It would have freaked me out a fortnight ago, but by now I knew my way round the menu, and was working the coffee machine like a pro, making sure I sent Seb or Saffron out to clear and wipe the tables regularly, so that we could keep on top of everything. 'We are rocking, guys,' I found myself saying more than once, with a triumphant note in my voice. 'We are doing this!'

It wasn't until after lunch that I realized I hadn't had a visit from Ed and his dog yet. Had I missed him, opening up so late? He'd come in early both times before. Surely he couldn't be staying away, after that perfect bacon roll I'd made him last time?

Mid-afternoon Amber shouted through that she was off to have a cigarette break outside. 'I'll cover in the kitchen,' I told Seb. It was reasonably quiet, now that the lunch rush was over. Hopefully I wouldn't have to actually *cook* anything. 'You and Saffron – wherever she's got to – can take orders, and keep things tidy here, okay?'

He bit his lip. 'I think Saffron's gone out,' he mumbled, not looking me in the eye.

I finished the cappuccino I was making and dusted it with chocolate powder. 'There you are. That's nine pounds seventy-five all together,' I said to my customer, then turned back to Seb. 'What do you mean, Saffron's gone out?' I asked, frowning. 'Gone out where?'

He hung his head, scratching the bum-fluff on his chin and looking decidedly awkward. 'I dunno. Forget I said anything,' he muttered, then went to serve the harassed-looking woman who was next in line. 'Hi. What would you like?'

'Tuna-mayo baguette, two ham sandwiches on granary, two pots of tea and a strawberry smoothie,' she rattled off, and I had to hurry into the kitchen to start making up the order, much as I wanted to press Seb as to what he meant. Why had he turned so shifty when I asked him about Saffron? Clearly something was going on – but what?

I found out thirty seconds later when I heard raised voices through the back kitchen window.

'What the *hell* do you think you're doing? Does Evie know you've got this stuff?' It was Amber's voice, loud, shocked and accusing.

I stopped buttering. Stuff? What stuff?

Then came Saffron's reply, lower and sneering: 'Mind your own business. This has nothing to do with you.'

Amber again: 'Well, that's where you're wrong, lady. It's got everything to do with me. Go back inside right now. You've got some explaining to do.'

Seb bustled into the kitchen. 'Tuna baguette, two ham on granary,' he said, sticking the order sheet on the spike.

'Yep, got it,' I murmured, barely hearing. I stood there,

frozen, the butter knife hovering over the baguette as foot-steps approached from outside.

Then the back door burst open and in came Saffron, followed by Amber. Amber's eyes were blazing, her mouth pulled taut in an angry line. 'Evie, did you or did you not give this stuff to Saffron? I've just caught her flogging it to her mates round the back.'

She dumped a carrier bag on the counter, which bulged with goodies. There were cans of soft drink, cakes I'd bought that morning, loads of crisps, several pasties . . .

I stared from the bag to Saffron, who scowled back at me, seemingly unrepentant.

'One bacon sandwich on white, one cheese salad on brown, two kids' jam sandwiches, all to go,' Seb an-nounced, rushing in with another order.

'I certainly *didn't* give this stuff to Saffron,' I said slowly, feeling a thump of anger inside. How dare she? How *dare* she steal from the café? All that time she'd been bunking off in the stock cupboard, she'd been secretly nicking bags of my food and drink. 'How long's this been going on for, then, your little racket?'

She scuffed her foot along the floor and shrugged as if she didn't care.

'Well, it ends right here,' I said, my voice shaking with rage. 'You're sacked, Saffron, as of this minute. Go on –

get out. I've enough to worry about, without my own staff pinching stock.'

'Suits me,' she muttered, pushing the bag off the counter so that it crashed to the floor. One of the crisp packets burst, spraying golden salty shards everywhere. 'This place is a fucking dump anyway, and you're not gonna last five minutes. I'm well shot of it.'

She flounced out, nose in the air. I felt like running after her and plunging the bread knife between her shoulder blades, the little madam.

'Bloody hell,' Amber said, picking up the cans of drink (now dented) and the food from the floor. 'With staff like that, who needs enemies?'

'Two cream teas, two rounds of white toast with jam,' Seb said, pink-cheeked as he came in again. 'And what's happened to Saffron?'

I blinked. 'I … um … seem to have fired her,' I said, feeling light-headed with the aftershock. I'd never done anything quite so managerial before. Had I been too hasty? Too severe? It wasn't as if I'd ever been Employee of the Year myself, throughout my crappy career history.

No, I thought, in the next moment. I hadn't been too quick to fire her. As well as the stock-pinching, there had also been the permanent bad attitude, the lateness, the time I'd spotted her trying to nick that fiver. It was a wonder she'd lasted as long as she did.

I gave myself a shake. 'Come on, we'll have a chat about it later,' I said briskly. 'Let's crack on with these orders before we get behind.'

'Hell's bells,' Amber groaned at twenty past six, when we had closed up for the night. 'Well, that was a day and a half.'

'Seventy, eighty, ninety, one hundred ... It's usually much worse,' I said, pausing from cashing up. 'Honestly, I know it was busy today and there was the horrible sacking incident, but apart from that, it actually felt like *fun*, having you in the kitchen instead of that pillock Carl.' I took out a wedge of notes and pressed them into her hand. 'Here, have some wages. You were ace today, chef. Thank you.'

She put the money back in the till. 'Don't be daft, you don't have to pay me,' she said. 'I'm your mate, I'm just here to muck in.'

'Yeah, but ...' I said, snatching the money and shoving it into her pocket. 'Amber, really—'

'No!' she said, yanking it out again and replacing it in the till. Then she slammed the till drawer shut and leaned against it, arms folded. 'Honestly. Just take me to the pub and buy me a beer. I'm cheap like that.'

'It'll be the same again tomorrow, though,' I warned. 'In fact, I think half-term must have started, so it'll be packed for the next week, if this weather holds. And we'll be short-staffed too, now that I've given Saffron the boot, so . . .'

'So I'll stay as long as I can,' she said, 'just until you've got your new chef in, or Carla starts screaming down the phone at me to come back to the shop. Or, of course, I get a call-back for this new play . . .' She pulled a face. 'We live in hope,' she said. 'Anyway. We did well today, didn't we? Good teamwork.'

She held up a hand and I high-fived it. 'Good team-work,' I agreed. 'And now let me buy you dinner and a large drink in the pub.'

'Done,' she said.

I finished cashing up while she went to shower and change. The takings were pretty good — certainly the best of any day I'd ever worked there. It made me wonder how much Saffron had helped herself to in the past. According to Seb, it had been going on for some time. 'I didn't want to tell on her, though,' he'd said, his neck turning red. 'She's the sort of person who . . .'

He didn't finish, but he didn't have to. Carrawen was a small village and I could just imagine how miserable she'd have made his life if he *had* dobbed her in, and she'd found out. Still, he didn't have to worry about her now. None of us had to worry about her now. She was out on her ear, and good riddance to her.

With that happy thought, I locked the till and went up to the flat, whistling tunelessly and feeling that everything might just have taken a turn for the better. The only tiny fly in the ointment was the fact that Ed hadn't shown up. Could it really be *disappointment* I was feeling, that he hadn't popped in that day?

Chapter Thirteen

The pub was full of sun-kissed holidaymakers, quite a few of whom I recognized. There was Mrs Egg-and-Cucumber-No-Crusts-Please telling off her boisterous kids, there was Ms Banana-Smoothie sipping a lurid cocktail with a gaggle of giggling mates, there was Mr Sausage-Sandwich supping a pint ... It was nice, walking in and not feeling such a stranger all of a sudden. It gave me a flush of pleasure to imagine that people might recognize me as Evie-from-the-Café. It made me feel I belonged in some small way.

We ordered some food and took our drinks outside to the small pub garden, which had picnic benches and sunshades set up. It still felt warm, although the first cool evening breezes were starting to stroke inland from the sea. By the looks of some of the lobsteresque punters, it had been scorching out on the beach earlier.

'So, what did you think?' I asked Amber, taking a swig of my gin and tonic. It was so icy and refreshing and delicious, it was hard to stop myself gulping down the whole thing in one long swallow. 'Of the café, I mean?'

'I think it's great,' she replied. 'Really fab. You could do so much with it. The menu's a bit basic — I think I'd put some paninis or jacket potatoes on there, for starters, and maybe even some evening meals, if you were planning to branch out into opening later ...'

I blinked. Opening later? Jo had never opened later.

'And some kind of revamp,' she went on. 'I mean, it's nice enough as it is, of course, but a lick of paint would freshen everything up, and maybe some new pictures on the walls.'

'Right,' I said, taken aback. I hadn't thought about any of these things; it had been enough for me to get to grips with the coffee machine. 'Remind me again why I'm doing this, and not you?'

She elbowed me. 'Ah, it's just because I'm coming in as an outsider,' she said. 'You're used to it always having been the same for years and years, aren't you? You're looking at it as your aunt's place that you've inherited, whereas I'm looking at it through a punter's eyes.'

I nodded, realizing that she was right. 'It does feel as if I'm walking in Jo's footsteps,' I admitted. 'I keep forgetting it's mine now, and that I can change things around.' I drank more gin. It was even more delicious than the first glug.

'You can totally change it around,' she said. 'You could turn it into a little bistro, serve yummy dinners – I bet there's nowhere else to eat around here, is there, other than this place? People would love it, sitting out on that deck in the evening, candles on the table...' She sipped her drink thoughtfully. 'Seriously, you should do it. Get some nice tablecloths, write up a posher menu, you could be quids in.'

'Since when did you become Jamie Oliver?' I asked. 'You're forgetting one small problem: I can't blooming cook.'

She winked. '*Janie* Oliver, if you don't mind,' she said. 'And once you hire your fab new chef, you can leave all the cooking to them, durrr.' She eyed my glass. 'Blimey, that went down quick. Want another?'

'I'll get them,' I told her. 'You're on freebies all night, remember. Back in a tick.'

I sauntered through to the bar, my mind freewheeling with possibilities. Amber was a genius! I loved the idea of opening the café up in the evenings, through the summer at least. Maybe just at weekends initially, I thought to myself, test the waters –

Then I froze in my tracks, all plans for a bistro forgotten. A familiar voice and then a familiar laugh seemed to go right through me, turning my blood to quick-setting cement. I stared into the depths of the pub, my heart thundering. Surely I'd got it wrong. Surely I'd imagined it.

But no. There at the bar, laughing with the barmaid about something, was none other than my long-lost teenage crush, Ryan Alexander. I was sure it was him. It was his laugh – his no-holds-barred, let-rip laugh. *Ryan Alexander!*

I stood there staring for a moment, my brain almost unable to comprehend what my eyes and ears were telling it. His hair was shorter than it had been – it no longer tumbled in waves to his jawline – but yes, it was definitely his profile. Definitely.

I hurried back out to the beer garden, my cheeks turning scarlet. 'Oh my God,' I said to Amber, sitting down again and cupping my hand around my face in a pathetic attempt to hide myself.

'That was quick,' she said, staring at me in confusion. 'Ah. You seem to have forgotten something. Like ... drinks?'

I couldn't talk about drinks. There was only one subject on my mind. 'Do you remember me telling you, ages back, about the surfer hunk I had a mad fling with?'

'The shagging-in-sand-dunes one?' Amber said. 'Course I do. You bent my ear about him for at least a year. I was sick of hearing about him after –' She broke off and clapped a hand to her mouth. 'Why are you bringing this up now?' she asked. 'Don't tell me . . .'

'Yes,' I said, feeling dazed and giggly. 'YES. He's here.'

'No WAY!' Her eyes were wide and round, like tawny marbles.

'Way,' I told her, excitement rising hysterically inside me. 'Yes way. I'm sure it's him I just clocked at the bar. He's actually here, in the village, in this pub, RIGHT NOW.'

'Oh. My. GOD.' Amber leaned over the table and grabbed my hands. 'This is too good to be true. Exit Matthew — and enter gorgeous surf-dude from the past, the one that got away. It's like something from a film.'

'I know,' I said. 'In a minute Hugh Grant's going to stroll in and Richard Curtis is going to shout "Cut" and . . .'

'Wow.' Amber shook her head. 'This is great. This is serendipity to the power of a million. This is going to be *fun*.'

There was a familiar look on her face. A familiar trouble-making look that made me nervous all of a sudden.

'Oh no, you don't,' I told her quickly. 'Uh-uh. Nose *out*, thank you very much. No interfering.' I pulled a face at her. 'Look, I only just split up with Matthew five minutes ago, remember. I am grieving and mourning, and need time to lick my wounds, and—'

'Licking *wounds*? There are way better things to lick,' she said with a snort. 'And besides, all this grieving and mourning and anguish — you know what the best solution to that is, don't you?'

'Yes, large amounts of wine and crying,' I replied smartly. 'And chocolate, and support from sympathetic best friends, who don't try to manipulate you emotionally and—'

'No,' she interrupted. 'No, no, no, no. The best solution is a rebound shag, or seven. Preferably with a hot ex-boyfriend who has made a surprising reappearance after many years. Result!' She clapped her hands together. 'Now we just have to hope he has a few hot surf-dude mates for me, and Bob's your avuncular relative.'

I groaned. 'Amber, no ... I'm so not up for any of this,' I told her. 'Really. Really and truly.'

She raised her eyebrows and gave me a knowing look. 'Best thing to do when you fall off a horse is get right back in the saddle,' was all she said. 'Or even, back in the sack.'

'No,' I said again, trying to sound as firm as was humanly possible. 'Absolutely not.'

'Ri-i-ight,' she drawled, as if she didn't believe me for a second. 'How did he look when you saw him, anyway? Still hot?'

I paused to think. In my haste to run away before he

glimpsed me, I'd barely taken in the details. Hearing his deep, throaty chuckle and seeing his profile – the strong jawline, the slightly too-large nose, the beefy shoulders – had been enough to rocket me back to my lusty adolescent romance with him. Oh. My. God.

'Maybe we should just head off to the flat,' I said uncertainly. 'I mean, I'm not exactly in a position for romance right now.'

'Who said anything about *romance*?' Amber snorted. 'Go on, get in there, missus. This could be just the rebound shag you've been waiting for. "Memories..."' she began warbling theatrically.

A couple of women at the next table were turning their heads and looking over at us, with bemused expressions on their faces. 'Shut up,' I hissed. 'For God's sake, let's just get out of here. I haven't shaved my legs for ages, let alone ... anything else.'

She gave a delighted-sounding laugh. 'Aha! So you *have* been thinking about getting nekkid with the guy at least.' She made little shooing movements with her hands. 'What are you waiting for? Go and reintroduce yourself. And don't come back until you have. I'm not dying of thirst or anything, there's no rush.'

I hesitated, biting my lip as I weighed up the options. Ryan and I were both adults. Where was the harm in a smile and a hello, for old times' sake? Chances were, he wouldn't even recognize me. But on the other hand ... Maybe he would remember that summer as fondly as I did.

'No spying,' I warned her. 'And no stirring.' I smoothed my skirt down self-consciously. I was wearing my favourite denim skirt and a black strappy vest-top. Not exactly top-of-the-range designer, but I'd brushed my hair at least and chucked on a string of shimmering blue beads. 'Do I look okay?'

'Sensational,' she replied. It was an ego-boosting lie, of course, but it helped.

'I'm still not sure this is a great idea,' I said weakly.

'Off you go,' was all she said. 'See you in a bit.'

I turned and began walking back to the bar, jittery and uncertain. Nothing was going to happen, of course. I was still getting over Matthew, who'd been a proper boyfriend, a long-term, live-with boyfriend, and not just a holiday fling who'd vanished into the surf one day like a mirage, never to be seen again. I'd just say a friendly hello, gosh-fancy-seeing-you-again kind of thing to Ryan as I ordered the drinks, and that would be all.

I went back inside, blinking as my eyes adjusted to the dingier light in there. He was still at the bar. Oh, shit. I'd half been hoping he'd have left so that I didn't have to go through with this. But there he was, still joking around with the barmaid. Okay ...

I cleared my throat. I was only going to say hello, for goodness' sake. And at least it would shut Amber up.

I stood behind him for a moment, pretending I was waiting to be served, but really sneaking the chance to look him over. The youth had turned into a man. He was wearing a blue shirt with white pin-stripes, and chinos. His surf-dude curls had been cut to a neat short back and sides, and his neck looked fat and red. In fact, it wasn't just his neck that appeared fat; he seemed bulkier all over than he had done as a teenager. Hell, didn't we all, though. It was unfair to compare someone with their nineteen-year-old self.

He was booming with laughter at something the bar-maid had said. 'You're such a chav,' he told her. 'You and your bargain flip-flops and your tatty red nail varnish.'

I glanced down at my own feet, which were working their very own bargain flip-flops and tatty red nail varnish look. Oh. Did that make me a chav too?

'Oi, don't be cheeky,' she told him. She gave him a bright smile and went off to serve someone else, but I had the feeling that her smile was fake and he'd actually hurt her. Hmm.

I took a deep breath. Right. Come on, Evie. Now or never. *Action!* Richard Curtis ordered in my head.

'Ryan,' I said tentatively, tapping him on the shoulder. 'Is that you?'

He turned and squinted at me. His face was craggy and well worn, and had seen too much sun, judging by the slightly leathery texture of his skin, but it was definitely him.

There was a flicker of recognition in his eyes. 'Hey, I remember you,' he said slowly. 'You worked at the café. Jo's daughter.'

'Niece,' I corrected, a smile spreading across my face. 'Evie.'

'Evie, that's it,' he said, and slapped his thigh. 'Holy shit! Talk about a blast from the past.' He stared at me from top to bottom, his eyes lingering on my chest. Yuck, I hated it when men did that. It wasn't even as if there was anything much to look at, in my case. 'Well, fancy seeing you again,' he said, his voice softer and smoother. 'Where have you been hiding all these years, then?'

'I –' I began, slightly creeped-out by the way his gaze kept returning to my boobs. Was he addressing *them* or me? It was hard to tell. 'I've been back in Oxford. How about you?'

'Oh, here, there and everywhere,' he said, with a casual wave of his hand. I took this to mean Hawaii and other surfing hot-spots, but then he said, 'Kent for a while. Home Counties. Wherever I lay my hat . . .'

'Right,' I said. 'So, what are you doing with yourself these days?'

'Sales,' he said grandly. 'I'm an account manager for an engineering firm. Doing pretty well, although I say so myself, ha-ha.' His fake laugh set my teeth on edge. 'But where are my manners?' he asked my breasts. 'Let me buy you a drink. We can reminisce about the old times.'

I hesitated. He was *really* creeping me out now. Someone seemed to have changed his setting to Sleaze and turned it up to max. 'Um . . .' I began, but before I could say anything else, I felt someone barge past me.

'Ryan, are you getting those drinks or what?' came a shrill voice, as a blonde-haired woman shoved her way through. She glared at me and then at him, and I recognized her, with a sinking feeling, as the woman who'd had a go at me in the village shop that day. Not Betty the shopkeeper, but the other one. And now she seemed intent on laying claim to Ryan too. Ah. Perhaps it was time to step away from the ex.

'Evie, this is my lovely wife, Marilyn,' Ryan said, putting a meaty arm round her shoulders. 'Marilyn, this is Evie. An old friend.' He winked at me, and I felt nauseous.

Marilyn's eyes scrunched into an even tighter glare, if that were possible. She seemed to be bristling with some pent-up rage as if she were longing to take a swing at me, and maybe one at her husband, for good measure. Oh God. I was totally regretting introducing myself now.

'Yes, I know who she is,' Marilyn said bitterly. The

coldness of her eyes made me squirm. 'She's the one who just sacked our Saffron today – that's who *she* is.'

There was a horrible lurching feeling inside me, as if the bottom of my stomach had fallen right away. '*Our* Saffron,' she'd said. Which I guessed meant they were Saffron's ... parents. Oh shit.

The look on Ryan's face changed. 'That was you?' he said, his eyes narrowing. 'You sacked her? She was very upset when she came home this afternoon. She's only a kid. Why the hell did you have to sack her?'

The colour surged into my cheeks. 'Why did I sack her? Because she was stealing my stock, and taking money out of the till, that's why,' I said defensively. 'I'm sorry, I didn't know she was your daughter, but—'

'That's rich, coming from you,' he sneered. 'I remember you helping yourself to stuff from there all the time, back when you were a teenager, that summer we –'

He broke off. Marilyn looked as if she were going to combust.

'I always checked with Jo first, before I took anything,' I replied, indignant at the very notion that Saffron and I had acted similarly in any way. 'And she was my aunt, she was family, it was different.'

'Well, we'll be pursuing this,' Marilyn spat. 'Unfair dismissal, that's what this is. You should be ashamed of yourself, lady. Jo would have been ashamed of you too.'

That was the last straw. 'Jo would have sacked her just like I did,' I retorted hotly, brimming over with anger. 'Jo would have sacked anyone she caught stealing. Face facts – your daughter's a nasty little thief, and good riddance to her. You're lucky I didn't go straight to the police.'

There was a horrible silence as I finished speaking – or shouting, rather. I glanced round to see that everyone in the vicinity was listening in, eyes glued to the slanging match. Oh, great. So much for me being Evie-from-the-Café, everybody's friend. I'd probably just lost half my clientele in one stroke.

Marilyn raised her hand as if she were about to slap me around the face, but Ryan grabbed her arm just in time. 'How dare you say that about my daughter,' she hissed. 'How DARE you!'

Ryan got to his feet. His eyes were flinty. 'You've changed,' he told me contemptuously. 'Come on, Marilyn.'

And with that, he took their drinks and they went back to their table.

I felt myself turn scarlet with embarrassment and stood there, staring after them like a prize pillock. Right. Okay. So that probably couldn't have gone any worse if we'd scripted it beforehand. *Bollocks.*

'Can I help you?' the barmaid asked, and I turned, trying to snap out of my daze. She saw me looking at Ryan and Marilyn (who were glaring daggers back) and clicked her tongue sympathetically. 'Ignore them,' she said in a low voice. 'She's a nasty old cow and he's just as bad. He's a car salesman over in Wadebridge, not an engineering manager, or whatever it was he said to you.'

'They aren't exactly the friendliest couple I've ever met,' I managed to say, trying to keep my tone light. Inside, my heart was thudding. I felt as if I'd just made some dangerous enemies.

'No,' she agreed. 'Stay away from them, that's my advice. I wish *I* could, but ...' She shrugged and indicated the bar. 'Anyway. What can I get you?'

I ordered the drinks, my face still searing, and went back to Amber, deliberately not looking in the direction of Ryan and Marilyn. What a prat I was. Fancy getting up my hopes for an old flame when everyone knew that first loves were best left in the past. What had I been thinking? And then for it to turn out that he and his bitch-wife were actually Saffron's *parents*. Typical Evie luck. Just typical. I glanced up at the sky as I went into the garden. I had a feeling that some celestial beings were playing tricks on me, and having a good old laugh at my expense. How else could things have gone so catastrophically wrong?

'Oh dear,' Amber said as I returned to the table. 'Is it a No on the rebound-shag front?'

I put her drink down in front of her and took a long, thirsty gulp of mine. 'Ha,' was all I could say.

She sipped her drink, looking as if she were trying not to laugh. 'So he's no longer a heart-throb, then?'

'He's fat,' I said, 'and sleazy, and he couldn't look me in the eye. And he was rude to the barmaid, and he's married to a woman who makes Nurse Ratched look like a pussycat. Oh, yeah, and they're Saffron's mum and dad. And I also managed to bellow out around the whole pub that their daughter was a . . . How did I put it? A nasty little thief.'

She burst out laughing. 'You didn't!'

'I bloody did.' I buried my head in my hands. Talk about a disaster. I couldn't believe how horrifically one innocent conversation had spiralled out of control. 'Honestly, Amber, I know what this place is like. Everyone will get to hear about it. Everyone will be bad-mouthing me. I'll be driven out of here with pitchforks by the end of the week, you wait.'

'Oh, love, no you won't,' she said, still gurgling with laughter.

'It's all right for you,' I snapped, irritated. 'This is all a big joke to you, isn't it? But I've got to live here. I'm supposed to be making a go of it here, and all I'm doing is making things worse on a daily basis.' I slammed my fist down on the table. 'Shit,' I moaned. 'What am I going to do?'

She put her arm around me, finally having stopped gurgling. 'Sorry,' she said. 'I shouldn't laugh—'

'No, you bloody shouldn't.'

'But you've got to admit it's kind of funny.'

I pulled a face. 'Yeah, absolutely hilarious,' I said.

She nudged me. 'Come on, grumps, it'll be all right.'

'Will it? Saffron's horrible mum was talking about making a claim for unfair dismissal just then – that's the last thing I want.'

'That's not going to happen,' Amber scoffed. 'Unfair dismissal – for stealing? She'd be laughed out of court. No chance. She's just trying to scare you.'

I sighed. 'What a disappointment,' I said. 'Ryan, I mean. Honestly, I've been having erotic dreams about that man for the last thirteen years. Never again.'

'They'll be nightmares now,' Amber said, with her usual frankness. 'Wake-up-screaming-in-the-middle-of-the-night nightmares, by the sound of it.'

'And what a let-down too,' I said. 'That whole precious first-love thing – the one that got away.' I gave a snort that a wild boar would have envied. 'After speaking to him just now, I'm bloody glad he got away. In fact, I wish he'd get away a bit further, and take his crappy wife and daughter with him.'

'Yeah,' Amber agreed. 'It's like all the pop stars I used

to fancy as a teenager. Seeing them get fat and bloated and start to lose their hair … It's all wrong. They should be preserved in aspic, those first crushes, and never allowed to age, let alone sire revolting children.'

'Quite,' I said. 'To think that the last time I saw Ryan, he had a six-pack and surfer shorts. Now he's just a porky middle-aged dad.'

Amber raised her glass. 'To *not* having married a porky, middle-aged dad,' she said solemnly, and I clinked mine against hers.

'To not having married a porky, middle-aged dad,' I echoed with a sigh.

Our food arrived – fish and chips twice – and we tucked in hungrily. It wasn't the most amazing dinner I've ever had: the chips were pale and slightly undercooked, and the fish batter was rather soggy. If I *did* start serving evening meals at the beach café, I thought, at least I could be pretty confident that the competition wasn't up to much.

Then I heard a man's voice behind me. 'Hello, stranger. When did you arrive back in town?'

We turned to see Ed with a pint of lager, and I couldn't help my spirits lifting two-hundredfold. 'Hello,' I said, twisting round on the bench. 'I was wondering what had happened to you.' I clamped my mouth shut quickly, hoping that didn't sound as if I was some kind of weird stalkery type. 'I mean—'

'I was wondering what had happened to you too,' he replied, thankfully, before I could dig myself further into a hole. 'First that jerk of a chef was back in the café, and then it was closed up, and...' He shrugged. 'I was starting to think you'd done a bunk.'

'No,' I said. 'Well, yes, but I'm back now. Back for the summer, bridges smouldering in ruins behind me all the way from here to Oxford.'

Amber stretched out a hand. 'Hello, by the way. I'm Amber, seeing as Evie has so rudely forgotten to introduce us.'

'Oh God, sorry,' I said, flustered. 'Ed, this is my best friend Amber, and Amber, this is Ed.'

'Nice to meet you,' he said. 'Mind if I join you?'

'Please do,' Amber said fervently. 'Evie's had a melt-down in the last five minutes, and I'm not sure I can stand it any more.' She stuck her tongue out at me cheekily and I blushed.

'Are you okay?' Ed said. 'Sorry — if this is a private moment, I can sit somewhere else, but—'

'No, stay,' I told him. 'It's cool. I've just ... made a prat of myself. Again.'

'She's just shouted at her long-lost ex and his evil wife, quite loudly in the bar,' Amber said. 'Slagged off their daughter in public, and probably made even more enemies amongst the locals. That's the gist, but—'

'Yeah, all right, all right,' I said sharply. 'He doesn't need to know every gory detail.'

Amber winked at me. 'Just making conversation,' she said. 'Who wants another drink, then?'

'Me,' I said, with rather too much desperation in my voice.

Ed was kind enough not to ask any more about what had happened with Ryan and Marilyn, thank goodness, and by the time Amber returned with our drinks, we were deep into a debate about which was better: swimming in the sea by moonlight or in full beaming sunshine, and any awkwardness was forgotten. Amber, inevitably, had something to say, and then we got into a debate about skinny-dipping, and the most daring places we'd all done it; and then we were off onto a conversation about other outrageous things we'd done, and we were laughing so much that time seemed to sprint along unnoticeably. Before I knew it, the sky was becoming darker and a chill was creeping in. I shivered and rubbed my bare arms, wishing I'd had the sense to bring along a cardigan or jacket.

'So, what do you do down here?' Amber asked Ed after a while. 'Are you working, or ...?'

She let the question tail off politely, and I noticed him give the faintest of grimaces. I pricked up my ears, waiting for his response. I was curious too. I didn't actually know much about him, I realized, apart from the fact that he'd gone skinny-dipping on Bondi Beach, he loved swimming in the sea when there was a full moon, and he'd once allowed himself to be made up as Barbara Cartland for a student party.

'I'm not working at the moment,' he said. 'Just dog-sitting for a mate. I was working in London, but ... not any more.'

I detected a certain awkwardness about him, as if he really didn't want to talk about this. Amber didn't seem to notice any such thing, though. 'Go on, then, don't leave us in suspenders: what happened? Where were you working?' She narrowed her eyes. 'Ah. Don't tell me. You're one of those disgraced bankers. A hedge-fund squillionaire who lost everything.'

'Amber!' I protested. 'Leave him alone.'

But he gave a hollow laugh. 'No, I'm not a disgraced banker,' he said. 'I was in the restaurant business actually.'

I did a double-take. A classic, staring, did-he-really-just-SAY-that? double-take.

'The *restaurant* business?' I screeched, leaning forward. No wonder he'd been such a perfectionist about his bacon roll. Had I actually been right first time, thinking he was a food critic? 'Why didn't you tell me before? I'd have been picking your brains for advice, if I'd known that.'

'Yeah,' Amber chimed in. 'She's been dying on her arse

out there – well, not today, obviously, with me mucking in, but ...' She grinned suddenly. 'Don't tell us. You're a chef.'

He nodded. 'Got it in one.'

I was still staring. And then laughing. 'Are you winding me up?'

'No *way*,' Amber squealed. She punched the air. 'Result! Oh, this is too good to be true. Well, there you go, Evie, problem solved. You need a new chef, and Ed here's out of work – perfect!'

'I never said I—' he began, but I was already talking over him.

'Oh, Ed, that's amazing,' I gushed. 'Would you really help me out? Carl quit without any notice, and Amber will have to go back to Oxford soon, and I'm advertising for a chef, but nobody's actually applied yet, and it'll probably take ages, so ... Would you?'

Ed didn't look quite as thrilled as I was at the turn this conversation had taken, I realized. In fact, he was positively squirming on the picnic bench, as if going back into a kitchen was the very last thing he wanted.

Unfortunately for him, I was drunk and desperate, and willing to grovel. 'Please?' I begged, putting my hands together in a mock prayer. 'Pretty please?'

He hesitated. 'Oh, all right,' he said. 'I suppose so. Not stupid hours, because I've got the dog to look after, but ... okay. Just for a few days, until you hire someone full-time. Nothing permanent.'

'Yay!' I yelled, throwing my arms around him. 'Ed, you're a life-saver. Oh, my goodness, this evening suddenly just got SO much better. And I'm totally going to buy you another drink immediately. What are you having?'

'Second thoughts,' he said, deadpan, pulling a face. 'And a pint of Stella.'

I got to my feet with some difficulty (I was more drunk than I'd thought) and saluted him. 'Coming right up,' I said, still beaming like a loon. 'Chef.'

Chapter Fourteen

Ed was certainly taking this seriously, I realized when he came into the café the following morning. We talked pasties, paninis and surfer specials, and he even agreed to try an evening menu one night. By the end of it I was practically fizzing with excitement. It was so useful to talk to somebody who actually knew about the food business, who could guide me through the choppy café waters, even if he *was* only going to be helping for a week or so. I was grateful for what I could get — so grateful in fact that I must have thanked him approximately nine thousand times while we chatted.

'It's fine, really,' he said in the end. 'To be honest, I've been getting a bit bored down here on my own for all this time. It'll be good to have something to do other than walking the dog and learning to surf.'

'Well, thank you again,' I said, shaking his hand as he got up to leave. His big, rough chef's hand. It was very manly, I found myself thinking, and blushed violently.

'I'll order the ingredients you need, and I'll see you tomorrow.'

I watched him lope off across the beach with the dog, and let out a girlish giggle, not quite able to believe my lucky break. This was going to be good, I thought. Really good. It was just what the café – and I – needed.

We had another busy day's work: it was the bank-holiday weekend, so the beach was packed. With a staff member down, we were working at full stretch, but it was worth it, not having to put up with Saffron's sulks and strops. But then at the end of his shift Seb said, calm as you like, 'So I won't be in for a couple of weeks now, all right? Because I've got my exams coming up after half-term, and Mum says I need to revise.'

'Your mum says you . . .' I echoed, my voice dying out midway through the sentence. 'Oh. Right. Seb, you could have told me this earlier, given me a bit of notice. I thought you were going to be here all week?'

He looked faintly surprised at the irritated tone in my voice. 'Oh, no. Sorry,' he said. 'I didn't think—'

'No,' I said grimly. 'Never mind. Best of luck in your exams, Seb.'

I shut the café door after him and let out a groan. 'One in, one out,' I muttered. 'Honestly, Amber, just when I think my luck has turned and I'm getting somewhere with this place, something else goes wrong.'

She was fiddling with her phone and didn't look up for a moment. 'Bollocks,' she muttered. 'Look, this isn't the greatest timing, I know, but Carla's just texted me.'

'Oh no,' I wailed. I knew what was coming.

'And she wants me back in the shop for Tuesday,' she went on. 'I'm sorry, mate. She can't get anyone to cover for me, and—'

'Don't worry,' I said. I felt like the captain of a sinking ship. Thank God for Ed stepping in, I thought again. If it wasn't for him, I'd be running a one-woman show – or not, of course. Actually, if it wasn't for him, I'd probably be running for the hills.

'So I'll do what I can before I go tomorrow, but...' She was all but wringing her hands, she looked so wretched.

'Don't worry,' I said again, as much to myself as to her. 'It'll be all right. I'll manage.' *I'll bloody have to*, I added under my breath. *I'll manage if it kills me.*

Amber had only been staying a few days, but it gave me a pang the next morning when I saw that she'd packed her toothbrush and shower gel away, in preparation for leaving later on. It had been brilliant, having her around with me, keeping me going with her non-stop sandwich-making, her crap jokes and her so-bad-it's-good singing.

'I'm going to miss you,' I said dolefully as we trooped downstairs from the flat. 'I wish you weren't going.'

'You'll be fine,' she said. 'You can do this, Evie. It's going to be great. You've got Ed on board, and he seems to know what he's doing – plus he's a bit of eye-candy around the place ...'

I gave her a look as I unlocked the inside door to the café. 'Don't start that again,' I warned her. 'I can see straight through you. Remember what happened last time you butted in, Cupid.'

We went through to the café and I saw something khaki-green through the glass doors outside. A sleeping bag on the deck. The girl I'd seen there before was back. I'd been in such a whirl lately that she had quite slipped my mind.

I hurried to unlock the front door. 'Amber, come here,' I called in a low voice. 'There's a kid asleep on the deck.'

The girl woke at the clicking of the lock and sat up, eyes wide and scared. And then, before I could push the door right open and stop her, she was up on her feet, out of the sleeping bag and hurrying away with it, like before. 'Wait,' I called, rushing out onto the deck. 'Come back!'

Amber was there beside me. 'Who is she?'

'I don't know,' I replied. 'Just some teenager. I've seen her here before, but she scarpered last time too.' I bit my lip, feeling helpless. I hated the thought of her sleeping rough. She was so young and vulnerable to be out on her own at night. 'Poor kid,' I said. 'I wonder where she's from?'

We watched her vanish from sight. 'It's that seaside-town thing, I guess,' Amber said. 'People come here hoping to pick up seasonal work, thinking that because it's a holiday place they'll have a nice time...' She shrugged. 'I hope she's okay.'

'I'll keep an eye out for her,' I said. 'I didn't mean to scare her away, I was going to see if she wanted some breakfast. God knows what she's doing for food, if she's got nowhere to sleep.'

We both stood there on the deck for a few moments. It was a cool, fresh start to the day, slightly overcast and grey. There wasn't a soul to be seen.

'I love it that you're right here, at the edge of the land,' Amber said dreamily, gazing out at the sea. 'I can't imagine living with a view where you could quite easily see nobody for hours on end. It must be amazing living here in the winter.'

I gulped. I hadn't even thought that far ahead. 'I don't know,' I said doubtfully. 'It would get pretty lonely, I think, stuck out here on your own.'

She elbowed me. 'Come on, cheer up,' she said. 'You've got all this on your doorstep, you're living in one of the most desirable and beautiful places in the whole country – things could be a lot worse, Evie Flynn. At least you don't have to drag yourself back to Oxford on bank-holiday trains later, like Muggins here.'

'I suppose,' I replied, realizing with a jolt that I'd barely thought of Oxford since we'd left it behind, three days earlier. I wondered what Matthew had been doing over the weekend. Had he planned something nice with Saul? He'd been talking about us all going for a bike ride together, now that Saul was getting so good without stabilizers. I imagined them setting off, maybe with a picnic, to have an adventure somewhere without me, and my eyes suddenly prickled with tears.

'You okay?' Amber said, putting a hand on my arm.

'Yeah,' I said. 'It's just ... Everything. Every now and then, I get hit by how much my life has changed in the last month. You know, back in April I was happy as anything, making plans with Matthew, and—'

'Well, no,' Amber cut in. 'I wouldn't say you were "happy as anything".'

I stopped. 'Wouldn't you?'

She shook her head. 'You didn't really want to do that teaching course, did you? It was obvious. You hated your temp job, and you and Matthew didn't seem all that wild about each other, either. Sorry,' she went on, seeing my jaw drop. 'Just telling it how I saw it. Whereas I think this place' – she swept her arm around, encompassing the sea, the beach, the café – 'is amazing. Mind-blowingly amazing. And I think you're really lucky, Evie. *Really* lucky.' She folded her arms across her chest as if she wasn't about to brook any arguments. 'So, are we ready for business then, or what? Our last day together for a while – let's make it a good one, shall we?'

I nodded, still processing her words. *Lucky*, she'd called me. Lucky? I hadn't felt lucky in all of this. I had felt overwhelmed, anxious and pretty bloody miserable at times. But yes, from an outsider's view, I supposed I could be described as lucky. The girl who'd slept outside the café probably would have swapped places like a shot. And that thought alone was enough to snap me out of the doldrums. 'I'm ready,' I said, wedging the door open and hanging up the 'Open' sign. 'Once more unto the breach, my friend.'

'Unto the beach, you mean,' she laughed, disappearing inside. 'I'm going to make up some sandwich fillings for later.'

I poured us each a coffee while we waited for the first customers, and counted my blessings. Amber was right. I was lucky that this opportunity had sailed right into my life. Now I just had to make sure it didn't sail right out again.

✻

We were crazily busy that bank-holiday Monday. This wasn't helped by three things: one, Amber and I running the show single-handed (or rather double-handed) most of the time; two, the food delivery arriving at twelve-thirty, which was of course our busiest point of the entire day; and three, my bloody sister Ruth rocking up unannounced, at the same time.

I could have wept when I saw her face there in the queue, about six people from the front (it was a long queue), glancing around the place and clocking everything in a single searching gaze: the crockery piling up on the unwiped tables, where I hadn't had time to go out and clear them; the mutters and moans from the queue about how long I was taking to serve everyone; and, worst of all, the harassed look on my face that undoubtedly said: I am stressed, I am stressed, I can't cope. AS USUAL.

Her face, on the other hand said: Oh dear. *Oops.* Evie's cocked up again. AS USUAL.

Thank heavens for Ed, who chose that moment to walk in. I thought for a moment he was a delusion, a mirage, brought on by my poor brain being flooded by stress chemicals. Then he spoke the magic words: 'Need a hand?'

'Yes, please,' I croaked, putting lids on the six takeaway teas and coffees I'd just made.

'I'll clear the tables,' he said, without even being asked.

If he hadn't just walked into the kitchen to grab a cloth, I think I might have grabbed *him* and kissed him right on the lips in gratitude.

It felt rather a blur, trying to take orders, make drinks, count out change and, above all, give off the impression that I was coping, coping, coping, for the benefit of Ruth, gloating there in the queue. It was like a bad dream, knowing that she was present while I was drowning so publicly. I wondered if it had even occurred to her to offer to help. I doubted it. She would be gleefully saving up all the details of my atrocious café management to report back to the rest of the family. 'Poor Evie. I don't think she *quite* knows what she's let herself in for, I'm afraid . . .' Ugh. I could hear her faux-sympathetic tone as clearly as if she was speaking the words out loud.

'Can I help you?' I turned to my next customer, who had approximately five thousand sandy children milling around her.

'We'd like some ice creams, please,' she said. 'What flavours do you want, kids?'

'Chocolate . . . no, strawberry. Actually, that green one.'

'I want crisps, not ice cream.'

'I need a wee.'

My smile was becoming fixed. The queue was becoming longer. And the grumbles were becoming louder too. Then I heard my sister's clear, ringing, teacher's voice above everyone else: 'Evie, we'll pop back later, when it's not so hectic,' she said over the crowd. And then, to the rest of the queue in general, 'She hasn't been working here very long. I'm sure you'll get served eventually, but don't be too hard on her, will you?'

My hackles went up so fast I was surprised they didn't rip right out of my skin. I also seemed to be making a low growling in my throat, like a rabid dog. 'Patronizing cow,' I muttered as she left, her kids in tow.

'Right, have we decided on ice creams, then?' Ed said, appearing beside me as if by magic. He smiled down upon the children waiting at the counter, then up at their mum. 'Do you know what – my favourite flavour is the toffee crunch. You get real toffee in it, *and* these yummy, crunchy biscuits. Who wants one of those?'

'ME!' the kids chorused, even the one who'd been eyeing up the crisps.

Their mum beamed in relief. 'Brilliant,' she said, batting her eyelashes at him. 'We'll have five of them then, please.'

With Ed beside me, we gradually whittled down the queue between us. He was great: always polite and friendly to the customers, but quick and efficient too, handling the food, drinks and money dexterously. It was like having a good fairy alongside me – well, no, not a *fairy*, exactly, I corrected myself, my eyes drifting to his tanned, muscular arms. A knight in shining armour with a flowery pinny on, who was a dab hand at working a coffee machine.

Once the queue was under control, he vanished into the kitchen to start making up the pasties, and I was finally able to let my breath out. Phew. That had been full-on, but we had just about managed, selling more sandwiches, drinks and cakes than I'd thought possible. Annie had brought in some new cakes: a ginger loaf and a Victoria sponge, both of which looked amazing. There were also chocolate brownies and rocky-road squares for anyone needing a chocolate fix, and they were all selling well. 'That was delicious,' one old lady said, beaming, as I cleared away her empty plate. 'The lightest sponge I've had for a long time. Have you got a new chef here?'

I smiled. 'There *is* a new lady doing our cakes, yes,' I said. 'I'll let her know that you enjoyed it.'

'Please do,' she said, her eyes twinkling behind her glasses. 'It really was very good.'

I felt a spring in my step as I walked away. Customer satisfaction rocked!

Amber came out from the kitchen and handed me a coffee. 'Here,' she said. 'I'm on the front line with you now. Old Gorgon Ramsay in there has kicked me out.'

'Oi, I heard that,' Ed shouted, with a laugh in his voice.

'I've changed my mind about you,' she called back, rolling her eyes. 'Dead bossy,' she added in a stage whisper.

I smiled. 'Takes one to know one,' I reminded her, and then, to the woman who'd just appeared at the counter, 'Hi, can I help you?'

She was tall and built like a swimmer, with broad shoulders and a body that tapered at the waist. She had long brown hair, bright-blue eyes and a voice that was pure Aussie, with every sentence ending in a question. 'Hi,' she said. 'I'm looking for a job, actually? I don't suppose this place is taking on any waitresses?'

My mouth opened in a dazed smile and I couldn't speak for a moment. 'Yes,' Amber said on my behalf. 'Yes, we are. Or rather, she is, cos I'm buggering off today.'

I managed to close my mouth and end my village-idiot impression. 'Have you got waitress experience?' I asked, trying to sound efficient and managerial. I thought back to all those times in my life I'd traipsed around cafés and restaurants asking for work, and hardly ever getting any. I'd had so many brush-offs, so many rejections, and it had been, on the whole, utterly demoralizing. From the way this woman's eyes lit up, I got the impression she'd been there, done that herself.

'Sure,' she said at once. 'I've had plenty, back home in Melbourne? And I've been working in a restaurant in the West End for the last six months?' She fumbled in a volu-minous blue leather bag that was slung over one shoulder and pulled out some stapled pieces of paper. 'Here, I've got a résumé, references, the lot,' she said.

'Thanks,' I said, taking the papers from her. Amber craned nosily over my shoulder to see too. I'd got as far as reading her name – Rachel – when a couple of families came through the door and walked up to the counter. 'Listen, Rachel, I'll look through this later and give you a bell. All right?'

'Cool,' she said. 'That would be awesome. I'll do anything – any hours, washing up, cleaning . . . ?' She grinned, a wide toothy grin, with dimples like brackets on either side. 'I'm a hard worker, and reliable too. Speak to you later?'

'Great, cheers,' I said, smiling. I liked her. I knew you had to go on more than just a gut feeling about a person when you were hiring them, but there was something very warm and likeable about her. I couldn't imagine her snarling at the customers or pilfering the stock like Saffron had. 'Speak to you later.'

She raised a hand in farewell and left the café, and I turned to my next customer. 'Hi, what can I get you?'

Ruth didn't show her face in the café again, but she did send me a text later in the afternoon.

Hope all ok. Are you surviving?! Will pop in this eve for a chat. R x

Are you surviving, indeed. I felt myself bristling at the

implied insult. We'd been absolutely fine after that busy spell she'd seen, thank you very much. 'And no, you bleeding won't pop in,' I muttered savagely under my breath, 'because I'm not going to be here.'

I texted back, *Sorry, out this eve. Tomorrow? E x*

It wasn't a lie, I had to take Amber to Exeter to get her train home. She'd protested that she'd be fine catching the train from Bodmin and there was no need to go out of my way, but the connections were going to be a nightmare, and I couldn't force a seven-hour journey on her, especially when she'd been such a brilliant friend in my hour of need lately. It was the least I could do.

Meanwhile, Ed had made the first batch of pasties – Mediterranean vegetarian, as well as chicken and vegetable – and they smelled utterly heavenly. 'Go, Ed; go, Ed; go, Ed . . .' Amber and I cheered, when the first tray came out of the oven. I clapped my hands, feeling slightly hysterical, wanting to laugh with joy and cry with relief at the same time.

He raised his eyebrows. 'What are you two like? You haven't even tried one yet. For all you know, I might have played arsenic roulette with this lot.'

'I'll take my chances,' Amber decided.

'Sod it, me too,' I said. 'They look good enough to risk my life over.'

He laughed and cut two of the pasties into three,

dividing them onto three plates so that we all had a taster of each. 'Cheers, ladies,' he said, bringing the plates out to us, and standing with us behind the main counter.

'Cheers, Ed,' I said. 'These look bloody amazing.' I picked up one-third of the chicken-and-vegetable pasty and blew on it to cool it down. It was crammed with pieces of chicken, cubes of potato, carrots, onion and peas, all held together by a covering of hot, golden pastry.

I nibbled the edge of it. The pastry was yummy – not so thick that it clogged up your mouth, but light and flaky; the perfect texture. I took a larger bite and tasted the rich gravy he'd made, some soft, juicy chicken and a piece of carrot. 'Mmm,' I said, leaning against the worktop as I savoured the flavours. It really was good. 'Oh, Ed. This is *lush.*'

'Totally lush,' Amber agreed, licking a splodge of tomato from the corner of her mouth. She was eating the veggie pasty. 'YUM.'

A customer approached the counter just then, a thirty-something bloke who looked bemused to see the three of us there, gorging ourselves on pasties and looking ever more blissed-out with each mouthful. 'I'll have whatever you're having,' he laughed. 'They smell great.'

It turned out that he was with some mates on a stag do, and he promptly ordered four of each flavour between them. 'Let us know what you think,' I said, bagging up the pasties. 'And if you're around for a few days, come back. We're rolling out lots of new flavours this week.'

'Will do,' he said.

The rest of the afternoon passed quickly, with the pasties all but selling out. The Victoria sponge and the brownies did really well too, and we had lots of great feedback from the customers. I was almost sorry to close up at five o'clock, especially as it meant my time with Amber was practically over.

'I wish I could stay longer,' she said, as we pulled away in my car half an hour later, with her luggage in the boot. She swung round in her seat for a last look at the café. 'It's been ace.'

'I wish you could stay longer too,' I said, suddenly misty-eyed as we drove through the village. 'I'm so glad you came, though. I couldn't have done it without you.'

'Ah, don't give me that,' she scoffed. 'You'd have done brilliantly whether I'd been here or not. And you probably wouldn't have insulted Saffron's parents quite so vociferously if I hadn't plied you with alcohol and forced you into speaking to the Ageing Surfer.'

I laughed. 'True, but I wouldn't have had Ed coming on board, either, if it wasn't for you interrogating him that night. And he's well worth a public showdown or two.'

'He is,' Amber agreed. 'Hey, and don't forget to ring that Aussie bird back, will you? She seemed all right. Are you going to give her a trial run?'

'Too right I am,' I replied. 'Her CV would have to be diabolical for me not to.' I gave a little sigh as we left the village behind. 'Besides, I need a mate around here, with you going, don't I?' I glanced across at her. 'Saying goodbye to you is going to feel like breaking my last link with Oxford.'

'No, it isn't,' she argued. 'It's not like you're never going to see me again. And besides...' She grinned cheekily. 'You've got your lovely sister in town, haven't you? That's one Oxford link still going strong.'

'Not if I've got anything to do with it,' I said darkly.

'Oh, don't let her get to you,' Amber said. 'You're every bit as good as she is, and don't you forget it. Has she ever run her own business? No. Has she ever had the balls to do anything spontaneous and reckless? No. Has she got anywhere near as cool a best mate as you have? No. I rest my case.'

'Thank you,' I said. 'I'll remind her of that when I see her.'

'You do that,' she replied. 'Ways to make a grown woman cry, numbers one, two and three.'

The bank-holiday traffic was predictably appalling and it took well over two hours to get to Exeter. I walked to the platform with her and had a big, squeezy goodbye.

'You're a café superstar,' she told me. 'And you're going to have a brilliant summer, I just know it.'

'You too,' I said. 'You're going to get the most amazing part in a West End show, and then a starring role in a Hollywood movie.'

'And you're going to win Café of the Year Award, and Rick Stein is going to beg you for advice,' she bantered. 'On his knees, I should think. And we're both going to live happily ever after.'

Chapter Fifteen

After Amber's train had pulled away and she was well and truly gone, I sat in the car and had a little moment of 'Aarrrgh!' to myself.

Aarrrgh – I had split up with Matthew.

Aarrrgh – I missed Saul so much.

Aarrrgh – I had given up my sensible Oxford life and leapt into the great Cornish unknown.

Aarrrgh – I didn't have any friends within three hundred miles.

Aarrrgh – I had to face Ruth tomorrow, and it was going to be awful.

Then I took a deep breath, counted to ten and puffed it all out again. And then I phoned Rachel the Aussie and gave her a job.

'Cool,' she said. 'When do you want me to start?'

'Tomorrow morning? Nine-thirty?'

'I'll be there.'

I clicked off the call. Well, that was something at least.

Then my phone buzzed with an incoming text. *Will take you out for supper tomorrow. Pick you up at seven? R x*

I wasn't sure why Ruth had taken to calling the evening meal 'supper' all of a sudden. Probably thought it made her sound more middle-class than she actually was. It had always been 'tea' in our house throughout our childhood, but there you go. I wasn't going to quibble about being taken out for 'supper', even if it was by my patronizing older sister.

I drove back to the café feeling quiet and contemplative. The sun was going down, and the sky was smeared with deep purple and crimson. 'Just me, now,' I said out loud. 'Just me.'

The words didn't sound quite so scary as I'd anticipated. In fact, I was surprised to feel a spark of excitement. Amber had been right earlier that morning when she said she didn't think I'd been happy in Oxford. In hindsight, I didn't think I had been, either. Yes, I'd been doing all the so-called right things, trying to please Matthew and my parents with my career choices, but in actual fact the thought of teacher training had bored me rigid, made me feel stifled.

Well, nobody was stifling me now. Nobody was telling me to do anything. It was all totally up to me — the trials and triumphs, the customers, costs and cakes. Feeling cheered, if slightly apprehensive at this, I put on some music and sang loudly all the way back to Carrawen Bay. Or rather, as I was starting to think of it, back home.

When I finally parked the car it was nearly ten o'clock and pretty much dark. I loved how much deeper and more velvety the darkness was here by the sea. There was none of the light pollution that you got in Oxford, the hazy amber glow, which meant the sky never quite hit its ultimate jet-black. Down here in the bay, the darkness all but swallowed you up: the sea was a deep, liquid black and you could smell its salty scent and hear its rhythmic rushing better than you could see it. Tonight there was a gleaming slice of moon up in the charcoal sky, and a sprinkling of bright silver stars.

I locked the car quickly, glancing around and feeling jittery, as my eyes strained uselessly to see into the shadowy corners of the parking area. It was daft, as this was surely way safer a place than our old street in Oxford, but all the same my senses felt on full alert as I walked around to the steps leading up to the deck and main entrance of the café.

I stopped abruptly as I reached the middle step and heard a movement from the deck above. A rustling sound. My heart lurched and I gripped the hand-rail, adrenaline spiking through my bloodstream. Was it rats? The wind blowing something about? Or a person? Had Saffron and her family come back seeking vengeance?

I climbed the next two steps, my legs feeling like jelly, and saw, to my horror, that through the shadowy near-darkness there was indeed a person on the deck.

'Oh, shit,' said the person in a scared, young voice, peering up at me.

It was the girl I'd seen before, the homeless girl who'd slept rough on the deck a few times. Now she was half in, half out of a sleeping bag, as if she were poised to take flight again. But I was blocking her way.

'I'm sorry,' she said, struggling to her feet and clutching up her bedding. 'I'm really sorry. I'll go, don't worry.'

'No, it's okay,' I said, not moving. I was so relieved that she wasn't some nutter about to attack me, or the café, that I felt my legs swaying beneath me. 'You don't have to go. Look – are you hungry? Have you had anything to eat?'

She stared at me suspiciously. Her face was largely in shadow, but her whole stance was wary and defensive: her arms were close to her body and I could feel how on edge she was, how much she wanted to run.

'Come in,' I said, when she didn't reply. I fumbled for the door keys in my bag. 'Come and have something to eat at least. We've got lots of leftover pasties, and cake as well.'

Still she hesitated. I walked onto the deck and felt her shrink away from me. I was tense too. I really didn't want her to bolt away again; I couldn't help feeling in part responsible for her, knowing that she had slept here before.

'Come on,' I said, slotting in the key and pushing the door open. 'We've got a new chef and he's amazing. Try one of the pasties he's made, at least.'

'Are you sure?' she asked, gripping her sleeping bag as if it were a shield.

'Totally sure.' I flicked the lights on and held the door open. I saw her glance through the window to the welcoming brightness of the lit café, and was sure she wouldn't be able to resist.

I was right.

'Thank you,' she murmured, head down, as she slipped in through the door after me. I could see her better now, and she was a tiny thing: skin and bone, with long tangled blonde hair, framing a thin face. How old was she? I wondered. It was hard to say for sure. Sixteen? Eighteen? Fourteen? There was a world-weariness about her that was heartbreaking, and I felt an uncomfortable pang inside when I thought back to my own teenage years – the comfortable, warm home my parents had provided, the soft bed, the meals on the table, the clothing allowance. What had gone wrong for this girl, that she was sleeping outside my café at night, that she had left her own home behind?

'Sit down,' I said. 'Let me get you a drink. Do you want something hot, or a cold drink? Or both?'

Her gaze went up to the chalked menu and she was silent for a moment. Then she turned her thin little face back to mine, a look of longing in her eyes. 'Could I ... could I have a hot chocolate? Please?'

Bless her. She was just a kid, after all. 'Of course you can,' I said, taking a mug, and scooping some chocolate powder into it. She was well spoken, I had noticed, and polite, with that 'please' on the end. Her accent was southern, but there was no West Country burr to it. 'I'm Evie by the way,' I said, stirring in the hot milk. 'Do you want squirty cream and marshmallows on this?'

'Yes, please,' she said, tucking a strand of hair behind her ear with a certain amount of self-consciousness. 'I'm Phoebe,' she said after a moment.

Who could tell if that was her real name, or if she was fobbing me off with a fake one, but whichever it was, I felt as if we'd made progress. I was Evie, she was Phoebe. Okay. That was a start, at least.

'Here you go,' I said, bringing her drink over. 'As for food, there are two different sorts of pasties, or cake, or I could make you some toast. What do you fancy?'

She took a tiny scoop of the cream with a teaspoon and licked it. A fleeting expression of pleasure passed over her face, but then the shutters came down and she was back to being wary. She mumbled something and her gaze fell to her dirty fingers, which she played with in her lap.

'What was that?' I asked. I was still standing, not sure she would feel comfortable if I sat down next to her. It was like trying to coax out a cautious animal from a hiding place, wanting it to know that you weren't going to hurt it.

'How much?' she muttered, still not making eye contact.

How much? Oh God, she thought I was going to charge her. 'Nothing,' I told her firmly. 'I didn't ask you in to make a sale. I asked you in because...' I shrugged helplessly. 'Because ever since I first saw you sleeping outside I've been worried about you.'

Her chin went up. 'You don't need to worry about me,' she said, with all the glacial, misdirected condescension that only a teenager could come out with. 'I'm fine.'

She so clearly *wasn't* fine, but I didn't think me pointing this out would help. 'Okay,' I said slowly. I went back behind the counter. 'I'm going to have some of this Victoria sponge,' I said, lifting off the glass lid. 'And I can tell you, it is absolutely delicious. Would you like me to cut you a slice as well?'

Again, there was the hesitation as if she was weighing up the balance. What was going through her head? I wondered. She was obviously tempted by the food, but was she worried that she would somehow owe me for it?

'It's a couple of days old,' I lied, 'so I'll probably have to throw it out tomorrow. You'd be doing me a favour, really, if you have some. I'd much rather it was eaten than wasted.'

'Yes, please,' she said quietly, sipping her drink.

'Right,' I said, cutting two slices and trying not to look too pleased. I wasn't going to say so yet, but now that I'd seen for myself just how young and vulnerable she was, there was no way I was going to let her sleep rough tonight. No way. I would get some food down her, see if she wanted a bath, then say she could stay in the spare room.

Matthew's horrified face appeared in my head. *Let her stay? You don't even know the girl. She's probably a drug addict. She'll rip you off, take your money and do a bunk. Don't be so ridiculous!*

Well, he had a point. I didn't know the girl, and yes, she might well be an addict, but she was also young and sleeping outside my café. Whoever she was, and whatever her situation, I couldn't just send her back into the night.

I slid the plates onto the table and sat down. 'There,' I said. 'You're lucky I'm not making the cakes myself any more; a lovely lady called Annie bakes them now. If this was one of my home-made efforts, it wouldn't taste half as nice, believe me.'

She wasn't listening, she was cramming one end of the slice into her mouth and chewing quickly. A flicker of bliss crossed her face and she suddenly looked much younger, like a kid eating birthday cake at a party tea. My heart ached, wondering why the hell she was out on the streets, and where her parents were. And what should I do, as the adult in this situation?

I toyed with my cake – I wasn't really hungry, and had only said I was having some in the hope that it would encourage her to accept a piece – while I thought. I didn't want to scare her off by getting heavy about contacting her parents or even the police, but all the same I felt morally responsible to do *something*.

'Look,' I said, after a while. 'Phoebe, I do have a spare room here, you know. You're welcome to stay if—'

Damn. It was too much, too soon. She was already getting to her feet, clutching that manky old sleeping bag. 'I'm fine,' she said. 'I told you, I'm fine.'

I got to my feet too, feeling the situation slipping away from me. 'I don't want you to have to sleep outside, though,' I said. She was hurrying towards the door, and I followed her. 'Look, why don't you stay tonight, I can wash your sleeping bag for you . . .'

'No,' she said stiffly. 'Thanks for the cake, but I've got to go now.'

'But where?' I cried, as she disappeared through the

door. 'Phoebe . . .' But she was already running down the steps and away. I'd scared her off. 'Come back any time,' I called out into the darkness. 'I mean it, any time!'

I heard her pattering over the sand, and then there was silence, save for the ssshhh-ssshhh-ssshhh of the sea. She'd gone.

I stayed on the deck for a few moments in case she changed her mind and came back, but she didn't. A cool breeze was blowing in off the sea, with a mist of spitty rain just starting, and I felt wretched and foolish at having driven her away into who knew what. Where was she going to sleep now? I hoped the rain wouldn't get any heavier. I hoped she knew somewhere else to go where she'd be sheltered.

The next morning I peered out of the window in case Phoebe had crept back in the night to sleep on the deck again, but there was no sign of her. It was cool and overcast, but according to the weather forecast, this was due to be the last dry day for a while, as it was meant to be turning showery. By my calculations, I reckoned that would mean another busy day on the beach, even if the sun didn't actually show itself. In classic British holiday-maker style, everyone would doggedly drag themselves to the sand, suffering goosebumps and wind burn, with freezing extremities for anyone crazy enough to get in the sea, all in the name of a seaside holiday. They would be queuing round the block for my teas, coffees and hot snacks, I could predict it already.

Ed came in at eight-thirty and began making pastry for a new batch of pasties. 'What are we having today, chef?' I asked, passing him a coffee.

'I'm doing lamb-and-mint, a classic Cornish and a veggie one,' he replied, rubbing butter into the flour.

'Brilliant,' I said. 'We've still got some of yesterday's too, so there'll be lots to choose from.'

He winked. 'That's the plan.'

'And we've got a new member of staff starting as well,' I said, loath to leave the kitchen just yet. I liked watching him work, I realized. Plus, I knew that in an hour or so the mid-morning rush would start and I wouldn't get a chance to chat to him until the lunchtime customers had all been served. 'Rachel, she's called. She's an Aussie, but has been waitressing in London. Some restaurant called Duke's in the West End, I think.'

'Oh yeah?' He didn't raise his head from his pastry-making, but I sensed him tense up for some reason.

'Yeah, have you heard of it?'

He shook his head, still not looking at me. 'Nope.'

My eyes narrowed as I watched him. I was sure he was lying. 'Oh my God, it's not the one you used to work at, is it?' I said, the words bursting out in a torrent. 'That would be a bit weird, wouldn't—'

'No, it's not the place I worked at,' he said shortly.

'What *was* the name of the restaurant where you were cheffing?' I asked curiously. It had struck me when I'd read through Rachel's CV that I actually knew next to nothing about Ed. No references, no career history, nothing. All I had was his say-so, and I'd let him take over the kitchen. Don't get me wrong, I was very grateful that he *had* taken over the kitchen and so far he had been fantastic there, but it had crossed my mind that this was not your typical business arrangement. Other café managers probably wouldn't have been so laid-back about letting a complete stranger become their chef, without finding out a few basic things first. Mind you, other café managers weren't scream-ing desperate, like I had been.

'Evie, I'd love to chat, but I really need to get on with these pasties,' he answered now, and I felt I was being politely but firmly blocked. 'Okay?'

I raised my eyebrows, but he still wasn't looking my way and didn't notice. 'Fine,' I said, walking briskly out of the kitchen. So he didn't want to talk about it. That was cool. That was okay. It wasn't like I'd officially employed him or anything, anyway. He was just doing me a favour, being here and helping out for a few days. I couldn't exactly throw a hissy fit and start demanding answers, could I?

All the same, even though it was none of my business, Ed's reticence was kind of strange. Kind of . . . mysterious. I made myself another cup of tea and began chalking up the new pasty fillings on the menu, trying to put the whole thing out of my head.

I opened the café at nine to a trickle of early, breakfast-seeking customers, then my new employee rocked up (five minutes early – perfect) and got stuck in straight away. I could tell almost immediately that she was one of those easy-going, unflappable types, who had a smile for every customer and wasn't scared to get her hands dirty. A million times better than sulky Saffron and nice-but-dim Seb, that was for sure.

'So how long have you been in the UK?' I asked, between customers.

'Six months,' she said. 'Mostly working in London, but I spent a few weeks up in Edinburgh and Glasgow seeing rellies and travelling around. It's great down here, though. Really beautiful. I'm a beach girl at heart – I've missed the sea.'

I smiled. 'I think I'm a beach girl at heart too,' I told her.

Between serving teas, coffees and pasties (the new ones

looked and smelled every bit as delicious as yesterday's), I found out that she still had six months before she had to return to Australia, and was now saving up for a jaunt around Europe before then. 'I'd love to go to Paris,' she sighed dreamily. 'And spend a week or two in Italy. And Amsterdam sounds cool, oh, and Barcelona...' She grinned. 'So it's awesome that you've given me a job here. I'll take as many shifts as you can chuck my way.'

'I might take you up on that,' I said.

Ed stayed in the kitchen most of the morning, but when I gave Rachel a break, at half-eleven, and was the only one behind the counter, he brought orders out to me, to save me dashing to and fro the whole time. He'd just carried through two hot Cornish pasties to go, when something strange happened.

'Hey,' said my customer, a middle-aged woman with white-blonde highlights, a St-Tropez tan and designer sunglasses propped on her head. She was staring at Ed. 'I know you from somewhere, don't I?'

She had one of those crisp, well-spoken voices that you can't help but pay attention to. Interested – and yes, all right, with some nosiness – I looked from her face to his, only to see Ed flush red and come over more awkward than I'd ever seen him. 'I don't think so,' he said quickly, passing over the bag of pasties and backing away.

'Yes, I've definitely seen you,' she persisted, her voice

clipped and self-assured. She tapped a polished red finger-nail on the counter thoughtfully. 'Definitely...' Then a look of triumph appeared on her face. 'That's it! Weren't you the chef from – oh, what's the name of that place?'

'No, sorry,' he said, edging away into the kitchen. 'I just work here. I'm not anybody.'

There was an awkward silence after he'd disappeared, and the woman stared after him, puzzled. 'Strange,' she said. 'I was sure it was him. I'm very good with faces usually.'

I bit my lip. Why was Ed being so damn shifty? 'That's four pounds, please,' I said politely.

She handed over the money, still looking perplexed. 'Could have sworn it was him,' she said to herself. 'Thank you.'

Ed didn't come out of the kitchen for the rest of the day. There was something odd going on, but I couldn't bring myself to ask why he was behaving so secretively. The last thing I wanted was for him to be annoyed by my questions and – God forbid – walk out, just when he was becoming so indispensable.

All the same, I wasn't a fool. Anyone could see there was something big that he wasn't telling me. I just had to find a way of discovering what the hell he had to be so mysterious about.

*

The afternoon passed without any huge dramas. The pasties were proving very popular, with the classic Cornish being our bestseller of the day, closely followed by the chicken-and-vegetable. I still hadn't decided on my own particular favourite. I thought it had been the chicken, until I'd tried a lamb-and-mint one on my lunch break, which had been so delicious, it had thrown me into turmoil. By the end of the day, we'd sold every last one of our pasties, and all the cakes too. Rachel had been fab: chatty and hard-working and, best of all, told me she had a mate, Leah, who was due to arrive in Cornwall imminently and would be looking for a job. 'So if you need another waitress, she's your woman,' she told me. 'Heaps of experience, hard-working and a good laugh.'

'Sounds just about perfect to me,' I replied. Result!

I was in such a cheerful mood that even the thought of going out with Ruth that evening didn't annoy me. 'I am just as good as you, Ruth,' I practised saying into the mirror after I'd put on my lippy. 'Just as good. Amber says so, so it must be true.'

Ruth drove a big Ford Galaxy, with Hugo and Isabelle strapped into the back seats, and Thea in the middle. She and her husband were in the front, so I pulled open the sliding door on the side and peered into the back. 'Evening, all,' I said. 'Are you having a lovely holiday?'

'Yeaaaahhh!' the kids chorused.

'We went to a fantastic castle today in Launceston, didn't we, children?' Ruth said. 'Super views from the keep.'

'And we went on a boat,' Isabelle said. 'But Hugo was a bit sick, weren't you, Hugo?'

Hugo ignored his sister. 'You get to sit next to Thea, Aunty Evie,' he said, leaning forward. He was only nine, but had a lofty air of authority about him; I could imagine him in the House of Commons addressing the Prime Minister in similar fashion in years to come. That was if he hadn't been elected Prime Minister himself, of course. Knowing Ruth, she was already grooming him for the top spot. 'Me and Isabelle don't like sitting with her, cos she's so naughty.'

'Yes, do hop in, and we can get going,' Ruth said, from the driver's seat.

Two-year-old Thea gave me a dazzling smile as I clambered inelegantly in. 'Nice dwess,' she said, reaching over and patting the fabric with a sticky hand. 'Nice dwess, Aunty Weevie.'

Hugo and Isabelle fell about in hoots of mirth behind us. 'Aunty *Weevie*! She thinks you do lots of wees!' Isabelle spluttered.

'Isabelle!' Ruth snapped, turning and glaring in disapproval. 'Let's not have any naughty words, please. Sorry, Evie. They're overexcited.'

'Oh, I don't mind,' I said, clipping on my seatbelt. 'As long as it's not Aunty Poovie, of course. I might have to put my foot down about being called that.'

There were shocked screams of delight from the back seat. 'Aunty *Poovie!*' Isabelle squealed, nearly wetting herself, while Hugo snorted with laughter, very much like a breathless warthog. 'Aunty POOVIE!'

A certain tightness appeared around my sister's mouth as she drove away. Oops. 'Evie, please don't encourage them,' she said in a strained voice. 'I do my best to keep toilet humour out of family life, but ...'

'Mummy say TOILET!' Thea announced joyfully, and then they were all off again. Their shrieks of laughter were infectious, and I couldn't help joining in.

'That's enough, kids,' Tim said, although I was sure I caught sight of him smirking to himself. 'Settle down.'

I felt partly to blame for the decline in conversational standards, and tried to make amends. 'So, whereabouts are you staying?' I asked politely, as Ruth left Carrawen and navigated a tight bend at a safe twenty-two miles per hour. A line of traffic was already building up behind us.

'A little cottage just outside Rock,' Ruth replied. 'We've been there the last few years too, so it's almost home-from-home now.'

I had a sudden image of her telling Oxford friends about 'their little place down in Cornwall', as if it was a second home that they owned, while omitting to mention that it belonged to somebody else and they were merely renting it. I was probably being unfair, though. Be *nice*, Evie, make an effort.

'Sounds good,' I said. 'And you're here for the whole week?'

'Yes, we're very lucky,' Ruth said. Much as I loved my sister (I did, honestly), I wished she didn't have such smugness in her voice. 'Tim's managed to get the full week off work, so we're staying until Saturday.' She frowned as she turned a corner and saw a juddering tractor ahead. 'Oh God, a tractor,' she said. 'That's all we need. I don't know how people stand driving around here.'

We slowed to a crawl in the wake of the tractor. The cars behind seized chances to overtake in daring bursts of acceleration, but Ruth didn't seem to consider this an option. I was starting to feel hungry, and slid an arm across my belly. This could turn out to be a long journey.

I turned to smile at Hugo and Isabelle. 'Anyone want a game of "I Spy"?'

'So,' Ruth said, some time later, when we were finally sitting in the restaurant, having ordered our food. 'This is nice.'

It *was* nice. 'Naice' even, if you had that kind of plummy accent, which plenty of the diners here did. It was a place in Tregarrow that had been recommended in Tim's AA holiday guide and was full of couples who bore distinct resemblances to Ruth and Tim, all wearing Boden, with confident-voiced prep-school children in tow, called things like Henry and Celia. By the time we'd arrived there, though, Thea had fallen asleep and was now grumpy and red-faced, Hugo and Isabelle were bored and complaining, and my tummy had been rumbling for at least twenty minutes. It had also started sheeting down with rain.

'Bit fancier than the café, eh?' Tim said condescendingly. 'You could get some tips from this place, Evie.'

'Mmm,' I said, trying not to rise to his jibe. Oh, sod it, I couldn't hold back. I was fed up with being talked down to, on my own turf as well. 'Different kind of outlet though, really, Tim,' I said, equally patronizingly. 'My customers come in off the beach, rather than dress up for the occasion, so you can't really compare. Although we are looking into expanding, to an evening opening, so ...'

'Are you?' Ruth asked in surprise. She shot an annoyed look over at Hugo, who was twirling his fork round and round, rather too near Isabelle. 'Give that to me,' she hissed, reaching over and snatching it from him. 'We don't want it going in someone's eye.'

'Yes,' I said. 'I've got this new chef in, who's keen to try an evening service at weekends, so I thought we'd give it a go.' Not that Ed and I had discussed the evening thing any further, I realized. I hoped he hadn't gone off the idea now that he'd actually had the experience of working alongside me. 'The thing about being your own boss,' I said loftily, well aware that I was sinking to their depths, 'is that you can change things around however you want to.' *Take that, you mere employees, you,* I wanted to add. *Shove that in your company pension plan.*

'Obviously you need to get the right menu for an evening service,' Tim said wisely. Clearly all his years as an academic had given him a razor-sharp insight into the restaurant business.

'Well, yes, obviously,' I replied, resisting the urge to add a rude 'DUH!'

'And obviously you need to have enough staff,' Ruth advised me. She gave a tinkling laugh. 'It looked pretty hectic when we came in yesterday – oh, I did feel for you. I could tell you were having a tough time.'

I could feel my fists clenching under the table. *You are every bit as good as she is,* Amber had told me. I was struggling to hang on to that now.

'I wanted to try the ice cream in your café, Aunty Evie, but Mummy said we couldn't,' Isabelle said, slipping her hand into mine.

I gave it a squeeze. 'Well, you'll have to come back another time then,' I told her, trying my damnedest not to let Ruth get to me. *Has she ever had the balls to do anything spontaneous or reckless? No.* 'We've got lots of yummy flavours, Izzy. Raspberry ripple, chocolate, mint choc-chip – what's your favourite?'

She smiled at me. She was sweet, Isabelle, with her freckles and dark bob, which fell into a fringe just above her eyes. 'Chocolate,' she said, her hazel eyes round and solemn.

Thea perked up from her high chair where she'd been playing with a little cuddly dog. 'Me want chocolate,' she said. 'Chocolate now?'

'Thea thinks we're going to have chocolate now!' Hugo guffawed, as if this was the most hilarious thing he'd ever heard. 'She thinks this is a chocolate restaurant, where all you get is chocolate!'

'Well, Thea is—' Ruth began.

'And everything is MADE of chocolate!' Isabelle interrupted. 'Even the chairs and table!' She pretended to nibble on the wooden table. 'Deeee-licious!'

'Ooh, that would be good,' I said, smiling at her. 'I'm going to eat your chair, Izzy. Yum-yum!'

'Stop that, Isabelle,' Tim snapped.

'I'm going to eat Thea's high chair, then she'll be able to escape and do naughty things,' Hugo said, leaning over and pretending to bite it.

Thea squealed in excitement and biffed him on the head with her spotty dog. I laughed – they were so much funnier than I'd remembered, my nephew and nieces – but Ruth and Tim had disapproving expressions.

'Behave yourselves,' Ruth hissed. 'This is a nice restaurant, it's not a . . . play-barn. People are looking.'

Nobody was looking at all, she was imagining it, but Isabelle, clearly in a silly mood now, pulled a funny face and waved. 'Hello, people,' she giggled.

'Hello, people-weeple,' Thea echoed.

'She said WEEPLE,' Hugo spluttered. 'That's what you call people who do lots of wees!'

'Hugo, Isabelle and Thea, that is ENOUGH,' Tim said in a dangerous-sounding low voice. The giggles and snorts stopped immediately, all gleefulness killed off in an instant.

'Sorry, Daddy,' Hugo said, looking down at his lap.

Our food arrived just then, so the moment was over, thank goodness. It was disconcerting, feeling that I had more in common with my nephew and nieces than my own sister and brother-in-law. What did that say about me? I wasn't sure I wanted to know the answer.

'So, did I tell you?' Ruth said, cutting Thea's food into small pieces. 'We saw Matthew in town on Saturday, with . . . Jasmine, is it? He said you two had split up.'

No, she hadn't told me. She knew perfectly well she hadn't told me. And Jasmine? Who was Jasmine? And why did Ruth think it was acceptable to casually lob other women's names into stories about Matthew across plates of overpriced chicken and chips?

'Mmm,' I said neutrally, sipping my wine. 'Yep.' I posted a shred of chicken into my mouth and chewed mechanically. 'This is delicious.'

'Saw him at the petrol station, as we were filling up to come down here,' Tim said. 'You know, the one just before you get to the ring road.'

'Ah,' I said, like I cared. Inside I was mentally combing through every single conversation I'd ever had with Matthew to see if I could find any memory of this Jasmine woman getting a mention. Who the hell was she, and what the hell was she doing in my boyfriend's car with him?

Ex-boyfriend's car, that was.

'They were off to Malvern, for a walking weekend, they said,' Ruth went on. Was she being completely insensitive, I wondered, or was she getting some kind of warped kick out of telling me all this? Putting me in my place as usual. Payback for the 'being my own boss' remark, no doubt. I wished she would shut her big lipsticked mouth. I didn't want to know. I did not want to know about walking weekends in Malvern with Jasmine.

Conversely, I did want to know, too. I wanted to know *everything*.

'Well, good luck to them,' I said, unable to help a tinge

of bitterness sliding into my voice. 'Matthew always was a boring old fart. He can take his walking weekends in Malvern and shove them up his – '

I stopped, aware of the saucer-eyed children hanging on my every word.

'Aunty Weevie say FART,' Thea announced.

'I think she was about to say something even RUDER,' Hugo spluttered.

Happily, this was enough for Ruth to decide to change the subject, and we talked about safer topics like gardening and her tennis lessons for the rest of the meal. Farts, wees and ex-boyfriend's arses didn't get a single look-in, and I wasn't sure who was more relieved, my sister or me. But she'd proved her point anyway. Once again she'd made it clear just who was superior within the family.

I am just as good as you, Ruth, I had said into the mirror that evening, but I wasn't. And I never would be, either, at this rate. I let out a sigh and ate my food without tasting any of it.

Chapter Sixteen

The drive back to the café was a quiet one. The children dozed off, and any attempts at conversation were hampered by the torrential rain that thundered against the car roof. I'd had enough of chit-chat anyway; my mind was spinning and spinning with this news about Matthew, completely distracting me from any other topic. Who was this Jasmine woman? Was she his new girlfriend, or just a friend? Could it have been some work outing, and he'd just happened to offer her a lift? Or was she the real reason he'd wanted to split up with me?

'Letting you go,' he'd said at the time, as if he were generously releasing me from the relationship against his wishes. Yeah, right. He was letting me go so that he could move on to a new model, more like.

I felt humiliated, as if he'd rubbed my nose in it, as if he'd deliberately staged a 'chance' meeting with my sister, so that I would discover he had a new girlfriend. And of all the ways to find out, of all the people to break that horrible news to me, Ruth was the worst person to do such a thing. That made the sting even more painful.

I hated the sound of Jasmine already. She sounded as boring as hell. Walking weekend in Malvern indeed. How middle-aged and dull could you get? I bet she wasn't the type for outrageous al-fresco sex on the Worcester Beacon, either. She'd probably pack a Thermos flask and a hypothermia blanket, just to be on the safe side. She probably had a first-aid kit tucked in a pocket of her big, sensible knickers, and one of those tragic hiking sticks. *My name is Jasmine, and I can bore people to tears with my encyclopaedic knowledge of lichen and birdsong. Would you like to go walking with me sometime?*

Well, they deserved each other. I just hoped for her sake that she was a neat freak like him. Bitchily I fantasized about her being a complete slob and driving him nuts with her slovenly habits. Or them both getting struck by lightning in a terrible storm as they stood on the top of British Camp. That would teach them. Fat lot of good Jasmine's first-aid kit and birdsong calls would be *then*.

She'd better be nice to Saul, this Jasmine, I thought grimly as we cruised through the dark, rain-sodden lanes. She'd better be bloody lovely to him. He deserved nothing less. I sighed, hating Matthew and hating Jasmine, wishing Ruth had kept her mouth shut and left me none the wiser.

I glanced over at Thea, who was fast asleep with her thumb in her mouth, her facial features slack, her eyelids just trembling slightly with some dream or other. She was so cute; how come I hadn't noticed it before? Just because Ruth was a pain in the arse, it didn't mean her kids were too. They had all been adorable tonight – really sweet and funny and giggly. Previously, round at Mum's for Sunday dinner or other family gatherings, the older two in particular had always been rather sensible and solemn; mini-Ruths, in fact. But they'd let their hair down tonight in true holiday style, and had been hilarious. It had made me miss Saul even more, spending time with them. I hoped he was okay, and having a fun half-term. I would write him a letter, I decided. Splitting up with Matthew didn't mean I had to lose touch with him too.

'Here we are,' Ruth said, and I jerked out of my thoughts. We were back at the café, and I hadn't even noticed us coming through Carrawen village.

I unclipped my seatbelt. 'Thanks for tonight,' I said politely. 'It was lovely to see you all. I hope you enjoy the rest of your holiday.'

'Lovely to see you too,' Ruth said, and Tim mumbled some nicety or other along the same lines.

'See you soon,' I said, pulling open the door. 'And you've got such fantastic kids, you really have. Say good-night to them from me, won't you?'

Ruth looked surprised and somewhat touched at my words. 'Will do,' she said. 'And thank you. Bye now.'

I jumped out, pulled the car door shut and gave a quick wave before hurrying up to the front door. It was still absolutely pelting down, and I suddenly thought about Phoebe and her sleeping bag. I hoped she would have somewhere warm and dry to go. *If she's on the deck tonight,* I thought to myself, *I am totally going to drag her in and make her stay this time. Absolutely no arguments.* But when I clattered up the steps to the deck, it was empty.

The next morning it was still raining heavily. The weather matched my mood. I hadn't slept well, tormented by images of Matthew kissing another woman. *Jasmine.* I had changed my mind about her being dull and frumpy. In my head she was now tall, slim and gorgeous, with waves of tumbling blonde hair. She was also an incredible career woman with loads of mates and an amazing social life, who helped out in an old people's home in her spare time and was always kind to animals. Even my imagination was against me, I thought miserably as I huffed downstairs to open the café.

'Bloody hell, what's up with you?' Ed said when he came in to start work and saw me sitting in one of the booths, nursing a coffee and glaring out to sea. The waves were surging and heaving in the bay, crashing over the rocks at the far spit-point.

'Nothing,' I muttered in reply.

'Not that long-lost ex of yours again, is it?' he asked, in an irritatingly cheerful voice. 'The one you shouted at in the pub the other week? Don't tell me you've gone and done it again?'

'No,' I snarled. 'It's not *him*.'

'Ah,' he said. He sat next to me and folded his arms as if we were discussing something trivial like the weather. 'Some other bastard, eh? Bloody men, what are they like? Complete and utter nightmares the lot of them.' He winked. 'Am I right?'

He was teasing me, and I wasn't in the mood for it. I slurped my coffee, scowling, and to my annoyance he burst out laughing.

'Oh, Evie, come on, I'm only winding you up,' he said. 'God, if looks could kill...' He elbowed me. 'All right, I get it, you don't want to talk about it. I will shut up. Okay?'

I managed a brief smile. 'Sorry,' I said. 'I'll be all right in a minute. I'm just — fed up. Ignore me.'

He made himself a coffee and sat back down with me. 'I need to get on with the pasties and baguette fillings in a minute,' he said, 'but we haven't spoken about the weekend yet, have we? Are you still on for opening up one evening for dinner?'

'Yes,' I said, forgetting my grump for a moment. 'Yes, definitely. I was just talking about that last night. The thing is, it's already Wednesday now, so we might be cutting it fine for this weekend.'

'Nah,' he said confidently. 'Plenty of time. And if we're going to do it, it really should be this Friday. Lots of people will be off home on Saturday, won't they, end of half-term week?'

'Oh, yeah,' I said. It was true. The bay was full of holidaymakers right now, and it would be quieter the following week when the kids were back at school. I sat up straighter, suddenly feeling ten times more alert. 'What, so you really reckon we could run a dinner menu this Friday? As in – two days' time?'

'No problem,' he said. 'Start telling people about it today, and we'll plan our menu and order the food later on. Maybe print up some fliers, give them out to people on the beach, that sort of thing.'

'Okay,' I said, Matthew temporarily forgotten. 'We can get some nice tablecloths too, and candles . . .'

'That's the spirit,' he said. 'Friday night it is, then. It'll be great.'

I smiled back at him. 'That's a plan,' I said, feeling much better.

Ed went into the kitchen just as Annie breezed in with her cake delivery. This time she'd brought one carrot cake with cream-cheese frosting and walnuts on top, and a chocolate sponge that she'd decorated with silver balls. 'I came over all kitsch,' she confessed with a laugh. 'You're lucky I didn't add on a few Jelly Tots too.' She'd also brought more flapjacks and some iced cookies, and I gave her a hug along with her pay.

'I love the silver balls,' I told her. 'And honestly, your baking has made such a difference to this place. People keep coming back for more, and word of mouth is definitely spreading. What with your cakes and Ed's pasties, we've had a brilliant few days.'

She beamed. 'I'm glad to hear it,' she said. 'Martha and her boyfriend, Jamie, have taken it upon themselves to be my chief testers and have been very strict with their critiques, so I'm pleased everyone else approves.'

'Well, pass on my thanks,' I said. 'Tell them there's a free coffee for them any time they're passing. And you too, of course – can I get you one while you're here?'

'Better not,' she said, glancing up at the clock. 'I need to get to the shop. But another time would be good – or maybe a drink one evening?'

'Sounds perfect,' I said. 'In fact, we're opening for dinner on Friday night, why don't you come along then? On the house, to say thank you for all your hard work.'

'Really? You're doing evening meals?' She sounded surprised. 'What a good idea. I'd love to come. Are you taking bookings, or . . .'

I grabbed a notepad that was stuffed down the side of

the till. 'We are now,' I told her. 'Shall I book you and Martha in?'

'Why not,' she said. 'Maybe make it a table for three, in case Jamie wants to come too. But I'll pay, obviously. You don't have to treat us.'

'Absolutely not,' I told her, writing down the booking. Then I heard Ed's warning voice from the kitchen. 'Evie,' he cautioned, 'you're not giving away all your profits, are you?'

Annie laughed. 'At least someone here is thinking about the business,' she said. 'I'd better dash. Traffic's going to be hideous today, with this rain. Let me know which cakes you want for Friday – and whether I can do anything to help with the desserts that evening too.'

'Will do,' I said. 'Cheers, Annie.'

I set out the cakes, then climbed onto a chair and chalked up 'Friday Night New Evening Menu – Taking Bookings Today!' on the blackboard. It was silly of me, I knew, but I couldn't help getting excited about it already. I hoped Jo was looking down and taking note of all this. I had the feeling she'd be cheering me on all the way.

Rachel came in soon afterwards, and I filled her in on the plan for Friday. 'So any chance you get, if you could mention it to the customers and try to take some book-ings, that would be brilliant,' I said. 'Mind you,' I went on, glancing out at the storm that was still raging, 'we'll be lucky to get any customers at all today, now that the weather's so abysmal.'

My words were like a prophecy of doom. The only person who came in before ten o'clock was the postman with a couple of letters. 'Thanks,' I said. 'I don't suppose I can tempt you with a coffee while you're here, can I? Or a hot pasty?'

He laughed ruefully. 'I'd love a coffee *and* a hot pasty, darling, but I've got to get on,' he said. 'Traffic's terrible. All the holiday crowd are trying to find museums and castles to keep dry in, and clogging up the roads.'

'Oh well,' I said. 'You can always come back on Friday night – we're having a special dinner menu then, if you're interested?'

'Sorry, love, I've got to crack on,' he said again, waving a hand as he walked away.

'Right, okay then,' I said as the door shut behind him. I wasn't used to having nothing to do. Ever since I'd started working here the café had been busy, busy, busy. Now I was twiddling my thumbs. 'Rachel, while it's so quiet I'm just going to get on the computer and design some fliers,' I said. 'Scream if we get a sudden deluge of ravenous punters, yeah?'

'Sure,' she said.

There was a tiny office just off the kitchen where Jo

had kept all her paperwork and filing. I'd hardly been in there since I'd moved down, and there was dust on the computer monitor. I brushed it off and turned the machine on, twirling in the swivel chair as it hummed into life. While I waited, I opened the letters that the postman had brought – four handwritten envelopes. It seemed strange to see my name there, with 'The Beach Café, Carrawen Bay' as the address underneath. I didn't recognize the writing. Were they bills from suppliers perhaps?

I ripped open the first envelope and pulled out the contents. Then my heart sank as I realized what it was: a letter of application for the chef's job and a CV. Of course, responses to my recruitment ad in the paper. Damn. I had secretly been hoping that nobody would apply, and I'd get to keep Ed for a while longer. Obviously not.

The PC was up and running now, so I stuffed the envelopes into my in-tray, meaning to look at them properly later. Then I typed up my flier, centred it all and changed the fonts a few times before sending it to print.

The café was still empty, so I opened up my emails. At the top of my in-box was one from Matthew. Fingers trembling with nervous anticipation, I clicked on his name to open the message. Was he writing to apologize for the Jasmine thing? Was he writing to say he'd changed his mind, Jasmine was a terrible mistake and I was the finest woman in the universe?

Was he hell. He was writing, I soon realized, to say that the electricity and gas bills were in, and my share of them came to £103.

'Well, you can whistle for that, mate,' I muttered furiously. 'Because you won't be getting anything from me now.'

Of all the flaming cheek. Honestly! Did he have no idea about tact, about relationship RULES? I had the moral high ground – twice over, actually, having first been dumped and then replaced so quickly. And he had the nerve to write to me, telling me I owed him?

Fired up with annoyance, I hit Reply and typed furiously.

Dear Matthew,
   You have got to be kidding. Do you really think you're going to get anything from me, now that I know all about you and Jasmine? DREAM ON.
                                        Evie

Before I knew what I was doing, I'd hit Send and the message had vanished. I imagined the look of distaste that would appear on his face as he read it. 'Well, sod you,' I said crossly to the computer screen. Then I picked up my fliers and went back into the café. Although it seemed rather deceitful, I didn't mention the application letters to Ed. I would tell him later, I assured myself. Of course I would.

Finally, at eleven o'clock, we had our first customer. It was a silver-haired lady wearing a long grey coat and a plastic see-through rainhood, which she untied and shook out, before coming over to the counter. 'Goodness,' she said, 'it's horrible out there.'

Rachel smiled politely at her. 'It sure is,' she said. 'But at least it's warm and dry in here. What can I get you?'

'Ooh, a cup of tea, and a piece of cake,' she said. 'Why not? When you reach my age, you've got to have the good stuff when you can. And that Victoria sponge looks lovely.'

'That's the spirit,' Rachel said, dropping a teabag into a teapot and setting a cup and saucer onto a tray.

'One slice of Victoria sponge coming right up,' I said, cutting it as Rachel made the tea. Then, because our customer looked rather frail and I wasn't sure she'd manage the tray, I went out from behind the counter and picked it up myself. 'Where would you like this?' I asked.

She pointed to the nearest table and I carried it over, setting out everything for her. 'Thank you, dear,' she said, gesturing at the empty seats. 'Do join me, if you're not too busy. I'd be glad of the company.'

'That's a good idea,' I said. 'Rachel, do you want to take your break now? I'm going to have a cup of tea myself, seeing as we're so quiet.'

'Then I'll join you,' Rachel said. 'I'll get the teas. Milk, no sugar, right?'

'Thanks,' I said.

The old lady introduced herself as Florence and told us that she'd moved down here from Coventry, with her husband, in March. 'We had our honeymoon in the bay, fifty years ago,' she said, eyes far-away, 'and came on lots of summer holidays here too with our son. It was always our dream to live here one day, so when we retired, Arthur – my husband – he said, "Come on, Flo, let's just do it. Let's live our dream."'

'Good for you two,' Rachel said warmly. 'I'm all for living out your dreams.'

'Me too,' I said. 'And how are you liking your new life down in Cornwall?'

Florence smiled, but it was a small, sad smile. 'It was lovely at first,' she said. 'We felt like a couple of kiddies, starting again. It was exciting. But . . .' She sighed, her fingers trembling as she cut the cake into smaller pieces. 'But just two weeks after we'd moved down here, Arthur got ill. He died last month. Very sudden. Very shocking.'

'Oh no,' I said, putting my hand on her arm. 'Oh, Florence, I'm so sorry.'

She nodded, unable to speak for a moment. 'I do miss him,' she said, her voice choked with emotion. She'd gone very pale. She dabbed her eyes with a tissue, then blew her nose and took a long, shuddering breath. 'I still don't know if I'm coming or going.'

'I bet you don't,' Rachel said sympathetically. 'Do you have family nearby, is there anyone who's been looking after you?'

She dabbed her eyes again. 'No,' she said. 'All our friends are back in Coventry, and it's too far for me to drive there. My son's in the States at the moment, he's working out there as a television producer, so there's just me.' She took a sip of tea, then gave us a watery smile. 'I'm sorry, girls. Listen to me, moping on and on at you. I'm just a silly old lady – don't take any notice.'

'You're not a silly old lady,' I said, squeezing her hand. 'You've had a really hard time, no wonder you're upset.'

'Yes,' she said. She took a dainty mouthful of the cake. 'This is very nice,' she said after a moment. 'Arthur would have loved it. Victoria sponge was always his favourite.'

'He was obviously a man of taste, then,' Rachel said.

Florence's eyes sparkled. 'Oh, he was,' she said. 'He was a wonderful man. But you don't want to hear me going on any more. Tell me all about yourselves instead, while I enjoy this cake.'

So we ended up having a good old chat, the three of us, while the rain continued to lash down outside. I moaned on for a bit about splitting up with Matthew, and the other two assured me it sounded as if I was better off without him. Then I made them both laugh by telling them about the Ryan disaster. 'Oops,' Florence giggled, her hand up to her mouth like a girl.

'I know the bloke you mean,' Rachel said. 'He tried it on with my mate in the pub the other week. Got a glass of beer over his head for his efforts.'

Now it was my turn to laugh. 'Don't mess with the Aussies,' I spluttered.

'Too right,' she said. Then, since we were getting confidential with each other and we still had no customers, she went on to tell us about her man troubles – how she'd originally come to the UK with her boyfriend Craig, whom she'd been with for years, but they'd split up two months ago. 'It was one of those stupid arguments that didn't really mean anything, but neither of us would back down,' she said, fiddling with the sugar packets. 'Too pig-headed, the pair of us. So when he ended up saying, "Fine, I'll go off on my own then", I blurted out, "Okay, you do that." And I haven't seen him since.'

'Oh dear,' Florence said. 'Never let the sun set on an argument, that was our motto.'

Rachel raised an eyebrow. 'Hmm. There have been quite a lot of sunsets since then, to be honest. And ... nothing. He's too stubborn to get in touch, and so am I.'

'Blimey,' I said. 'Not even one drunken phone call or text? You are hardcore, missus.'

For the first time since I'd met her, Rachel suddenly seemed vulnerable. 'I miss him, though,' she said. 'And I wish I hadn't left it so long. I wish I'd had the guts to smooth things over there and then, rather than digging my heels in.'

'Where is he now?' I asked. 'Why don't you get in touch?'

'He's still in London, according to Facebook,' she said, and gave a sigh. 'I should get in touch, shouldn't I?'

'Yes,' Florence and I chorused, Florence with such severity in her voice that I wanted to giggle. 'Swallow your pride,' she added in a gentler tone. 'You can't leave things this way.'

Rachel nodded. 'It has got kind of ridiculous,' she agreed. 'I guess I should make the first move.'

'Good girl,' Florence said, patting Rachel on the arm. She was sweet, I thought to myself affectionately. Exactly the nice, caring sort of grandma figure I'd always wanted, dispensing kindly advice from all her years of wisdom.

A couple of dog-walkers came in just then, wanting to warm up with coffees and pasties, and Rachel went to serve them, glad of the chance to duck out of the conversation, no doubt.

'I suppose I should go home,' Florence said. 'Thank

you for sitting with me and chatting, it has been a real pleasure. I'm so glad I braved the rain to come out. I try and go somewhere every day for a little walk, otherwise the walls start closing in on me. But now I know how friendly you are in here, and how delicious the cake is, I'll definitely be back.'

'You do that,' I said, helping her on with her coat. 'Any time, Florence. It's been lovely to meet you.'

'Well, I might pop in on Tuesday, then,' she said. 'It's my birthday and I don't know what else to do with myself.'

'Definitely,' I said. 'We can have a little celebration for you right here, can't we?'

She smiled, and it was like the sun coming out. 'That would be wonderful,' she said, her knotty old fingers shaking as she did up her buttons. 'I would like that very much.'

An hour or so later, the sun really did come out, and we had a steady stream of people popping in for lunches and drinks. I booked two more tables for Friday evening, and we gave out lots more fliers. 'Now it really is official,' I said to Ed later in the afternoon, when I brought some orders in to him. 'We've got proper bookings for Friday night – from people I don't even know! No turning back now.'

*

Ed knocked off at about three so that he could go and walk the dog, and Rachel and I covered the last two hours of the shift, which tended to be the quietest part of the day. Ed had said he'd come back and sort out Friday's evening menu with me later, so I got stuck into the cleaning up while I waited. I actually rather liked scrubbing the kitchen and café area every night. Matthew would have been shocked if he could have seen me sluicing down the walls, floor and countertops, washing, mopping and bleaching, when I'd never bothered doing such things in our Oxford home, but I took a peculiar sort of pride in making it all perfect here, staying in control. Germs begone!

On this particular evening I'd turned up the radio and was singing along loudly to Beyoncé as I mopped the floors, and yes, all right, I was even dancing a bit with my mop and shaking my thing, as if I were some bootylicious megastar rather than Mrs Mop in my old denim shorts and a pink vest-top. And of course, wouldn't you just know it, at the exact moment I'd thrown back my head to hit the high notes, I heard a knocking at the glass door and spun round to see Ed standing there, looking very much as if he were trying not to laugh at me.

Actually he didn't even try very hard, now that I thought about it. He was laughing into his hand, as if *that* disguised anything. I went to unlock the door, feeling like the ultimate prat. The Prat Factor, that's what I had.

'Evening,' I said, pretending I was completely cool about him seeing me singing and dancing with a mop, even though something inside me had keeled over and died. (My dignity, namely.)

'Hello,' he said. 'Is this the right place for the *Cornwall's Got Talent* auditions?'

Very funny. I decided to play him at his own game. 'It is, actually,' I replied. 'Can I take the name of your act?'

'Um, yes, it's ... Edvis,' he said. 'Ah-ha-ha,' he added, with a diabolical Elvis lip-curl.

I burst out laughing as he launched into the worst hip gyrations I'd ever seen. 'Oh God, I thought you'd slipped a disc there for a minute,' I spluttered, when he stopped and struck a dramatic pose. 'Well, you've failed the audition, I'm afraid, but come in anyway. I was just finishing off the cleaning,' I went on, unnecessarily, mop still in hand. 'Help yourself to a drink of anything and have a seat, I'm almost done.'

I heard him humming 'All Shook Up' as I sloshed the mop around the last corners, and then the sound of a cork being pulled out of a bottle. 'I brought my own, I hope you don't mind,' he said.

'Course I don't mind,' I called back, hearing the wine

glug-glug-glugging into a glass. 'As long as you pour me one, of course.'

'Coming right up.'

I tipped the mop-water away, wiped my hands on my shorts and went to join him. We clinked our wine glasses and smiled at each other. He *was* rather easy on the eye, it had to be said, I found myself thinking. And he had what my mum would have called 'a lovely smile', which lit up his whole face.

'So, let's talk menus, shall we?' Ed said, as if I needed prompting.

Of course. Menus. 'Let's,' I agreed. 'I guess we want to keep it fairly simple.'

'Absolutely,' he said. 'I'm thinking three starters, three mains and three desserts. No need for anything bigger or fancier, right?'

'Right.'

'And we're aiming squarely at holidaymakers,' he went on. 'People who'll want to treat themselves, have something they might not have at home. We need to give them an experience.'

'Let's hope it's not diarrhoea,' I quipped. Clearly the younger and more puerile members of my extended family had been a bad influence on me lately. I would have to put in a complaint to Ruth. 'Sorry. You're right, of course. An experience — and it should be a Cornish one, too. So let's have some fresh fish for one of the mains, one veggie dish and one meaty dinner for the carnivores. All lovely local Cornish ingredients.' I grinned at him. 'In other words, fish and chips, egg and chips or sausage and chips, yeah?'

He batted me over the head with his notepad. 'Tell you what, while our punters are eating their egg and chips, maybe you can go around entertaining them with your "jokes".' He did that thing with his second and third fingers to show he meant jokes in the loosest sense of the word. 'We'll save the mop-dancing and karaoke for the dessert course.'

I laughed. 'They might even pay me extra to stop,' I said.

'Now there's an idea,' he said deadpan, putting a pound coin on the table.

I looked from the coin to his face and laughed again. 'Jealousy is a terrible thing, Edvis,' I told him, pretending to be sorrowful. 'All right, let's get this menu on the road then.'

We finally agreed on red snapper, classic steak (from the happiest and most well-looked-after of Cornish cows) and a mushroom risotto for our mains, a couple of different bruschettas or crab pâté for a starter, followed by a choice of toffee pudding, apple pie and ice cream for our desserts. During this time we had somehow necked most of the Sauvignon Blanc between us and had taken the piss out of each other non-stop. All Ed's earlier awkwardness and shifty behaviour had completely vanished, and we'd had a real laugh. I thought of the job applications that I hadn't even read through yet, and felt a pang of sadness that this was only a temporary arrangement. He was so funny and interested in the business, and moreover a bloody great chef, that already I couldn't imagine working with anybody else.

'Brilliant,' I said, rising unsteadily to my feet. 'Fabulous. I'm going to walk up to Betty's shop right now and see if she'll take a few leaflets off our hands, and leave some in the pub too. You wait, we're going to be packed on Friday, and they're all going to *love* it.'

He was smiling at me, his eyes soft and crinkling at the edges.

'What?' I asked.

'Nothing,' he said, getting up too and tucking his notebook in his back pocket. 'I'll see you tomorrow.'

I thrust some leaflets into his hand. 'Here,' I said. 'You can deliver these to your neighbours, yeah?'

His fingers closed around mine, and for a second I felt a spark of something between us. Something intense. Something heady. Something – yes, romantic, even.

Then, just as suddenly, he withdrew his hand. 'Will do,' he said, turning and heading off in such a business-like fashion that I was left feeling rather dazed, and wondering if I'd imagined the whole thing. Probably. I was a bit tipsy, that was all.

'Right,' I said aloud to myself as the door shut behind him. 'Well, that's that, then.'

I cleared away our wine glasses, then headed out on a leaflet drop.

I stopped at Betty's shop first, bracing myself for some rude comment about how I'd insulted Saffron's family or committed some other terrible crime. I hoped she wouldn't turf me out again. She'd been civil to me, if not over-friendly recently, but I wasn't counting my chickens that I'd won her over yet by any means.

'I'm closing in two minutes,' she said as I walked in. She was glaring as if I was the most inconvenient thing that had ever happened to her in her 'convenience' store. Excellent customer service as usual, from the sweet-talking Betty.

'It's all right, I'm not buying anything,' I said as I approached the counter, which probably wasn't the best reply, in hindsight. Her eyes became flintier and her bosoms were thrust out like offensive weapons. I was quailing in my flip-flops, but told myself it was just plain ridiculous to be scared. We were two grown women, for goodness' sake. How bad could this be?

'Betty, I was wondering if I could leave some of these

leaflets here,' I said, in my nicest, most non-confrontational voice. 'We're opening the café for dinner on Friday night, and trying to drum up some bookings. Is that okay?'

She sneered at the leaflet I held out, pointedly not taking it from me. 'Was this his idea then, that bloke you've got working for you?' she asked.

I stared at her, slightly nonplussed. 'Well … it was a joint idea,' I said. 'But I think it could be really good. Might bring some more people to the village,' I added, hoping to lead her into thinking she could actually benefit from this too.

She shook her head. 'There's something not right about him,' she said darkly. 'People are saying he's not who he makes out. I wouldn't trust him, if I were you.'

I bristled, certain that this was the exact same bitchy, gossipy tone of voice she'd used when talking to people about *me*. I might not have retaliated if I hadn't polished off a good half-bottle of wine within the last hour, but as it was, I couldn't help a reply bursting out of me. 'Well, I *do* trust him,' I told her, snatching my leaflets away again. 'He's a really great guy, and an excellent chef.' I was just about to add a 'So NER', but managed to shut my mouth in time.

She raised her eyebrows, folding her fat arms across her chest, so that her large bust rested upon them like a shelf. 'Don't say I didn't warn you,' she said shortly, and began tidying the counter display with excess fussiness. 'Anything else?'

'No,' I said turning on my heel and walking away. 'Nothing else.'

Chapter Seventeen

The leaflets didn't exactly get welcomed with open arms at the Golden Fleece, either. 'I would take some, but I don't think our landlady would be too chuffed,' the tall, good-looking lad behind the bar said. 'We do our own evening food here, you see, so . . .'

He was polite, at least, which was more than Betty had been. 'Fair enough,' I said, feeling stupid for having asked in the first place. 'I hadn't thought about that. No worries.' Then I spotted his name badge: Jamie. 'Oh, are you Martha's boyfriend? The artist?'

He seemed pleased to be referred to as that. 'Yeah, that's me,' he said. 'You're Evie, right? The one Annie's been baking for?'

'The very same,' I said. 'Hey, Martha was telling me you're going to have your artwork in an exhibition soon – how cool is that! I loved the painting they've got in their – ' I stopped talking, as his face had fallen and his whole body seemed to sag. Oh dear. What had I said?

'It's been cancelled,' he said, dejection written all over him. 'The council have had their arts budget slashed, so the exhibition isn't going ahead any more.'

'Oh no!' I felt gutted for him, he looked so downcast. 'What a shame,' I said. 'That's really bad luck. Still, you've got talent. I've seen it, they've seen it, other people will recognize it too. I'm sure this isn't the end for you.'

He didn't look particularly optimistic. 'That's what Martha keeps saying, but...' He shrugged. 'I dunno. It's just so disappointing. I was really looking forward to showing my work to people, getting it seen, you know.'

I nodded sympathetically. I could imagine just how frustrated he must have felt, to have had this exhibition within touching distance and then have it taken away from him. It was almost worse, having had your hopes raised and then dashed, than nothing happening at all.

'I'm sure,' I said. 'But don't give up. You *are* good, and you never know what's around the corner.' I gave him a smile, hoping that sounded encouraging rather than patronizing. 'Nice to meet you anyway. Always a free coffee for you and Martha in the café.'

'Cheers,' he said.

It was raining again as I headed for home, and my toes slithered wetly in my flip-flops. The warm tipsiness I'd felt earlier had disappeared, and I couldn't wait to get back in the flat and into my PJs, with a cup of tea and some trashy

TV to watch. That was one advantage of living on my own, at least – I was able to catch up on all my soaps and TV dramas again, free from Matthew's pained looks and tuts of disapproval.

But then, as I reached the deck outside the café, I saw that Phoebe was back. She was sitting against the front wall, hunched up with her arms round her knees, as the rain spattered down around her. Tonight there was no jumping up and running away. Tonight she seemed defeated and weary, looking up at me as if to say, *Well, here I am again. What are you going to do about it?*

I unlocked the door and pushed it open. 'Do you want to come in?' I asked. She nodded, and in we both went.

'Thank you,' she mumbled. She stood there, limp, her sleeping bag trailing on the floor.

'Look,' I said, turning the lights on. 'I don't know you, and you don't know me, but I can't let you sleep out there in this weather. There's a spare room here, and you're welcome to stay. You can have some food and a bath too, if you want. What do you think?'

She nodded again. Bless her, she seemed broken – all the fight had gone from her.

'Okay,' I said. I think we both felt a bit weird and awkward about the situation. 'Come upstairs then, I'll run you a bath and show you where everything is.'

It struck me again as I led her through to the flat that,

yes, I was taking a risk here, asking this girl in when I didn't know a thing about her. For all I knew, I could wake up the next day and find that all my worldly possessions had been stolen, and I would never see her again. But my gut instinct was that it would be fine, and she wouldn't do any such thing. And she was only a kid. How could I do anything else, other than take her in? It wasn't as if I had anything worth pinching really anyway. If she was after jewels and solid silver cutlery, she'd been camping outside the wrong place.

I set the bath running, poured in a splosh of bubbles and found her some clean towels and pyjamas, as well as a dressing gown that had once belonged to Jo. 'There,' I said. 'You have a good old soak. I'll make you something to eat once you're out, okay?'

She nodded shyly. 'Thank you,' she said again.

'No problem,' I said, leaving her to it.

I had a sudden memory of being that sort of age myself, when I'd had a massive row with my parents about going to Glastonbury with my mates. In the end, I'd stormed off to the festival in a rage, ignoring the fact that they'd forbidden me to go. (They were worried I would get in with the so-called 'wrong crowd'. Ha! Too late. I was already part of the so-called wrong crowd, and having a whale of a time with them.) After the festival weekend was over, I couldn't face going back to Oxford and had hitched down to Cornwall instead, seeking refuge at Jo's. I'd turned up knackered, smelly and practically penniless, and she'd simply taken me in, without any judgement or questions. The next morning she'd been on my case about phoning home, yes, but I was always grateful thereafter for that one night of pure acceptance, when she'd opened her doors to me without any hassle.

While Phoebe was in the bath, I called Amber for a chat, which involved a moan about Matthew, a rant about Ruth and some pondering about Ed. She promised she'd accidentally-on-purpose spill a drink on Matthew and Jasmine if she ever saw them in town together, which made me feel better. Then she made me laugh, telling me about her new audition for an advert promoting indigestion tablets and the anguished faces she'd had to pull in front of the casting team. 'Could have been worse,' she said. 'My agent wanted to put me forward for the haemorrhoid-cream ad too, but they clashed, so I got to choose. Don't LAUGH!' she scolded, as I couldn't help a splutter of amusement. 'You wait, this will pay off one day, when I get snapped up for stardom.'

'Yeah,' I said. 'Absolutely. Any day now.'

When we'd finished chatting it was still quiet in the bathroom, so I grudgingly opened the CVs I'd received for the chef's job and flicked through them: *Mark Albury, aged fifty-five, previous catering experience: chef for some pub in Devon.*

Catherine Walcott, aged twenty-two, previous catering experience: none, but she'd been a waitress and she was a quick learner (smiley face and exclamation mark). Jason Grimshaw, aged thirty, previous catering experience: working in a chippy in Wadebridge. Vicki Groves, aged forty-two, previous catering experience: cooking for her four children and baking for the school PTA on numerous occasions.

I put my head in my hands, not feeling enthused about any of them. Mark Albury did have good experience, admittedly, but he seemed to have worked in about ten different places over the last decade. That wasn't a good sign, surely? Catherine Walcott had irritated me without even having met her, and would need complete training from scratch, which I didn't have the time or experience for. Then there was the chip-meister, and mumsy Vicki, neither of whom filled me with any kind of excitement. Hopefully some stronger applications would come through the post over the next week or so. Or maybe Ed would reconsider and . . .

I heard the bathroom door opening and light footsteps padding out. 'I'm down in the café,' I shouted, stuffing the letters into a folder.

Phoebe emerged, swamped in Jo's big red dressing gown, with her hair twisted up in a towel turban. 'That was so nice,' she said gratefully. 'Thank you.' Her face was pink and shiny, and she looked wholesome and healthy, as if she'd just showered after a stint of horseriding or gymnastics, rather than having been out on the streets for days on end.

'You're welcome,' I said. 'Um...' It was odd, being hostess to a complete stranger. What would Jo have done? Well, she'd have fed her for a start. 'What can I get you to eat?' I asked, prompted by this thought. 'Cheese toastie? Scrambled egg? Pasty?'

'Scrambled egg, please,' she said. 'Do you want me to help?'

'All right then,' I said, surprised at being asked. 'Come through to the kitchen and we'll do it together.'

I got her whisking the eggs while I slotted some bread in the toaster and melted butter in a pan. Then she poured in the eggs and I handed her a wooden spoon to stir them, while I buttered her toast. 'Scrambled eggs on toast is always easier with two people,' she said chattily while she stirred. 'It's kind of a rush, doing it all on your own.'

'It is,' I agreed, holding back from asking whom she usually made scrambled eggs with. Her mum, her dad, a sister? 'That looks perfect,' was all I said, eyeing the pan. 'Do you want to dish it onto the toast?'

I poured her some juice and we went back through to the seating area, where she dug into the food with gusto. There was colour in her cheeks now, and she looked a different creature from the bedraggled, pitiful girl who'd been outside with her sleeping bag. It still felt strange, sitting there with her, but at the same time I was sure I was doing the right thing, doing what Jo would have done.

'Nice?' I asked, watching her eat.

She nodded. 'Really nice,' she replied. 'Thank you for this, and for the bath. It's really kind of you.'

'You're welcome,' I told her.

I hesitated, wanting to tackle the big, unspoken subject of why she had been on the streets for God-knows-how-long and what her plans were, but I wasn't sure how best to go about it. I was pretty certain she wasn't going to make a bolt for the door like last time, especially now that she was in a dressing gown, but all the same I didn't want to make her feel backed into a corner and wary of me all over again.

'Listen,' I said. 'You don't have to tell me anything you don't want to, but ... what happened? How come you've been sleeping rough?'

She stopped chewing immediately and tensed up. Oh no. Had I blown it again?

She put down her knife and fork. 'Because I hate my mum,' she said sullenly after a moment. 'And I just...' Her eyes glittered with emotion, and a hard, defensive look came over her face. 'I'd just had enough.'

'Right,' I said, deliberately not asking anything else just yet. I was hoping she'd fill in the blanks for me.

'It's just — she's such a fucking *snob*,' she burst out. 'Sorry,' she added in a mutter. 'But she is. She has no idea.'

'So, what, you just walked out, did you? Had a row or something?'

'Yeah.' She scooped some more egg into her mouth and I thought that was all she was going to say, but then she carried on. 'We had a massive row because she didn't like the girls I've been hanging around with. She doesn't think they're good enough for me, or some crap like that. Well, they *are*. They're my *friends*. So . . .' She shrugged. 'We had a fight, and I just . . . ran away.'

'Wow,' I said. 'So I take it you're not from Cornwall, then.' I already knew she wouldn't be. There was a toughness about her, an edge, which made it clear she was a city girl.

She shook her head. 'London,' she said, still glowering.

'It's a long way to come,' I said. There was a moment's silence as if she was too polite to tell me I was stating the bleeding obvious. 'Have you spoken to your mum since you walked out?' I asked gently.

'No way,' she spat.

'So she doesn't know where you are?'

'Nope. Not a clue.' She seemed proud of the fact. Her chin was up, she was bristling, on the defensive.

I bit back all my other questions, not wanting to interrogate her too much. Not yet anyway. She looked as if she was on the verge of flouncing back out into the rain, dressing gown and all. 'Want anything else to eat?' I asked instead.

She shook her head. 'No. Thank you.'

'Well, I'm glad you came here,' I said, getting up and taking her empty plate. 'This café is a special place, you know. My aunt used to run it, and back when I was a teenager, and having all sorts of problems with *my* mum, and my so-called perfect big sisters, she took me under her wing and let me stay.'

Phoebe was staring at me anxiously, and I couldn't tell if she'd even listened to a word of my little speech. 'Evie, you're not going to ... phone the police about me or anything, are you?'

I paused. 'No,' I said finally. 'I'm not going to phone the police. But I do think it would be the right thing for you to phone your mum. You don't have to tell her where you are, but just let her know that you're safe, and that you're okay. She must be going out of her mind with worry. Don't you think?'

There was a silence. She was studying her nails with fierce concentration as if all the solutions to the world's problems had been encrypted on them, and she was the only person who could decipher the code.

'Think about it,' I urged. 'You don't have to do anything now, but just think about it, at least. Yeah?'

She nodded, still not looking at me. 'Yeah,' she said. 'I'll think about it.'

The following morning when I woke up, Phoebe had vanished again. I'd kind of expected it, to be honest; she was like the cat who walked by himself, not the sort to get too comfortable in a place and let her guard down. She'd left a paper napkin on the table with 'THANK YOU' written on it and some kisses. She'd also washed up and dried the dirty dishes from last night's scrambled egg, and left them tidily on the worktop. However much she loathed her mum, the woman had certainly brought her up to have good manners.

It wasn't raining now, so wherever she'd gone she wouldn't be getting cold and wet at least. I wondered if she'd be back again tonight, or if my nagging about her mum had put her off.

Still, I'd done my best. She'd been fed and watered, and she'd slept the night in a bed, with a roof over her head. I hoped the reminder of creature comforts might be enough for her to stop being so stubborn and patch things up with her family.

Martha came in at around eleven that morning, holding hands with Jamie, and I couldn't help comparing the two girls. Martha seemed so happy and chilled in contrast to prickly, vulnerable Phoebe. 'Hi there,' I said. 'Haven't seen you for a while. How's half-term going?'

Martha pulled a face. 'I've been revising for my exams all week, but Jamie persuaded me to STEP AWAY from the textbooks and get some fresh air.'

'I've got a day off from the pub,' he said, 'so I thought we'd hit the beach. Looks a good day for surfing – the waves are huge.'

'I noticed,' Rachel said longingly, butting in. Then she looked embarrassed. 'Sorry, that was really nosy of me, eavesdropping.' She smiled at them. 'I'm Rachel. Frustrated surfer. Jealous!'

'This is Martha and Jamie,' I said. 'Martha's Annie's daughter – you know, our cake lady? And Jamie's a fantastic artist who also works in the pub.'

'Ah, that's where I recognize you from,' Rachel said. 'The Fleece, right?'

'That's the one,' he said.

I made their coffees while the three of them chatted. 'What sort of art do you do?' Rachel asked, and Jamie started telling her about his paintings, his expression a mixture of enthusiasm for what he did and a 'been crushed' look about his eyes. He was still nursing his disappoint-ment about the exhibition being dropped, I thought sympathetically.

As I turned to set the coffees on the counter, I noticed – for what seemed like the hundredth time – the flaking paint on the nearest wall, and Amber's words came back to me. *You should do the place up. A lick of paint, some pictures on the walls* . . .

And in the very next moment an idea burst into my head. Such a good idea, and such a blindingly obvious solution, that I almost dropped the cup I was holding in excitement.

'Hey,' I said, interrupting him. 'I've just thought.' The words bubbled out of me in my enthusiasm to speak. 'Why don't we put up some of your work here in the café, Jamie? I've been thinking for ages that it needs brightening up, and I reckon your paintings would look wonderful in here. And if people want to buy them – even better!'

His mouth dropped open in surprise, and then he did a quick, sweeping glance around the room, as if imagining his artwork on the walls. 'Really?' he asked. 'Are you serious?'

'Of course I'm serious,' I said. 'It's a no-brainer! The café will look fab for having some cool paintings up. The customers will love it. And it'll be like you having your own private exhibition – for as long as you want.'

He didn't speak for a moment. He looked stunned, as if I'd just whopped him in the face with a menu.

'That would be amazing,' Martha said, clutching at his arm. 'How cool is that, Jay? Your own show, right here in the bay.'

'Awesome,' Rachel agreed. 'Local artist, local café — what's not to love?'

'If you wanted to, we could even open up one evening specially,' I said, the idea developing in my head as I spoke. 'Like a little launch party: you could get all your mates to come, your art teacher, whoever you want. We could have some nibbles and wine, make a real night of it. Hopefully sell some pieces, and then have the others on show over the summer. If that's all right with you, of course,' I added hastily, suddenly realizing that he still hadn't said anything.

He bit his lip and for a second I thought he might actually cry. 'Would you really do all that?' he asked in the end. 'Do you mean it?'

'Yes,' I said. 'Of course I mean it. I thought the picture at Annie and Martha's house was fantastic — I'd be honoured to have your work on my walls. And everyone deserves a break. It's really nice for me to be able to help you. If that's what you want.'

'Wow,' he said, and his face split with a broad grin. 'Oh wow, Evie, that sounds brilliant. Absolutely brilliant. I don't know what to say.'

'Say yes,' Martha prompted helpfully.

'Yes,' he said, laughing. 'Yes, yes, yes. And thank you. This could be really cool!'

I was grinning too. The delight on his face, the surprise and happiness he so clearly felt, made me in turn feel brilliant as well. 'Fab,' I said. 'Then let's do it. Have a think about what would be the best date for you, and we can make plans.'

They took their coffees, Jamie still looking rather dazed. 'Okay,' he said. 'I'll have a look at my shifts next week and get back to you. Thank you.'

They wandered away, Martha already flipping through a little diary and both of them leaning in to pore over its pages. I felt excited too: for Jamie, as well as for the future of the café. An evening menu, an art show – what else could I do here? I could hire out the space for local groups, evening classes, children's parties … All of a sudden the possibilities seemed endless. *This is only the beginning*, I thought happily, before turning to my next customer with a smile. 'What can I get you?'

It was another busy day, with lots of customers all wanting food. As ever, this was a double-edged sword – I was thrilled that we were so in demand, and that I was starting to recognize repeat customers who'd returned because they'd enjoyed our pasties, baguettes and cakes (hurrah!), but it was hard work too, and stressful trying to keep on top of the cleaning up as well as the constant stream of orders. I was also conscious that, as the employer of Rachel and Ed, I had to make sure they had regular breaks throughout the day. The last thing I wanted was to be running some kind of sweatshop where I worked my staff into the ground.

So with all that going through my head, when Phoebe walked into the café later that afternoon and began clearing dirty plates and cups from the tables without even being asked, I wasn't sure if I was more surprised or grateful. 'Hi,' I said, with some bemusement as she passed me on her way to the kitchen, her arms full of crockery. 'Um, what are you doing?'

She gave me a shy little smile. 'Just ... wanted to say thank you,' she said. 'For last night. And I've got nothing else to do, so I thought I might as well help. Is that okay?'

'Hell, yes,' I replied. 'Ed – the chef – will tell you what to do with that lot. There's a spare apron in the kitchen you can put on, to protect your clothes. Thanks, hon.'

'Okay,' she said, disappearing into the kitchen.

She was a total godsend that afternoon, Phoebe. She was sweet and polite to the customers, she worked tire-lessly, and she even helped behind the counter when Rachel went off for a break. At the end of the day I put an arm around her and hugged her. 'You're a superstar,' I said. 'Thank you. I think every café deserves a Phoebe.'

She laughed. 'I enjoyed it,' she said.

'Watch it,' Ed warned, overhearing. 'She'll be roping you in every day, if you start talking like that.'

'I don't mind,' she shrugged. 'It's not like I've got anything better to do.'

I looked at her consideringly. 'Well, we could use an extra pair of hands, to be honest,' I said. 'But I don't want to take advantage of you, so we'd have to work something out . . .' I bit my lip, my thoughts a muddle. I didn't even know how old she was, and whether I'd be breaking any employment laws by having her working for me. 'Let's talk about it later. Do you want to stay again, or have you got somewhere else to go?'

I saw Ed's eyebrows shoot up at this, and he glanced from me to Phoebe in surprise.

She nodded, looking up at me through her eyelashes. 'Do you mind?'

'No,' I replied. 'I don't mind. Although I hope you realize I'm going to be on your case about phoning your mum . . .'

'I thought you might say that,' she replied. I could see her weighing everything up, her face impassive as she thought. Then she nodded again. 'Okay. That's cool.'

'Yeah? You'll give her a ring?' I hadn't been expecting that.

'Yeah,' she said. 'I'm not going to tell her where I am,' she added quickly. 'Because I'm not going back, ever. But I will let her know I'm okay. Just so she's not freaking out about it.'

I gave her another hug. 'That's brilliant, Phoebe,' I said. 'Really brilliant, and really mature. I think you're doing the right thing.'

That evening, while Phoebe was upstairs phoning home, I sat down in the café with a pad of paper and pen. Encouraging Phoebe to reconnect with her mum had reminded me that I wanted to keep in touch with my surrogate boy, Saul, and I soon became engrossed in writing him a long, chatty letter, telling him all about the beach, and the café, and what I'd been doing here. *If you're ever in Cornwall on holiday with your mum or dad, do give them my address, as it would be lovely to see you again*, I wrote at the end. I was pretty certain that Matthew would never come down to this part of the country while I was in it – beach holidays weren't his thing, plus I knew damn well he'd give me a wide berth for fear of any embarrassing emotional scenes that might arise. As for Emily, Saul's mum, I wasn't sure what she would think of my letter, but I hoped she'd read between the lines and realize just how fond I was of her fabulous son, and that that would make it all right by her.

Phoebe came downstairs just as I was signing off *Lots of love, Evie*, and sat at the table next to me. 'Well?' I asked. 'How did it go?'

She shrugged. 'All right.'

'She was pleased to hear from you, though, I bet?'

She looked very small and young all of a sudden. 'She started to cry,' she told me, and her own bottom lip trembled momentarily as if she might burst into tears as well.

'Oh gosh,' I said, putting an arm around her. 'She must have been so worried.'

'She kept asking where I was and what I'd been doing, and said she'd been doing her nut she was so worried; that she'd reported me to the police as a missing person, and that I'd been on the news, and everyone had been out looking for me.' Her face crumpled up. 'And then she was sort of shouting at me, like she was really angry with me, and then saying sorry, and how much she loved me, and that she wanted me to come home . . .' She seemed shell-shocked. 'I didn't know what to say.'

'Well, she knows you're all right, that's the main thing,' I said. 'And you can think about everything else in time. How did you leave things at the end of the conversation?'

I noticed she was fiddling with a scrunched-up tissue in

her lap, and my heart gave a twist. She must have had a little sob upstairs on her own, poor thing. 'She asked me to come back and I said no,' she replied. 'And that was when she started crying and saying, "Please, please, please", and telling me she loved me.'

'That must have been a bit heavy,' I put in, seeing that her lip was going again.

'And then she asked if I would phone her again in a few days, so that she could make sure I was all right.'

'See, she *does* care,' I felt obliged to say. 'Did you agree to that?'

She nodded. 'I had to,' she mumbled. 'She was so upset. I've never heard her like that.' She shook her head, lost in thought. 'I can't believe there was something about me on *telly*. How weird is that?'

My arm was still around her and I gave her a squeeze. 'You must have known she'd be upset, you running away,' I said gently. 'Any mother would be the same. But it's just because she loves you so much, I'm sure.'

My mobile started ringing then. 'Talk of the devil,' I said, seeing my parents' number flashing up on the screen. 'Hi, Mum,' I said, answering. 'How are you?'

'Well, I'm fine, darling, but how are *you*?' she gushed. 'Ruth rang to say you were having a dreadful time with the café, that it had all been going horribly wrong, and that you were finding it a terrible struggle . . .'

Did she now. 'Mum, it's fine,' I tried saying, but she was in full flow, barely pausing for breath.

'Dad and I have been discussing it, and we don't want you to have a miserable time there this summer, especially if you've changed your mind about coming back to start your teaching degree. Which is another thing Ruth told us, so—'

'Mum, listen, it's really fine,' I said again, starting to feel exasperated. I ran my finger across my throat as if slitting it, and rolled my eyes at Phoebe, who giggled. She scribbled something on a paper napkin and skipped away. *It's just cos she loves u*, she'd written — my own words, parroted back at me.

I stifled a laugh. 'What's so funny?' Mum demanded. 'I don't think this is a laughing matter, Evie!'

'Oh, Mum, stop worrying,' I said affectionately. 'Honestly, I'm having a great time. Ruth's exaggerating, that's all. She caught me at a busy moment. You and Dad should come down for a visit, when you break up for the summer holidays. See for yourself how well the café's doing.'

The funny thing was, I meant every word of it, I wasn't just fobbing her off with a line. I really *was* having a good time now that I'd found my feet, and genuinely did want to show the café off to my parents, wanted to prove that I was actually making a success of something for once, despite their doom-laden predictions. I launched into descriptions of our upcoming evening menu, plans for Jamie's art exhibition, Annie's cakes and Ed's all-round brilliance. 'And we're bringing in a profit,' I said proudly. 'So there's nothing to worry about. How are you and Dad?'

As I listened to tales of Dad's gardening achievements and news about the dog's latest adventure, my own words about the café kept coming back to me. I'd come a long way in a short time, I realized, feeling a flush of pleasure and pride. And best of all, for the first time in my life I'd found a job and a way of living that I actually felt passionate about.

'Are you still there?' Mum asked, when I failed to respond properly to whatever domestic bombshell she'd just recounted.

'Yes,' I said, gazing out of the window and admiring the sunset, which was just like a peach melba, with its golden and raspberry-coloured streaks. 'I'm still here.'

I smiled to myself. *Still here.* I liked the sound of that.

Chapter Eighteen

The next day was Friday, and I was filled with a churning mixture of excitement and nerves about our dinner menu that evening. The order from the cash-and-carry had been delivered, we'd booked two-thirds of the tables, and Annie had promised to pick up some tea-lights and fresh flowers from Wadebridge, but I still had the feeling I'd forgotten something important.

'Have you contacted the local paper?' Rachel asked. 'You should invite them along. With a photographer, preferably, to try and drum up some publicity. Get in touch with the local radio station too, see if they'll give you a mention.'

'Ooh, that's a good idea,' I said.

She grinned. 'I used to work at a marketing agency, for my sins,' she confessed. 'Old habits die hard. I can write up a press release if you want and email it around?'

'Fantastic,' I said. 'Thanks, Rachel.'

Phoebe hadn't vanished at the crack of dawn today,

which I was pleased about. She was making herself useful again, wiping tables and clearing them, and loading and unloading the dishwasher, even wiping down the laminated menus when she ran out of other jobs to do.

'Menus!' I exclaimed, noticing what she was doing. 'I need to type one up for tonight.'

'I can do that for you,' she said, overhearing me.

'You should have a break,' I told her. 'I haven't seen you stop moving since we opened up. Go on, take yourself off to the beach with a drink. But thanks,' I said. 'You're a trooper – and you too, Rach. I don't know what I'd do without you both.'

Ruth, Tim and the kids came in and, miracle of the year, we weren't rushed off our feet at the time, so I was able to make a big fuss of them all and let them spend ages choosing their ice creams. I felt a flush of pride as I handed over the cones, and made drinks for Ruth and Tim. *I am capable, I am managing, look at me, just like a proper café owner*, I thought with a secret smile to myself. I hoped *this* would get reported back to Mum, after the scaremongering earlier in the week.

'Those cakes look amazing,' Ruth said, looking longingly at them.

'They are,' I told her. 'Annie's been making them – remember Annie, Jo's friend? They're as delicious as they look, and you know what they say...' I winked at her. 'Nothing has calories when you're on holiday.'

She laughed. 'I wish! But go on then, you've twisted my arm. A slice of that chocolate cake, please.'

'Better make that two slices,' Tim put in. 'We *are* on holiday, like you say, and we'll be back at the gym tomorrow.'

'Wise choice,' I said. 'You'll be glad you made that decision.'

The children all hugged me when they left – rather stickily, it had to be said, especially Thea, who insisted on kissing me repeatedly with her ice-creamy lips – and I was surprised to realize that I actually felt sorry to see them go.

'I'm down here all summer, so if you fancy coming back for another visit, you're very welcome,' I found myself saying. It had been the first time in my life that I'd ever invited Ruth anywhere. 'Mum and Dad are hopefully going to pop down soon too. I'm not sure what Lou's plans are for the holidays . . .'

'One more kiss, Aunty Weevie,' Thea demanded, turning her chocolatey face up in my direction. I obliged, feeling quite a lot of the chocolate transfer itself to me in a rather wet and smeary fashion.

'Hope I can see you again before too long, anyway,' I said.

'Yes, that would be lovely,' Ruth agreed. 'You are lucky, living here, Evie. I'm almost envious!'

I loved that 'almost', as if she couldn't quite bring herself to be fully envious. 'I am lucky,' I agreed. 'I'm having a really good time here now.'

She dabbed briskly at my face with a Wet Wipe, as if I were one of her children. 'Oh dear, sorry. Thea is the muckiest child on this planet.'

'Aunty Evie,' Isabelle said shyly, pressing herself against me. 'I want to have my own café at the seaside when I'm a grown-up lady, just like you.'

I gave her a squeeze. 'That would be wonderful,' I said, having a flashback to saying exactly the same thing to Jo, when I'd been around Izzy's age. 'We could be neighbours, couldn't we?'

Her eyes shone. 'Yes!'

They trooped off, with lots of waving and kiss-blowing, and I felt a warmth spread through me. For once, it had been as if Ruth and I were actually on an equal footing, rather than her looking down on me from her position on high as the 'success story' patronizing the 'screw-up'. There she had been with her family in my café, and nothing – absolutely nothing – had gone wrong. Her kids had liked coming in to see Aunty Evie, just as I'd always liked coming to see Jo. There was a nice symmetry about it, a continuity that pleased me. *When I'm a grown-up lady, just like you*, Isabelle had said, and for once I did feel grown-up, as if I'd passed some kind of test, after all the black-sheep years.

'How adorable,' Rachel said, smiling at me as Isabelle darted back for one last beaming wave through the window. 'And how cool, having an aunty who has her own beach café. Much boasting back at school, I reckon.'

Her words made me glow with pleasure. 'Do you think?' I asked. 'Fancy Isabelle saying she wanted to be like me when she grew up. No one's ever wanted to be like me — ever.'

'You're a role model now,' Rachel teased. 'Wouldn't you say, Pheebs?'

'A total role model,' Phoebe smiled, then she launched into the *Jungle Book* song. 'It's true-ooh-ooh, we wanna be like you-ooh-ooh . . .'

I elbowed her, laughing. 'Enough! Stop it,' I said, secretly loving every minute of it though. A role model! I would treasure Isabelle's remark for a long, long time, I knew that already. Being looked up to by my niece felt like the nicest compliment I'd had in ages.

That afternoon, once we'd closed the café and Rachel had left, Phoebe helped me cover the tables with some sweet red-and-white gingham tablecloths that I'd bought from the cash-and-carry, and then we dissected the bunches of flowers Annie had dropped off, making lots of smaller posies with just one or two flowers and some leaves, and putting them into stem vases. After that, I printed off the menus, set the tables with cutlery and tea-lights, hung some fairy lights around the counter and threaded another string along the balcony that enclosed the deck. Then I ran to get changed into a plain black shift-dress and bung on some make-up.

'What else do you want me to do?' Phoebe asked.

I smiled at her – my loyal, tireless new assistant. 'Phoebe, you don't have to do anything, love,' I said. 'You've worked your butt off all day. You can have your dinner here, as one of the guests, if you want. God knows you've earned it, all the work you've done.'

Her face darkened. 'I want to help,' she said stubbornly. 'Don't you trust me?'

'Of course I do!' I told her. 'I'm just saying, you don't have to. Don't feel you have to slave all day because you've stayed here a couple of nights.' I looked at her, standing there mulishly with her arms crossed over her chest. 'But if you really want to help—'

'I said I did, didn't I?'

'Then I'll give you some tables to waitress. That would be brilliant.' I wasn't sure why she was being so tetchy all of a sudden, when she'd been so eager to please for the rest of the day. I put a hand on her shoulder. 'Are you okay?'

'Yeah,' she muttered. 'It's just ... I don't want to be a burden.'

'You're not a burden,' I told her.

'It's been really kind of you letting me stay, but—'

'But what?' Then I got it, why she was being so uptight. 'Look, if you're worried I'm going to chuck you out on a whim, don't be – because I'm not. All right? You can stay all weekend, and if you pitch in and help, that's brilliant and I'll appreciate it. But you know that you can't stay with me forever, so –' I broke off. It was difficult, finding the right words. I didn't want to hurt her feelings or push her away, but at the same time I needed to be upfront and lay out the facts. 'So you need to start thinking ahead, making plans,' I told her. I softened, seeing the panicked look that appeared on her face. 'I'll help you, whether you decide to stay in Cornwall, or go home, but you've got to make some decisions. You can't just be on the run forever.'

She hung her head and said nothing.

'What's happening about school, for instance?' I asked. 'I don't even know how old you are, Phoebe. Are you going to stay on in education, or look for work, or claim benefits, or—'

'I don't know!' she cried. 'I don't know, all right?'

Just at that moment, Ed walked in and, with a sob, Phoebe ran past him and out through the door. I let out a groan. 'Aarrrgh,' I said, running my hands through my hair. 'I think I just handled that really badly.'

'What's going on? What's the story with her, anyway?' he asked.

I explained briefly, feeling wretched and useless. 'And now she's flounced off again, and...' I sighed. 'I know she's not my responsibility, but I just want her to be all right. She's so *young*. Too young to be living on her own down here. I wish she could sort things out at home, but...'

He glanced up at the wall clock and I followed his gaze. It was twenty to seven, and we'd be opening up before long. 'Leave her be,' he said. 'We've got too much to do here to start chasing around after her.'

'I know, but...'

'But nothing,' he said gently. 'Look, you've been really kind to her. You've been more generous than lots of people would have been in your position. She knows that. She also knows that what you said is right, that she does have to make some decisions and sort herself out. So put her out of your mind for now, and let's focus on tonight. This is a big night for us. We need to be on top form if we're going to make this work.'

I nodded. He was right. 'Come on, then,' he said. 'The clock's ticking. Have a deep breath, and let's get started.'

The first customers to arrive, just after seven o'clock, were Annie, Martha and Jamie, and as I ushered them in, I saw the café through their eyes, and felt a huge rush of pride. The tables looked so smart with their tablecloths and flower-filled vases, and the candles and fairy lights lent the room a soft, pretty glow. 'Isn't this wonderful?' Annie said, hugging me. 'Jo would have loved what you've done, Evie.'

'It's great,' Martha smiled. 'Really posh — like a restaurant!'

I winked at her. 'It'll be even posher with some paintings on the walls, right, Jamie?'

He grinned. 'None posher,' he said. 'By the way, is it all right if we have the show next Tuesday evening?'

'Sounds good to me,' I said. 'Will that give you enough time to invite everyone you want?'

'Yeah, plenty,' he said. 'Thanks again, Evie. I can't wait.'

I showed them to their table and gave them some menus, and then the next group of people arrived, and then the next. Rachel and I were soon busy taking orders, serving drinks and bringing out the starters. We were running as a BYO, so people had brought along their own bottles of wine for which we charged a small corkage fee. Soon the wine was flowing, the room was filling up and there was a pleasant buzz of conversation and low laughter, and the clink and scrape of cutlery.

More people arrived, some without having booked, meaning that it wasn't long before every single table was full, inside and out. Rachel and I were madly busy, hurrying from table to kitchen, from kitchen to table, fetching and carrying as fast as we could go.

It was hectic, and we were only just keeping on top of everything, but it was all good. Our customers seemed to be enjoying themselves, eating everything on their plates and telling me how delicious the crab pâté was, and how gorgeous the café looked, and asking if this was going to be a regular thing, opening in the evening, because they'd definitely be back, if so. And I was buzzing with adrenaline and happiness and pride, lapping it up, and loving being able to pass all the compliments on to Ed. In fact, I loved everything about the evening at that point. I loved bringing out the plates of amazing-looking food and hearing people saying, 'Oooh!' when I set them down. I loved having the backdrop of the sun setting into the sea as people ate and drank, and the sky gradually turning from pink to purple to navy. I loved the smells of the main courses mingling with the smells of perfume and aftershave. It gave me a kick that people had dressed up in evening clothes to come to my little café on the bay.

There was no sign of Phoebe, though. Every time I had to serve one of the tables outside on the deck, I found myself looking out for her on the beach, wondering where she'd gone. But then in the next moment I'd be asked for more bread, or for tomato ketchup, or another drinks order, and I'd have to snap out of my thoughts and hurry away again, back in waitress mode.

Then things started to go wrong, typically all at once. First somebody accidentally spilled their glass of wine over me, which wasn't a total disaster, but it wasn't the nicest sensation to feel red wine dripping into my shoes. Then, when I returned from cleaning myself up, there was a complaint about a steak not being cooked to the customer's taste, and I had to take it back. ('There's always one,' Ed muttered, tossing it into the frying pan and whacking up the heat.) Then Rachel dropped a salt shaker, sending a long white trail of salt across the floor, which had to be swept up, and then lots of people seemed to finish their main courses at the same time, and all needed their tables clearing and their dessert orders taking simultaneously.

I felt as if everyone was trying to catch my eye and beckon me over for different things, and was becoming more exhausted and stressed and ragged by the second. My feet were killing me, I could feel my face turning pink and the room felt hot, too hot. Two people came through the door just then – more people who hadn't booked – and I bustled over, all set to apologize that we were full, and could they come back later? Then I noticed that the taller, bulkier one had a large camera, which he was taking out of a bag, and the other had a notepad and pen. Oh, my goodness, was it really the local news guys? Had Rachel's press release actually worked?

'Hi, I'm Joe and this is Paul, we're from the *North Cornwall Gazette*,' the guy with the notepad said. He had a small, ratty sort of face with patchy brown hair and quick, interested eyes that seemed to take in everything. 'Is it okay if we get a few pictures?'

'Of course,' I said, trying to smooth my hair back into place, and hoping I still had some make-up left on. 'No problem. What sort of thing do you want?'

The cameraman – Paul – wanted a shot of the whole room, with everyone raising their wine glasses in his direction (miraculously, they all obliged), and then one of me, Rachel and Ed. 'Sure,' I said. 'I'll just drag him out of the kitchen.'

I hurried in to see him plating up some steaks and a snapper. 'Ed,' I said, 'some guys from the local paper are here. Could you come out for a quick photo?'

He glanced up at me. 'These are ready for table three,' he said, snatching another order and grabbing two more plates. 'Sorry, I'm too busy to do anything else right now.'

'It'll only be for a minute,' I told him, picking up the steaks and carefully balancing them, before taking the snapper. 'Please? The more pictures they take, the better chance there is of them using one, and the more space we'll get in the newspaper.'

He shook his head, stirring the risotto and ladling a steaming scoop of it onto a plate. 'Sorry,' he said again.

Frustrated, I delivered the food to table three, then went back to Paul, the cameraman. 'He's really busy in there,' I said. 'Can it just be a photo of me and Rachel?'

The cameraman duly clicked off a shot of us standing in front of the counter. I noticed several tables needed their plates clearing, while others had finished their drinks. *Hurry up*, I thought, becoming increasingly agitated. He seemed pleasant enough, but there was a slowness about him that put me on edge. Rachel obviously felt the same way, because she dashed back into the fray like a spring being released as soon as the cameraman thanked us.

'Could I take a snap of the chef in action, if he's too busy to come out?' Paul asked, and Joe nodded. 'That would be good,' he said. 'And maybe a quick interview, if you've both got a minute?'

'I'll see,' I said, heading towards the kitchen again, feeling slightly desperate at the sight of all the plates and glasses building up on the tables.

'Excuse me,' someone called, waving.

'Two minutes!' I promised, smiling and hoping it didn't look too much like a grimace. I stuck my head into the kitchen and realized that Paul and Joe had both followed me.

'All right, mate, can we just get a photo for the newspaper?' Paul asked, holding his camera to his face and lumbering towards Ed.

To my surprise – and, to be honest, my embarrassment – Ed flung up a hand in classic 'protecting myself from the paps' pose and swung round away from them. 'I said I was too fucking busy, all right? Not now!'

Blood throbbed in my face at his aggressive tone of voice. I couldn't believe he'd been so damn rude to these guys, when they were only doing their job – and, more to the point, when they were doing us a favour, coming out here in the first place. Didn't he care about the café? I'd thought he did, but maybe I'd got it wrong.

'Sorry,' I said, ushering them away. I tried to make a joke of it. 'You know how temperamental chefs can be. Listen, if I give you my email address, do you want to send some questions over and we can do the interview that way? Or on the phone later? It's just that we're quite busy . . .'

I sensed that ratty Joe in particular had had his interest piqued by Ed's show of temper. I could almost imagine a pair of whiskers twitching on his face, his nose trying to sniff out a story. 'Sure, whatever,' he said. His eyes narrowed and he glanced back towards the kitchen as if something was bothering him. 'Where do I recognize that guy from?' he muttered. He chewed the end of his pen and looked at me. 'What did you say his name was? Your chef?'

'Ed,' I replied, and then, because I knew he was going to ask Ed's second name and I didn't want to make even more of a prat of myself by replying that I didn't actually know (great boss I was), I added, 'Jones. Ed Jones.'

'Ed Jones, okay.' He scribbled it down. 'Doesn't ring a bell, but he's very familiar . . .'

'Can I get some service here?' someone called out. I spun round to see a red-faced man waving an empty glass in the air.

'I'll be right with you,' I said, my polite smile feeling more fake and fragile by the second. I was delighted that the local press had taken an interest in our opening night, of course, but I was now terrified they might write less than flattering things, having seen us at our most hectic (and rude, when you had Ed in the equation). I really wanted them to sod off now. Rachel was dashing back and forth like a blur, doing all the waitressing single-handedly and being generally amazing, but she couldn't manage on her own for much longer. Everything seemed to be hanging by a thread and we were only a split-second away from all-out disaster.

Then Phoebe walked in. 'Sorry,' she muttered as she

went past me. She washed her hands, put on an apron and promptly got stuck in, clearing away empty plates and glasses with efficiency and speed. I could have kissed her for her perfect timing, and for saving me from my own nervous breakdown, if it weren't for the fact that I still had the press guys standing next to me. 'Well, thanks for stopping by,' I said to them. 'I'd offer you a table for dinner, but we're actually fully booked right now. However, if you'd like to wait and sample the food, you'd be very welcome.'

'It's all right, love, I've got a date with the pub,' Joe said. He handed me a business card. 'Give me a ring about this interview, yeah?'

'Will do,' I said. 'And do take one of these menus, if you want to write about our range of food.' I thrust the printed paper into his hand before he could say no, and thankfully watched them leave. Yikes! What had just happened there, with Ed? It had been excruciating. I really hoped they wouldn't turn the article into a slagging-off, or just ditch the coverage altogether. Why had he been so rude to them, so belligerent?

Still, no time to think about that now. My customers needed me, and I had to whizz round and take orders for desserts and coffees, before anyone had a chance to complain about slow service. 'Thanks,' I said to Phoebe as we passed each other. 'You're a life-saver.'

With Phoebe, Rachel and me on board, we were soon back on top of things, and then the first diners had finished, and were paying and, joy of joys, leaving big fat tips. 'That was delicious,' Annie said, hugging me as she pressed some notes into my hand.

I deliberately hadn't given her a bill, so I tried to return the money. 'Oi,' I said. 'Yours was meant to be on the house, as a thank-you for your amazing baking. Have this back.'

'No,' she said. 'Absolutely not. You've earned every penny of that. We've had a lovely night.'

'Thank you,' I said. 'I'm glad. And thanks for coming.'

'I'll drop in tomorrow, so we can chat about Tuesday,' Jamie said.

'Definitely,' I told him. 'Look forward to it. Bye.'

Other people left and new people arrived to fill the tables all over again, but I was starting to feel more relaxed, as if we were into the swing of things now. As fast as a table was cleared, it was relaid with clean cutlery and menus, and we managed to keep abreast of the orders. And then, all of a sudden, I realized I was actually enjoying myself again, feeling upbeat about the evening after a few hair-raising moments had threatened to derail the whole thing.

Okay, so maybe I was biased, but it did seem as if everyone was having a good time: every table deep in conversation, lingering over coffees and last glasses of wine, as the sky turned completely black outside. It struck me how lucky we were that it had been a warm, still evening, meaning that diners could eat outside on the deck. If it had suddenly started raining when we'd been full, there would have been no means of shelter out there, and no room for them to come inside. The situation could quite easily have descended into utter farce. I giggled in horror, imagining the awful scenes that might have taken place, and sent up a grateful little prayer to the god of café owners, thanking him or her for keeping my customers dry.

By eleven o'clock we were done, and the four of us collapsed into a booth, knackered but exultant. 'Brilliant,' I said, high-fiving them all, aware that my face was shiny, my dress still smelled of wine, and my hair was all but standing on end from where I'd been running my fingers through it in moments of stress. I didn't care in the slightest, though. 'Absolutely brilliant! You all played a blinder — everyone had such a great night.' I couldn't quite bring myself to look at Ed. I still wasn't sure what to make of his outburst to the press. I mean, yeah, everyone knew that chefs were prone to diva-like behaviour, but honestly. It was only the *North Cornwall Gazette*, for heaven's sake, not some sleazy gossip rag trying to stitch us up, or run a damaging exposé.

'Whew,' Rachel said, letting her heels fall off with a thunk-thunk to the floor and wiggling her toes. 'We did it. No dramas, no disasters. And a visit from the local press – how cool is that?'

'Yeah,' I said, still not catching Ed's eye. 'That was really ... cool. I just hope I don't look too manic in that photo.'

'What photo?' Phoebe asked. She had gone very pale. 'For the newspaper?'

'Yeah,' I told her, then realized she was probably freaking out that her mum might get to see it and track her down. 'But don't worry, they left just after you arrived.'

'Well, all in all, I think this evening calls for a celebratory something,' Ed said, getting to his feet and loping into the kitchen.

'Good on ya!' Rachel shouted after him, and grinned at Phoebe and me. 'I'm always up for a celebratory something.'

'I hope it's the rest of that toffee pudding he's bringing out,' Phoebe said, licking her lips. 'That looked totally yum, didn't it?'

I smiled at her, but said nothing. I wished I could be as exuberant as they were. Yes, I felt triumphant that the evening had gone well on the whole, but I was too discomfited by Ed's strange behaviour to chill out totally and enjoy our success. Still, now that Phoebe had mentioned the pudding, I realized I quite fancied some too. I was absolutely famished.

I kicked off my shoes and tucked my feet up under me on the seat, hoping to force myself into a better mood. 'Toffee pudding would hit the spot,' I said. 'I've been ravenous all evening – I was too nervous to eat before we opened up, and the smell of all that amazing food has just been . . .'

My voice trailed away as I saw that Ed was re-emerging with a bottle of bubbly and some glasses.

'Oh Ed,' I said, touched by the gesture. 'Is that what I think it is?'

He nodded, his eyes seeking out mine, a slight anxiety about his gaze, as if he knew that he'd pissed me off. 'Do you mean, is this the finest cava that Betty's shop can manage? Yes,' he replied. 'You bet it is. I thought we all deserved a treat after that.' He glanced at Phoebe. 'Well, those of us who are old enough, that is.'

'I reckon she could have a small glass,' I decided. 'What do you say, Pheebs?'

She smiled. 'Sounds great.'

Ed poured the foaming fizz into the tall champagne glasses he'd unearthed and we all held them up together. 'To the four of us,' I said. 'For making the Beach Café's first evening venture such a success. Thank you and cheers!'

'Cheers!' everyone chorused.

'And to Evie,' Ed added. 'For being a great boss, and a great person.'

'CHEERS!' Rachel and Phoebe chimed in, clinking their glasses against mine.

Tears rushed to my eyes. It was silly to get so emotional, I knew, but no one had ever called me a great boss before. I wasn't even sure if anyone had ever called me a great person, either, come to think of it. Mind you, I thought in the next breath, he was probably just trying to butter me up, apologize for what had happened – and if that was the case, platitudes weren't quite good enough.

'Aw, shucks,' I said. 'Well, because I'm a so-called great boss, I'm going to insist we all finish tonight's leftovers. I, for one, am having me a bit of that sticky toffee pudding. I reckon it will go perfectly with this bubbly. Who's joining me?'

By the time we'd sunk the bottle of cava and worked our way through the leftover crab pâté and French bread, mushroom risotto, salad and puddings, it was nearly midnight, and we were all flagging. 'We'll open a bit later tomorrow,' I decided. 'Is ten-thirty all right for everyone?'

'Cool,' said Rachel. 'Sounds good to me.'

Rachel and Phoebe took the dishes and glasses away, and Ed cleared his throat. 'You're probably wondering why I overreacted to those journalists,' he said awkwardly.

'Well, yes, you could say it had crossed my mind,' I replied.

'I'm sorry I lost my temper with them,' he said. 'I've had a few run-ins with the press before, and don't trust any of them.'

'Ed,' I said, exasperated, 'they're from the *North Cornwall Gazette*, not the *News of the World*. They just wanted a photo and two lines from you that they could put in the article. It was a really good publicity opportunity, but...'

'I know,' he said. 'And I'm sorry. It's just—'

Frustratingly, before he could finish his sentence Rachel reappeared, slinging on her jacket, and he fell silent. 'Well, I'm off,' she said. 'Ed, d'you mind walking me back to the main street? There's no moon tonight, and it's totally black out there.'

'Sure,' he said. The perfect gentleman.

I said goodnight to them both, feeling more baffled than ever. Why had Ed had 'run-ins' with the press previously? What was his story?

I locked up after they'd gone and realized that Phoebe was hanging around, looking rather self-conscious, the smile no longer on her face. Oh God, was she hoping to have a big Life Chat now? I wasn't sure if I could cope with any more high drama tonight.

'Let's hit the sack,' I said, pre-empting her. 'We'll have a talk tomorrow, okay?'

'Okay,' she said quickly, sounding relieved. 'And, Evie – I'm sorry I stormed out earlier.'

'No worries,' I told her. 'I'm glad you decided to come back. You were a massive help this evening. We couldn't have done it without you.'

'That's okay,' she said. 'I'm going to bed then. Goodnight.'

'Goodnight, Phoebe.'

I couldn't get to sleep immediately once I shut my eyes in the darkness of my bedroom. I was so revved up from the mad long adrenaline rush of the last four or five hours, and so stuffed with leftover food, that I felt too wired to doze off, and my mind kept replaying all the details over and over again. It had been knackering and stressful at times, but overall I'd really enjoyed it, and so too had the customers it seemed. I felt proud of myself and my little team for pulling it off. We did it! But what the hell had happened with Ed? Really – what had all that been about?

I had to get some straight answers from him, I decided. I had to just pin him down and get the truth out of him. Who was he, and why did he keep acting so suspiciously?

Chapter Nineteen

Saturday was cool and cloudy, and the beach was deserted compared with how crammed it had been the previous week. I guessed that lots of families had gone home, with work and school starting the following Monday.

It felt rather like clearing up after a house party, taking down the fairy lights and putting away the candles and vases from the night before. I bundled up the tablecloths to go into the washing machine, while Phoebe collected all the used menus. 'What do you want me to do with these?' she asked. 'Bin? Or will you use them again next week?'

I bit my lip. Would there even *be* an evening opening next week? I wasn't sure I'd still have Ed in my kitchen then, and I doubted I'd have hired anyone new to replace him, either. 'Bin,' I said after a moment. 'Oh, but ... maybe just keep one, as a souvenir.'

The café seemed plain and unadorned once again after we'd removed all its frippery and trimmings, like a party girl waking with a hangover and pasty skin. I was glad more than ever that we'd have Jamie's paintings on the walls soon; seeing the place dressed up for the evening had made me realize how tatty around the edges it was in broad daylight. Some striking pieces of art would be the perfect distraction from the tired old paintwork elsewhere.

Ed and Rachel arrived within minutes of each other just before ten o'clock, so I didn't get the chance to press Ed on his strange behaviour and rudeness towards the press guys. He seemed in a subdued mood anyway, not up for the usual banter, and kept himself to himself. Perhaps I was being unfair on him, I thought. Perhaps I had been expecting too much. He was only helping me out for a week or two, after all – it wasn't like he was an equal partner in the business, or had any long-term interest in it. Why should he care if some guys from the local rag had showed up? No skin off his nose what they wrote.

But ... all the same. We were mates, weren't we? You didn't shaft a mate when they were getting a lucky break from the media, did you?

I tried to put it out of my head and act normally, but I felt that things were strained between us, as if it was on his mind, too. It was annoying, as well, when he'd seemed as if he was about to explain himself last night, until Rachel had interrupted our conversation. What had he been about to say? And would he attempt to say it again if he got the chance today?

Jamie and Martha dropped in that morning to discuss Jamie's forthcoming art show, and we sat down with coffees and a notepad to formalize everything. 'Lindsay, the landlady at the pub, says she'll donate some wine,' he told me, 'and Annie says she'll make a load of cakes too. The only thing is . . .' He shifted uncomfortably. 'I'm worried that there's nothing in this for you. I mean, do you want to charge people to come in, or can I give you a cut of the paintings that are sold, or . . . ?'

'Oh,' I said blankly. 'I hadn't even thought about that. No, you don't need to give me any commission – they're your paintings.' I felt awkward myself then. 'Jamie, I didn't suggest this because I wanted to make any money out of you. I just wanted to help.'

'I told you,' Martha said to him.

He smiled sheepishly. 'Thanks,' he said. 'I really appreci-ate it.'

'And I *am* going to have the coolest paintings on my walls, remember,' I told him. 'That's what I get out of this: some funky artwork livening up the café. That's good enough for me.'

Ed left as usual at about three – 'dog o'clock' as he called it – and I watched him lope away, feeling frustrated. We hadn't managed to speak properly all day and now he'd gone. By tomorrow I was sure it would feel too late to pick up the threads of the photographer-meltdown conversation again.

The sun came out at around four, and suddenly the beach was bathed in beautiful golden light, yet still it and the café remained quiet. A few customers had dropped by for cake and coffee, but the pace felt laid-back and easy after the frantic rushing around of Friday night. I wiped down the tables in a leisurely fashion while Phoebe and Rachel chatted behind the counter.

'I'm definitely going for a swim after work today,' I heard Rachel say as they both gazed out at the glittering water. 'Look at that, mate. A proper beach, that is. Almost as good as the ones in Oz.'

'A swim would be good,' Phoebe said, with a trace of longing in her voice. 'I haven't swum in the sea for ages.'

'Well, come with me, then,' Rachel said. 'Fancy it?'

'Yeah, but . . .'

I glanced up to see Phoebe's troubled expression. 'I don't have a cozzie,' she said after a moment. 'And don't suggest skinny-dipping, cos that is so not going to happen.'

Rachel laughed. 'You can borrow my flatmate Gina's,' she said. 'She's tiny like you, and she won't mind a bit. Come over to our place after work and I'll fix you up.'

Phoebe beamed. 'Cool!' she said.

I straightened up, one hand on my back. 'We can call it a day now, if you want,' I suggested. 'We're not busy, and you did both bust a gut for me last night. Go on, you two have your swim, make the most of the sun. I can manage here.'

Phoebe looked all giggly and excited at the thought of leaving with cool surfer-chick Rachel, and they were only too pleased to say goodbye and head off. The last customers left, and I closed up, enjoying being able to call the shots and finish early. Now what to do, though? I turned the sign on the door to 'Closed', then hovered there for a moment, staring out at the beach. It did look wonderful down there, the most exquisite afternoon sunshine drenching everything in clear golden light, like a picture postcard, or the perfect photograph.

Then I smiled, knowing exactly what I wanted to do.

Half an hour later I was on the cliff path looking down at the beach through the viewfinder of my trusty old camera. Jo had given me this camera when I was twenty-five, and for a couple of years after that it had been practically a permanent fixture in my hand. It was an old-fashioned Leica that Jo had picked up second-hand (they didn't come cheap), but I hadn't realized just how good a piece of kit it was until the first photos had come back from the chemist's with every image sharp and clean, the colours bright and true. After that I was hooked, and began documenting every important event of my life: birthdays, weddings, holidays, the changing of the seasons, anything that caught my eye in fact.

I had a skinny silver digital camera too, which Matthew had given me a few Christmases ago, but I still preferred the black bulk of the Leica in my hand, the old-fashioned rolls of film and that crystal-clear viewfinder, through which I had seen so many sights. It was old-fashioned and unsexy to all but the camera buffs of the world. I loved it.

I took some shots of the bay, then wandered further around the headland, crouching near the cliff edge to click off a few frames of the sea below as it dashed and foamed against the rocks. Now that I had my back to the bay, there wasn't another person in sight – just me and my camera, and the salty wind tugging at my hair. It was wild and deserted up here, with scratchy, coarse grass and scrubby-looking gorse, which had been battered by the wind into strangely flattened shapes. I found my barren surroundings dramatic and beautiful, especially when you could turn one hundred and eighty degrees and be faced by the bustling village of Carrawen and the golden, shining beach by contrast.

I wriggled onto my belly, propping myself up on my elbows to get the angle of the shot right, concentrating hard on catching the exact moment when the waves exploded against the cliff wall. There!

'Not about to chuck yourself in, are you?'

The voice gave me such a start that I almost dropped the camera into the sea. I whipped my head around, and saw that Ryan was standing behind me, one eyebrow cocked, a lazy sort of smirk on his face.

'Oh God,' I said, getting up inelegantly, caught off-guard by his sudden appearance. 'You nearly gave me a heart attack. What are you doing up here?'

'I saw your note,' he said, still with that smirky leer. 'The one you left on the door?'

'The one I left on the ... Oh,' I said. I'd scrawled a note for Phoebe – *Gone for walk on cliffs, come and find me!* – in case she got back before I did, not wanting her to be sitting around locked out for ages. But why the hell would Ryan think the note was intended for *him*? And why had he come to the café in the first place? 'That note was for ... Never mind.'

'So here I am,' he said, not seeming to have heard. 'Back in our special place, just me and you.' He took a step nearer, his eyes roaming suggestively over my body, and I was about to step back in horror when I remembered that I was near the edge of the cliff. I dodged sideways instead. Oh God, talk about getting the wrong end of the stick. Yes, this *had* been our special place once upon a time, as had all sorts of deserted beauty spots around here, but surely he didn't think for a minute that my note was some kind of come-on, to *him? Gone for walk on cliffs, come and find me!*

Oh, man. Perhaps if you were as self-obsessed and as much of a jerk as Ryan seemed to be these days, then you *would* take it as a nod and a wink and a lick of the lips. But he had got it so badly wrong, I didn't know where to begin.

'Ryan, the note wasn't for you,' I said, wanting to clear this up fast, before it could escalate any further. 'It was for a friend – a female friend who's staying with me.'

'I still have happy memories of those days,' he said, not listening apparently. He was drunk, I could smell the alcohol on his breath. His eyes were bloodshot, and there was a dirty mark on the front of his polo shirt, as if he'd spilled his lunch down himself. 'Me and you together, our own summer of love. Remember?'

Yikes, he was starting to freak me out. I wished it wasn't so lonely and deserted up here. There was a glint in his eyes that made me think he wanted to re-enact our so-called summer of love right here, right now – about as repulsive an idea as it was possible to have.

I glanced at my watch. 'I'd better get back,' I said casually, hoping he couldn't hear the giveaway thump of my heart. 'Nice to see you again anyway.'

He blocked the path and took hold of my wrist. 'Wait,'

he said. His fingers were pudgy, but he had a strong grip. There was a coldness about him, as if I'd offended him, and I suddenly felt afraid. This clifftop, which had seemed so tranquil and beautiful just minutes earlier, now seemed a place of potential danger. 'We haven't finished talking yet.'

Adrenaline ricocheted through me and my heart thudded to a faster beat. I tried to yank my arm away, but he held on. 'Let go of me,' I said firmly, as if I was speaking to a naughty child. 'I mean it. Let go of me right now. Or … or I'll tell Marilyn.'

He laughed. 'Tell her what? That you lured me up here with your little note, that you—'

'Ryan, let go,' I said louder, trying again to wrest my hand from his grasp. 'That note wasn't for you, I didn't lure you anywhere.' I was dimly aware of crunching footsteps approaching along the path, and I raised my voice until it was a shout. 'LET GO OF ME!'

He dropped my hand. 'All right, no need to—'

'What's going on? Evie, are you okay?' It was Ed, rounding the corner and hurrying over, with Lola at his side.

I sagged with relief, my knees not seeming able to support me any longer. 'Hi,' I said stupidly. Lola bounded up to me and pushed her nose into my hand, her body warm against my bare legs, her tail wagging in delight.

'Are you all right?' Ed asked again, glowering at Ryan as if he was about to swing a punch. 'I thought I heard shouting.'

'Yeah,' I said. 'I think Ryan here got the wrong end of the stick. I think . . .' I swallowed, trying to recover myself. 'No harm done.'

'Are you sure?' Ed asked, still glaring at Ryan. He was all but squaring up to the man. 'Because if I hear you've been messing about with Evie . . .'

Ryan put his hands up, all innocence. 'I haven't done anything,' he blustered, glancing sideways at me. Then he licked his lips, looking nervous all of a sudden. 'You won't really tell Marilyn, will you? She'd kill me if—'

'No,' I said, my fear of him draining away. He was pathetic. A sleazy, overweight creep whose wife had him by the *cojones*. 'Just go away, Ryan.'

He put his head down and shambled off. The whole episode felt surreal – him clutching at me, me yelling at him – and it had been so sudden and so peculiar that already it seemed as if it hadn't really happened, that I'd dreamed the entire thing. 'Bloody hell,' I said, light-headed with what might have been. Nothing too serious had happened, but what if Ed hadn't come around the corner just then? The way Ryan had gripped my wrist had been uncomfortably hard; I didn't like to think what his next move might have been.

'That looked a bit full-on,' Ed said, his eyes on me. 'What the hell was he doing?'

I explained about the note and Ryan's obvious misinterpretation, and how the situation had just started turning nasty. I shivered. 'Was I glad to see you turn up, Ed,' I said. Then I stopped myself, realizing I'd been here before. Damsel in distress, being rescued by a bloke: it was Matthew and the elf dress all over again. What was wrong with me that I ended up in these ridiculous situations?

I shook myself briskly. I didn't need rescuing again. It was independence all the way for me, from now on, end of story.

'So, what brings you up here anyway?' I asked, forcing a change of subject. I didn't want to talk about how vulnerable I'd felt two minutes earlier, how panicky I'd been. 'Is this where you and Lola come for your walkies?'

He grimaced. 'Well, we do sometimes, but I was actually looking for you. I saw Pheebs and Rachel down on the beach and wanted to catch you for a chat in private. About last night. I know I've got some explaining to do.'

Last night? My mind went blank. Oh, of course, *last night*! It seemed so long ago now that the journalist had been sniffing around, and that Ed had all but pushed him out the kitchen. 'Yeah,' I said slowly. 'You do really, don't you?'

Standing up on the clifftop seemed the wrong place to

be having this conversation, though. Anyone could wander along and interrupt; I didn't want Ed to be put off again. 'Why don't we go back to the café and talk about it there,' I suggested. I pointed at the camera. 'I promise I won't try and take a photo of you.'

He smiled weakly at my rubbish joke. 'Good idea,' he said, whistling to Lola, who'd gone to sniff at a rabbit hole. 'Let's do it.'

We wandered back together, and he began asking about my camera and what I'd been taking photos of up on the cliffs. We got into a conversation about photography, and the type of pictures we both liked best, and by the time we'd got back to the café he was offering to give me surfing lessons if I gave him photography lessons. I agreed, laughing, because I knew it wouldn't really happen, that it was one of those stupid things you went along with at the time. Besides, he was only here a few weeks longer, wasn't he, while he was dog-sitting. I had a sudden pang at how much I would miss him when he left Carrawen, and stopped laughing abruptly.

Nevertheless, the awkwardness from earlier had melted away by now, and it felt as if we were mates again. My note was still on the café door, but there was a new line written underneath it – *Gone to Rachel's becos her mate is making us curry! She says you are welcome too!* – in Phoebe's rounded, girlish hand, followed by an address.

I smiled. 'She's sweet, isn't she?' I said, taking down the note and unlocking the door. 'Come on in. Fancy a drink?'

A brief chat over a glass of wine, that was what I'd envisaged, followed by an early night and nine hours' sleep. But no. As I was pouring the wine, Ed asked something about my sisters, and then somehow or other we ended up having this whole conversation about siblings and families, which turned into stories from childhood, through to embarrassing teenager anecdotes, and then more widely, on to stuff like music and books and films. By now, of course, I had completely forgotten the point of him coming here, and that he hadn't actually explained his odd behaviour the night before. He seemed to have forgotten too. It was only when I was trying to persuade him that *Grease* was a way better film than *Citizen Kane*, for oh, so many reasons, that we realized we'd sunk two bottles of wine and were both ravenous. How had that happened?

'I'll make us something if you like,' he said, getting to his feet and lurching rather unsteadily towards the kitchen. 'What do you fancy?'

The dog lifted her head drowsily from where she'd dozed off under the table and watched him go. I was watching him too, but for some reason my eyes had gravitated to his bottom. What did I fancy? Um...

'Anything,' I replied, dragging my gaze away and blinking hurriedly. What was wrong with me? I was as bad as Colin the Human Slimeball, perving after my own chef. 'A piece of toast or something. A sandwich,' I said, following him into the kitchen. Gawd, I thought, as I bashed my hip on the doorway, unable to walk in a straight line. I was kind of squiffy, it had to be said.

He gave me a look. 'Is that what you usually have for dinner: a piece of toast?' he asked. 'Don't tell me you've got this great big kitchen, with every utensil a chef could ever desire, and all you make yourself is *toast*?'

I shrugged guiltily. 'Yeah,' I admitted. 'Sometimes with cheese on top,' I added, as if that made it all right.

He rolled his eyes heavenwards. 'What are you like?' he laughed. 'God!'

But then he caught my gaze and everything went a bit strange, as if we couldn't stop looking at one another. He was smiling at me, his eyes crinkling at the edges, and it was so full-on all of a sudden that my insides turned swimmy and I started to worry I was going cross-eyed.

'What *are* you like?' he repeated softly and reached a hand to my face, his fingers just caressing my skin with their tips.

A shiver rippled through me and my heart seemed to stop beating. And then he leaned forwards and kissed me, his arm encircling me so that I was pulled in against him.

His lips were soft and I shut my eyes, and then the blood was rushing around my face, pulsing beneath my skin, and my heart *was* beating after all – it was pounding in fact – and I could hardly breathe because it felt so good and so natural to be kissing him, right there in my kitchen . . .

Then he drew away, looking agonized. 'Oh God, I'm sorry, Evie,' he said. 'I shouldn't have done that. I'm really sorry.'

'No,' I said, grabbing his hand, 'don't be sorry.' I was about to tell him how much I'd been enjoying it – and hell, let's just carry on with that kissing thing – but the words died in my throat as I noticed how mortified he looked, as if kissing me had been a truly terrible idea. Maybe it had been a truly terrible *experience* for him too, I couldn't tell from his expression. Either way, he was clearly regretting it, big time.

I looked at the floor. 'You're probably right,' I said miserably. 'We're both a bit tipsy. Got carried away.'

'Yes,' he agreed. He cleared his throat. 'That's right. I know you've just come out of a relationship, and . . . and so have I. Not the best time for either of us.'

It was news to me about his relationship, but I tried to look nonchalant. 'We're as bad as each other,' I said breezily. 'Rebounding all over the place like a couple of . . . of . . . balls.' I cringed at the terrible choice of word. 'Well, not *balls* as in *balls*,' I said, then groaned. 'Oh God,

345

Evie, just shut up. Sorry,' I garbled. 'Drunk and lost the plot, that's me. But anyway. No more kissing – I get it. Not practical, if we're both going to work together. So . . .' I closed my eyes, wishing with every ounce of my being that a kindly relationship-god might come to my rescue with a lightning bolt, or an earth tremor, or some other distraction. Unfortunately not.

'I probably should make a move,' he was saying. 'Home, I mean', as if there was any danger I might think he meant making a move on *me*.

'Yeah,' I agreed, nodding far more vigorously than I needed to. 'Home. Of course. Don't worry about the toast, I'll make my own. Oh!' I had just remembered about the explaining he was meant to have done – his whole reason for coming back and having a drink in the first place. I shook the thought out of my head. I wasn't going to ask him about all that now, I decided. That could wait for another day. Right now I wanted him to go, so that I could be on my own and get my head around the fact that we'd just had the most erotic kissing session I'd ever had, right here in this kitchen.

'Oh?' he prompted.

I gave him a super-fake smile. 'Nothing,' I said. 'I'll see you tomorrow.'

I stayed in the kitchen while he left with Lola, then cradled my head in my hands and let out a gigantic groan.

It was the damsel-in-distress thing that had kicked this all off, it had to be. I must have some faulty wiring somewhere in my brain that was causing these mad, lusty feelings to course through my body whenever somebody rescued me from a perilous situation. Either that, or I was far too drunk for my own good and needed to go to bed.

I made myself some toast while I thought about it, the feeling of his body against mine still making me tingle all over.

Chapter Twenty

I woke up the next morning feeling embarrassed and slightly sick that I'd kissed Ed during a mad Pinot moment. *What are you like?* he'd said in that teasing, affectionate way. It was a good question. What *was* I like, getting into a drunken clinch with him at the drop of a hat. Matthew hadn't even crossed my mind until Ed had broken away and started mumbling about us both being on the rebound. I'd been too engrossed in that kiss, the sudden leap of blood I'd felt, the excitement that had fluttered up through me. Not him, though. His thoughts had turned to his ex, whoever the hell she was. I wondered if she was the reason he'd run off to Cornwall in the first place. Had she broken his heart? He'd said something about wanting to get away from London, back when Amber and I had first spoken to him in the pub, hadn't he? Typical. The first decent kiss I'd had in ages, and it was with a guy who was clearly hung up on his ex. No wonder he'd left in such a hurry last night; probably couldn't wait to get away from me.

Ten minutes after he'd left the door had opened again, and my spirits had soared — he'd come back! — but it was only Phoebe, of course. Thankfully she'd been so full of tales of swimming and curry, and Rachel's cool backpacker flatmates, that she hadn't noticed the flush on my cheeks or the slightly deranged look in my eyes. I'd made my excuses and crawled off to bed, where the kiss had swum around and around in my head, even making its way into my dreams, where it had developed into a full-blown X-rated scene, with clothes flying off in all directions, and ... well, you get the picture.

And now it was the cold light of day, and Ed and I were due to work together again in just a couple of hours. That was going to be ... interesting. I would need to resurrect all my old acting skills if I was going to get through the shift without giving away how I felt about him now.

I sat up and pulled on my dressing gown, not quite sure how I *did* feel about him now. I had wanted to kiss him (and the rest), and found him attractive, and funny, and *nice*, but ... It was complicated. Too complicated to think about coherently with a hangover, that was for sure. Anyway. These things happened. We were both adults and could get over it. Right?

Ed gave me a look when he came into work that morning — a swift, searching, are-we-cool? sort of look — to which

I responded with a quick, business-like smile, hopefully conveying the message: *You bet we are cool, never been cooler, cool as the coolest cucumber, that's me.* We were busy in the café that day, without a lot of downtime to chat, so there wasn't the ideal moment for either of us to refer to what had happened in any greater depth. This was probably for the best, I figured. I mean, nobody likes those excruciating kinds of conversation, do they? We'd already done the *Oops. Sorry we kissed. Shouldn't have done* thing. I didn't want him to go on about what a mistake it had been, all over again. Because, in all honesty, it hadn't felt much of a mistake to me at the time. It had felt really lovely.

At the end of the Sunday shift I gave Rachel and Ed their wages, making sure that Rachel had her tips from Friday night. 'The café will be closed tomorrow,' I said. 'We all need a day off. So I'll see you both on Tuesday morning, okay?'

'A day off!' Ed said teasingly. 'What are you going to do with yourself?'

'I have no idea,' I replied. 'Get on the beach and work on my tan, hopefully. I'm pale as anything, being in here all week. And actually...' I swallowed. I had to be honest with him, lay all the cards on the table. 'I've got some job applications that I should look through too. People who want to take the chef's job here.' I plastered on a false, bright smile. 'So you won't have to put up with working with me for too much longer, you'll be glad to hear.'

'Oh,' he said. He looked hurt, which I hadn't been expecting. I hoped he didn't think I was booting him out because of the kiss. I so *wasn't*. If anything, the kiss had made me want him to stay even more. He rolled his eyes. 'Oh well, thank God for that,' he said jokily. 'It's been a nightmare.'

There was a rather strained silence. 'You did say you only wanted to be here a week or two, didn't you?' I said, just to be certain.

'Yeah, absolutely,' he replied. 'I'm sure you can find someone much more suitable than me, someone who won't bite journalists' heads off or—'

'I'm sure we *won't* find anyone better than you,' I told him. 'But needs must, and all that.'

'Right,' he said stiffly. 'Well, enjoy your head-hunting then. See you Tuesday.'

'See you Tuesday,' Rachel echoed, waving a hand. 'And thanks for the money. I'll try not to spend it all in the pub tonight.'

I watched them go, feeling as if Ed had completely misread me. Surely he didn't think I wanted to get rid of him because of the journalist debacle? It had annoyed me, yes, but not enough to give him the boot. I didn't *want* him to go; I really liked him. I'd come to rely on him, to trust his judgement as a colleague and a friend. But . . .

I sighed. Perhaps it was as well to get another chef in fast, after that kiss. It had made it hard to concentrate all day, being in close proximity to him, especially when I'd taken orders into the kitchen where it had all kicked off between us.

'They're nice, those two, aren't they?' Phoebe said, interrupting my thoughts. 'Rachel and Ed, I mean. Really friendly.'

'Yeah, they're great,' I said, wondering where this was going. She was looking out of the window at the big waves outside, and there was something wistful and far-away about her face. Was she homesick? I wondered. 'What are your friends like back home?' I asked.

Her eyes lit up. 'They're fab,' she said. 'Really funny and mad. We all hang out together and borrow each other's clothes and do each other's hair. Polly is the craziest one, she's just totally outrageous like, oh my God, is she for real, kind of thing. And Rosa is like the most beautiful person in the world, and all the boys fancy her big time. Zoe is arty and wears weird vintage stuff, but always looks amazing, and Sasha is really brainy like this mega-geek who can remember loads of phone numbers and stuff, but so gobby she's always getting into trouble.' She wrapped her arms around herself as she stood there.

'I kind of miss them,' she said after a moment. 'I wish they were all here as well. We'd have a right laugh.'

'I know what you mean,' I said. 'I miss my friends, especially my best friend Amber. It's hard coming somewhere new, where you don't know anybody, isn't it?' I got my phone from my pocket and held it out to her. 'Why don't you give one of them a ring for a gossip?' I suggested.

'Really?' she asked. She was looking at my phone so yearningly, it was as if she could have eaten it. 'Are you sure? Oh, cool, thanks.'

I busied myself with the cashing up while she took the phone upstairs to find the number on her out-of-credit mobile. I could hear snatches of laughter and conversation floating down every now and then. 'No WAY!' I heard her squeal. 'Oh. My. GOD!'

I smiled to myself. It was nice to hear her sounding like a teenager for once, all giggly and high-pitched, rather than a stressed-out mini grown-up having to tough it out independently.

I made a plate of salad and helped myself to the last chicken pasty we had, then poured a glass of cold rosé and took the whole lot outside onto the deck. The sea was wild and bucking, with romping great waves, and the surfers were out riding them, their black wetsuits glistening in the surf like sealskin, their boards becoming part of their bodies as they rode in, arms outstretched, muscles taut. One of them had a dog that was bounding about excitedly in the shallows, tail wagging, barking for joy, and with a sudden jolt I realized that it was Lola, Ed's dog. Did that mean Ed was one of the surfers?

My heart was pounding that extra bit quicker as I peered down at the sea, trying to pick him out. Then I saw Lola going mental as one particular surfer swerved into shore, and then he was laughing and petting her, while her tail was a frenzy of happiness. Ah. Gotcha.

I sipped my wine and watched him, a blush creeping into my cheeks. He was the only one not in a wetsuit, and my eyes were drawn to his lean, flat torso and his muscular arms, all tanned an even, golden brown above the long black trunks he was wearing. Water dripped off him as he picked up his board and waded back into the waves. *Phwooarr*, I found myself thinking, remembering the kiss and my dirty dream, and then jerked in my seat, cross with myself. No, not 'Phwooarr'! He was my *chef*, my *employee*, not an object of lust to perv over, I reminded myself sternly. An employee nursing a broken heart, no less.

But then again ... 'Corrrr,' I marvelled, forgetting all of this in an instant, as he paddled out on his board, then waited for the next big wave to roll in. He had a lovely back and shoulders – rippling and beefy. Who would have thought, to look at him in his chef whites?

Moments later, the sea bulged and rocked with the force of an incoming wave – whoosh, there it went – and there he went too, up on his board as the wave crested, holding his balance as he surged into shore, bringing him and a couple of other guys racing in with it. I realized I was holding my breath as I watched, only to let it all out in a rush of relief as he reached the shallows and Lola bounded up to greet him.

She wasn't the only one to run over to him. Another surfer, clad in a black and electric-blue wetsuit, jumped off her board and high-fived him, and I was sure I heard them both laughing over the roar of the waves. It was Rachel.

Oh, right. Oh. Well, she had said she was a surfer, hadn't she? So it shouldn't have been all that surprising that they were down there together, but ...

They hadn't asked me, I thought childishly. I hadn't been invited. Was it wrong of me to feel a prickle of jealousy at them enjoying themselves – frolicking, you could even say – in the surf, when they hadn't thought to mention it to me? Don't say he was rebounding from his ex, to me, to *her*?

Phoebe skipped out onto the deck just then, looking happier than I'd ever seen her. 'Okay?' I asked, needlessly. I turned my head away from the surfers, not wanting to see any more. Blood was throbbing around my face and throat, and I kept replaying the images I'd just seen. A variation of a childhood song began running through my head: '*Ed and Rachel splashing in the sea, S-U-R-F-I-N-G . . .*'

Phoebe beamed. 'Awesome. I just talked to Zoe, and it was so cool to get all her gossip and hear what's been happening. She's like totally loved up with Max, this boy in our year, and she asked him to her birthday party as a dare, and he said YES! So she's freaking out about it now and doesn't know what to wear, and doesn't know what to *think*, and . . .'

'When's her party?' I asked casually.

'It's next Saturday,' she replied, biting her thumbnail. She slumped into a chair and dangled her legs over its arm. 'I wish I could go.'

'Then go,' I said. 'What's stopping you?'

She swung an arm around indicating the beach. 'Well, cos I'm here. But . . .'

I sipped my wine, catching her gaze. 'Come on. You might as well tell me what happened at home. Were things really so bad that you can't go back for Zoe's party? Don't you think she needs you to be her right-hand gal, and help her and lovely Max get together?'

It all sounded a bit *Hollyoaks* to me, but Phoebe really did seem to be dithering at this. 'Well . . .'

'I know you and your mum fell out, but couldn't you

stay with Zoe for a while, or one of your other mates? Just until you sort things out with your family?'

She tipped her head back and stared up at the sky. 'I guess,' she said tentatively. 'The thing is . . .' And then the whole story poured out in a gush of words: how she'd always felt overlooked by her parents because her brother was disabled, and needed lots of extra care and attention, and how he took up most of their time. How she got fed up with feeling as if nobody cared about her, or asked how her day was, because they were so busy with Isaac. Why she had stopped bothering trying to do well at school, because she didn't think anyone was interested.

'Why bother trying to do well? For yourself, of course,' I put in, but she wasn't listening.

'I started hanging around with Zoe and that lot, who are a "bad influence", according to my mum,' she went on, contempt in her voice. 'And, finally, I felt like I was getting a reaction from Mum and Dad. For the first time ever they actually noticed what I was doing, what I was wearing, where I was going. I wasn't "good little Phoebe" any more.' She propped her head on one hand, her expression hard. 'But the thing was, the more they went on at me, the more I felt like pissing them off. So . . .'

'So it became a vicious circle,' I said sympathetically.

'Yeah,' she said. She stared out to sea, shivering as a

sudden breeze swept in from the waves. 'And then, when I ran away, I thought they'd probably be glad I'd gone, glad they wouldn't have to worry about me any more, now that they only had precious Isaac to bother about.'

'No way,' I said firmly. 'There's no way they'd think that. Look, you said yourself how upset your mum was on the phone. She's probably been feeling massive guilt that it's come to this. She and your dad must be desperate for you to come home and try again.'

She shook her head. 'I don't think so,' she said, her voice icy. I could see right through her, though, and was sure this was her hurt pride speaking.

'What did Zoe say about you running away?' I asked after a minute of silence.

'She said they were all freaked out, they missed me, and . . .' She stumbled over the words. 'She said it wasn't the same without me.'

'Of course it isn't!'

'And she also said, if I wasn't going to come back, could she have my hair straighteners, because they're better than hers,' she added, and a smile twisted her mouth upwards. 'Cheeky cow.'

'Well, that alone is worth going back for,' I told her. 'You can't have one of your mates sneaking off with your good hair straighteners behind your back, can you?'

'No.'

There was a pause. 'I do really want to go to Zoe's party,' she mumbled.

'I think you should,' I replied. I pushed my phone back across the table to her. 'Go on. Ring your mum again. Tell her what you told me – get it all off your chest. Zoe needs you. Your hair straighteners need you. Your mum and dad and brother need you. I know you might not believe me, but it's true.'

I could tell by her face she was torn, really torn. Then she moved the phone back towards me. 'Maybe tomorrow,' she replied.

'Okay,' I said, not daring to push it any more. This much was a major breakthrough in itself, getting her even to consider the idea.

Then she was peering down at the sea. 'Hey, look! There's Ed, surfing.'

I turned back towards the water, grateful for the excuse to look, but at the same time not sure I wanted to see. What if Ed and Rachel were now writhing in the shallows together, snogging and getting it on, like a scene from *Blue Lagoon*?

Phoebe leaned over the balcony, waving both arms above her head. 'Hellooooo!' she bellowed.

Ed had just fallen off his surfboard, by the look of things, and was laughing. He waved back, then beckoned us down. 'Come on in, you two,' he yelled. 'Water's lovely.'

He was looking straight at me. 'How about that first surfing lesson?'

'Ha-ha-ha – I don't think so,' I said nervously to Phoebe. There was no way I was going to let him see me in my swimming costume, with my milk-white legs and cake-eater's belly, especially now that I'd seen just how buff and hunky he looked in his. 'Maybe tomorrow,' I called back, smiling, but crossing my fingers under the table. 'And maybe never,' I muttered. I didn't want to scare any small children with my beached-whale surfing attempts.

'There's Rachel too,' Phoebe realized. 'Whoa, check her out, she's awesome! *Hello, Rachel,*' she shouted, waving again. 'Ooh,' she said to me, 'do you think there's a thing going on between those two?'

I swallowed, feeling awkward. 'Dunno,' I mumbled.

'God, he's quite fit, isn't he, old Ed?' she went on, still leaning over, eyes fixed on their figures in the surf. 'Nice bod. Look at his bum! Well juicy.'

I snorted, imagining Ed's face if he could have heard her. Talking to her mate on the phone seemed to have transformed Phoebe into a different person – ten times livelier and cheekier. 'Well juicy?' I echoed, pulling a face at her. 'What are you like?'

'Bit old for me, though,' she went on, still gazing down at him.

'You don't say.' I smiled at her. 'Are there any boys back home you've got your eye on, who might be at this party, then?'

'Well ... sort of.' She sat down again, Ed and his juicy bum forgotten, as she told me about this boy she liked called Will, and how she'd fancied him for ages. He was totally hot apparently, but he'd been going out with Darcey Sheldon, who was queen bee of the whole school, so Phoebe didn't think she had a chance – until Zoe had said just five minutes ago that she'd seen them arguing outside McDonald's yesterday. Now Phoebe was hoping Will would dump Darcey and then ...

I raised my eyebrows. 'You'd better get in there quick, girl,' I told her. 'Forget your hair straighteners, and helping out your mate. That's the best reason of all for going back to London, I reckon.'

She laughed. 'Yeah,' she said. 'Maybe.'

We sat out on the deck for a while longer, me with my wine, Phoebe with a Diet Coke, and she was chattier than I'd ever known her to be. She told me all about her mum, who ran a gift shop in Chelsea, and her dad, who was a journalist for *The Times*; and how she was in the middle of doing her A-levels and wanted to go into fashion design. The more she talked, the more I think she was convincing herself that it would be okay to go home, that it was maybe the right thing to do. I got the impression that what bothered her most was the idea that she'd be backing down somehow, losing face and letting her parents 'win', but I hoped she would decide that was a small price to pay ultimately.

She flung her arms around me when it got late and we both went up to bed. 'Thanks, Evie,' she said. 'You are the coolest grown-up I've ever met.'

I hugged her back. 'And you are definitely the coolest teenager I've ever met,' I told her. 'Goodnight.'

Chapter Twenty-One

On Monday, Phoebe went off to the beach first thing – it was a glorious day – while I got down to the thorny problem of my chef-hunt. I'd had another couple of job applications, but none were leaping out at me as must-employ types. The problem was, I wanted Ed – in more ways than one. After seeing him surfing, I'd had another enjoyably rude dream about him, where we'd been on the beach together and he'd ripped off my bikini (and hadn't burst out laughing: this *was* a dream, after all) and then he'd ravished me on the sand, and I'd woken up, absolutely panting and yearning like something from a bad porn movie, and slightly concerned that I might have shouted his name out in my sleep and woken Phoebe.

The dream had disturbed me. It had been so real and so vivid, and I had imagined it all in such detail, too: him wrapping his arms around me, the feeling of his weight on my naked body, squeezing that juicy bum of his (Phoebe was dead right about that), even the noise he made when he came (quite loud and caveman-ish, if you must know). And of course, being a dream, there was no problem with sand creeping into intimate, sensitive areas. It had been wonderful.

I sighed. What an idiot I was, getting my knickers in a twist over him when he clearly wasn't interested. It would be better for both of us if I found a new chef, so that he didn't have to put up with me lusting over him every day. It was the grown-up, business-like thing to do. So I picked up the phone and called three of the applicants – the pub-restaurant chef, the chip-meister, and a woman who worked in a deli in Wadebridge – and invited them all in for an interview the following Monday.

There. I'd done it now. With a bit of luck, one of my interviewees would fit the bill perfectly, and I could let Ed go. Feeling strangely miserable about this, I took myself off to the beach with a big floppy sun hat and a fat novel, trying to put the whole thing out of my mind. *Aaaand relax*, I ordered myself, stretching out on the towel in the sunshine. If only it was that easy.

That evening Phoebe came in tanned and sandy, her hair tangled with salty sea water, and glowing with happiness. She'd bumped into Rachel, it turned out, and the two of them had gone out on a boat with a couple of Rachel's backpacker mates all day. I had a pang of missing my own friends as she described their exploits, and wished I'd been there too. 'It was so cool,' she said. 'We were diving and snorkelling, and we had a picnic on this deserted bay, just along the coast – I loved it.' She smiled at me, her eyes sparkling greener than ever, now that her face was so brown. 'It was the perfect end to my Cornwall adventure.'

My eyebrows shot up. 'The perfect end ... You're going home?'

'Yeah,' she said. 'Talking to you yesterday and Rachel today, it just made my mind up. Friends and family are what it's all about. And Will Francis too, obvs.'

I laughed. 'Oh, *obvs*,' I replied. 'So, what's the plan? Have you phoned home? When are you going?'

'Mum and Dad are coming to get me tomorrow. Both of them.' She made a sarcastic *wow* face. 'Both taking time off work, and everything. Even leaving Isaac at home with my gran for the night. Cos I'm *that* important.'

I nudged her. 'You *are* important, Pheebs. Don't you forget that, now.' There was a moment's silence and I realized just how much I would miss her. Yeah, she'd been prickly and suspicious at first, and yeah, she was melodramatic and overemotional, but she was a sweetheart too – sparky and funny. 'Oh God, I'm gonna miss you,' I said, putting an arm around her. 'And not just because you're an ace waitress. Come on. If this is your last night with me, I'm going to take you out to dinner. Have a shower and get yourself dolled up. We're going to the Fleece.'

The following day the café was open again. Annie came in with some lovely new cakes, including a cheesecake with fresh strawberries. Rachel and Ed arrived promptly for work, and I was able to be perfectly cool and professional with Ed, despite images of my X-rated dreams flashing into my head the moment I saw him. Rachel seemed all giggly and excitable for some reason, and at one point I even caught her singing along to a slushy ballad on the radio, as if she were thoroughly loved up herself. It gave me a strange feeling. *Do you think there's a thing going on between those two?* Phoebe had asked, when we'd seen Ed and Rachel splashing about in the surf together, and I'd dismissed it at the time as being impossible. But she did seem suspiciously chirpy today...

No. Surely not. I was imagining things, having delusions like a madwoman.

Phoebe spent the entire morning watching the door, as her parents had arranged to meet her in the café. 'I'm actually quite looking forward to seeing them again,' she'd told me in the pub the night before. 'I know it's not suddenly going to be like, amazing between us, but ... you know, I've made my point. Things are definitely going to be different. Better.'

'Pheebs,' I said to her now, seeing her eyes on the door for the millionth time, 'I'm sure your mum and dad will be keen to see you, but it'll take them – what? Five hours to get to Carrawen from London, I reckon. Even with the best will in the world, they won't be here before this afternoon.'

She grinned. 'Yeah, I know. I'm just twitchy,' she said.

At about eleven o'clock Florence, the sweet silver-haired lady who'd been in the week before, appeared. 'Happy birthday!' I said, remembering in the nick of time the conversation we'd had last time. 'What can I get you? Surely you're going to have a piece of cake on your birthday – my treat?'

Her face creased into a smile. 'That would be lovely,' she said. 'And a pot of tea, please.'

I took it over to her and, as we were fairly quiet, sat down opposite her. 'How are things?' I asked her. 'Have you had a nice week?'

'Well, it's been quiet, you know,' she said, daintily cutting her cake into small pieces. 'Trying to keep myself busy, but . . .'

'Not painting the town red, then,' I said, smiling at her.

'Not exactly,' she said, pouring tea into her cup.

'You know, Florence, I've been thinking about what you were saying last time you were in,' I told her. 'About feeling a bit lonely because you didn't really know many people here. Well, the circumstances are slightly different for me, but I do understand how you feel. I'm new to the area too, and miss my old friends.'

She tilted her head expectantly, her eyes bright and bird-like, but said nothing.

'So I was wondering...' I began, hoping I wasn't about to say something laughably stupid, 'about having an open house here in the café one night a week. Women only. Just somewhere that people can come and have a chat and a piece of cake, bring a bottle of wine maybe, and get to know each other. A girls'-night-in sort of thing for whoever fancies it.' I was about to go on, but she interrupted me.

'What a lovely idea,' she said. 'I'd be all for it. It is beautiful, this part of the world, but there isn't a huge amount going on in the evening. No bingo, no social club. It's what the community needs, something like this.'

I could have hugged her. It was exactly what I hoped she'd say. 'Brilliant,' I replied. 'I was thinking maybe this Thursday night for our first get-together. What do you reckon?'

She nodded. 'Perfect. I'll look forward to that. Girls' night, eh?' She giggled, looking twenty years younger as she did so. 'Arthur would have loved that – me off on a girls' night at the age of seventy-two!'

'You're as young as you feel,' I reminded her. 'Oh, and Florence, if you're at a loose end tonight, a lad in the village is having an art show here. Seven o'clock. Free wine and nibbles. Might be nice to spend your birthday evening down here?'

She looked delighted. 'That would be wonderful,' she said. 'I've been dreading today, spending it without Arthur. My son said he'd phone later on from America, but it's not the same as actually being with people. I'd love to come along.'

Rachel was clearing tables nearby and strolled over. 'Hey, Florence,' she said. 'I owe you a thank-you. After what you said last week, I plucked up the courage to contact my ex.'

'Oooh!' said Florence, pleased. 'Good for you. And what happened?'

'We've made up,' she replied, grinning from ear to ear. 'We had a really long talk last night, and both said sorry. Best of all, he's coming to Cornwall next week!'

'Oh, wow!' I said. 'That's fab news.' So *that* was why she'd been so I'm-in-the-mood-for-lurve. And of course she and Ed *weren't* having a wild fling, after all. Never believed it for a second anyway. *Obvs*, as Phoebe would say.

'Splendid,' Florence agreed. 'Well done. Now don't you feel better for taking my advice?'

'I do,' Rachel said. 'I feel so much better.' She bent down and kissed Florence on the cheek. 'Thank you. You're my new life-guru, is that all right?'

'Oh my!' Florence said, turning a little pink. 'I'm not quite sure what one of those is, but I'm happy that you're happy, Rachel. And I'm glad that he's seen sense too. Marvellous.'

'I love a happy ending,' I said, smiling at both of them. 'Good on you, Rach.'

'Thanks,' she beamed. 'The world is a better place when you're in love. Wouldn't you agree, Ed?' she called over as he came out of the kitchen.

He shrugged, looking rather bad-tempered. 'How the hell should I know?' he muttered, dumping an order on the counter.

Ouch. I found myself wincing, but Rachel merely seemed amused. 'Oh dear,' she said in a stage whisper, 'there's someone who could do with some of your love-life advice, Florence.'

'Goodness,' she said, eyes twinkling. 'A nice-looking lad like him, you'd have thought he'd have the ladies flocking around him.'

I could feel my cheeks turning red. She was probably right. For all I knew, he might be the number one

Carrawen hottie, with girls constantly falling at his feet. And here was me, with my silly great crush on him. 'I'd better get back to work,' I said lightly, before we had to talk about it any more.

Phoebe got increasingly excited as we neared midday, but from then onwards she sank further and further into gloom. 'Where *are* they?' she kept fretting, every half an hour or so. 'Why aren't they here yet?'

'Pheebs, it's a long drive, mate,' Rachel reminded her. 'Give them a chance. Even if they set off first thing, they'll have had to stop for lunch and petrol at some point.'

'It's true,' I told her. 'They could be a while yet. Go and have your lunch break, and put them out of your mind. They'll be here before too long, I'm sure.'

'I hope they do turn up soon,' Rachel said to me as Phoebe reluctantly sloped off. 'She's spent all this time being mad with them – I'd hate for them to screw things up, just as she's come round to making peace.'

'I know,' I said. 'She's going to take it so personally if they arrive really late – she'll think the worst, that they don't care, and then they'll be back to square one.' I sighed. 'Come on, Mum and Dad. Don't let her down now.'

At three o'clock, just as I thought Phoebe was about to burst into tears with every new tick of the clock, in came a well-dressed couple in their forties. The woman had the same high cheekbones and fair hair as Phoebe, only hers was styled in a chic graduated bob. The resemblance was unmistakable, though. She had a brisk, searching manner as she walked in – and then her eyes fell upon Phoebe, who had her arms full of crockery, and she let out a little cry.

'Oh, darling,' the woman said, rushing towards Phoebe, who dumped the crockery unseeingly on the nearest table and ran to meet her. 'Oh, Phoebe!'

There was a tangle of arms, a tight embrace, muffled words of greeting. I could hear one or both of them crying. I had a lump in my throat, and exchanged a watery-eyed look with Rachel.

'Hello, pickle,' the man said gruffly, putting his arms around them and kissing the top of Phoebe's head. He was wearing a short-sleeved shirt, smart trousers and expensive-looking shoes, and looked completely out of place in my café.

'This is Evie,' Phoebe said when they'd all hugged and kissed and exclaimed over one another. She was pink-cheeked and tearful-looking, as if it was all a bit much for her. 'She let me stay with her. Evie, this is my mum and dad, Maria and Bradley.'

'Hi,' I said, but Maria had already invited herself around

the counter and hugged me so hard it took my breath away.

'Thank you,' she said, squeezing me fiercely. 'Oh, thank you, Evie. I can never repay you for your kindness.' She crossed herself quickly. 'When I think of my little girl out there on the streets at night...' She shook her head and I could see that she was welling up. 'Thank God for you. Thank God for you!'

'It's fine,' I said. 'She's a lovely girl.'

'I hope she didn't give you any trouble,' Maria said, holding my hand and gazing intensely into my eyes. 'I hope she didn't make a nuisance of herself?'

Bloody hell, I thought, slightly stunned at the question. Leave her alone. You've only just got her back, don't go driving her away again. 'She's been great,' I said, glancing over at Phoebe, whose mouth had drooped somewhat, her expression turning hurt. 'Fantastic. No trouble at all.'

'We'd like to give you some money for looking after her,' Bradley said, getting his wallet out of his trouser pocket and pulling out a wedge of notes.

I cringed. 'Really – no,' I said, embarrassed. 'There's no need at all. She's been a pleasure. And she's worked her socks off in here for me, so please, put your money away.'

'Can I get you guys a drink while you're here?' Rachel asked brightly, before an awkward silence could develop.

'Some coffee would be wonderful,' Maria said, still with her arm around Phoebe. There was a tiredness visible in her face now that she'd stopped beaming. She must have gone through hell, I thought, with a twist of sympathy. So must he. No wonder they were slightly over the top; I'd have been screaming hysterically, in their shoes. 'Thanks, hon.'

'A flat white for me, no sugar,' Bradley added. 'Thank you.'

'Where are you staying tonight?' I asked them politely as Rachel got to work.

'We're staying in The Excelsior, just along the coast,' Maria said, gesturing behind her.

I tried – and failed – to stop my jaw from dropping. The Excelsior was seriously expensive and seriously cool. All sorts of famous people had stayed there.

'Lovely room overlooking the beach, a wonderful view,' Maria went on. 'We've booked you in there too, Phoebe, for tonight. We don't want to put Evie out any more.'

'She wouldn't be—' I began, but Phoebe was making a choking sound in her throat.

'You checked into your hotel before you came to find me?' she asked in disbelief.

I froze, only just registering what Phoebe had realized, and felt appalled. In fact, I wanted to snatch Phoebe away from these monstrous, unfeeling parents of hers.

'Only for a minute,' Maria said. 'You know what I'm like, I was bursting for … Only for a minute,' she said again, her voice faltering. 'We did come straight over afterwards.'

'Have a seat,' I told them. 'We'll bring the coffees over.' I busied myself getting out a tray and wiping it down. 'Bloody hell,' I muttered to Rachel. 'Poor old Pheebs. I feel like I'm sending her back into the firing line.'

'I know what you mean,' she murmured. 'Not the cuddliest types, are they?'

'About as cuddly as a pair of snakes,' I replied under my breath.

I brought over the drinks with a selection of cakes, too, in case they were hungry. 'Honestly, we've been worried *sick*,' I heard Maria saying tightly to Phoebe as I approached, her mouth shrivelled, as if she'd been sucking on a lemon. 'What were you *thinking*?'

Poor Phoebe looked as if she might burst into tears. I put down the drinks and cakes, then hesitated, knowing that I should butt out of this private family drama, but not sure whether I could keep my mouth shut. Guess what? I couldn't.

'I get that this has been a difficult time for you,' I blurted out before I could help myself, 'but it's not exactly been a picnic for Phoebe, either.'

There was a moment's silence and Bradley turned his

eyes – his cold, rather dead-looking eyes on me – in what felt like horrible slow motion.

'I mean, when I found her, she was sleeping *outside*.' My voice had become shrill. 'She was sleeping out in the rain and the cold for night after night – she wasn't doing it for fun, you know. She was doing it because she was desperate.'

Oh God. Shut up, Evie. Phoebe looked as if she was folding into herself with embarrassment. That was the last thing I wanted.

'Well, I appreciate your concern,' Maria said frostily, 'but...'

'I hope you'll get on better now, that's all,' I interrupted her. 'Because I think she's lovely. She's really grown-up, she's fun, she's loyal, she's a bloody hard worker – she's a credit to you. And I know it must have been awful, her running away, I get that, but you've found her now, so I hope you...' I swallowed. 'I hope you can treasure her. I would.'

There was another moment of awful, tense silence and my heart pounded. Maria's eyes were hooded as she stirred her coffee briskly and I wondered for a split-second if she might throw it in my face.

'Sorry,' I muttered, holding the tray to my chest. 'None of my business. I'll just—'

I was about to walk off and hide in the kitchen when

Phoebe spoke. 'Thank you, Evie,' she said, her voice small and cracked.

'My pleasure,' I replied, trying to signal to her with my eyes that I was sorry if I'd just made everything worse. I really hoped not.

I went back to the counter, adrenaline whooshing as if I'd just been in a fight, and helped Rachel serve the customers. We had a rush on, and I was whizzing back and forth from the kitchen for a few minutes – and in that time Phoebe and her family vanished. I didn't even get to say a proper goodbye.

I went over to the table with a heavy heart. I really must have pissed them off. Then I saw the pile of bank notes tucked neatly under one of the cake plates. I counted them, my heart racing. Two hundred quid. It felt like blood-money.

I hurried out to the deck, but they'd gone, disappeared from view. Then I ran through the kitchen and out the back, just in time to see a year-old silver Audi pulling out of the car park and accelerating away. I waved frantic-ally, but the car had tinted windows and I couldn't tell if anyone had seen me. I sighed, feeling as if I'd failed somehow, as if I'd fallen at the very last fence.

As soon as the café was officially closed that evening, Jamie, Martha and one of Jamie's mates, who seemed to be called Boz, arrived with boxes of artwork. Boz had brought along a drill too, but quickly proved himself to be a total incompetent with power tools, gouging huge holes in the wall and spraying everything with plaster dust.

'Boz,' I wailed. 'Have you any idea how to work that thing? I do want the wall to stay standing, please. You're like a bloody woodpecker!'

'Give it here,' Ed said, wandering through from the kitchen. The feminist in me wanted to grab the drill from Boz and say to Ed, 'It's all right, I can manage', but the realist in me knew that actually I'd probably make even more of a bodge-job than bodger Boz.

Boz handed over the drill, and Ed went round making ten neat holes where the pictures were to go, pushed a Rawlplug into each one and then searched around for the screws. 'What?' he said, when he saw me looking at him.

I laughed, slightly embarrassed. 'Nothing,' I said. 'Just ... you being all capable and manly.'

He laughed too. 'I am always capable and manly,' he reminded me.

'Yeah, yeah,' I scoffed. 'Modest too, right?'

'Naturally.'

I was excited about hanging up the pictures – hell, I was excited about seeing the pictures full stop. It had crossed my mind earlier that I'd offered to have all this artwork on my walls without even giving it the once-over in advance. Pretty dumb really. Once again a case of my mouth working before my brain could catch up. What if, I'd agonized the night before, the paintings were awful? Or offensive? What if they depicted grisly scenes, or had loads of expletives daubed across them? This really could be another own goal for Evie Flynn, unprofessional café manager extraordinaire. But on the other hand . . .

I gasped as Jamie pulled the dustsheet off one of the largest paintings. It was a beautiful sea scene of blues and greens, with iridescent shells and bright-shimmering fish. It was calming, serene and eye-catching. You could almost hear the sound of the water when you looked at it.

On the other hand, I thought to myself with a smile, I might just have scored a hat-trick.

Once Jamie was happy with the arrangement of the canvases, he set about putting numbered stickers next to them, and pinned up a price sheet. The smallest canvases were very reasonable at £50 each, I thought, with the medium-sized pieces priced at £150, and the two largest paintings at £250. They were all underwater scenes, similar in style, but with different colours and subjects, making each piece unique. They worked brilliantly as a collection.

'Oh, my goodness,' I said, gazing at the display of colour around my walls. 'Jamie, don't they look wonderful? Doesn't the café look fantastic?'

He was still tweaking the canvases, making tiny adjustments to them, standing back with his head on one side and his eyes narrowed, considering the composition of the arrangement from all angles. Then he smiled. 'It's amazing, having them together like this,' he said. 'I've never actually seen them as a collection, all up at the same time.'

Martha was beaming. 'Now we just need people to buy them all and commission you to do loads more,' she said proudly.

'Well, not straight away, I hope,' I said, then clapped a hand to my mouth, feeling bad. 'Sorry, that came out wrong. I'm just being selfish, because I want to have them here for a little while.'

Jamie grinned. 'Don't worry,' he said. 'If they all sell, I'll just paint you some more.'

'I'll take you up on that,' I said. I gazed around, loving the way the café had been brought to life by the artwork. It looked classier somehow, more upmarket, more cool. What do you reckon, Jo? I thought, smiling to myself. Check out our café now!

Lindsay, Jamie's boss from the Golden Fleece, who had brassy-blonde hair, a capacious bosom and high red heels, arrived with some wine she was donating, and a boxload of small plastic wine glasses. 'Put me down for one of those little canvases, Jay,' she said. 'The one with the pink coral. It'll look lovely in my bathroom.'

'Really? Thank you.' Jamie looked delighted, and Martha immediately went bustling over with her stickers to put a red dot next to the canvas in question.

'Sold! To the lady with the wine,' she cheered.

Lindsay grinned. 'My pleasure,' she said. 'I'd love to stay, but I've got to get back to the pub. Have a great night, though.' She elbowed me. 'Looking great in here, kid,' she said. 'You're doing a smashing job, I keep hearing.'

'Really?' I blurted out in surprise. 'I mean – thank you. Thanks, Lindsay.'

Annie was next to arrive, with some boxes of cupcakes. She'd iced them in the same shades of blue and green as the paintings, and had found some tiny white sugar decorations in the shape of seashells. 'Oh, they're gorgeous,' I sighed, helping her to set them out on plates. 'You're a legend, Annie. A domestic-goddess legend!'

We dragged all the chairs and tables to one end of the café so that there was enough floor space for everyone to wander around and admire the artwork, and I poured out some glasses of wine and set them on the counter, along with the plates of cakes, so that people could help themselves. The only thing missing was Phoebe, I realized with a pang. I wondered if she was sitting through a painful dinner at the Excelsior right now. I hoped she'd be okay.

And then all of a sudden it was seven o'clock, and the first people began arriving.

Chapter Twenty-Two

A shamble – it was the best way to describe them collectively – of Jamie's mates were the first official guests to saunter in: gangly and seemingly awkward in their lanky frames, as if they still felt like little boys inside. They all had similar floppy hair and mumbly voices, and proceeded to take the piss out of Jamie in the way that teenage lads do, although you could tell it was affectionate and that they were actually more than a little proud of their talented mate. 'He's only got blue and green in his paintbox, poor sod,' one of them quipped, looking around at the underwater paintings. 'We should have a whip-round for you, Jay, get you a few other colours.'

'Ah, look, Giz, he's done a portrait of you here,' said another, pointing to one picture that had a large orange fish with thick, fleshy lips and a slightly vacant expression. I couldn't help a snigger as I realized who 'Giz' was – a lanky guy with a curtain of dark, greasy hair and a strikingly similar blankness about his face.

'Mate, I knew you'd come in handy for something one day,' Jamie said, slapping him on the back and laughing. 'Cornwall's Next Top Model.'

'Gerroff,' grumbled Giz good-naturedly, shrugging him – and all the teasing – off.

A couple of Jamie's teachers walked in next – both in their fifties and smartly dressed, and the lads promptly reverted to behaving like schoolboys. 'All right, miss?' they said politely, as if butter wouldn't melt.

Then came a load of Martha's friends, all with long swishy hair and sparkly flip-flops, who clustered together giggling and drank the wine too quickly, as if they were worried somebody would ask their age and take it away from them.

The room was filling up, and the atmosphere felt good – pleasantly buzzy and friendly. It was a balmy evening, with mellow golden light from the sun dancing in streaks on the waves outside. I was thoroughly enjoying myself in my role as hostess. This was what the café was all about: bringing the community together for a special occasion. I hardly recognized anyone – and really, why should I? They were all villagers who had their own kettles and cake tins to turn to in their homes; they didn't need to come to the café in the way that the holidaymakers and day-trippers did. I liked the thought that, although by day the café was for the beach-goers, by evening it could be a place for the locals themselves to meet.

This notion was clearly occurring to everyone else at the same time, almost visibly travelling around the room like a thought-wave. Within the space of the next hour one of Jamie's mates asked if I'd consider letting them use the café as a place for their band to practise one evening a week, as their parents were all fed up with the racket; then one of the teachers asked if her book group could have their monthly meeting here too. 'We've been getting together in the pub, but it's so noisy in there, we can't hear ourselves think, let alone discuss the finer points of narrative structure,' she said to me. Then her eyes twinkled conspiratorially. 'Not to mention everybody's gossip too, of course. This place would be perfect.'

'Fine by me.' I said to them both. 'Of course. Any time!'

Florence came along then, just as I was talking to the book-group lady – Elizabeth, her name was – and I introduced the two of them. 'Florence is fairly new to the village,' I said. 'She doesn't know many people here yet.' And Elizabeth, bless her, promptly invited Florence to come along to their next book-group meeting, right there on the spot. 'We're reading the new Kate Atkinson,' she said. 'I can lend you my copy if you want?'

'That would be lovely,' Florence said happily. 'Thank you very much.'

I left them chatting in order to go on wine duty and top up people's glasses. Lots more guests had arrived, and Jamie was looking flushed and exhilarated as he talked about the paintings with a group of people. For all the crowd, though, I didn't see any more red dots by the pictures; only the one by the pink-coral piece that Lindsay had claimed. I hoped there would be at least one more sale, for Jamie's sake. He'd said earlier that having the paintings on show was what mattered most to him, but all the same ... I decided I'd buy one of them if nobody else did. Sod it, we'd done well lately, especially with our Friday-night takings, and they were genuinely striking pieces of artwork.

I was just gazing around, wondering which one I'd choose, when I saw that Ed had arrived and was speaking to a woman I didn't recognize. I hesitated, wanting to go over and say hi, but feeling slightly self-conscious about it too. If it hadn't been for that stupid kiss, I wouldn't have thought twice about joining him, but now ... I bit my lip. He looked gorgeous in a short-sleeved summery shirt with the top two buttons undone, and a pair of smart dark-blue jeans. My skin felt hot just looking at him.

I was plucking up the courage to go over — hell, it would be the normal thing to do, wouldn't it? Staying away would only make it seem a bigger drama than it needed to be — when Rachel walked in with a tall, slim woman who had cropped black hair and large brown eyes. 'Evie! I want you to meet Leah,' she said when she saw me, grabbing the woman's arm and pulling her over. 'Leah's my mate from Melbourne, who's just arrived in the bay. Remember me saying that she was hoping to find some work here? Well, now that Phoebe's gone, if you need another waitress, then . . .'

'Then I'm your woman,' Leah said with a smile, showing even white teeth. Dimples flashed in her olive-skinned face as she turned her friendly gaze on me. 'Hi, Evie. Awesome place you've got here.'

I smiled back, getting a good vibe about her. Call me a pushover, but I did love it when people were complimentary about the café. It had become so tightly bound up with who I was, that it felt like personal praise. Oh, what the hell, I thought. You had to go with your instincts sometimes, and if she was Rachel's mate, she was probably all right. 'Hi, Leah,' I said. 'Nice to meet you, and welcome to Carrawen! Why don't you drop in tomorrow morning and we can have a chat about work then?'

'Cool,' she said. 'Thanks very much.'

I went to refill my glass — the wine that Lindsay had provided was slipping down very easily, that was for sure — then picked up the bottle to do the rounds and see if anyone else wanted a top-up. Then I stopped in my tracks, staring in horror at the person who'd just arrived, almost expecting sinister music to start playing. It was Betty. Horrible, evil Betty from the shop. The last person I'd expected to see crossing my threshold. What was she doing *here*?

I watched her covertly. She was all dolled up for a change – I'd only ever seen her in her nylon overall and polo-neck before. Tonight she was wearing a rather lurid flowered dress, wedge-heeled espadrilles and a chunky silver necklace. She'd set her hair in curls and was wearing lipstick. Bloody hell. It was like having the Bride of Frankenstein totter in. Whose benefit was this for? I wondered. And, again, what the hell was she *doing* here?

Something else was strange about her. Something that didn't quite look right. Ah. That was it. She was *smiling*. I'd never seen her mouth in any shape other than a snarl or a sneer before, but tonight she was smiling around at the paintings, her face practically glowing with appreciation. Blimey. Don't tell me she was an art buff on the quiet? Don't tell me we had the West Country's answer to Brian Sewell right here in Carrawen?

She was scouring the room now as if searching for someone, and then she made a beeline for Jamie, who was deep in conversation with an earnest-looking woman, who was – ooh! –actually getting out a cheque book.

Oh yes, I thought, stifling a whoop. Jamie had made a sale. And then, in the next instant – *oh no. Betty, no! Step away from the artist, Betty,* I urged telepathically, *don't wreck Jamie's big moment, for heaven's sake.* Knowing her, she was probably going to say something crushing and spiteful about the whole evening, and the cheque-book lady would have second thoughts. Knowing Betty, the smile on her face was an evil one, a gloating bad-fairy one, and she'd burst into a horrible cackle any second: mwah-ha-ha-hah!

I had to stop her. I stepped blindly towards Betty, but she was pretty nifty on her wedges, heading straight for Jamie like a woman on a mission. Then I heard something deeply weird.

'Hello, Mum,' said Jamie.

I almost fell over in shock. Hello, Mum? Betty was Jamie's *mum*? No way. No WAY! I thought for a second my brain might explode. How could this be possible? It was a small village, yes, and lots of people knew everyone else. Lots of people seemed to be related to each other, but all the same ... How had I missed this one?

Then I got the fear. *Shit!* Had I said anything awful about her in front of him? Probably, knowing my big mouth. Almost certainly in fact. Oh Gawd...

'Come and meet Verity,' Jamie was saying, putting an arm around Betty as she reached him. 'Verity, this is my mum, Betty. And, Mum, guess what, Verity's just bought one of my paintings.'

My mouth was hanging open and I quickly snapped it

shut. Jamie had sold a painting! That was wonderful. But oh, my goodness ... I was still reeling from the Betty bombshell. How come I hadn't been told about this? How come Jamie was so sweet and normal, when his mum was such an old witch?

Florence had appeared in front of me, and I blinked. *Come on, Evie. Pull yourself together.*

'I'm having a lovely time,' she said, twinkling at me. 'Thank you so much for inviting me, dear. I've met some very friendly people and I've even bought one of the little canvases as a present to myself.'

'Brilliant,' I said warmly. 'I'm really glad. So it's turned out to be a good birthday, then?'

'Oh, it has,' she replied. 'A very good birthday. And I had some wonderful news earlier from my son too, when he phoned – he's going to be back in the UK soon, working on a new documentary. I can't wait to see him.'

'Oh, that's fab,' I said. Her eyes were moist with emotion, bless her, and it made me feel sniffly just looking at her. 'I'm so pleased, Florence.'

'He couldn't believe it when I told him I was going out to an art exhibition tonight,' she giggled. 'He said, "Really, Mum? Good for you!"' She grinned. 'I'm so glad you asked me along this evening. I'd have been twiddling my thumbs and feeling miserable, if I'd stayed in at home.'

'Well, I'm really glad you came,' I told her. 'And do

spread the word about our girls' night in, won't you? Invite anyone you want to. The more the merrier, I say.'

I broke off then, because I could see Betty approaching us. She looked uncharacteristically nervous, her face florid, her lipsticked mouth in a tense, puckered circle. 'Have you got a minute?' she asked.

'Sure,' I said. 'Florence, would you excuse us?'

Betty and I stepped to one side, away from the throng. She cleared her throat self-consciously and fiddled with one of her Pat-Butcheresque earrings. 'I want to say thank you,' she began quietly. 'Thank you for giving my Jay a chance. He's absolutely over the moon with all this. Over the moon.'

I was — there is no other word for it — gobsmacked. Utterly gobsmacked. Betty ... being nice. Betty ... saying thank you! Had the body-snatchers had a day trip to Carrawen Bay recently? Was this really a Cyborg in front of me, wearing the lurid dress and lippy?

I realized I was staring. 'It's my pleasure,' I told her quickly. 'He's a lovely lad, and his paintings are great. He deserves a break.'

She was twisting her hands now, looking incredibly uncomfortable. There was a sheen of sweat on her face. 'The other thing is: I'm sorry. I ...' She was struggling to force the words out. 'I've been a bit unfair on you. Mis-judged you. And ...'

Oh, my word. Weirder and weirder. Had that really been a 'sorry' as well as a 'thank you' she'd squeezed out from that cat's bum of a mouth? I half-expected lightning to strike the café, like some biblical end-of-world scenario.

'And I'm sorry,' she said again.

Bloody *hell*. Bloody HELL! I thought I might fall over with the shock. Was there something hallucinogenic in the wine that meant I was imagining this conversation? She was looking so awkward that I took pity on her. 'No hard feelings,' I said, once I'd got my breath back from this unexpected turn of events.

'I was very fond of your aunt,' she went on. 'Very sad to see her go. And when you came in, I thought you were going to muck it all up and . . .' She shook her head, her eyes down. I had never seen her so humble. Meek, even. Evil Betty – meek! 'Well, I was wrong. I got you wrong. What you've done for Jamie, what you've done for the café, it's really good.'

'Thanks, Betty,' I said, still somewhat dazed. 'I appreciate that.' Then, to lighten things up a bit – the atmosphere between us had become very sombre, very confessional – I added, 'Right! Well, I reckon we both deserve a drink after that, wouldn't you say?' and poured us each a large slosh of wine. 'Cheers,' I said, clinking mine against hers. 'To Jamie – and to a great night.'

'Cheers,' she said. 'I'm so proud of him, I can't tell you. Just so proud.'

The evening was getting stranger by the minute, but I was enjoying myself. And having Betty, my former nemesis, on side could only be a good thing, couldn't it?

By nine o'clock four of Jamie's paintings had been sold, and he'd had praise and compliments coming out of his ears. Someone had even expressed an interest in commissioning him to paint a mural in their bathroom. To say he was jubilant was a massive understatement. I was jubilant, too. The whole night had been a roaring success. Everyone seemed to have enjoyed themselves, and I had mingled my little socks off, meeting lots of friendly locals, who all kept telling me how proud Jo would have been of me, and how wonderful it was to see the café doing so well. I had invited lots of women to the café's inaugural 'girls' night in' too, including (after my fifth glass of wine) Betty, the village matriarch herself. Who would have predicted *that* at the start of the evening?

Ed, Annie, Martha, Jamie and my new mate Betty helped me clear the empty glasses and plates, then said goodbye and went home. All except Ed, that was. We looked at each other in a strange, self-conscious silence and I felt myself blush.

'Fancy a stroll on the beach?' he asked, after a moment, grabbing one of the half-empty wine bottles that had been left. 'It's a beautiful evening.'

It *was* a beautiful evening – the sky aflame with red and scarlet, the air still warm, with just the faintest of breezes. And Ed was looking every bit as gorgeous too, I thought to myself.

'Yes,' I said. 'Oh yes.' Then I said 'Yes' a third time for good measure and laughed.

'I'll take that as a yes, then,' he said, and held out his hand.

I took it. And we walked down to the beach together.

'I loved it this evening,' he said, as if there was nothing out of the ordinary about us holding hands. I, on the other hand, could hardly breathe for the excited, tingly feelings that were running through my whole body. *We are holding hands*, I kept saying in my head. *I am holding hands with Ed. What does this mean? Has he stopped brooding about his ex? What is going to happen?*

'What was that?' I said, trying to shut out the giddy voice in my mind. 'You loved the evening? Oh, so did I. Wasn't it great? All those people. And Jamie's face! He looked so happy.'

'He did,' he said. 'It all came together perfectly, didn't it?' He squeezed my hand, then suddenly stopped walking and gestured towards the dune on our right. 'Okay, this looks a good spot. Let's sit here.'

I was so enjoying the walking hand-in-hand thing that I almost protested at having to stop, but managed to avoid blurting out anything stupid. 'Good idea,' I said, trying to sound casual.

We sat down in the cool, gritty sand, with the dune behind us. A breeze whispered through the hard, spiky grass that grew there, and the rushing of the waves on the shore sounded dream-like and hypnotic. The sky was getting darker by the minute, and I could see the first faint spangles of starlight emerging. How I loved living by the beach, I thought happily. I couldn't imagine being back in a city again now.

Ed poured us each a glass of wine and we clinked them together. 'Cheers,' he said. 'Cheers to the café, and to you too, Evie. You're what makes it something really special.'

'Oh, Ed,' I said, embarrassed and pleased at the same time. 'I don't know about that . . .'

'Well, I do,' he said. 'You were the one who made tonight happen, who brought everybody together. You were just . . . *sparkling* tonight.'

I blushed and opened my mouth to say something self-deprecating, but he was still talking.

'I've been down here for – what? – six weeks now, and

that was the first time I've really been aware of the community, all the links between people. And they all enjoyed it too, you could tell.'

'I loved seeing so many villagers coming in,' I agreed. 'They were so friendly, weren't they? It made me feel part of the bay, like I belonged here. And so many of them talked to me about Jo, too – my aunt who used to run the café. I kept getting the feeling that she was there as well, somehow, looking down on us, and raising a glass to everyone probably.'

The bottle was between us, wedged into the sand, and he moved it to his far side, so that he could edge closer to me. 'Listen, about what happened the other night,' he began. 'I'm sorry I pounced on you like that, but ...'

I cringed. He was *sorry*. That was not what I wanted to hear. 'Oh God, don't start that again,' I said, my words tumbling out in embarrassment. 'I know it was a mistake, I know you didn't mean to, and probably wish you hadn't, but—'

'The thing was,' he said. 'It wasn't a mistake.' And before I could say anything else, he'd turned towards me, taken my face in his hands and was kissing me.

I kissed him back. He wrapped his arms around me and we kissed and kissed, and it felt amazing – every bit as brilliant as it had in the kitchen. It felt right, like we belonged together, like it had been written in the stars that this should happen. Was happening. Was still happening ...

He broke off and smiled at me. The sky was a deep, dark blue around us, but I could see the softness in his eyes, and felt utterly melty inside, my nerve endings all a-tremble. Whoa. He was a good kisser. A fantastic kisser.

'You're a fantastic kisser,' I said, feeling drunk and dizzied, unable to stop the words coming out all by themselves.

He laughed. 'You're not bad yourself,' he replied. He traced a finger down the side of my face, and every cell of me seemed to quiver.

'Okay, so is this the part where you say that we shouldn't be kissing any more, because of that rebound thing? And then I start talking about balls, and embarrass myself, and it all goes awkward and weird?' I forced a little laugh but my heart was racing painfully. I genuinely needed to know.

He shook his head. 'No,' he said. 'This is the bit where I tell you that I'm falling in love with you.'

I laughed, then. I know this wasn't an appropriate response, but it caught me so off-guard that it was more a reflex reaction out of embarrassment. Besides, his words sounded like something from a film.

'Don't laugh,' he scolded. 'You're not supposed to laugh!'

'Sorry,' I said. 'I just...' I smiled at him. 'Go on, say it again, and I promise I won't laugh next time.'

He rolled his eyes. 'God, you make things difficult sometimes. All right. I'll say it again.' He cupped my face with one hand and looked deep into my eyes. 'Evie Flynn, I'm falling in love with you,' he said.

This time I didn't laugh. A shiver went through me, followed by a deep yearning instead. 'Ed,' I said, reckless-ness coursing through me as I made a decision there and then. 'Shall we go back to mine?'

Chapter Twenty-Three

I'm not going to tell you exactly what happened next. Not all of it anyway. Some things have to be kept private, right? But I will just say that events became so passionate and urgent once we'd got back inside the café, that before I knew it the main counter ended up being christened in a rather special way. *Evie Flynn, you hussy,* I thought to myself as our clothes were hurled across the café floor. There was a split-second where the sensible part of my brain flashed up the query: *Is this too soon? Are we rushing into things? Should we do the hand-holding and kissing for a while longer before we actually get naked?*

The lusty part of my brain dismissed such nonsense immediately. *Oh, shut up! I can't wait a second longer. I fancy this man like crazy. And I ... oooh ...*

So. Ahem. Yes. Hot, frantic, juicy sex on the counter was the order of the day. (*Today's special ...*) And it was good. Seriously good. I can also confirm that my dreamy imaginings of his caveman noise weren't too far off the mark. Oh, and that the bacon sandwiches he made us afterwards were the finest I'd ever eaten, even if I did get the giggles seeing him stark-bollock-naked apart from his chef's apron.

He brandished the spatula at me when he heard me giggling. 'Hot fat on the genitals is no laughing matter,' he said sternly.

'Sorry,' I said, 'but I can't take you seriously when your bum's hanging out the back like that, with the apron strings dangling between your cheeks.' I giggled again. 'It's a good look, though, really. Straight out of a dodgy calendar.'

He struck a pose. 'What do you think, Mr October?'

'Mr Cocktober, more like,' I said childishly, laughing at my own crap joke. I pulled on an apron myself and did a matching stupid pose – hand on hip, looking over one shoulder flirtily and putting a finger to my lips. 'Miss Aug-arse-t,' I said demurely.

'Like it,' he said, raising an eyebrow. 'Like it very much actually.'

We sat munching our bacon sarnies in one of the booths, his arm around me, me snuggled against him. I wasn't sure which was tastier: the bacon or him. 'So . . .' I began, then stopped myself. I was just about to do that classic post-coital confessional thing, where you start telling each other secrets and intimate stuff, but at the last second I wasn't sure whether Ed would be game. Maybe we didn't know each other well enough yet, despite having shagged each other in a mad frenzy minutes earlier. I didn't want to break the spell we'd just woven by giving him the third degree now.

'So,' he replied. He swallowed the last of his sandwich and gave me a squeeze. 'I guess I'd better get back. The poor dog will be wondering what I'm doing.'

I felt my shoulders sag with disappointment. I'd forgotten about the dog. I'd kind of assumed that Ed would stay over the whole night, that we'd cuddle up in my bed and hopefully have sex again – maybe slower and more tender this time, gazing into each other's eyes, watching each other's reactions. Obviously he had different ideas. Oka-a-a-ay.

I'm falling in love with you, he'd said up on the dunes, and the words stung as I recalled them now. Had it just been a line to get my kit off? And now that he'd realized what an easy lay I was, he was going to sod off back to his place? Great – that really seemed the sort of behaviour of someone in love. Looked like I should have held out and kept us at the kissing stage for longer after all, rather than throwing caution to the wind, and my clothes to the floor.

Bollocks.

'Right,' I said, trying to sound like I wasn't bothered.

I got up quickly so that his arm jerked away from me. 'Yep.' I busied myself with the plates, standing so that he couldn't see my bare bottom, and wishing I was wearing something more substantial than this ridiculous apron get-up. I felt very drunk, very tired and very naked and just wanted him to go all of a sudden. 'I guess I'll see you tomorrow then.'

He stared at me. 'Wait, Evie, why are you being so prickly?' he said, clutching at my arm.

Him grabbing me like that made my fingers slip on the plates, and in the next instant they'd shattered on the tiled floor with a horrible crash. I felt like crying. This was all going wrong.

'Bloody hell,' I muttered under my breath, feeling the worst mood ever brewing.

'I wish I *could* stay, honestly,' he said, still holding my arm. 'Really. I'm not about one-night stands, that isn't me. I really like you, Evie. I thought we had something good going and I'd love to ... see what happens next.'

'What happens next is I've got to sweep up these broken plates before we cut our bare feet on them,' I said grumpily, still not looking at him. There was a pause and I felt a horrible black stew of bitterness churning around inside me. Then I raised my eyes to him. Maybe I was being unfair. He did *look* sincere, I acknowledged begrudgingly. 'Sorry,' I said after a moment. 'I'm just knackered and . . .' I shrugged, looking away again and feeling vulnerable. I didn't want to come across as needy and clinging, I wanted to be super-cool and in control. This was not easy. 'I just thought you were going to stay,' I said gruffly in the end.

'I'd love to stay,' he said. 'Evie, I would, but . . . Another time, yeah?' He reached up and touched my face, and my insides did that gooey, dissolving thing again.

I nodded, feeling slightly better. 'Another time,' I agreed. I was looking forward to it already.

Once we'd swept up and he'd gone (after a lovely, lingering kiss in the doorway), I went upstairs to bed, but I was so wired with what had just happened that sleep seemed impossible. My mind seemed to have reverted into teen-agerhood and kept repeating *Oh my God!* over and over again, interspersed with *I shagged Ed – it was amazing!*

It was difficult to stop myself from texting Amber to tell her. I so badly wanted to! But it was two in the morning, and I knew she slept with her mobile near her bed, so I'd wake her up, and then she'd probably be so monstrously pissed off with me that she wouldn't be properly excited on my behalf. That was not a good end result for anyone.

I'd email her instead, I decided, throwing off the covers and padding downstairs. I'd send her a long juicy message and get it all out of my system, thus hopefully short-circuiting the *Oh my God!* loop still rebounding around my head. And then I would sleep. Hopefully, with another disgustingly dirty dream about Ed to entertain me between now and when my alarm went off.

I switched on the PC and made myself a hot chocolate while I waited for it to start up. I opened my email account and was just about to hit the New Message option when something in the in-box caught my eye. An email from Amber – with 'Ed' as the subject matter. Ooh! Coincidence or what? Had she somehow telepathically picked up our shagging exploits?

I clicked on it, intrigued. And then, as I read her message, I felt myself stiffen and my heart sank to the floor. The *Oh my God!* loop stopped abruptly, and a new one appeared in its place. *Oh, shit. Oh, shit. Oh, shit!*

> *Hi Evie,*
>
> *How's it going? Tried phoning you earlier, but the phone rang and rang. Off gallivanting are you, madam? (And when are you gonna get that answerphone sorted out FFS? Twenty-first century now, you know.)*
>
> *I was hoping to chat, as I've got something serious to tell you. I don't quite know how to say this, so I'll just come out with it. I've found out something really awful about Ed. I remembered you saying he was being cagey about the restaurant where he used to work, and now I know why. One of those weird things: Carla*

*and I were clearing out the stock room at the shop and there was
a pile of old newspapers that hadn't gone in the recycling. Managed
to knock over a bucket of water, so spread one out to soak it up —
and there was a picture of ED in the paper. Thought I was
imagining it, but definitely him. Turns out he was charged with
assault a few months ago, and the restaurant — his restaurant —
went bust. All sorts of dodgy dealings uncovered in the paperwork
too: a big financial mess. He is now bankrupt, and the whole thing
sounds pretty nasty. His real name is Ed Gray, so google him and
you'll see what I mean.*

*Sorry to be the bearer of bad news, but I do think it all sounds
v dodge. Best to get a new chef in asap, I reckon. Don't touch him
with a bargepole!*

On a more cheery note, I . . .

I couldn't take in any more. My head was spinning,
as if I'd just come off the waltzers at a fairground. Ed —
my Ed — charged with assault? Bankrupt? Dodgy financial
dealings? No. No! I couldn't believe it. Didn't want to
believe it. Please let it not be true . . .

I leaned back in the chair, unable to equate this
bombshell with the Ed that I'd grown to know and —
yes, all right, fall in love with. Not to mention having had
recent rampant sex with in my actual workplace a mere
two hours ago. This couldn't be real. I was in some sort
of weird dream, that was it. I was drunk and dozing, and
my mind was playing crazy tricks on me.

I pinched myself. Ow. Okay, not a dream, then. I was actually sitting here, in real life, and the bomb had just dropped.

I read through Amber's email again, trying to unravel it more slowly this time, in case I'd got it all wrong. I hadn't. The words were every bit as ugly and shocking as they had been two minutes ago. *Shit.* If it was true, then ... I stopped myself before I got any further. It couldn't be true. It just couldn't. Newspapers made mistakes all the time, didn't they? And maybe Amber herself had got the wrong end of the stick. She'd used the newspaper to mop up some water, after all – maybe the water had smudged the newsprint and the photo, maybe it wasn't even Ed in the first place.

Maybe.

But the more I thought about Amber's words, the more I had the creeping dread that, actually, there might just be a ring of truth in them. I hated to admit it, but the facts fitted: he had a temper, I'd seen that for myself when I thought he was going to punch Ryan. And there was the way he'd been so paranoid about customers recognizing him, the way he'd refused to have his photo taken for the newspaper – it fitted. Why else would a chef as talented as Ed run off down to Cornwall in the first place and hide himself for weeks on end, if he wasn't ashamed of what had happened? So much for my theory that he'd left London because of a broken heart. This was way messier.

'Oh, *bollocks*,' I moaned, feeling despairing. No wonder he hadn't wanted to tell me anything about his restaurant. No wonder he hadn't given me so much as a full name. I put my head in my hands, badly wanting all of this not to be true. Well, there was only one way to find out.

I opened up a new page on the browser, brought up Google, then hesitated. I felt cowardly, hunting him down online like this. Shouldn't I just go straight to him and ask him, hear it from the horse's mouth?

Yes. Of course I should. It was absolutely right that I did. But it was two in the morning, and I couldn't wait any longer. I needed to know everything right now, before my brain imploded with questions.

Ed Gray chef, I typed into the search box, hating myself a bit for it. Then, before I could change my mind, I clicked the Search tab.

A second later the screen was full of links. I forced myself to look at them. There were links to the *Guardian*, *The Times*, BBC News, *Independent*, and I caught sight of the words 'bankrupt' and 'violent misconduct' before I'd even got halfway down the page. I wanted to cry. Right, so it looked as if it *was* all true. These were good, reputable sources. They couldn't all have got the story wrong, it was there in black and white again and again. Now what should I do?

Don't touch him with a bargepole, Amber had advised. Well, it was a bit late for that, wasn't it?

It was the middle of the night, I had drunk gallons of wine, and I should have crawled back to bed and conked out to give my brain a rest. But obviously I wasn't going to do that. Obviously I wasn't going to rest until I'd obsessively combed through every single article about Ed, gleaning every fact it was possible to glean, and torturing myself just a little bit more with each passing website.

Three o'clock came and went, and my hot chocolate sat there, undrunk and no longer fitting its description. This is what I found out: Ed had owned and managed a West End restaurant called Silvers, which served modern British cuisine with a twist, according to the online *Time Out* review. Its average score on the Toptable website was four stars. 'Great food, we'll be back,' one reviewer had written. (Not now, they wouldn't, I thought darkly.) As well as all that, I'd also discovered that Ed had run the place with his wife – yes, his *wife* – Melissa, although they had split up, since the allegations of Ed's violence. ('OUT OF THE FRYING PAN' the headline in the *Sun* had read.) She had filed for divorce, he had filed for bankruptcy, and then they had both gone into hiding.

What a lovely story. What perfect bedtime reading. The only thing missing was 'And they all lived miserably ever after'.

My mind was still whirling, trying to make sense of it. Betty had hinted there was something dodgy about him, hadn't she? I remembered. Had she known all along? And why had Ed wanted to get involved with my café in the first place, given what had happened to Silvers? Was it all some elaborate scam, one of those 'long con' tricks you saw on *Hustle*, where he'd planned to fleece me the whole time? Was I being set up?

No. Surely not. I wasn't that bad a judge of character, was I? I had trusted him, I liked him, he had seemed genuine to me. But then again, he *had* turned out to be a violent criminal, and I hadn't spotted that one, had I?

Face it, Evie. Once a sucker, always a sucker.

I turned off the PC when my brain started to ache, and sloped off upstairs, to spend the rest of the night tossing and turning and trying not to weep into the pillow.

I must have dropped off eventually, because I woke with yet another roaring hangover, feeling as if I was about to expire any second, with a raging thirst and a pounding head. The events of the night before tumbled into my mind one after another, resulting in a crescendo of despair.

Hurrah — Jamie's party!

Oo-er – shagging Ed!

Oh shit – turned out he was a lying, violent, bankrupt crook.

Uggghh – I had the worst hangover ever and felt like never getting up again.

'It's great to be alive,' I croaked sarcastically and shut my eyes, hoping I'd completely imagined the later events of the night before. But I hadn't, had I? Not even my own evil imagination could punish me so viciously with such a God-awful twist of events. What was worse, I realized with a groan, was that I was going to have to confront Ed with what I'd found out. How could I not? How could I pretend everything was normal?

Oh, fabulous. Today was already a complete write-off and I'd only been awake two minutes.

Somehow or other I forced myself into the shower, where I scrubbed fiercely at my skin as if I could scrub off my memories of the way Ed had touched me, the way his body had felt against mine. Nope, it wasn't working. In fact, just thinking of those things only made me feel even more gutted that our fledgling relationship had collapsed so quickly. Oh, Ed ... Why did you have to turn out so *bad*? I thought wretchedly. Especially when I'd thought you were so damn good, too.

I couldn't stomach any breakfast. Had no enthusiasm

whatsoever for the thought of dishing up food and drinks all day. Had no enthusiasm for anything, come to think of it, other than returning to the solace of my bed and staying there for several months. I looked pale and pasty and rough as old boots. For the first time ever, I seriously considered not opening up the café at all, just hanging up the 'Closed' sign and shutting everyone out.

Then I imagined Jo's look of disappointment if I did such a thing. Remembered the nice words everyone had said about the café last night. Remembered that, at the end of the day, I was a businesswoman and I just had to view this as an unfortunate business experience. Forget romance, forget lovey-dovey nonsense. It was all a load of cobblers – and high time I realized as much. And I'd done nothing wrong in this mess; it was Ed who'd tried to pull the wool over my eyes. I would hold my head high, tell him to sling his hook, and take on one of my chef applicants in his place.

'Just an unfortunate business experience,' I muttered to myself as I went to switch on the coffee machine. Happened to everyone. I'd get over it in time. Eventually.

Then I froze. The two aprons were there on the counter, the ones Ed and I had worn the night before. Mr – what had I called him? – Cocktober, that was it, I remembered with a grimace. It didn't seem all that funny any more. In fact, it made me want to cry. I snatched them up and stuffed them into the washing machine in the kitchen, out of my sight.

'Morning, gorgeous!'

I heard Ed's voice and his footsteps, and stiffened. How I wished I hadn't found out all that stuff last night. If I'd still been in the dark about his past I could have called back, 'Morning, handsome!' or something equally light-hearted and flirty right then; we could have had a smooch and a fumble right here in the kitchen, smiled into each other's eyes, felt happy and smitten, and probably ragingly horny too.

Instead, I felt hollow. There was an ache inside me, and not just from my hangover toxins. He should have told me, I thought miserably. He shouldn't have played me for a fool.

'Morning,' I said quietly, pushing shut the washing-machine door. Deep breath, Evie. Might as well get this over with.

He stopped in the doorway when he saw my face. 'Are you all right?' he asked, concerned.

I shook my head. 'No,' I replied. 'Not really. Ed—'

'If this is about me not staying, I'm so sorry,' he interrupted. 'I felt horrible, walking off last night. I've only got another week dog-sitting, and after that I'll be able—'

'No,' I said, cutting him off. 'It's not that.'

There was an awkward silence then. 'Oh,' he said, confused. 'Well, what's up? You're not regretting what we did, are you?'

'No,' I said. 'Well ... no. I don't regret having sex with you, anyway.'

He flinched as if he didn't like my turn of phrase. Tough. The gloves were off now. 'Evie, you seem really cold. What's going on? I don't understand.'

I folded my arms across my chest. 'I don't understand either, Ed Gray,' I said, spitting his name out. 'I don't understand why you didn't tell me about your *wife*, and about your restaurant going bust, and you facing assault charges. I don't understand that at all.'

There was a terrible, throbbing silence when I'd finished speaking. He looked aghast, and my heart sank a little bit further. So it was true, then. Even though I'd seen all the damning news articles and photos of him online with my own eyes, there was still a tiny piece of me that had hoped it wasn't really true. Wrong again, Evie.

'How did you ... I mean, when did you...' His voice trailed away, and he hung his head. I'd never seen him so unsure of himself, so broken-looking. 'It's not what you think,' he said after a moment.

'Really,' I said flatly. 'The thing is, Ed, I don't know *what* to think.' I took a deep breath, hating this conversation already. 'I liked you. I really did. I thought you were a good person. But now I've seen all that stuff online, I—'

He looked up sharply. 'What do you mean?'

Now it was my turn to be hesitant, as I saw the defensive, almost angry light in his eyes. 'I couldn't sleep last night, so I went to check my emails,' I began, deciding not to add in the bit about wanting to write a gooey, gossipy email about him. 'My friend, Amber, had emailed me saying she'd seen something about you in the papers, and . . .'

He was bristling now, his jaw set, his body tense as if he was about to fly into a rage. 'Oh, right, let me guess, you decided to do some detective work, did you? Did a spot of googling and found out some juicy titbits?' He slammed a fist down on the worktop, and I stepped back, remembering the assault allegations and feeling jumpy. 'Well, that's great. Really glad you did that. Made your mind up about me now, have you? It's all there in black and white, so it must be true.'

'Stop shouting at me,' I said. 'And yes, all right, I did look you up. And it's lucky I did! Were you going to tell me any of that stuff, or were you just going to keep stringing me along like an idiot?'

There was silence for a moment. I was starting to think he was going to agree that, yes, he *had* been planning to string me along like an idiot, when he shook his head.

'What's the point?' he muttered bitterly. 'What's the fucking point?'

He stormed towards the door and I stared at him, my brain catching up a second later. 'Wait – what are you doing?' I called after him. 'Where are you going?'

'Where do you think?' he shouted over his shoulder. 'I can't stay here if you believe all that stuff.' He stopped at the door and looked at me, his eyes cold, as if he hated me. 'I quit.'

And with that, he walked out of the café, while I was left gawping after him, my mouth open in shock. Right. Okay. So what now? Had I just lost my chef as well as everything else?

I put a hand to my face, reeling. Well, it looked like I had. And really, what else had I expected? Him to say, *Oops, yes, you got me, but it doesn't change anything, does it?* It wasn't exactly a surprise, him leaping on the defensive and making a quick exit. I would have done too, if someone had just rumbled me as a violent, lying criminal.

I felt a twist inside, though, as those words came into my head. Because I still couldn't quite apply them to Ed in any real sense. He didn't seem like a bad guy. He had always been so lovely. *Yeah, but he didn't actually deny any of it, did he?* my brain pointed out helpfully. *Didn't seem in a hurry to give his side of the story. Talk about shifty. Talk about acting guilty!*

I let out a groan and went to make myself an espresso.

A triple one. I needed something to jerk me out of myself, to shock my body into remembering that it was awake and needed to function properly. One thing was for sure: with the argument hanging over me, and no chef on the premises, it was going to be one long mutha of a day.

The door opened and I turned hopefully. Was Ed walking back in to make amends, to explain?

No. It was Rachel and Leah, both looking annoyingly cheerful and hangover-free. Damn. 'Morning,' I said, trying to hide my disappointment.

'Hi, Evie,' they chorused.

I found myself glancing quickly at the counter, my guilty conscience suddenly nagging that I might have left a pair of knickers on it, or there might be a smear of ... well, you know. Dried fluids. It looked clean enough, but I would make sure to give it a surreptitious scrub-down when I got the chance.

'Um, coffee?' I said, remembering my manners.

I made us all drinks, then showed Leah the ropes. 'I don't think Ed's going to come in today, so I'll ring a temp agency, see if we can get someone to cover for him,' I said, making this up as I went along. 'But I may have to step into the kitchen to do the lunches if not, okay? Rachel will look after you, though, so let's see how we go.'

Let's blag it as usual, in other words, I thought grimly to myself. Although hanging out in the kitchen on my own did have a certain appeal, I had to admit. Not half as much appeal as Ed being there, doing the cheffing, but at least I wouldn't have to wear my serving-the-public face all day. At least I could keep my head down and stay behind the scenes. Mind you, it did mean I would have to do all the cooking, I realized a split-second later. I wasn't sure I could stomach the smell of frying eggs and bacon, without vomiting everywhere.

I didn't have any luck with the three temp agencies I tried. 'Might be able to get you something tomorrow,' was the best offer I had.

'Yes, please,' I said wearily, although privately I was hoping it wouldn't come to that. Surely Ed would come back and we could sort things out?

The sound of the café door opening interrupted my thoughts, and I left the office quickly, hoping it was Ed, reappearing purely thanks to the force of my telepathy. *I didn't mean what I said. Sorry to walk out on you. The least I can do is explain . . .*

It wasn't Ed. Still, it was the next best thing at least – Phoebe. She came in on her own, looking rather uncertain. She was wearing a khaki vest-top with a denim skirt and purple sequinned Converse on her feet; all clothes I didn't recognize. Her parents must have brought them for her.

'Hi,' I said hurrying over. 'Are you okay? I'm so glad you came in; I would have hated you to disappear back to

London without a proper goodbye.' I hugged her tightly, feeling emotional about the thought of her going. Her hair was glossy and smooth, and she smelled clean and perfumed. All traces of the beach bum had gone; this was a city girl who'd come in today.

'I'm all right,' she said. 'We've had a chat. Things are ... cool.'

'You're sure? I hope I didn't put my foot in it yesterday,' I said. 'I just ... I just didn't want them to have a go at you. But I'm sorry if I made things tricky.'

'It's okay,' she said, and then a dimple flashed in her cheek as she smiled. 'I kind of liked it, actually, you having a pop at them. It was well cool.'

'Oh Gawd,' I groaned. 'I didn't mean to have a pop, I just wanted to stick up for you.' I shrugged. 'I think you're worth sticking up for, Pheebs, that's all.'

'Thanks,' she said. 'And thanks for everything else too. I really liked staying here with you.'

'You're welcome,' I told her. 'I loved having you.' I could feel myself welling up; I'd never been any good at goodbyes. 'And listen, keep in touch, yeah? If you need a job when you've done your A-levels next summer, and fancy some time in Cornwall, you know where I am. You're always welcome.'

She threw her arms around me in another hug, and I

felt a massive lump in my throat. 'Thanks,' she said, her voice muffled in my shoulder.

'Take care of yourself,' I said, my voice cracking on the words.

Rachel came over and said her goodbyes too, and then Phoebe put her head into the kitchen. 'Oh! Where's Ed?' she asked in surprise. 'Isn't he here today?'

I forced a bright smile on my face. 'Not working today,' I said casually. 'I'll tell him you said goodbye.' *If I ever see him again, that is.*

We waved Phoebe off, and I slunk into the kitchen, making myself a large cup of tea and wishing things didn't have to change. My whole life had been constant change in the last few months – it was exhausting.

'Two bacon rolls, Evie,' Rachel said just then, bustling in and sticking an order sheet on the spike. 'One white, one brown.'

I blinked away the tears that had been lurking in the corners of my eyes. 'Coming up!' I said, whacking on the grill, peeling some rashers from the packet, and trying to stop myself thinking about Phoebe and Ed, and everything else that was making me feel sad.

The thing was – as the rational part of my mind insisted on pointing out pedantically – the thing was, I was always going to find out about Ed's dodgy past sometime. It wasn't something that anyone could hide forever. And maybe, despite how horrible things felt now, maybe it was all for the best. I'd found out, I was dealing with it, the shock and misery would wear off at some point and we'd all move on. Better to know now than before I fell any deeper in love with him, right?

'One bacon-and-egg roll on white, two wholemeal toast to go,' Leah said, coming in just then with another order.

'One cheese-and-ham toastie on white to go,' Rachel added, two seconds later.

Okay. I was now officially too busy to think about Ed – or anything else – any more. And that was a good thing. I made the orders on automatic pilot, trying not to gag, and, wonder of wonders, they actually looked edible and I didn't set the kitchen on fire or anything awful. I wasn't going to be able to manage any new pasties – I knew my limits – but we had some left over from yesterday and that would just have to do.

Hell, I'd come a long way in my few weeks as owner of the beach café, I said to myself, flipping the bacon in rather a professional way. Ed? Who cared about Ed anyway?

It turned out to be one of the most stressful days I'd ever had in the café. Try as I might, I couldn't help but hope that Ed would appear and we could sort things out, but by midday miserable reality had set in, and I'd given up on him showing his face. The pasties had sold out by one o'clock, and then I got totally stressed out by all my sandwich orders, especially as we ran out of egg mayo, tuna mayo and pesto chicken in quick succession, and I had to speedily make up more batches of each. It was a hot, muggy day, the kitchen felt airless and sticky, and we had customers queuing out the door at some points, despite Rachel's best efforts. Leah was great, but she was inevitably a bit slower, it being her first day.

By the time it got to five o'clock and we'd cleaned up, and Rachel and Leah had left, I sat down in a booth and absolutely bawled my eyes out. Everything came out: my tiredness, my upset at last night's discovery, the horrible-ness of my confrontation with Ed first thing, and the misery that had kicked in afterwards, not to mention the three painful fat burns I had on my wrist from frying eggs all morning.

Ed had seemed so furious that I'd looked him up online, but really, what did he expect, when I'd found out something so awful about him? How could I *not* have looked him up, after Amber's email? And shouldn't he have mentioned his dodgy past to me in the first place? What a mug I had been, letting him waltz into the kitchen without even running a few basic checks on him. I'd ignored all the warning signs until it was too late. And now I was paying the penalty, big style.

Yet for all of that, for everything I'd found out, it was his kindness that I kept remembering. The way he'd helped me so much, and made the café a better place alongside me. He'd been a mate and an ally, as well as anything else, which made the betrayal a million times worse. How could I ever trust anyone again?

I had been thinking about him all day, wondering what he was doing, how he was feeling. Was he packing up to leave Cornwall and hide out somewhere else? Did he feel hounded, now that I'd uncovered the truth? I hoped he knew me better than to think I'd start spreading gossip around the village, but the way he'd looked at me just before he'd stormed out – it was as if he couldn't stand the sight of me. Maybe he thought that I *was* that kind of evil gossip-monger. Maybe he had already gone.

Deep down, I was still holding out a tiny, feeble hope that he would come over that evening, to talk. Surely we couldn't leave things as they were, with that furious conversation the last one we ever had? I would have gone over to his place if I had the faintest clue where he lived, but surprise, surprise, I didn't know his address, along with all those other pieces of information I hadn't had. Like the wife, et cetera.

I ran myself a bath. *It'll be typical*, I thought, *I'll just get into the bath and there'll be a knock downstairs, and it'll be him.*

I got into the bath, braced to leap out again instantly and rush to the front door in my dressing gown. No knock came.

Afterwards I put on a hair-conditioning treatment and some cosy pyjamas, and settled down on the sofa in front of *Coronation Street*. *It'll be typical*, I thought, *if I'm sitting here with my hair in a towel, and he knocks at the door and sees me looking like a madwoman.*

I waited. I even turned the volume down slightly so that I wouldn't miss any knocks at the door. No knocks came.

Once *Corrie* was over, and I'd washed out the conditioner and had had a long and rather mournful chat on the phone with Amber, I felt wrung out. I really wanted an early night, but I knew that if I went to bed, then – sod's law – there would be a knock at the door and yadda yadda. I forced myself to stay up until nine-thirty, then admitted defeat and faced up to the facts. He wasn't coming. There wouldn't be any knocking at my door tonight. *Forget it, Evie. Go to sleep. Maybe he'll be back tomorrow.*

I sank into bed and tried to get comfortable, but I couldn't help one horrible thought that seemed to have jammed on replay in my head. *If Ed didn't come back tomorrow ... what then?*

Chapter Twenty-Four

Thursday began as another crappy kind of day. Again, no sign of Ed. Again, horrible muggy weather, with barely a breath of wind to stir up the soupy air. A chef from the temping agency arrived at about eleven o'clock, which was something, though. Her name was Wendy and she was about my mum's age, built like a wrestler with black-inked tattoos down her arms, and dyed-black hair held back with a pink plastic hair-band. 'All right, pet,' she said in a Marlboro-roughened northern accent when Rachel brought her into the kitchen. She stuck out a meaty paw and nearly broke my fingers with her iron grip when I shook it.

'Hi,' I said, temporarily losing all the blood circulation in my hand. 'I'm Evie. Thanks for coming in. What are you like at making pasties?'

'Pasties? Champion, love,' she assured me. 'Let me wash my hands and I'll get stuck in.'

Wendy was a breath of fresh air. She was hard-working,

made a decent pasty – albeit not with the same flair as Ed – and had the dirtiest, most gravelly laugh I'd ever heard. She lived in Tregarrow, a couple of miles away, and had been a school dinner lady for the last ten years, until budget cuts meant that she'd been made redundant a few weeks ago.

'I miss my kiddies,' she said sadly. 'Never had any of my own, and you get right fond of the little buggers when you see them day in, day out.'

'So are you looking for a full-time job now?' I asked casually, wondering if the answer to my long-term cheffing problems was standing right in front of me.

She shook her head. 'Not really, love,' she replied. 'My hubby's not well, so I can't leave him for hours on end. School dinners were great for me – just a couple of hours out, and then back home. And this sort of thing is perfect, popping over to you for a half-day. But any more than that ...' She shook her head. 'No. He has all these hospital appointments and what-not, you see, so I can't do regular shifts.' She elbowed me with one of her huge fleshy elbows. 'Don't tell me, you were just about to snap me up and all,' she said, guffawing.

I smiled at her. 'Unlucky for me, eh?' I said. 'But lucky for your husband.'

She winked. 'And doesn't he know it,' she told me, wielding her rolling pin on the pastry.

Another good thing happened shortly after Wendy's arrival. The postman brought a letter with an Oxford postmark and, when I turned it over curiously, I read 'From Saul', in wobbly handwriting, followed by his address. The café was fairly quiet, so I seized the chance to duck into the office and open it in private. Two letters fell out, one from Saul and one from his mum, Emily. I read Saul's first.

Dear Evie,

Thank you for my letter. I am learning about the Romans in school. They were COOL. And I scored two goals in football club yesterday. Dad read me more of the Moomins but didn't do the proper voices like you, so Mum is reading it to me now. Thingumy and Bob are really funny!

Mum says we can visit you at the seaside!

Love Saul

PS I miss you.

PPS This is a picture of the Lego dragon I made. xxxxxx

I sat still for a moment, reading the words again and feeling choked up, imagining his little face screwed up in concentration, tongue poking out of his mouth as he sat there writing it all down. Did he mean that, about coming to visit, or was it one of those vague parent-promises he'd misinterpreted?

I read the letter from Emily to find out.

Dear Evie,

Saul was so chuffed with the letter — thank you. It was really kind of you. He does genuinely miss you, and I'm not surprised — Matthew's new girlfriend is like a wet lettuce, really drippy and bland. Wondering if this is his midlife crisis?!

Funnily enough, my sister Amanda lives not too far from you, in Bude, and we're going to be over there for a week in August. Would love to pop in and say hello, if that's okay. Saul is really impressed that you have your own café, right on the beach, and has been talking about it non-stop since you wrote!

All the best, Emily

She'd written her mobile number on the bottom, and it felt like a hand outstretched in friendship. The thought of seeing my Saul again made me fill up with pure, golden happiness. I hadn't lost him. I could keep in contact with him. And Emily had sounded genuinely matey in her letter, which was great.

'It's not all bad,' I muttered to myself, walking back out to rejoin my team. It was only the new Ed-shaped hole in my life that kept me from smiling.

Wendy went home after she'd made lots of lovely pasties, and she agreed to come in between eleven and two again for the next three days, an arrangement that suited us both. I now felt confident about handling the breakfast orders on my own first thing, and then she'd be there to cover the lunch rush when I needed her. I wrapped up a couple of cakes in a paper bag and gave them to her as she was leaving. 'For you and your husband,' I told her. 'And I'll see you tomorrow.'

'Ah, cheers, love,' she said, giving me a smacker of a kiss on the cheek. 'Ta-ra for now.'

The rest of the afternoon passed without incident, but I had the same hollow feeling as the day before by the time I closed up. Why hadn't Ed come back? Was that really it – everything over between us, after one five-minute argument? He obviously didn't think much of me, if he didn't even consider it worth his while to explain the full story, present some kind of defence case.

Well, sod him, I thought crossly. I didn't want that kind of person in my kitchen, or in my life. I had Wendy the Muscles now, I had my letter from Saul, I had my girls' night in to prepare for. I didn't need Ed or his baggage weighing me down.

I wasn't quite sure what to expect from the girls' night in that evening. Martha and Annie had said they'd come along, as had Florence. I hadn't seen Betty since Jamie's party, so I wasn't sure if she was still planning to drop by or not. So potentially it would just be a small gathering, but that was cool, I didn't mind.

I pushed the tables together to make for more convivial seating, lit a few candles and flicked on some fairy lights, then arranged some cupcakes in a tempting display on the counter so that people could help themselves. I wanted the evening to be informal and enjoyable for everyone, and to make the space seem homely, so that people felt like guests rather than customers. Because of this I'd decided not to charge for the cakes, and had asked people to bring their own wine, if they wanted it. I hoped it would work, and that everyone would like to meet on a regular basis. I certainly would.

Annie and Martha were the first to arrive, Annie bringing with her a tray of iced chocolate brownies. 'I can't let you give all your profits away,' she said, setting them out on a plate, 'so I thought I'd contribute something.'

Florence came in next with Elizabeth and some other women, Michaela and Alison, who were from the book group, bearing wine and Kettle Chips. Florence was all excited because she'd just heard that her son, Francis, was back on UK soil and heading for Cornwall right now, to stay with her for a few days. 'I've turned on my mobile phone and everything,' she said, showing me. 'So if he gets to the bay early, he can let me know.' She winked. 'I told him he might have to wait outside in his car, though, as I don't want to miss any of the girls' night in!'

I laughed. 'Good for you,' I said. 'I'm glad you've got your priorities right.'

Moments later, Annie's neighbour Tess appeared with another friend, Helena, and Betty walked in, with her sister Nora. Next came Rachel, Leah and some of their back-packer mates with a box of white wine between them and bags of Doritos. Suddenly the room was full, and everyone was chatting.

Look at this, I thought to myself, feeling a rush of pleasure at the sight of all these women, from teenagers to grand-mothers, right here under my roof. People were laughing, swapping stories, catching up with old friends and making new ones. It was exactly what I wanted. It was perfect. Well, it would have been, if there hadn't still been that dull ache of sadness inside me, which meant that some-times I drifted away from what people were saying, caught up in doleful wonderings about Ed.

'When's Ed coming back, Evie?' Rachel asked me then, dragging me into the conversation. 'Is he ill, or just having some time off?'

'Um . . . I'm not sure,' I said cautiously.

'He was meant to be going back to London anyway next week, wasn't he?' Rachel said, frowning as she thought. 'I'm sure he said something like that.'

I shrugged, feeling miserable. I had no idea. What a surprise, something else he hadn't told me. 'Your guess is as good as mine.'

'Well, he's cancelled his newspaper order,' Betty put in,

overhearing. 'Came in this morning to say he didn't want it any more.'

I felt sick at these words and slumped back against my seat. So he really was off, just like that, without so much as a goodbye. Didn't Tuesday night mean *anything* to him? 'Nice of him to tell me,' I muttered.

There was an awkward moment. 'Did you two fall out?' Rachel asked tentatively.

'Kind of,' I replied. I didn't want to get into the full story – Ed would hate me even more for gossiping – but the people at my end of the table (Rachel, Leah, a Kiwi called Suze, Florence, Betty and Nora) all looked so sympathetic, and I *had* just drunk a glass of wine very quickly, and this *was* a girls' night, where you were allowed to go into affairs-of-the-heart stuff, so . . .

'We had a bit of a fling,' I confessed. You could almost hear the sucked-back 'Ooooh's, the rustle of clothes as everyone leaned closer in, not wanting to miss a syllable of gossip. 'I thought we'd really hit it off, you know, things felt so good between us.'

'So what went wrong?' Leah asked.

I sighed. 'We had an argument,' I said. 'I can't tell you what it's about, but Ed was *mahoosively* pissed off and stormed out.' I shrugged. 'And I haven't seen him since.'

'Oh dear,' Florence said, looking concerned. 'Have you tried to make up with him, say sorry? Don't let the sun go down on an argument, that's what Arthur and I always used to say.'

I gave her a small smile. 'I would if I could, but I don't even know where he lives.'

'Ah, but I do,' Betty said eagerly. 'He's up on Bay View Terrace, number eleven, I think.'

I swung round to face her. 'Really? That's his address?'

'Yes,' she said. 'He's been getting the paper delivered up there while he's been in the village.'

Everyone started talking at once. 'You should go round – it's not far. He might not have gone anywhere.'

'Go and sort it out, these things are much better once you start talking about them.'

'He's mad about you, anyone can see that. Go on, go and make your peace.'

This last was Rachel, and I felt tears prickle my eyes at her words. 'Do you think so?' I asked, twisting the stem of my wine glass between my fingers.

'Yeah!' she replied. 'He's totally got the hots for you. Hundred per cent. I've seen the way he looks at you.'

My heart gave a huge thump. Decision made. I would take control, seize the day, just do it! Maybe I needed another glass of wine first, though. Dutch courage and all that. 'Right, then. I'll go later on tonight, when this is finished,' I said.

'No, you won't,' Betty said bossily. 'You'll go right now. We'll keep an eye on things here for you.'

I dithered. What to do? There wasn't that much to keep an eye on, to be honest. People could help themselves to the cakes, and everyone was drinking their own wine, so . . .

'Go,' Florence told me. 'Just go. Tell him you're sorry and that you want to make up.'

'The best part of breaking up,' someone warbled, 'is when you're making up . . .'

I laughed and stood up. 'Okay, okay. I'll go.'

A cheer went around the room and I clapped my hands to my face, feeling flustered and excited and more than a little nervous. 'I won't be long,' I told them.

'Take as long as you need,' Florence replied.

'Good luck,' Rachel and Leah shouted after me.

And with that, I headed out into the night. Eleven, Bay View Terrace, here I come!

It was about nine o'clock by now, but still as humid and oppressive as it had been all day. Someone – Annie, I think – had been saying there had been a severe weather warning on the early-evening forecast about very heavy rain in the south-west, and I could feel the thunderous conditions building in the air. The pavements were dusty and dry as I walked up the main street, and my face felt hot. I hadn't even bothered looking in the mirror to check I looked all right, I realized, so keen was I to get over to Ed's and talk to him. I patted my hair down as I climbed the steep main street, sending up a little prayer to the Goddess of Vanity that I didn't look completely minging. Ah. Bay View Terrace – there it was, up on the right.

My heart was really thumping as I turned into the small, quiet road, full of whitewashed terraced cottages. There were no lamp lights on this street, and the sky was dusky, filling the gardens with shadows. I could hardly breathe with nerves as I passed each house – number one, two, three – and started to wonder what on earth I was going to say to him when he answered the door. Four, five, six. What if he slammed the door in my face and refused to speak to me? Seven, eight, nine, ten.

Well, I was just about to find out. Number eleven – this was it.

I went up the small path to the house, then stopped. The house was as pretty and sweet as its neighbours, with rampant wisteria up its front wall, and a sprawling rose bush under the front window. I could smell the perfume from the velvety white roses that bloomed there. Unlike its neighbours, there were no lights on in this house, though. The curtains in the front rooms were still open.

Disappointment slid through me as I clocked just how empty and silent the house seemed. Was he even in?

I knocked at the door, listening for Lola's bark and the sound of any life from within. There was silence. Maybe they were in the back garden, I told myself. Or maybe he'd gone to the pub.

But as I stood there in the warm, fragrant evening light, knocking again – and again – I remembered what Betty had said about cancelling his newspaper, and realized I was too late. He *had* already left the bay. Had he gone back to Melissa, his wife? I wondered despondently. Or had he gone someplace different altogether, making moves on a new sucker like me?

'Bastard,' I said, kicking the doorstep vehemently. And then I walked back towards the café, trying not to cry.

I was so caught up with my own misery that I nearly jumped out of my skin when I reached the café's little car park and saw a figure moving out from the shadows next to a car I didn't recognize. 'Oh!' I gasped, my hand flying up to my throat, and my heart skidding into a faster beat. Was it Ed? I wondered, my breath catching in my throat. Or was it, in fact, some deranged nutter on the prowl? Not Ryan again, surely?

'Sorry, didn't mean to startle you,' the man called, stepping towards me. It was getting darker by the minute, but he looked about forty, tall and slim, dressed in jeans and a long-sleeved grey top. 'This is the Beach Café, right? Carrawen Bay?'

'Yes, that's right,' I said. 'Can I help you?'

'Oh, great,' he said. 'Yes. I think my mum's in there? I was just coming to surprise her.' He held out a hand. 'Francis.'

I smiled at him. 'Florence's son,' I said, shaking it. 'I'm Evie, manager of the café. Come with me, she's having a girls' night in inside.'

He grinned broadly. 'She mentioned it on the phone,' he said. 'She was all excited. Are you sure I'm allowed in?'

'I think we can make an exception for long-lost sons,' I said. 'Come on, it's this way.'

We walked round to the front of the café and I showed him in. A squeal went up from Florence and she hurried over excitedly to throw her arms around him. A big 'Aahh' sighed out around the room from everyone else, then I felt numerous eyes slide towards me, wanting to know what had happened.

'Well?' Rachel prompted.

I made a thumbs-down gesture. 'Not there,' I said. 'I think he's done a bunk, left town.'

An 'Awww' of sympathy went around the room now. It was like being in a pantomime, although unfortunately nobody shouted out an excited 'He's behind you!'

'The rotten sod,' Betty said, clucking indignantly. She shook her head. 'Never did trust him, mind. Always thought there was something shifty about him myself.'

Florence and her son had finished their embrace and she looked around the room, eyes shining. 'Everyone, I want you to meet my son, Francis. Francis, these are all my new friends.' She began introducing everyone individually, and I could see Francis's eyes almost popping out of his head in surprise that his mum suddenly had so many pals of all ages.

'Wow,' he said at the end. 'And is this a regular thing, you ladies meeting up for cake and gossip like this?'

There was a slight hesitation and, again, I felt all eyes on me. 'Well, I hope it'll be a regular thing,' I replied after a moment. 'This is actually our first get-together, but I'd love this to be a place for all the Carrawen Bay girls to drop by and have a natter on a Thursday evening. So why not?'

Somebody gave a whoop, and then somebody else started clapping, and before I knew it, everyone was clapping and cheering at this news. I smiled, feeling the hairs on the back of my neck prickling. It felt ... lovely. Like I belonged.

Annie passed me a glass of wine. 'Cheers, everyone,' she said, holding her own glass in the air. 'I think this is the start of the Carrawen Bay Thursday Club, don't you?'

And then we were all raising our glasses and toasting each other and it felt wonderful. Screw lying Ed. Forget sneaking-away-into-the-night Ed. I had all these fabulous women around me – and a rather stunned-looking Francis – and that was good enough for me.

Chapter Twenty-Five

The next day — Friday — it started to rain. At first, I was glad that the humidity had been blown away by the cool, wet breezes sweeping in off the sea, but after it had poured down solidly for four hours with no sign of a let-up, I found myself wishing it would stop. Rachel, Leah and I were twiddling our thumbs with no customers to serve, and we ended up giving the seating area a thorough 'deep-clean' for want of anything else to do, scrubbing the walls and skirting boards, even the chairs themselves. I was determined to keep myself distracted by work. As soon as I stopped, that was when the sad thoughts about Ed began to creep into my head again.

By the time Wendy turned up, we'd still only had a handful of customers, so I told her to make up just half the usual number of pasties, as there was no way we'd need our full quota with weather like this.

'"Summertime..."' I heard her crooning, in her deep,

throaty voice. ' "And the living is rainy . . ." You've gotta love our crappy British summer, haven't you?'

At midday Francis walked in, dripping wet despite the large black umbrella he carried. 'Hello there,' I said in surprise. 'Everything all right? What can I get you?'

'A coffee and a few words, if that's okay,' he said, shaking the umbrella and spraying water everywhere.

'Bad luck to have an umbrella up indoors,' Wendy muttered lugubriously from where she had come out from the kitchen to chat with us.

He raised an eyebrow at her and grinned. 'Bad luck to come back to Britain just as the weather turns too,' he said. 'I've left a heatwave behind in the States, apparently.'

I poured him a coffee and then led him to one of the booths by the windows, my eye drawn to the spitting grey waves as they roared in and out, and the rain, which was still sheeting down. God, it looked awful out there, the water levels rising ominously. I wondered what on earth Francis wanted to talk about, which was so urgent that he'd run through this downpour to get here.

'Thanks,' he said, ripping open a sugar sachet and stirring the contents in. 'Okay, so here's the thing. I don't know if my mum told you, but I'm a television producer—'

'She did,' I interrupted. 'Very proud, too.'

He smiled. 'Thanks. Well, I've been commissioned to make a new documentary series for Channel 4, about society in the twenty-first century. Broken Britain, the collapse of society, why no one speaks to each other any more, let alone knows their neighbours.' He wrinkled his nose. 'But I'm presenting the flipside too: how you do still get these great, thriving communities where people help and support each other.'

'Sounds good,' I commented.

'I was planning to start filming in Bristol and London, capture some of the communities there – there's a massive Portuguese population around Stockwell in south London, for example – and contrast their unity with the more disparate neighbourhoods in nearby areas. I wasn't planning to do any work here at all, just have a few days with Mum, but . . .'

'But?' I prompted, wondering where this was going.

'When I walked in here last night, and saw Mum surrounded by so many nice people, I was really moved,' he said. 'Relieved too – I know she's found it tough since Dad died, being cut off from me and all her old friends. So for me to come here and see that, actually, she's doing okay, it felt amazing. I hadn't expected to find the sort of close-knit community I was looking for, right here on Mum's doorstep – let alone for her to be involved in it.'

I sipped my coffee. 'She's a nice lady,' I said. 'I'm glad she's finding her feet now.'

'So,' he went on, propping an elbow on the table and

fixing me with an intense look, 'I'd like to do some filming for the documentary here in the bay, and I was wondering if I could focus in on this place as a centre for the community. Perhaps I could come along to your next — what was it? Thursday Club night? Or Mum mentioned that the book group was meeting here, or . . .'

'Hang on, hang on,' I said, wondering if I'd misheard. 'You want to film stuff here in the café, for a programme that's going out on Channel 4?'

He nodded. 'It's for the new *Dispatches* season,' he said. 'Is that okay?'

'Wow,' I said, still not quite taking this in. 'Really? Wow!' I found that I was giggling like an idiot. 'Oh God. I need to get my hair cut,' I blurted out, then felt embarrassed at my own vanity. 'I mean . . . Yes, please! WOW!' I jumped up from my seat and called over to Rachel and Leah. 'Guess what, guys? We're going to be on telly!'

They both squealed, and then Wendy rushed out from the kitchen, all flustered, and said, did she have time to put some make-up on, because there was no way she was going on t'box without her No. 7 on her face, and we all got slightly overexcited and screechy. What amazing publicity this would be for the café, I kept thinking. A little slot on primetime national TV — how good was that?

Francis was laughing. 'Why don't you guys come and

join us,' he said, waving them all over. 'Tell me what you think we should film.'

More squeals and giggles as Rachel, Leah and Wendy promptly dashed across to the booth and squeezed in with us. 'Wait till my hubby hears about this,' Wendy said, eyes glittering with excitement. 'Am I glad I said yes to your temp job here, Evie. Now, Francis,' she went on, addressing him sternly, 'are you sure you can't do the whole programme about us? I think we've got a lot to offer Channel 4, personally speaking.'

I spluttered into my coffee at the startled look on Francis's face, liking Wendy more and more by the hour. Unlike another chef I could mention, she didn't seem in the least bit camera-shy.

Francis said that making the decision to film here would rather 'bugger up the filming schedule', as he put it, but he thought he could get the film crew here for the following Tuesday. 'We're meant to be putting together a piece about the Afro-Caribbean community in St Pauls in Bristol then, but we can push that back until Wednesday or Thursday at a pinch,' he said. 'So if there's any chance you could have your ladies' night on Tuesday instead, then we can get some of that on film.' We also talked about him filming interviews with other community figures, like Lindsay from the pub, the head of the local primary school, and Betty, in her position as Retail Queen. He was interested in the coexistence of the public and private faces of the village, he said: how there was one level of activity that was all about the holidaymakers enjoying themselves, and a separate, more hidden level pertaining to the villagers' lives. All sounded good to me.

I could feel Wendy drooping beside me as we discussed these ideas, though, and after a while I clicked why – she had realized she wasn't actually going to be present for any of the filming in the café. 'Wendy, you'll have to come along on Tuesday evening,' I told her. 'It's our soon-to-be famous girls' night in – bring a bottle and some munchies, and you can have a good old chat with the Carrawen Bay ladies.'

'Even if I'm not actually from the village?' she asked, and I was about to tease her that, oh yes, actually, if she wasn't from the village, she wouldn't be allowed in, when I detected a certain vulnerability in her face. I wondered how often she got to have a night out, given that she seemed to be caring for her husband so much of the time.

'Of course,' I told her. 'Especially if you bring along some tasty nibbles to share. You'll have a whole load of new best friends in no time.'

She looked much perkier at this. 'Fab,' she said. 'Then count me in. I'll wear me poshest frock and all. Now, Francis, you just make sure you get my best side on film, won't you?' she said, wagging a finger at him. 'And for

God's sake, please don't film me when I've got me gob full of cake, whatever you do. Channel 4 won't know what's hit it!'

Francis laughed and we exchanged a smile. Wendy was going to be telly gold, I knew it already.

Word about the television programme spread around the village like wildfire and all the locals seemed hugely excited by the idea. 'Just what Carrawen Bay needs, some good publicity,' Betty said, her face creasing with smiles, when I popped into the shop later that day. 'This programme could put us right on the map, boost our tourist numbers ten times over.'

'I know, it's going to be great,' I said happily. 'I can't believe my little café is going to be on Channel 4. I wish Jo could have been here to see it.'

'She would have been so proud, lovey. So proud,' she said. 'Oh, and have you seen the *Gazette* today? Nice review of your restaurant evening.' She grabbed one of the newspapers and flicked through to find it, page after page after page, until she'd almost reached the sports news at the end. 'There you are,' she said finally, jabbing a finger at the paper.

I leaned over to see. In amongst some lurid ads for other restaurants, the horoscopes, and a piece about a production on at the theatre in Newquay, there was a small picture of Rachel and me, rather pink in the cheeks, under the caption 'FULL HOUSE FOR BEACH CAFÉ'S EVENING MENU'. I scanned quickly through the text, my heart thumping.

> New owner of the Beach Café in Carrawen Bay,
> Evie Flynn, aged 39 . . .

'Thirty-NINE?' I squawked. 'I'm thirty-two, the cheeky buggers.'

> . . . has begun an evening menu for diners looking for fresh, local food served in a beautiful beach-side setting.

'They've just copied out the press release,' I realized, rolling my eyes. Still, it could have been worse.

> With reasonable prices and a simple, seasonal menu, diners can enjoy great food while the sun sets in picturesque Carrawen Bay. The café operates on a BYO basis (bring your own alcohol) and charges a £2 fee for corkage. We can certainly vouch for a buzzy, friendly atmosphere with plenty of happy-looking customers. For bookings, telephone . . .

The smile slipped from my face. It was that 'For bookings' line that did for me. Because who could say when I'd ever run an evening menu there again, now that

Ed had vanished? Fabulous as Wendy was, I couldn't ask her to come and do an evening shift every week. In the meantime, what would I say when people phoned up to book a table? *Oh, sorry. We only managed to open one Friday night after all. Too ambitious for my own good, that's me!*

I stared at the picture of Rachel and me and felt a pang for that crazy, hectic evening, and the feelings of triumph that had followed. It was obvious now why Ed hadn't wanted to have his photo taken, of course.

'Thanks, Betty,' I said, trying not to get maudlin. 'I'll take a copy.' I'd snip out the cutting and put it in a scrapbook, I decided. And maybe one of the interviewees I had coming in on Monday would be up for trying another weekend evening menu with me. Surely one of them would do the job. I'd just have to hope so.

The weekend passed, and still Ed didn't get in touch or show his face. I was resigned to the fact that he'd gone now, but it didn't make me feel any better. In fact, I felt more of a fool with every day that went by. I'd been vulnerable, on the rebound from Matthew, I realized miserably, and he'd taken advantage. 'It was my fault just as much, though,' I moaned on the phone to Amber. 'He didn't force me into anything, I was fair game. I just . . . thought he was better than that. When, in fact, it turned out he was nothing but—'

'A cockhead,' Amber suggested helpfully.

'Yes, exactly,' I said. 'A total cockhead disguised as a nice guy. A wolf in chef's clothing.'

She was having a better time of it than me, luckily for her. She'd had a call-back from the BBC for a second audition for a new role they were casting in *Holby City*. 'I am bricking it,' she said cheerfully, 'but excited too. This could be it, Evie. I know I always say it, but this really could be it!'

'Oooh, matron,' I said in my best, fruity Kenneth Williams voice. 'Fingers crossed here for you.'

My sister Louise surprised me by phoning for a chat the same evening. 'When can we come and see you?' she asked. 'Ruth's kids haven't stopped going on about visiting your café, and mine are all desperate to come down.'

'Really?' I asked in surprise. A warm feeling swelled inside me.

'Yeah! It feels like ages since we saw you, Evie, it's been weird without you here.'

'Has it?'

'Yes, of course! And I was really sorry to hear about Matthew, by the way. What a jerk. I never thought he was good enough for you, anyway.'

'Didn't you? I mean ... thanks.' I realized I was gaping at all the revelations that were coming down the phone line and was glad nobody was there to see me.

'So, when can we come?' she asked. 'How about the last weekend in June?'

'Lovely,' I said, still feeling somewhat stunned. Louise and her kids wanted to see me. Me, the black sheep! I know that in most normal families this wouldn't be anything out of the ordinary, but it felt like a moon-landing for me. I found myself smiling whenever I remembered the conversation for the rest of the evening.

On Monday the café was closed, and I interviewed my shortlist for the chef's job. The Wadebridge deli-worker informed me that she wouldn't be available to work weekends or school holidays (which just so happened to be our busiest times). The chip-meister smelled distinctly alcoholic, despite the Polo mint he was crunching. The fifty-something ex-pub chef had a horrendous personal-hygiene problem and confessed that he'd lost his last job because of a brawl he'd had with the restaurant manager. 'We were only mucking about,' he said unconvincingly, as I sat there, goggling in horror. 'I didn't hurt him or anything.'

In a nutshell, they were all hopeless. And as if that wasn't enough, I had a surprise visit from Carl, who walked in as I was halfway through the third interview, asking if he could have his old job back as he'd been unexpectedly 'let go' from his new place of work. The ex-pub chef swung round so aggressively that I thought he was going to challenge Carl to a duel for the position. 'Carl, I am actually interviewing for the chef's job right now,' I told him, rattled. 'And I'm afraid the answer in your case is no.'

'But—' he began.

The ex-pub chef rose threateningly in his chair. 'You heard her,' he said. I half-expected him to start cracking his knuckles. 'Beat it.'

The whole interviewing experience was utterly depressing. I couldn't believe there wasn't a single suitable candidate who could hold a candle to Ed's prowess. I'd been bloody lucky with Ed, I realized. I missed him more than ever. I called Wendy at home and begged her to make me some more pasties for the next week, then rang round the recruitment agencies again to see if they had anyone who might be interested in the job long-term. They didn't seem hopeful. 'We'll see what we can do,' the last one said. 'But you are kind of cut off there. It's harder to place people when they need their own transport to get to and from work.'

I sank into gloom. Maybe I had been aiming too high. Maybe this was why Jo had ended up taking on no-hopers like Carl and Saffron. Maybe I'd dismissed Carl too hastily earlier on when he'd turned up, cap in hand. Should I give him another chance after all?

I sighed heavily, gazing out of the window at the rain,

which had just started lashing down again. Rehiring Carl felt like a step back, though. I might be desperate, but I wasn't that desperate. No. Onwards and upwards, Evie, I reminded myself. Tomorrow I had the TV crew coming, and the girls' night in to look forward to. It was going to be a fab evening – it seemed as if every woman in the village was booking in emergency cuts and blow-dries with Sheena, the mobile hairdresser, and excitedly discussing what they would wear, in anticipation of being on the telly. The café was thriving, the community had accepted me, there was lots of good stuff happening too.

Onwards and upwards. I'd just keep repeating it to myself until I finally believed it.

I slept badly on Monday night. Not only was I tossing and turning, kept awake by worrying that I'd never get a chef as good as Ed, and thinking about all the things I wanted to do to make the café look perfect for the next day's filming, but the rain was absolutely hammering down again, and a ferocious wind blasted around the café. The building was a rather higgledy-piggledy structure, with new and old parts. The kitchen and the main area of the café were single-storey, having been added on as later extensions to the original walls, whereas its older middle section, where the flat was, consisted of two storeys, like a ship's bridge. On this night, with the wind howling around, and the building creaking and groaning, it really did feel like being aboard a ship, on a stormy sea. In the end I stuffed in some earplugs to block out the noise, put the pillow over my head and finally fell asleep.

When I woke the next morning the sun was shining, and I smiled at the thought of the camera crew arriving in Carrawen within the next few hours and capturing it on film in all its sunlit beauty. Hurrah! Forget the chef problem, today was the day my beach café would be filmed for Channel 4. I felt rather like an expectant bride waking up on the morning of her wedding, all jittery and excited, and hoping that everything would go perfectly. *Please* let everything go perfectly, I said under my breath. It would be just my luck if some disaster happened on film – like a plague of rats or locusts emerging from my kitchen – and for it then to be shown on national television. Kiss your café career goodbye, in other words.

But that was not going to happen. That would *not* happen today. The universe had given me a lucky break, sending Francis my way, and I was going to prove to the entire country that the Beach Café in Carrawen Bay was the most desirable place to hang out in Cornwall.

I jumped in the shower, then sauntered down to breakfast. And that was when I let out a scream of shock and dismay, followed by quite a lot of swearing and wanting to cry. Oh my *Godddd*...

'No,' I gasped, tears springing to my eyes. 'Oh no.' Not today! Why did this have to happen today?

It seemed that the storm had been even worse than I'd thought. It also seemed that my earplugs had proved to be the industrial-strength variety, capable of blocking out even the loudest sounds – like that of half my café roof collapsing in the night.

Because, yes, disaster had struck all right. The universe was pointing and laughing at me, clutching its sides with glee at the latest spanner it had just lobbed into the works. I kept looking up and looking down, hoping I had made some mistake, that I was dreaming or that it was a bizarre trick of the light, but no. There really was a whopping great hole in my roof. You could actually see the mild blue sky through it. And there really were great lumps of plaster on the floor, right in the middle of the café, with huge surrounding pools of rainwater turning them into islands in a lake.

Shit. And double shit. And shit to the power of a million billion zillion. I double-checked, up and down. The hole was still there. The carnage on the floor was still there.

I sagged in dismay, clutching at the wall for support. Tears spilled down my face. No telly programme now. No glorious girls' night triumph now. How could I even open up the place, when customers ran the risk of having chunks of the ceiling dropping on their heads? It was all off. So much for feeling like a bride on her wedding morning — now I just felt like a bride who'd been jilted at the altar, with the happy-ever-after she'd been promised snatched away from her at the last moment.

Okay. Pull yourself together, Evie. Got to do something about this. Be practical, start sorting it out. Worse things happened. Maybe the TV people would wait a few days until I'd got the roof repaired and everything cleaned up. But oh, of all the days for things to go pear-shaped...

After a few minutes' hand-wringing, I did what every competent, hard-headed, go-getting businessperson does in a crisis. I phoned my dad.

'Is your insurance up to date?' he asked first of all. Good question. I hadn't got a clue.

'Yes,' I said, crossing my fingers.

'If there's a lot of damage, you need to get them out to look at the problem. Don't just start work without their say-so,' he told me. 'You might not be covered, if you go ahead without them agreeing to the repairs.'

I sighed. 'But I need to get it fixed for tonight, Dad, there's a television crew filming here, and—'

He snorted. 'Tonight? You'll be lucky,' he said.

I rang the insurance company (I *was* up-to-date with my payments, thankfully). They said it would be two days before someone could inspect the property, in order for me to put a claim through. I told them I didn't have two days. Two days was out of the question. I pleaded with them to come round sooner, like in the next hour. I actually used the phrase 'I'm begging you' and let rip some blatant snivelling.

The woman on the end of the line didn't quite snigger at my cluelessness, but I reckon it was a close thing. 'I'm sorry,' she cooed, sounding as if she couldn't care less. 'The earliest we can come is Thursday.'

I put the phone down and burst into tears all over again.

Bollocks. Now what?

Chapter Twenty-Six

I was just on the verge of hyperventilating in despair when Rachel and Leah turned up for work. 'Holy crap, what happened here?' Rachel asked, wide-eyed when I let her in. 'Was this from the storm last night?'

'Oh my *God*,' Leah cried. 'What a mess.' Then she looked even more horror-struck. 'But what about our filming?'

I sighed. 'I guess the filming's off,' I replied gloomily. 'I won't be covered by my insurer unless I go through their stupid slow process, and I just can't afford to get someone to come in and fix it otherwise.' I raked my hands through my hair. 'I guess I could climb onto the roof and try to patch up the hole myself, but ...'

Rachel shook her head. 'No way, Evie,' she said. 'You don't want to do that.'

'No,' I agreed, 'and it's not just the roof outside – it's the ceiling in here that's a massive problem too. Loads of plaster has already come down; I don't know how much more will – ' I broke off, jumping as a large lump of grey plaster suddenly plummeted from the edge of the hole and smashed onto the wet floor, as if proving my point. Leah screamed and we all backed away in alarm, eyeing the ceiling warily as if the whole thing might come down on us.

'Oh, man,' I moaned. 'Look, maybe you should both go. It's probably not safe to be in here. We're not going to be able to open up today, now that this has happened.' I felt like crying, not really knowing what to do.

'Aw, mate,' Rachel said, putting her arm around me. 'I was really looking forward to this, too. The café's big day.'

'I know,' I said. 'I can't believe it. These things always happen to me. Me and my stupid big dreams . . .'

'Well, we've got today,' Leah said, hands on her hips. 'They're not filming until tonight, so . . .' She gazed up at the hole in the roof again, her expression turning doubtful. 'Surely we can do *something* about this? There must be a local builder who could pay an emergency call.'

'I've got to think about the costs, though,' I told her, also staring up at the hole. The blue sky seemed to mock me through it. 'It could be hundreds or thousands of pounds to fix it, and I don't have that sort of cash knocking around.' I sighed again. 'I'm just going to have to hang on for the insurance people to cough up. See if Francis can wait a while.'

Rachel's mouth twisted as if she thought this was unlikely, but didn't have the heart to say so. 'Mmm,' she said. 'He did seem kind of in a rush, though, didn't he?'

There was a doleful silence for a moment, and I was about to send them away, give them the next few days off, when Leah spoke. 'I've got an idea,' she said thoughtfully. 'Why don't we get Jono to take a look? He's worked on building sites in the past, he might have some advice for you.'

Jono was one of their backpacker mates, I seemed to remember. 'Well, that would be something,' I agreed. 'He'd know more about it than we do, he might have an idea of the costs it would involve. Is he around today?'

'He was still in bed when we left,' Rachel said. 'Leah, do you want to go and drag him out? Get Craig and the other guys too. I'll stay and give you a hand clearing up in here, Evie.'

Leah vanished. 'Thanks,' I said. 'I'll get the mop and brush.' Then I stopped. 'Did you say Craig was here? As in your Craig?'

She blushed violently. 'Yeah,' she said. 'He got here yesterday. It is *so* good to see him again.'

I hugged her, momentarily forgetting my ruined café. 'Oh, that's fab,' I said. 'Yay for you and Craig! So things are okay, are they?'

'Yes,' she said, beaming. 'Really okay. It wasn't until I

saw him that I realized just how much I missed him. I'm totally stoked to have him back.'

'Aww, look at you going all red and soppy,' I teased her. 'I'm impressed that you tore yourself away from him. Florence will be chuffed for you too, won't she?'

We began cleaning up cautiously, avoiding standing underneath the gaping hole in the ceiling as we slowly mopped the huge lake of water that had gathered on the floor. Annie arrived soon afterwards, laden with new cakes, and gave a cry of shock when she saw what had happened. 'Oh, no!' she exclaimed, eyes wide in dismay. 'Oh, what a shame. Of all the times for it to happen too, just before your big night.'

'I know,' I said. She'd had her hair done, I noticed, and felt even worse. I knew Annie didn't have a huge amount of money to spare for trivial things like haircuts. She must have been really excited about the TV show to have done that. 'I don't suppose you know a nice friendly roofer who'd be able to come in and sort this out on the cheap?' I asked, pulling a face as I heard how pathetic and desperate I sounded.

'I don't,' she admitted, setting the cake boxes down on a table and frowning, 'but ... let me think. Who might be able to help?' Her face cleared. 'Well, I don't know a roofer myself, but I know someone who will. Could be worth a try.'

'Who?' I asked.

'Give me two minutes,' she said. There was a twinkle in her eye. 'I'm not promising anything, but ... two minutes!'

And then she was dashing out of the café before I could ask her anything else and hurrying away towards the main street.

I felt a flicker of hope flare up inside, but as two minutes turned into five, and then ten, this brief burst of optimism gradually leaked away. Rachel and I were still trying to clear the water from the floor, but there was a lot of it, and the soggy plaster left dirty grey smears on the tiles.

Then the door opened again. 'We're closed,' I said automatically as I turned. Then I straightened up, feeling almost embarrassed as I saw that it was Francis, with a couple of blokes.

'We just came by to confirm details for tonight,' he said, then stopped, taking in the scene of devastation. 'Oh,' he said. 'Oh, dear.'

'Yes,' I said, my spirits sinking all over again as I saw the café through his eyes. 'I was going to phone you, Francis. I think we might have to call tonight off, after all. Can we delay the filming for a day or so until I get this sorted out?' I crossed my fingers behind the mop handle, but he was shaking his head.

'Sorry,' he said. 'We're so tight already, what with

bringing in this extra piece in the first place, that I don't really think . . .' He exchanged glances with his crew.

'I guess we could just change the location,' one of them suggested. 'Film at the local pub or – '

Francis didn't look convinced. 'It was this place, though, that I really wanted,' he said. 'The atmosphere won't be the same in the pub. Too noisy, for one thing, and it won't be that whole community vibe that we're looking for. Damn it.' He frowned, scratching his head.

I saw that some of the crew were looking really pissed off, obviously not in the least bit happy about having been dragged all the way down here to Cornwall on Francis's whim, only for the whole thing to backfire before it had even happened.

'Sorry,' I said wretchedly. 'I'm trying to get the problem sorted, but . . .'

I broke off and stared as I noticed through the window that a group of people were approaching along the beach, heading straight for the café. There were Annie and Leah, but also a number of blokes I didn't recognize, some of whom were carrying toolkits. Others were speaking into their phones. 'Hold on,' I muttered to myself. 'What's all this about?'

Rachel peered out of the window. 'Well, there's Craig and Jono,' she said, pointing them out at the front, 'and as for the others – well, it looks like the cavalry to me.'

She grinned at Francis. 'I reckon you're about to see the Carrawen Bay community swinging into action,' she laughed. 'In fact, maybe you should start filming right now.'

I clapped a hand to my mouth in disbelief. 'Oh, my goodness,' I murmured. 'Are they really all here for me?' I let out a shocked giggle. 'No way. No way!'

Rachel squeezed my hand. 'You'd better believe it, darl',' she laughed, and then ran out onto the deck. 'Hey, guys. Up here!'

She was right. It really *was* the Carrawen Bay cavalry – or, to be more precise, Rachel's bloke Craig (who was gorgeous), Jono from Auckland, Betty's husband Alec, who was a retired handyman, Tim the chippy and Wes the builder. 'This is just the start of it,' Annie said, beaming, as they all came up the steps to the café door. 'As soon as I told Betty the girls' night in was in jeopardy, she got straight on the phone. Calling in any number of Alec's mates, she is. Word's gone round – everyone's going to pitch in and get this sorted for you.'

My mouth hung open and I could hardly speak for a moment, I felt so stunned, so overwhelmed at people's generosity and willingness to help. Then my dad's words came back to me, about the insurers not covering the costs if I didn't go with their approved tradesmen. 'Wait,' I said, almost embarrassed to start quibbling about money when they'd all come to my rescue so quickly. 'Um … How much is this going to cost? I mean, this is brilliant, don't get me wrong. But I'm not the richest businesswoman in the world, so –'

Betty's husband laughed. 'Bless ya, darlin',' he said with a Cornish twang as thick as clotted cream. 'After what you did for our Jamie, my missus would knock my block off if I tried to charge you anything. Besides,' he elbowed me and winked at his mates, 'I've got some of the lads coming round tonight to watch the boxing. We've been looking forward to having Betty out the house for the evening. Although, ssshhh, you didn't hear me say that, right?'

I laughed. 'Didn't hear a thing,' I assured him.

'We'll get it done for you, pet, don't worry,' Tim the chippy said. He was in his fifties, at a guess, a short, wiry bloke with a shock of silvery hair and eyes that shone blue against his nut-brown tan. 'We've got Bob, our roofing guy, on his way too, and one of the lads will do the plastering for you later.'

'This is amazing,' I heard Francis say in a low voice to his team. 'This is perfect for the programme. We're on.'

And so it began: the amazing clear-up by the Carrawen cavalry. It wasn't just builders who turned up to help, either. Word had obviously gone from house to house and all sorts of people appeared to muck in. Jamie and his mates arrived, the book-group ladies brought mops, buckets and disinfectant, and Lindsay from the pub even sent her cleaner along with instructions to help, as well as a bottle of wine for me. ('In case of emergency, break open and drink,' she had written on the label.) Meanwhile, Francis and his crew got the cameras going and filmed the whole thing.

I was kept busy in the kitchen, serving everyone free drinks, cakes and sandwiches, as the very least I could do. Wendy, when she arrived, went round taking orders for pasties (hamming up shamelessly in front of the cameras), then cooked everyone's special requests. 'Isn't this lovely?' she beamed. 'Like it must have been in the Blitz.'

I couldn't agree more. In fact, I couldn't quite believe that this was all happening – that so many people had come out to help me. Here I was, the damsel in distress again, but this time I hadn't needed a bloke to rescue me. This time the whole village had hurried to my aid. Talk about heart-warming. Talk about awe-inspiring. There I'd been, just an hour or so ago, cursing my rotten bad luck, when in fact, it turned out that I was the luckiest woman alive, having these amazing people around me, who'd heard what had happened and come to help.

I had such a lump in my throat as I passed coffees around to the builders, the cleaners, and all the other mucker-inners that I could hardly speak. Not so long ago, I'd been wondering if this was a bad dream. Now I was convinced it had to be a good dream. A really lovely, feel-good, couldn't-possibly-be-true dream.

Then I heard a familiar voice from behind me. 'Evie. Oh my God! What's going on in here?'

And I knew I absolutely had to be dreaming then, because the voice sounded very much like Ed's, which was obviously impossible. I was probably feverish, I decided, ignoring the voice. Addled with the shock. Because Ed had done a bunk, hadn't he, so there was no way . . .

'Evie,' the voice said again, and then he was standing in front of me, and my eyes snapped as wide as they'd go, as if they couldn't quite take in what they were seeing, as if they hadn't expected ever to be looking at him again.

'Oh,' I said stupidly, and then, 'You're back', even more stupidly.

'What the hell happened here?' he asked, staring around at the mob of people and at the damaged ceiling.

My shock at seeing him gave way to a sudden flare of anger. Did he really think he could waltz in again just like that? 'What the hell happened to *you*?' I countered, quite rudely, to be honest.

He hung his head at the sharpness in my voice. He looked tired, I realized, with a day or two of stubble on his chin, and bags under his eyes. 'I'm sorry,' he said. 'Sorry I walked out, and sorry I wasn't straight with you from the start. I should have told you everything earlier, but—'

'Mind your backs!' called Tim the chippy, coming in with some lengths of wood, and we moved out of the way to let him through.

'Look, I can't really chat right now,' I said to Ed, 'but don't run off on me again, will you? I do want to talk to you about all of this.'

He nodded. 'I want to talk too,' he said seriously. 'And I'm not running anywhere. What can I do to help?'

'Go and introduce yourself to Wendy in the kitchen,' I told him. 'You're going to love her.'

In just a few hours the café was as good as new. The hole in the roof had been patched up and waterproofed, with new shingles hammered onto it. The ceiling inside had been repaired and replastered. 'You'll have to leave that to dry out,' said the plasterer – Mark, I think his name was, one of the book-group ladies' husbands anyway. 'Couple of days should do it, and then you'll be able to paint over it.'

Slightly overcome by now, I hugged everybody and tried to pay them for the time they'd spent helping out, but not a single person would take my money. 'You're all right, love,' one of the builders said. 'But you know, my daughter's got her twenty-first coming up. Would it be all right if we had a do for her here in the café?'

'Of course, absolutely!' I replied, delighted. 'It would be

my pleasure. Let me know the date you want and we can talk about the details, yeah?'

Tim the chippy wanted to know if I was going to open the café for evening sessions again, and I couldn't bring myself to look across at Ed, who was hanging around rather self-consciously in the background, as if he didn't know what to do with himself. 'I'm not sure,' I admitted honestly. 'But if we do, Tim, bring your wife along and you can both have dinner on the house, okay? Same goes for all of you. I owe every single one of you. Thank you. You're all superstars!'

I felt so worn out with such an extraordinary sequence of events – and was so desperate to talk to Ed, moreover – that once the building work was finished, I decided to close the café for the rest of the day. I couldn't cope with the thought of serving up pasties and ice creams as if nothing had ever happened. By the way Rachel snuggled up to Craig, I didn't think she minded all that much about having the afternoon off. 'See you later for our girls' night,' I told her, Leah and Wendy as they left.

Francis and his crew packed up, all looking pleased as punch. 'Wow!' said Trev the sound man, grinning. 'That was so cool. Are you sure you didn't arrange all of that to make for good telly?'

I laughed. 'As if,' I said. Then I groaned, realizing

belatedly that I hadn't a scrap of make-up on, and that I hadn't blow-dried my hair into any kind of sane style earlier that morning. Mmm. Looking foxy for your TV debut there, Evie. 'In fact,' I said, gazing down at myself and clocking, too late, the tatty denim shorts and purple T-shirt I was wearing, which were now spattered with plaster dust and bleach, 'I don't know if you'll be able to call it "good telly" when I'm looking such a total minger. Damn! Where's Hair and Make-up when you need them?'

They all laughed. 'I'll scrub up for this evening,' I vowed and then, suddenly worried that they might feel they'd spent enough time in my café for one day, added, 'You will be back later, won't you? For the girls' night in?'

'Oh yes,' Francis said. 'We're all looking forward to it. See you later, Evie.'

Then they went, and it was just Ed and me left standing there awkwardly. The café felt very quiet and empty, having been full of so much activity previously. I swallowed. 'So . . .' I began, just as he said, 'Well . . .' in a similarly self-conscious fashion.

We both laughed, rather nervously, and looked at each other properly for the first time. He was still as gorgeous as ever, I thought, my heart quickening, and I still fancied him every bit as much as I had on that fateful night when we'd slept together. I felt the spark between us, that pulse of desire, as strong as ever and yet —

And yet.

I still didn't know where he'd been, what he'd been doing, I reminded myself. This was the man who'd thrown me into turmoil, who'd made me cry into my pillow the last few nights. Once bitten, twice shy, I thought, dropping my gaze. I wouldn't let myself be fooled again.

'Is it very cheeky for me to make us both a coffee?' he asked, breaking the silence.

'No,' I replied, trying to sound breezy and in control of the situation. 'Although personally I reckon my roof caving in, and being filmed for Channel 4 looking like a dog's breakfast, calls for something stronger. Want a beer?'

'You don't look like a dog's breakfast, Evie,' he said. 'But, yes, I'd love one. Please.'

I took a couple of bottles of San Miguel out of the fridge – yes, all right, it was for reasons of Dutch courage as well – and cracked them both open. Then we sat down at one of the booths opposite each other, bottles on the table. Okay. I was half-expecting some kind of ritual fanfare. *Let the explanations begin!*

He cleared his throat. 'I've been in London for the last few days,' he said without preamble. 'Had some stuff to do – meetings with my solicitor and accountant. And yesterday I was in court, too.' He looked pained suddenly, raised his eyes to the ceiling and then back to me. His hands were trembling. 'I don't blame you for reading that stuff about me online,' he said shakily. 'I would have done the same thing. I should just have told you from the start. In fact, I fully intended to tell you everything that night I came round and we ended up getting drunk and kissing each other. But I just . . .' His head went down. 'I lost my bottle at the last minute.'

I felt sorry for him, I couldn't help it. 'Tell me now,' I urged. 'What happened?'

He heaved a huge sigh. 'It's a mess,' he said. 'But the gist is, I was running Silvers, the restaurant, with my then-wife, Melissa. To start with, we were doing great. Good reviews, busy every weekend, all ticking along perfectly.' He grimaced. 'Well, that's what I thought anyway. Unfortunately, it turned out that Melissa was having an affair with one of our suppliers, and the two of them had hatched a plot to stitch me up.'

I sipped my beer as I listened, keeping my gaze steady on him.

'She'd always done the books, but what I didn't know was that she'd begun channelling money to him, overpaying him massively, basically,' he went on. 'The thing was, the business was all in my name and I signed all these accounts off. I didn't bother checking every detail of them because . . . well, I trusted her.'

I nodded. That was fair enough.

'Then the tax office called the accounts in for an

inquiry. They obviously suspected something dodgy was going on,' he said. 'Even though she was the one who'd been fraudulent, in the eyes of the law, I was the one who was culpable, because the accounts were in my name.'

'Shit,' I said. 'But couldn't you just tell them it wasn't you?'

He shook his head. 'It doesn't work like that, unfortunately,' he said. He looked so miserable I wanted to hug him. No, I didn't, I reminded myself quickly. No hugging. Facts first, before anything else. 'It all came out, then – that she was having this affair and had been planning to leave me for months.'

I couldn't help wincing. *Major* betrayal. *Major* stab in the back. 'Ouch,' I said quietly. Matthew might have been a pillock, but at least he hadn't done me over quite so spectacularly. 'What, and you had to take the rap?'

He pulled a face. 'I didn't want to,' he said. 'In fact, my solicitor was urging me to bring her into the picture, to grass her up and twist things so that the focus was on her.'

'Well, yeah, quite right too,' I said. 'So why didn't you?'

'The thing was,' he said, looking away, 'the thing was . . . she told me she was pregnant.'

'Ahh.'

'And I couldn't bear the thought of any child of ours growing up and discovering that we'd had this huge public court case tearing each other to shreds – which is what would have happened.'

'So you took the rap,' I said, understanding. It was pretty noble of him, I thought.

He nodded. 'Yeah,' he said. 'Well, I did until I discovered that it wasn't actually my child she was carrying. That was her first mistake in the whole bloody saga – telling me that the baby was Aidan's child. *Is* Aidan's child, rather. She was born two weeks ago. And when I found this out, a couple of months ago, it changed everything. Which is why I went on a bender and punched Aidan in the face.'

It was all falling into place. 'The assault charge,' I said, putting the pieces together in my head.

'Yes,' he said. 'I'm not proud of it, but...' He took a large swig of beer. 'Well, all right, I did kind of enjoy smashing him in the face actually. I should have done it a long time ago.'

'So what happened yesterday in court?' I asked.

He smiled, but it was a hard smile, and there was bitterness in his eyes. 'The assault charge was dropped,' he said, 'and the fraud conviction overturned. The police have taken Aidan and Melissa in for questioning, and I'm in the clear.'

'Bloody hell,' I said, staring at him. 'What a nightmare.' No wonder he'd sought refuge down in Cornwall. And no wonder he hadn't volunteered any of this information to me, either.

'So I'm sorry I wasn't exactly forthcoming about myself, but now you know.' His expression had turned anxious as if he was afraid of my judgement.

'Thank you for telling me,' I said, my voice sounding formal, even to my ears. 'And what happens now? How much longer have you got dog-sitting and ... what will you do when your time's up here?'

'Well...' He reached over and took my hand. 'That's what I wanted to talk to you about.'

I felt fluttery and fizzy inside as his long, strong fingers wrapped themselves around mine. 'Yes?' I prompted, my heart going crazy all of a sudden.

'I've come to really love it down here,' he said, gazing into my eyes. I felt as if the walls of the café had suddenly vanished, that there were only the two of us in the world, looking at each other in that moment. 'I love working in the café, I really like the people here – I mean, what happened today, it was just amazing. You'd never get that in London.'

I tried to make a joke of it, suddenly overwhelmed by the intensity of his gaze. 'Ah, it was only because they wanted to get on telly,' I said with a little laugh.

He shook his head. 'No,' he said. 'Well, yeah, partly,

but it was also because of you. Because you're so special and ... lovely.'

I blushed, feeling my cheeks flame at his compliment, and at the tenderness of his voice.

'Seriously,' he said. 'I went away to London, and all I could think about was how much I missed this place. How much I missed you. I've not been able to think straight or make decisions about the future, with this court case hanging over me. I was scared it might all go wrong, that I might end up charged, even in prison. But now that it's over, it's like a fog has cleared. I want to make plans, I want to look ahead again, I want to –' He squeezed my hand and it was as if a surge of electricity went through me. 'I want to be with you.'

I couldn't help it, I let out a noise that was half a laugh and half a cry, I felt so happy, so emotional about what he was saying to me. 'I want that too,' I said. 'I missed you so much. When you walked out I felt awful, like I'd wrecked everything, like I never really knew you at all. And now you're back, and I'm so glad you're back, and ...'

And then we were kissing and kissing, and I knew that this was it, this was my happy-ever-after. And I felt like that bride on her wedding day once more – as if this was the very best and most perfect day of my life, after all.

Epilogue

Three months later

'Ssshhh, it's about to start.'

'Oh my God! Quick, anyone want another drink?'

'No, just sit down, and hurry up. Where's Mum gone? Mum! It's starting! Get over here now.'

It was a Thursday night at the end of September, and the Golden Fleece was packed out, not a spare seat to be had. Lindsay had set up the big screen, which she usually saved just for England matches, and a huge cheer went up as the Channel 4 ident appeared on it.

'Here we go!'

'Now on Channel 4, it's time for *Dispatches*,' the continuity woman said smoothly. Somebody whooped. 'And tonight's programme is called *Britain: United We Stand?*'

Everyone cheered again, and Ed grinned at me. We were in the pub to watch the documentary that Francis and his team had made, and afterwards, because it was the end of the season, we were throwing a party on the beach to celebrate what an amazing summer we'd had. I'd put the money from Phoebe's parents towards a buffet, booze and fireworks, and I couldn't wait.

It had been the best summer of my life. As soon as his mates had returned from their travels and he'd handed back the dog, Ed had moved in with me and had been at my side ever since. I loved him. I absolutely loved him. He made me laugh, he made me happy, and I fancied him more than any man I'd ever met. Those post-coital bacon sandwiches of his were pretty unbeatable too.

With him back in the sack – I mean, saddle – alongside me, we'd pushed the café along together. We contracted out the pasties to Wendy, who made them up at home and delivered batches every day or two; we had branched out into catering for weddings and parties; and we'd splashed out on a new gazebo for the deck area, so that we could run an evening menu every Friday and Saturday night of the summer, whatever the weather. We were going from strength to strength and, after Phoebe's dad sent one of his colleagues from *The Times* to review the café for the Saturday colour supplement one day in August, we'd been rushed off our feet for the rest of the season.

Ed, on the advice of his solicitor, had pressed for damages following the court case, and we'd recently heard that he was going to be receiving a large sum of cash in February. He'd asked me how I'd feel about him investing money in expanding the café and I'd hesitated initially, remembering what Jo had always said: *Never confuse business with your love life.* But then I'd looked at his earnest, lovely face and I knew that Jo would have been delighted I'd met such a good, good man. 'That sounds brilliant,' I'd told him happily.

'The only thing is,' he'd said, 'we might need to have a long, hot holiday while the building work is taking place. I reckon there'd be enough money to go somewhere really amazing for a few weeks. What do you think?'

'I think – you're ace,' I'd replied, throwing my arms around him. 'You know, I've always wanted to go to India . . .'

He'd grinned. 'Then let's do it,' he said. 'I can never say no to a Goan fish curry.'

In the meantime we were going to take things down a gear at the café, opening at weekends only, and having some time off during the week. Our Thursday ladies' night was still as popular as ever, and I'd been thinking of starting a photography club one evening in the café too. Ed had been asked if he'd run a cookery course for the villagers and was also teaching me to surf. It was all good.

Meanwhile, onscreen, the programme had begun, with the camera panning around a deserted-looking housing estate. There were smashed windows, litter blew about the pavement, and the small play-park had been vandalized and was covered in graffiti. 'The politicians and historians tell us that society has broken down,' went the commentary, 'that there's no such thing as community any more, that our population has become insular, man desensitized to fellow man. The original purpose of this documentary was to examine the causes of this so-called broken society, and to look at the effects it has had on us all.'

'Cheery,' someone commented, to a ripple of giggles.

'However,' the voiceover continued, 'as we travelled around the country, from inner cities to rural countryside, from industrial centres to holiday destinations' — a shot flashed up of the bay and everyone let out what can only be described as squeals — 'we began to question the validity of this original assumption. We began to wonder whether Britain really was quite so broken after all. Our first stop was Bristol, where we visited the area of St Pauls . . .'

The screen showed streets of Georgian and Victorian houses, and I felt my concentration lapse, too jittery to listen properly as the commentary went through a brief history of this part of the city. 'Yeah, yeah, get to the good bit,' someone muttered behind me, and I laughed, agreeing entirely.

My phone buzzed with a text from my mum. *Can't wait*

to see your café on TV, darling, it read. *Dad and I watching, and so proud of you. Xxx*

I was still getting used to my parents being proud of me. It was a new experience for us all, and one that made me feel warm inside. They'd come to stay in August, and had just radiated pride and happiness from the moment they had stepped into the café. 'You're in your element here, just like Jo was,' Mum had said, more than once, marvelling at all the events we were running, and how brisk trade was. 'You're doing so *well*, Evie!'

'We're so happy for you,' Dad had said, hugging me. 'Well done, love.'

Their words had wrapped around me like the warmest, cosiest blanket. Maybe I was just a big old saddo for still wanting my parents to be proud of me, but damn it, it felt so good. No longer was I the black sheep of the family or a failure. I felt like an equal at last, that I'd found my niche and was thriving. Louise and her family had come to stay for a couple of weekends too, as had Ruth again, and I found myself in the new and rather lovely position of 'favourite aunty'. Sure, I think the free ice creams had helped swing this honour, but it was still wonderful to feel loved.

I read the text from my mum again, feeling choked up, and showed Amber, who was sitting next to me. 'Bless her,' she said. 'Well, I'm proud too, mate. The girl's done good.'

'And so have you,' I reminded her. 'Miss New Nurse on *Holby City*! I'm going to be flogging your autograph once you've gone, you know.'

She laughed and pretended to scoff, but I could tell she was dead chuffed. After all her millions of auditions and try-outs and bit parts, Amber had finally struck gold with a six-month contract to appear in *Holby City* as the outspoken new ward sister that everyone loved to hate. Her first episode had just gone out and she'd picked up some fab reviews on the back of it. The tabloids and magazines were already queuing up to interview her and, best of all, she was acting with a hot bloke called David, who played one of the male nurses. According to Amber, there was definitely some offscreen chemistry between them and she was crossing her fingers for some steamy games of doctors and nurses in private in the very near future.

Up on the TV, the St Pauls footage had finished, and the pub went silent as we waited to see where the focus of the documentary would be next. 'Coming up: a piece of Portugal in south London, and why the locals all like to be beside this particular seaside,' went the commentary. The whole pub cheered once more as there was a two-second flash of the bay onscreen.

The adverts began and there was a rush for the bar. Then I heard familiar Aussie voices, as Rachel and Leah burst into the pub, with Craig and Luke close behind. 'We haven't missed it, have we?' Rachel cried anxiously, glancing up at the telly.

'Don't worry, we haven't been on yet,' I said, smiling over at her. Craig and Rachel had been happily together ever since he'd appeared in Carrawen, and Leah had met Luke a month ago at a surfing festival in Newquay. By one of those perfect coincidences, they lived about twenty minutes away from each other in Melbourne. It was definitely fate. I was really going to miss Rachel and Leah, my right-hand girls. They were heading off at the weekend for a whistle-stop tour of Europe with their men, having worked tirelessly and cheerfully all summer for us. The café wasn't going to be the same without them. But all good things had to come to an end, right?

Well, not always. The good thing I'd had with Saul, for example, seemed to be carrying on, with or without Matthew chaperoning us. True to her promise, Emily had brought him to visit me, and I'd almost cried with happiness to see him again. Ed had taken up the reins in the café while I spent a lovely afternoon with Saul, Emily and Dan on the beach, making sandcastles, paddling and teaching Saul to bodysurf. 'Thank you for this,' I said to Emily, while Saul and Dan busied themselves digging a ginormous trench down to the sea. 'I've really missed spending time with Saul. He's just the nicest boy in the world.'

'Oh, he is, isn't he?' Emily replied, smiling, as we watched him chatting to a boy who'd come to help with the digging. 'He's been so excited about seeing you again, too. And . . .' She fiddled with her sunglasses as she tried to find the right words. 'And it's nice to get to know you better as well, Evie. Matthew was an idiot, letting you go. And letting me go too, come to that. I can't think what he sees in this Jasmine woman. She's got about as much personality as . . . as a tin of magnolia paint. Not a patch on either of us, frankly.'

I'd laughed, liking Emily much more now that she was in laid-back holiday mode. 'Well, his loss,' I said. 'Although I can't imagine being with Matthew any more, I must say. I don't think we were right for each other at all.'

She raised an eyebrow. 'But all's well that ends well, right? Looks like everything's turned out pretty bloody brilliantly for you since you broke up.'

I smiled and held up crossed fingers. 'So far so good,' I said.

Back in the pub, an excited hush fell over everyone as the second part of the programme started. 'Here we go,' Ed said, nudging me. Then, to cheers and shouts, the screen showed our bay, the camera panning from one side of the beach to the other. 'Tucked away in north Cornwall is the small seaside village of Carrawen Bay,' went the commentary. 'To the public, it's an idyllic resort with a pretty beach and thatched cottages. But what about the people who live there all year round? Has the local community been splintered by second-home owners and the hordes of holidaymakers?'

'Course it hasn't,' somebody shouted, and the whole pub laughed.

'We met the manager of the local café, Evie Flynn, who, as a newcomer to the village herself, is passionate about keeping the Carrawen community alive and kicking,' the commentary went on. I blushed furiously as an image of me behind the café counter appeared onscreen. Somebody wolf-whistled and I could hardly bring myself to watch, peeping out through my fingers at the TV. 'By day, Evie serves the holidaymakers their Cornish pasties and cream teas, but in the evenings she has made the café a centre where the villagers can get together. The book group meets here, as does the local band, and Evie also holds a regular "girls' night in" evening for the women of Carrawen Bay.' An enormous scream went up as some footage appeared of our Tuesday girls' night, the one I'd thought couldn't possibly happen after the roof came down the night before.

'There's me!'

'Look at Wendy!'

'There's Flo, looking glam.'

'And our Nora!'

'In fact,' continued the voiceover, 'on the day we arrived to start filming in Carrawen, there had been a heavy storm and the café had been damaged. And something extraordinary happened.'

Now the screen showed Alec and Jono hard at work on the roof, Tim sawing pieces of wood to fit the ceiling repairs, other people cleaning the floor, Wendy handing out her pasties with a wink and a wiggle . . .

Tears filled my eyes, remembering that day, and I gripped Ed's hand. He squeezed it tight and gave me a kiss.

'Who can say Britain is broken, when a whole village comes to help a friend in need?' asked the voiceover man, and I had to blow my nose, feeling quite overcome. Who indeed?

When the programme finished, I think everyone felt emotional. Carrawen Bay had been on primetime TV – and hadn't we done well? Hadn't we shown the world that our village, our community, our people, were all things to be proud of?

OMG just saw u on TV came a text from Phoebe. *U R*

FAMOUS! I smiled. Phoebe had phoned a few times during the summer, and was doing okay. She'd moved out of her parents' house for a while to stay with her friend Zoe, but she was loved up with the legendary Will Francis, the hottest seventeen-year-old in Earlsfield, so things weren't all bad. She was back at college and sounded happy, which was the main thing.

I stood on my chair, feeling tipsy and exultant. 'Who's up for a party on the beach?' I yelled. The cheers in reply almost blasted me off my feet. I grinned. 'I was hoping you'd say that. Come on, then. To the beach!'

Ed, Amber and I led the way, hand-in-hand, down to the bay, a happy crowd following. The sky was growing darker and the first cool breezes of autumn slipped around us, the light summer evenings already long gone, but the beach was as full of people as if it was a blazing hot afternoon. Craig, Luke and some of the other guys got a bonfire roaring, Elizabeth from the book group popped the first champagne cork, and soon everyone was tucking into hot dogs, spicy pumpkin soup and ginger cake, their faces lit by the golden glow of the fire.

There was Annie, who'd saved enough money from her cake-baking to take herself and Martha away for a holiday abroad, for the first time ever. There was Jamie, who had sold at least twenty of his paintings through the café over the summer and was starting a fine-art degree course at

Falmouth in a few weeks. There was Florence, surrounded by a group of new friends, and there was even Seb, who'd got ten straight As in his GCSEs, bless him.

I looked around at all these people I'd got to know and I felt a strong and wonderful sense that I belonged here, with them. This was my home, these were my friends, and there was nowhere on Earth I'd rather be.

'Cheers to us all,' Ed called out, raising his glass in the air. 'Cheers!'

'CHEERS!' everyone called back in a joyful roar.

Ed leaned down and kissed me, and I kissed him back. And I knew that even though I'd just had the best summer of my life, the following autumn and winter and spring were going to be every bit as good, with this man by my side. I couldn't wait to find out what happened next.

Lucy Diamond's five favourite beaches

Like Evie, I'm a beach bum at heart and can think of nothing better than swimming in the sea or soaking up the rays on the sand. Here are my favourite beaches, and the reasons why:

Coogee Beach, Sydney, Australia

I lived a stone's throw from this beach for three months while I was working in Sydney, and will probably never live anywhere as beautiful again! As well as sunbathing and beach barbecues, I also loved swimming in the open pool carved into the rocks at one side. Oh, and of course, raucous nights at the famous CBH bar too.

Brighton Beach, Brighton, England

We lived in Brighton for five years and I have a very soft spot for this beach. Perfect for people-watching, strolling along the prom or whiling away a sunny afternoon at one of the many funky beachside cafés and bars. Fab.

Haad Rin Beach, Koh Phangan, Thailand

I stayed in a wooden shack on this beach for a couple of weeks while I was travelling. It was wonderful opening the little shutters every morning and seeing the sea just metres away. I went to one of the legendary Full Moon beach parties there too, dancing till the sun rose. Unforgettable.

Sennen Cove, Cornwall, England

My parents went here for their honeymoon and took us back to Sennen for many family holidays when I was growing up. I have happy memories of surfing with my dad, swimming and sandcastle-building. And fish and chips for tea, of course!

Lyme Regis, Dorset, England

My husband proposed to me on the Cobb at Lyme Regis and it was one of the most romantic moments of my life. A lovely beach with an old-fashioned seaside feel and lots of character.

How to make the perfect Cornish Cream Tea

CLASSIC SCONE RECIPE

(serves 8)

350 g self-raising flour
¼ tsp salt
1 tsp baking powder
85 g butter
3 tbsp caster sugar
175 ml milk
1 beaten egg (to glaze)

Heat the oven to 220°C/gas mark 7. Mix the flour, salt and baking powder. Cut the butter into cubes then rub in to the flour mixture until it resembles breadcrumbs. Stir in the sugar, then make a well in the mixture.

Warm the milk then pour it into the dry mix and stir to combine to a dough.

Sprinkle your work surface and hands with flour, then tip out the dough. Fold it over a few times, then pat into a round approximately 4 cm deep.

Take a 5 cm cutter and dip it into some flour. Cut four scones from this round, then reshape the remaining mixture to cut another four. Brush the tops with the beaten egg, and put on a baking tray.

Bake for 10 minutes until risen and golden.

Serve your scones warm or cold, with butter, clotted cream and jam, plus a pot of tea and your nicest crockery. Sea view preferable but not essential. Enjoy!